Praise for David Lagercrantz

and THE MILLENNIUM SERIES

"Lagercrantz has more than met the challenge. Larsson's brainchildren are in good hands and may have even come up a bit in the world." —*The Wall Street Journal*

"Lisbeth Salander remains, in Lagercrantz's hands, the most enigmatic and fascinating anti-heroine in fiction." —*Financial Times*

"Masterful. . . . Intricate and ambitious. . . . Salander is an extraordinary heroine whose hacker skills are more relevant than ever in an increasingly high-tech surveillance society." —*The Atlantic*

"Lagercrantz pulls it off, and with a great deal of style. . . . Elegantly paced, slickly executed, and properly thrilling. . . . A welcome treat." —*The Guardian*

"Action-packed and thoroughly enjoyable. . . . Lisbeth Salander and Mikael Blomkvist [are] in the hands of a writer worthy of their story."
—William O'Connor, *The Daily Beast*

David Lagercrantz

THE GIRL WHO TAKES AN EYE FOR AN EYE

David Lagercrantz was born in 1962 and is an acclaimed author and journalist. He has written numerous biographies (including the internationally bestselling *I Am Zlatan Ibrahimović*, for which he was the ghostwriter) and four novels, including *Fall of Man in Wilmslow* and the number one bestselling *The Girl in the Spider's Web*.

www.davidlagercrantz.com

THE GIRL WHO TAKES
AN EYE FOR AN EYE

THE GIRL WHO TAKES AN EYE FOR AN EYE

David Lagercrantz

Translated from the Swedish by George Goulding

PENGUIN

an imprint of Penguin Canada,
a division of Penguin Random House Canada Limited

Penguin Canada, 320 Front Street West, Suite 1400,
Toronto, Ontario M5V 3B6, Canada

First published in Viking hardcover by Penguin Canada, 2017.
Originally published as *Mannen som sötke sin skugga* in Sweden in 2017
by Norstedts, Stockholm. Copyright © 2017 by Norstedts Agency.
This translation is simultaneously published in hardcover in the United States by
Alfred A. Knopf, a division of Penguin Random House LLC,
New York, and in Great Britain by MacLehose Press, an imprint of
Quercus Publishing Ltd, London, by agreement with Norstedts Agency. Published by
arrangement with Quercus Publishing PLC (U.K.).

Published in this edition, 2018

1 2 3 4 5 6 7 8 9 10

Translation copyright © 2017 by George Goulding

Cover design: Peter Mendelsund

Printed and bound in the United States of America

Library and Archives Canada Cataloguing in Publication available upon request.

ISBN 978-0-7352-3300-3
eBook ISBN 978-0-7352-3299-0

www.penguinrandomhouse.ca

Penguin
Random House
PENGUIN CANADA

CONTINUING CHARACTERS IN THE MILLENNIUM SERIES

LISBETH SALANDER, an exceptionally talented hacker and mathematical genius, tattooed and with a troubled past, driven by a need for justice.

MIKAEL BLOMKVIST, a leading investigative journalist at *Millennium* magazine. Salander helped him research one of the biggest stories of his career, about the disappearance of Harriet Vanger. He later helped clear her of murder and vindicate her in a legal battle over her right to determine her own affairs. Sometimes nicknamed "Kalle Blomkvist," after a boy detective who appears in several novels by Astrid Lindgren.

ALEXANDER ZALACHENKO, also known as Zala, or his alias Karl Axel Bodin. A Russian spy who defected to Sweden and was protected for years by a special group within Säpo. He was the head of a criminal empire and the father of Lisbeth Salander, who tried to kill him for the violent abuse of her mother. In the end he was executed by a member of Säpo.

CAMILLA SALANDER, Lisbeth's beautiful and manipulative twin sister, from whom she is estranged. Known to be linked to criminal gangs and thought to live in Moscow.

AGNETA SALANDER, Lisbeth and Camilla's mother, who was incapacitated by Zalachenko's beatings and died in a nursing home at the age of forty-three.

HOLGER PALMGREN, Salander's former guardian, a lawyer. One of the few people who knows Salander well and whom she trusts.

DRAGAN ARMANSKY, Salander's former employer, the head of Milton Security. Another of the few she trusts.

PETER TELEBORIAN, Salander's sadistic child psychiatrist. Chief prosecution witness in Salander's competency hearing.

ERIKA BERGER, editor-in-chief of *Millennium* magazine, a close friend and occasional lover of Blomkvist.

ANDREI ZANDER, a young and talented journalist at *Millennium* magazine who was murdered by Camilla.

ANNIKA GIANNINI, Blomkvist's sister, a defence lawyer who has represented Salander.

SVAVELSJÖ M.C., a thuggish motorcycle gang associated with Zalachenko and Camilla. Some of its members have been seriously injured in past encounters with Salander.

HACKER REPUBLIC, a coalition of hackers, among whom Salander, who goes by the handle "Wasp," is the star. Includes Plague and Trinity.

SÄPO, the Swedish Security Police, which harboured a secret faction known as "the Section," dedicated to protecting Zalachenko.

JAN BUBLANSKI, chief inspector with the Stockholm police who headed the team investigating the Salander case. Known as "Officer Bubble."

SONJA MODIG, a police inspector who has worked closely with Bublanski for several years, along with CURT SVENS-SON, AMANDA FLOD and JERKER HOLMBERG.

RICHARD EKSTRÖM, the chief prosecutor who has brought Salander to trial on multiple occasions.

FRANS BALDER, a professor of computer sciences and leading authority on research into artificial intelligence. He was murdered for information he was about to publish with *Millennium* magazine. AUGUST, his supremely gifted, autistic son, was rescued by Salander from Camilla's criminal associates and sent abroad for his protection, along with his mother, HANNA.

FARAH SHARIF, a professor of computer sciences who was a friend and colleague of Frans Balder since their student days. Engaged to marry Jan Bublanski.

THE GIRL WHO TAKES
AN EYE FOR AN EYE

PROLOGUE

Holger Palmgren was sitting in his wheelchair in the visitors' room.

"Why is that dragon tattoo so important to you?" he said. "I've always wanted to know."

"It had to do with my mother."

"With Agneta?"

"I was little, maybe six. I ran away from home."

"There was a woman who used to stop by to see you, wasn't there? It's coming back to me now. She had some kind of birthmark."

"It looked like a burn on her throat."

"As if a dragon had breathed fire on her."

PART I

THE DRAGON

JUNE 12–20

Sten Sture the Elder had a statue put up in 1489 to celebrate his victory over the King of Denmark at the Battle of Brunkeberg.

The statue—which stands in Storkyrkan, the cathedral in Stockholm—is of Saint George on horseback, his sword raised. Beneath him lies a dying dragon.

Next to them stands a woman in Burgundian attire. She is the maiden being saved by the knight in this dramatic scene and is thought to be modelled on Sten Sture the Elder's wife, Ingeborg Åkesdotter.

The maiden's expression is strangely unconcerned.

CHAPTER 1

June 12

Lisbeth Salander was on her way back to her cell from the gym and the showers when she was stopped in the corridor by the warden. Alvar Olsen was blathering on about something, gesticulating wildly and waving a set of papers. But Salander could not hear a word he said. It was 7:30 p.m.

That was the most dangerous time at Flodberga Prison. Seven-thirty p.m. was when the daily freight train thundered past; the walls shook and keys rattled and the place smelled of sweat and perfume. All the worst abuses took place then, masked by the racket from the railway and in the general confusion just before the cell doors were shut. Salander always let her gaze wander back and forth over the unit at this time of day and it was probably no coincidence that she caught sight of Faria Kazi.

Faria was young and beautiful, from Bangladesh, and she was sitting in her cell. From where Salander and Olsen stood, all Salander could see was her face. Someone was slapping Faria. Her head kept jerking from side to side, though the blows were not that hard—there was something almost routine about them. It was clear from Faria's humiliated expression that the abuse had been going on for a long time and had broken her will to resist.

No hands were raised to try to stop the slapping, and in Faria's eyes there was no indication of surprise, only a mute, dull fear. This terror was part of her life. Salander could see that just by studying her face, and it matched what she had observed during her weeks at the prison.

"Will you look at that," she said, pointing into Faria's cell.

But by the time Olsen had turned to look, it was over. Salander disappeared into her own cell and closed the door. She could hear voices and muffled laughter in the corridor and outside the freight train clanging by, shaking the walls. She stood in front of the shiny washbasin and narrow bed, the bookshelf and desk strewn with pages of her quantum mechanical calculations. Did she feel like doing more work on loop quantum gravity theory? She realized she was holding something and looked down at her hand.

It was the same sheaf of papers that Olsen had been waving around, and that did, after all, make her a little curious. But it was some sort of rubbish with coffee cup rings all over the cover page: an intelligence test. Ridiculous. She hated to be prodded and measured.

She dropped the papers which spread like a fan on the concrete floor. For a brief moment they vanished from her mind as her thoughts went back to Faria Kazi. Salander had not seen who was hitting her. But she knew perfectly well who it was. Although at first prison life had not interested Salander, reluctantly she had been drawn in, decoding the visible and invisible signals one by one. By now she understood who called the shots.

This was called the B Unit, the secure section. It was considered the safest place in the institution, and to a visitor that might have been how it seemed. There were more guards, more controls and more rehabilitation programmes here than anywhere else in the prison. But anyone who took a closer look would realize there was something rotten about the place. The guards put on an act, exuding authority, and they even pretended to care. But in fact they were cowards who had lost control, and they had ceded power to their chief antagonists, gang leader Benito Andersson and her mob.

During the day Benito kept a low profile and behaved like a model prisoner, but after the evening meal, when the inmates could exercise or receive visits, she took over. At this time of day her reign of terror was uncontested, just before the doors were locked for the night. As the prisoners roamed between cells, making threats and promises in whispered tones, Benito's gang kept to one side, their victims to the other.

The fact that Salander was in prison at all was a major scandal. But circumstances had hardly been on her side, nor had she put up a very convincing fight. The interlude seemed absurd to her, but she also thought she might just as well be in jail as anywhere else.

She had been sentenced to two months for unlawful

use of property and reckless endangerment in the dramatic events following the murder of Professor Frans Balder. Salander had taken it upon herself to hide his eight-year-old autistic son and refused to cooperate with the police because she believed—quite rightly—that the police investigation had been betrayed. No-one disputed that she went to heroic lengths to save the child's life. Even so, Chief Prosecutor Richard Ekström led the case with great conviction, and the court ultimately found against her, although one of the lay judges dissented. Salander's lawyer, Annika Giannini, had done an outstanding job. But she got virtually no help from her client, so that in the end Salander did not stand a chance. She maintained a sullen silence throughout the trial and refused to appeal the verdict. She simply wanted to get the business over with.

At first she was sent to Björngärda Gård open prison, where she had a lot of freedom. Then new information surfaced, suggesting there were people who wanted to harm her. This was not entirely unexpected, given the enemies she had made, so she was transferred to the secure wing at Flodberga.

Salander had no problem sharing space with Sweden's most notorious female criminals. She was constantly surrounded by guards, and no assaults or violence had been reported in the unit for many years. Records also showed that an impressive number of inmates had been rehabilitated. But those statistics all came from the time before the arrival of Benito Andersson.

· · ·

From the day Salander arrived at the prison, she faced a variety of provocations. She was a high-profile prisoner known from media coverage, not to mention the rumours that spread through the underworld. Only a few days earlier, Benito had put a note in her hand which read: FRIEND OR ENEMY? Salander had thrown it away after a minute—it took about fifty-eight seconds before she could be bothered to read it.

She had no interest in power struggles or alliances. She concentrated on observing and learning, and by now she felt she had learned more than enough. She stared blankly at her bookshelf, stocked with the essays on quantum field theory she had ordered before she landed inside. In the cupboard on the left were two changes of prison clothes, all stamped with the initials of the prison service, plus some underwear and two pairs of sneakers. There was nothing on the walls, not a single reminder of life on the outside. She cared no more for the surroundings in her cell than those in her home on Fiskargatan.

Cell doors were being shut along the corridor and normally that meant some freedom for Salander. When the noise died down, she could lose herself in mathematics—in attempts to combine quantum mechanics with the theory of relativity—and forget the world around her. But tonight was different. She was irritated, and not just because of the abuse of Faria Kazi or the rampant corruption in the unit.

She could not stop thinking about the visit six days earlier from Holger Palmgren, her old guardian from the time when the authorities had decided she was incapable of taking care of herself. The visit had been a major production. Palmgren was entirely dependent on home aides and assistants and hardly ever left his apartment in Liljeholmen. But he had been adamant. The social service's subsidized transport service brought him in his wheelchair, as he wheezed into an oxygen mask. Salander was glad to see him.

She and Palmgren had spoken of old times and he had become sentimental and emotional. There was just one thing that troubled Salander. Palmgren told her that a woman by the name of Maj-Britt Torell had been to see him. She used to be a secretary at St. Stefan's psychiatric clinic for children, where Salander had been a patient. The woman had read about Salander in the newspapers and brought Palmgren some documents which she believed he might find interesting. According to Palmgren it was more of the same old horror stories about how Salander had been strapped to her bed in the clinic and subjected to the worst kind of psychological abuse. "Nothing you need to see," he said. Still, something must have stood out, because when Palmgren asked about her dragon tattoo and the woman with the birthmark, he said:

"Wasn't she from the Registry?"

"What's that?"

"The Registry for the Study of Genetics and Social Environment in Uppsala? I thought I read that somewhere."

"The name must have been in those new documents," she said.

"You think so? Perhaps I'm just muddling it all up."

Perhaps he was. Palmgren had grown old. Yet the information stuck in Salander's mind. It had gnawed at her while she trained on the speedball in the gym in the afternoons and worked in the ceramics workshop in the mornings. It gnawed away at her now as she stood in her cell looking down at the floor.

Somehow the I.Q. test which lay spread across the concrete no longer seemed irrelevant, but rather a continuation of her conversation with Palmgren. For a moment Salander could not grasp why. Then she remembered that the woman with the birthmark had given her all kinds of tests in those days. They always ended in arguments and eventually with Salander, at the age of just six, escaping into the night.

Yet what was most striking about these memories was not the tests or her running away, but the growing suspicion that there was something fundamental about her childhood she did not understand. She knew she had to find out more.

True, she would soon be outside again and free to do as she wanted. But she also knew she had leverage with Warden Olsen. This was not the first time he had chosen to turn a blind eye to abuses, and the unit he headed, still a source of pride in the prison service, was in a state of moral decay. Salander guessed she could get Olsen to give her access to something no-one else in the prison was allowed—an Internet connection.

She listened for sounds in the corridor. Muttered curses could be heard, along with doors being slammed, keys rattling and footsteps tapping off into the distance. Then silence fell. The only noise came from the ventilation system. It was broken—the air was stifling, unbearable—but still humming away. Salander looked at the papers on the floor and thought about Benito, Faria Kazi and Alvar Olsen—and the woman with the fiery birthmark on her throat.

She bent to pick up the test, sat down at the desk and scribbled out some answers. Then she pressed the intercom button by the steel door. Olsen picked up after a long interval, sounding nervous. She said she needed to talk to him right away.

"It's important," she said.

CHAPTER 2

June 12

Olsen wanted to go home. He wanted to get away. But first he had to do his shift and deal with his paperwork and call his nine-year-old daughter, Vilda, to say good night. His mother's sister Kerstin was looking after her and, as always, he had told his aunt to lock the apartment using the extra security lock.

Olsen had been head of the maximum security unit at Flodberga for twelve years and had long been proud of his position. He was a compassionate person who sided with the underdog. As a young man he had even rescued his mother from alcoholism. So it was no surprise that he joined the prison service and before long made a name for himself. But by now there was very little left of his youthful idealism.

The first major blow came early. His wife left him—and their daughter—to move to Åre with her former boss. But in the end it was Benito who robbed him of his illusions. He used to say that there is some good in every criminal. But although boyfriends, girlfriends, lawyers, therapists, forensic psychiatrists and even a couple of priests had done their utmost, there was no good to be found in Benito.

She was originally called Beatrice, and later took the name of a certain Italian fascist. These days she had a swastika tattooed on her throat, a crew cut and an unhealthy, pallid complexion. Yet she was by no means hideous to look at. She was built like a wrestler, but there was something graceful about her. Quite a few people were captivated by her imposing manner. Most were simply terrified.

Benito had—so it was rumoured—murdered three people with a pair of daggers she called Kerises, and there was so much talk about them that they became part of the menacing atmosphere in the unit. Everyone said the worst that could happen was for Benito to pronounce that she had her dagger pointed at you, because then you were sentenced to death, or already as good as dead. Most of that was bullshit, of course, but even though the knives were a safe distance from the prison, the myths surrounding them spread terror along the corridor. It was a disgrace, a major scandal. Olsen had, in effect, capitulated.

He should have been well equipped to deal with her. He was six foot four, 194 pounds, and his body was fit and toned. As a teenager he had beaten up any bastard who tried to get at his mother. But he did have one weak point: he was a single father. A year ago Benito had come up to him in the prison garden and whispered a chillingly accurate description of every passageway and set of stairs Olsen would take each morning when he dropped his daughter in class 3A on the third floor of Fridhemsskolan in Örebro.

"I've got my dagger pointed at your little girl," she said.

And that was all it took. Olsen lost his grip on the unit and the decay spread down the hierarchy. He did not doubt that some of his colleagues—that coward Fred Strömmer, for instance—had become downright corrupt. Things were never worse than now, during the summer, when the prison was full of incompetent, frightened temporary staff. Tension rose in the oxygen-starved corridors. Olsen lost count of the number of times he had vowed to restore order. Yet he succeeded in doing nothing at all. The situation was not helped by the fact that the prison governor, Rikard Fager, was an idiot. Fager cared only about the façade, which was still nice and shiny, however rotten the inside.

Every afternoon Olsen succumbed to the paralyzing effect of Benito's eyes, and in keeping with the psychology of oppression he became weaker every time he backed down, as if the blood were being drained from him. Worst of all, he was unable to protect Faria.

Faria had been sent to prison for killing her older brother: she pushed him through a large plate-glass window in the Stockholm suburb of Sickla. Yet there was no sign of anything aggressive or violent about her. Most of the time she sat in her cell and read or cried, and she was only in maximum security because she was both suicidal and under threat. She was a human wreck, abandoned by society. She had absolutely no swagger in the prison corridor, no steely look that would command respect, just a fragile beauty which drew the tormentors and sadists. Olsen loathed himself for not doing anything about it.

The only constructive thing he had attempted lately was to connect with the new arrival, Lisbeth Salander. No small task. Salander was a tough bitch and there was just as much talk about her as there was about Benito. Some admired Salander, others thought she was an arrogant little shit, and others still worried about losing their place in the hierarchy. Every muscle in Benito's body was spoiling for a fight, and Olsen had no doubt she was collecting information on Salander through her contacts outside the prison walls, just as she had done on him and on everybody else of interest to her in the unit.

But so far nothing had happened, not even when Salander was given permission, despite her high-security classification, to work in the garden and ceramic workshop. Her ceramic vases were the worst he had ever seen. She was not exactly sociable either. She appeared to be living in a world of her own and ignored any looks or remarks that came her way, including furtive shoving and punches from Benito. Salander shook them off as if they were dust or bird droppings.

The only one she looked out for was Faria Kazi. Salander kept a close eye on her and probably understood how serious the situation was. This could lead to some sort of confrontation. Olsen could not be sure, but it was a constant anxiety.

Olsen was proud of the programmes he had drawn up for each inmate. No-one was automatically put to work. Each prisoner got her own schedule—depending on her individual problems and needs. Some inmates studied full- or part-time and were offered vocational guidance; others were in rehabilitation programmes and had sessions with psychologists and counsellors. Judging by Salander's file, they should be giving her a chance to complete her education. She had not been to secondary school or even finished primary school and, except for a brief spell working for a security company, she did not seem to have held any real job. She had had a string of run-ins with the authorities, although this was her first prison sentence. In fact it would be easy to dismiss her as an idler, but that was clearly not an accurate picture. Not just because the evening papers described her as some sort of action hero. It was her general appearance, and one incident in particular, that stuck in his mind.

That episode was the only positive, surprising thing that had happened in the unit for the past year. It had taken place a few days before, in the dining hall after the early dinner. It was 5:00 p.m. and rain was falling outside. The prisoners had cleared their plates and glasses, washed and tidied the dishes, and Olsen had been sitting by himself in a chair next to the sink. He really had no business being there; he took his meals with the staff in another part of the prison and the inmates looked after the dining hall themselves. Josefin and Tine—allies of Benito's—were given the privilege of looking after the catering. They had their own budget, ordered supplies, kept the place clean and saw to it that there was enough food for everyone. In prison, food means power, and it was inevitable that people like Benito got more while others got less. Which was why Olsen liked to keep an eye on the kitchen.

The unit's only knife was stored there too. It was not sharp and it was attached to a steel wire, but it could still cause damage. On that particular day he kept looking over at it while trying to do some work.

Olsen badly wanted to get away from Flodberga. He wanted a better job. But for a man without a college education who had only ever worked in the prison service, there were not so many options. He had signed up for a correspondence course in business administration and—with the smell of potato pancakes and jam still hanging in the air— now began to read up on the pricing of stock options in the security markets, even if he could not understand much and had no clue how to do the exercises in the teaching manual. That was when Salander came in to help herself to more food.

She was looking down at the floor and seemed sulky and detached. Since Olsen had no desire to make a fool of himself with yet another failed attempt at establishing contact, he kept working at his calculations. He was rubbing things out and scribbling revisions, and this obviously irritated her. She came closer and glowered, which embarrassed him. It was not the first time he had felt embarrassed around her. He was about to get up and go back to his office when Salander seized his pencil and scrawled some figures in his book.

"Black-Scholes equations are over-rated crap when the market is as volatile as it is now," she said and walked off as if he didn't exist.

· · ·

It was later in the evening, as he sat by his computer, that he realized not only had she given the right answers to his exercises in no time at all, she had also, with a natural authority, trashed a Nobel Prize–winning model for the valuation of financial derivatives. This was different from the humiliation and defeat he normally suffered in the unit. His dream was that this would be the beginning of a connection between the two of them, maybe even a turning point in her own life where she would recognize how talented she was.

He thought for a long time about his next move. How could he boost her motivation? Then an idea came to him—an I.Q. test. There was a stack of old test papers in his office; various forensic psychiatrists had used them to assess the degree of psychopathy and alexithymia and narcissism— and whatever else—they thought Benito might be suffering from.

Olsen had tried a number of the evaluations himself and concluded that someone who solved mathematical problems as easily as Salander could reasonably be expected to do well on the test. Who knows, it might actually come to mean something to her. And so he had waited for her in the corridor at what he thought was a good time. He even imagined he could see a new openness in her face, and paid her a compliment. He felt sure he had gotten through to her.

She took the test papers from him. But then the train came clanging by, and as her body stiffened and a dark look came into her eyes, all he could do was stammer and let her turn away. He ordered his colleagues to lock the cells while he went into his office behind a massive glass door in the so-called administration section. Olsen was the only member of the staff with his own room. Its windows overlooked the exercise yard with its steel fence and grey concrete wall. It was not much larger than the cells and no more pleasant either, but it did have a computer with an Internet connection and a couple of C.C.T.V. monitors, as well as a few bits and pieces which made the room feel cosier.

It was 7:45 p.m. The cells were locked. The train was gone, racing towards Stockholm, and his colleagues were sitting in the coffee room chatting. He himself was writing in the diary he kept about life in the prison. It did not make him feel any better; his diary entries were no longer entirely truthful. He looked over at the bulletin board, at the pictures of Vilda and of his mother, who had been dead for four years now.

Outside, the garden lay like an oasis in the barren prison landscape. There was not a cloud in the sky. He looked at his watch. It was time to call home and say good night to Vilda. He was just picking up the phone when the intercom alarm went off. The display showed that the call came from cell number seven, Salander's, which both intrigued him and made him anxious. The inmates knew they were not to disturb the staff unnecessarily. Salander had never before used the alarm. Nor did she strike him as someone quick to complain. Could something have happened?

He spoke into the intercom. "What's the matter?"

"Come here. It's important."

"What's so important?"

"You gave me an I.Q. test, didn't you?"

"Right, I thought you'd be good at it."

"Could you check my answers?"

Again Olsen looked at his watch. Surely to God she couldn't have finished the test already?

"Let's wait until tomorrow," he said. "Then you'll have time to go through your answers more carefully."

"That would be like cheating, I'd have an unfair advantage," she said.

"Fine, I'm coming," he said after a pause.

Why had he agreed? Immediately he wondered if he was being rash. On the other hand, he would regret not going, given how badly he wanted her to find the test stimulating.

He retrieved the crib sheet from his desk's bottom-right-hand drawer and when he was sure he looked presentable, he opened the sally port gates leading to the maximum security unit using his chip card and personal code. Walking along the corridor, he glanced up at the black cameras in the ceiling and felt along his belt. Pepper spray and truncheon, his bunch of keys and a radio, plus the grey box with the alarm button. He may have been hopelessly idealistic, but he was not naïve. Prisoners could put on an obsequious, pleading act, only to manipulate the shirt off your back. Olsen was always on his guard.

As he approached the cell door he grew more anxious. Maybe he should have brought a colleague with him, as regulations required. However intelligent Salander might be, she could not possibly have churned out the answers that quickly. She had to have a hidden agenda—he was by now convinced of that. He opened the hatch in her cell door and looked inside. Salander was standing by her desk and gave him a smile, or something close to a smile, which restored his cautious optimism.

"OK, I'm coming in. Keep your distance."

He rolled back the locks, still prepared for anything, but nothing happened. Salander was stock-still.

"So?" he said.

"Interesting test," she said. "Will you check it for me?"

"I have the answers here." He waved the crib sheet, and added: "You did it really fast, so don't be disappointed if the result isn't great."

He tried a tentative grin and she smiled again. But this time it made him uncomfortable. She seemed to be scrutinizing him, and he didn't like the scheming look in her eye. Was she up to something? It would not surprise him at all if some infernal plan was being hatched. On the other hand, she was small and skinny. He was much bigger, armed and trained to deal with critical situations. There was no danger, surely.

With some apprehension he took the test papers from Salander, smiling awkwardly, and glanced through the answers while keeping a careful eye on her. Perhaps there was nothing to be concerned about after all. She looked expectantly at him, as if to say: Am I good, or what?

Her handwriting was appalling. The test papers were covered in smudged, hurried scrawls. Without lowering his guard, he compared her answers, one by one, with the crib sheet. At first he simply noted that she seemed to have gotten most of it right. Then he could not help but be utterly amazed. She had correctly answered even the most difficult questions, the ones towards the end, and he had never heard of that before. He was just about to say something effusive when all of a sudden he found himself unable to breathe.

CHAPTER 3

June 12

Salander examined Olsen with care. He seemed to be on the alert. He was tall and fit, and had a truncheon, pepper spray and a remote alarm hanging from his belt. He would probably sooner die of shame than let himself be overpowered, but she knew he had his weaknesses.

He had the same weaknesses all men had, and he was burdened with guilt. Guilt and shame—she could take advantage of both. She would hit him, put pressure on him, and Olsen would get what he deserved. She scrutinized his eyes and stomach. His abdomen was not an ideal target, it was hard and muscular. In fact it was a bloody washboard. But even abs like that can be vulnerable, so she waited and eventually got her reward.

Olsen gasped, perhaps in surprise. As he breathed out, the alertness left his body and at that precise instant Salander punched him in the solar plexus. She punched twice, hard and unerringly, and then she took aim at his shoulder, at the exact point her boxing trainer Obinze had shown her. She struck him again with a wild and brutal force.

She realized at once that she had hit her target. The shoulder was dislocated and Olsen doubled over, panting, unable even to scream. He was struggling to stay on his feet. After only a second or two he toppled and collapsed onto the concrete floor with a dull thud. Salander stepped forward. She had to make sure he would not do anything silly with his hands.

"Quiet," she said.

It was an unnecessary command. Olsen was incapable of emitting even a squeak. The air had gone out of him. His shoulder throbbed with pain and he could see a flickering light above him.

"If you behave yourself and don't touch your belt, I won't hit you again," Salander said, and snatched the I.Q. test out of his hand.

Olsen thought he could make out sounds from beyond the cell door. Was it a television in a neighbouring cell? Or some colleagues talking in the corridor? Impossible to tell; he was too dazed. He considered screaming for help. But the pain had invaded his mind, and he could not think straight. He had only a blurred vision of Salander and felt frightened and confused. His hand may have moved towards the alarm, more as a reflex than in any conscious act. But it never got there. There was another blow to his stomach and he curled up in a fetal position and gasped for air.

"You see?" Salander said quietly. "Not a good idea. But I don't really like hurting you. Weren't you a little hero once upon a time, who saved his mother or something? That's what I heard. Now this unit of yours has gone to hell, and you left Faria Kazi in the lurch—again. I have to warn you, I don't like it."

He could think of nothing to say.

"That woman has been through enough. It's got to stop," she said, and Olsen nodded without really knowing why. "We're already seeing eye to eye. Did you read about me in the papers?"

He nodded again, now keeping his hands well away from his belt.

"Good. Then you know that I stop at nothing. And I mean, *nothing*. But maybe we can make a deal."

"What?" He barely managed to utter the word.

"I'll help you get this place back into shape and make sure Benito and her sidekicks don't come anywhere near Faria Kazi, and you . . . you're going to lend me a computer."

"No way. You"—he caught his breath—"assaulted me. You're in serious trouble."

"*You're* the one in trouble," she said. "You don't lift a finger to stop the bullying and abuse in here. Do you have any idea what a disgrace that is? The pride of the prison service has ended up in the hands of a little Mussolini!"

"But—"

"Shut it. I'm going to help you fix this. But first you're going to take me to a computer with an Internet connection."

"That is *not* happening," he said in a voice that tried to sound tough. "There are cameras all over this corridor. You're screwed."

"Then we're both screwed and that's just fine by me," she said.

At that moment, Olsen remembered Mikael Blomkvist. During the short time that Salander had been a prisoner, the famous journalist had already visited her two or three times. The last thing Olsen wanted was Blomkvist digging around in his dirty linen. What should he do? He was in far too much pain for rational thought. Instead he held his shoulder and stomach and said, without really knowing what he meant by it:

"I can't guarantee anything."

"Neither can I, so we're square. Let's get going."

"What if we run into another staff member in the admin section?" he said.

"You'll think of something. The I.Q. test was such an inspired idea, after all."

He struggled to his feet and lurched to one side. The bulb in the ceiling seemed to be spinning above him. He felt sick. "One minute, I have to . . ."

She helped him straighten up and smoothed his hair, as if to tidy his appearance. Then she hit him again, scaring him half to death. But this time there was no pain. She had put his shoulder back in place.

"Come on," she said.

He thought about pressing the alarm and bawling for help. He considered hitting her with his truncheon and using the pepper spray. But instead he walked down the corridor with Salander as if nothing had happened. As he opened the sally port gates, he prayed they wouldn't meet anybody. But of course they bumped into his colleague Harriet Lindfors, who was so slippery he could not know whether she sided with Benito or with the authorities. He had the feeling she went with whichever was likely to give her the best opportunity at any given moment.

"Hi," Olsen managed.

Harriet had her hair in a ponytail and her expression was severe. The days when he had found her attractive seemed far off.

"Where are you going?" she said. He may have been her boss, Olsen realized, but there was no way he could challenge Harriet's questioning look. He could only mumble:

"We're going to . . . We thought we'd . . ."

Using the I.Q. test as an excuse flashed through his mind, but he knew it would not work.

". . . ring Salander's lawyer," he said.

Olsen knew this was not very convincing either, and he probably also looked pale and bleary-eyed. All he wanted was to sink to the ground and shout for help, but he pulled himself together and added with unexpected authority:

"He's flying to Jakarta tomorrow morning."

He had no idea where Jakarta came from, but it was sufficiently specific and exotic to sound credible.

"OK, I see," Harriet said in a tone more appropriate to her status, and she left them. As soon as they could be sure she was out of sight, they continued on their way.

Olsen's office was sacred ground. The door was always closed and it was off-limits to inmates, who were certainly not allowed to make calls from there. But that was where they were heading. Maybe the guys in the control centre had already seen them crossing to the staff side after the doors closed. Any minute now someone would be along to see what was going on. It would not look good, but it might be for the best. He fingered his belt and thought about sounding the alarm. But he was too ashamed and, though he would never admit it, fascinated. Whatever would she think of next?

He unlocked the door and let her into the office, and for the first time it struck him that it was a pretty sad sight. How pathetic to have big photos of his mother pinned to the bulletin board, larger even than the photographs of Vilda. He should have taken them down a long time ago. For that matter he should have resigned and never had anything more to do with criminals. But there he stood. He closed the door as Salander fixed him with a dark, resolute look.

"I have a problem," she said.

"And what's that?"

"You."

"Why am I the problem?"

"If I send you out, you'll call for help. But if you stay here, you'll see what I'm doing."

"Why, what are you going to do? Something illegal?"

"Probably," she said.

And then he must have done something wrong again. Either that, or she was completely insane. She punched him in the solar plexus for the third or fourth time and once again he collapsed, gulping for breath, bracing for another blow. But instead Salander bent down and with a swift movement undid his belt and put it on the desk. He drew himself up, in spite of the pain, and glared at her.

It felt as if they might fly at each other. But she disarmed him yet again by glancing over at his bulletin board.

"Is that your mother there in the picture? You saved her, right?"

He did not answer. He was still considering launching himself at her.

"Is that your mum?" she asked again. He nodded.

"Is she dead?"

"Yes."

"But she's important to you, right? In that case you'll understand. I have to find some information, and you're going to let me do it."

"Why would I do that?"

"Because you've already let things go too far in here. In return, I'll help you bring down Benito."

"That woman is ruthless."

"So am I," she said.

Salander had a point. He was in over his head. He had allowed her access and lied to Harriet. He did not have much to lose, so when she asked him for his computer log-in, he simply gave it to her.

Her hands moved at bewildering speed over the keyboard, and he was spellbound by them. For what felt like an age, she seemed to be searching aimlessly, skipping through various home pages in Uppsala, those of the university hospital and the university itself. It was only when she came across a site for an antiquated-looking place—the Institute for Medical Genetics—that she paused and keyed in a few commands. Within seconds the screen went totally black. She was motionless, her breathing heavy and her fingers hovering over the keyboard, like a pianist preparing for a difficult piece.

Then she hammered something out with astonishing speed, rows of white numbers and letters on the black screen. Soon after, the computer began to write by itself, spewing a flood of symbols, incomprehensible programme codes and commands. He could understand only the occasional English word—Connecting database, Search, Query and Response—and then Bypassing security, which was more than a little alarming. She waited, drumming her fingers on the table impatiently. "Shit!" A window had popped up that read ACCESS DENIED. She tried several more times until at last a ripple went across the screen, disappearing inwards, and then a flash of colour: ACCESS GRANTED. Soon things began to happen which Olsen had not imagined possible. It was as if Salander was drawn through a wormhole into cyber worlds belonging to another time, a time long before the Internet.

She flicked past old, scanned documents and lists of names recorded with a typewriter or ballpoint pen. These were followed by columns of numbers and notes, which looked like test results. Some of the documents were stamped CONFIDENTIAL. He saw her own name among many others, and a whole series of reports. It was as if she had turned the computer into a snake which moved soundlessly through secret archives and sealed vaults. She kept going for hours, on and on.

He still had no idea what she was up to, though he could tell from her body language and her muttering that she did not quite reach her goal. After four and a half hours she gave up. He heaved a sigh of relief. He needed to pee. He needed to get home and see that Vilda was alright and go to sleep and forget about the world. But Salander told him to sit still and shut up. She had one more thing to do. She rebooted and typed in some new commands. He realized to his horror that she was trying to hack into the prison's computer system.

"Don't do it," he said.

"You don't like the prison governor, do you?"

"What?"

"Me neither," she said. And then she did something he did not want to see.

She began to read Rikard Fager's e-mails and files. And he just let her. Not only because he hated the man who ran Flodberga, or because everything had already gone too far. It was the way she used the computer. It seemed like an extension of her body, an instrument she played like a virtuoso, and this made him trust her. Maybe it was irrational; he had no idea. But he let her keep going, launching new attacks.

The monitor went black again, and once more those words: ACCESS GRANTED. What the hell? There on the screen he saw the corridor in the unit right outside. It lay still and dark. She played the same sequence of film several times, as if expanding it. For a long while Olsen sat with his hands in his lap and his eyes closed, hoping that this agony would soon be over.

At 1:52 a.m. Salander stood up abruptly and muttered, "Thank you." Without asking what she had done, he escorted her past the sally port gates back to her cell and wished her good night. Then he drove home and hardly slept—except for a short while just before dawn, when he dreamed about Benito and her daggers.

CHAPTER 4

June 17–18

Fridays were Lisbeth days.

Once a week on a Friday afternoon Blomkvist went to visit Salander in jail. He looked forward to it, especially now that he had come to terms with the situation and stopped being so angry. It had taken a while.

The prosecution and the verdict against her had made him furious. He ranted and raved on television and in the newspapers. But when eventually he realized that Salander herself did not care, he came to see her point of view. So long as she could keep on with her quantum physics and her workouts, it made no difference whether she was in prison or anywhere else. Perhaps she even saw her time inside as an experience, an opportunity. She was funny that way. She took life as it came, and often when he worried about her she just smiled at him, even when she was transferred to Flodberga.

Blomkvist did not like Flodberga. Nobody did. It was the only maximum security women's prison in Sweden, and Salander had ended up there because Ingemar Eneroth, the head of the national prison service, had insisted it was the safest place for her. Both Säpo and D.G.S.E., the French intelligence service, had picked up threats against her, said to come from her sister Camilla's criminal network in Russia.

It could well be true. It could also be bullshit. But since Salander had no objection to being transferred, that's what happened, and in any case there was not much left of her sentence. Maybe it was fine after all. Salander had seemed in unusually good spirits the previous Friday. And prison meals could be classified as health food compared to the junk she ordinarily stuffed herself with.

Blomkvist was on the train to Örebro, going through the July issue of *Millennium* on his laptop. It was due to go to the printers at the end of the day. The rain was pouring down outside. According to the forecasts, this would be the hottest summer in years. But the rain had been relentless, falling day after day, and Blomkvist longed to escape to his house on Sandhamn to find some peace. He had been working hard. *Millennium*'s finances were in good shape. After his revelations about senior figures within the U.S. National Security Agency colluding with organized crime syndicates in Russia to steal corporate secrets all over the world, the magazine's star had risen again. But their success had also brought worries. Blomkvist and the editorial management were under pressure to bring the magazine more into the digital landscape. It was a positive development, inevitable in the new media climate, but incredibly time-consuming. Discussions about social media strategy interfered with his concentration. He had begun to dig into several good stories, but had not gotten to the bottom of any of them.

It didn't help that the person who had handed him the scoop about the N.S.A.—Salander—was behind bars. He was in her debt.

He looked out the train window, badly wanting to be left in peace. Wishful thinking. The elderly lady sitting next to him, who had been asking incessant questions, now wanted to know where he was going. He tried to be evasive. She meant well, like most people who bothered him these days, but he was relieved when he had to cut their conversation short to get off at Örebro. He ran through the rain to catch his connecting bus. It was ridiculous to have to travel for forty minutes in an old Scania bus without air-conditioning, given that the prison was situated so close to the railway line, but there was no nearby train station. It was 5:40 p.m. by the time he began to make out the dull-grey concrete wall of the prison. At twenty-three feet high, ribbed and curved, it looked like a gigantic wave frozen in the middle of a terrifying assault on the open plain. The pine forest was a mere line on the distant horizon and there was not another human dwelling in sight. The prison entrance gate was so close to the railway-crossing barriers that there was only room for one car at a time to pass in front of it.

Blomkvist stepped off the bus and was let through the steel gates. He made his way to the guard post and put his phone and keys in a grey locker. As he went through the security check it felt as though they were deliberately giving him a hard time, as so often happened. A man in his thirties with a tattoo and a crew cut even grabbed his crotch. Then a drug-sniffer dog was led in, a black Labrador. Did they really imagine he would try to smuggle drugs into the prison?

He chose to ignore it all and set off down the endless corridors with a taller and slightly more pleasant prison officer. The sally port gates were opened automatically by staff in the monitoring centre, who were following their progress via C.C.T.V. cameras in the ceiling. It was a while before they arrived at the visitors' section, and he was kept waiting for a long time.

So it was hard to say exactly when he noticed something was amiss.

It was probably when Olsen appeared. Olsen was sweating profusely and seemed uneasy. He uttered a few polite remarks as he ushered Blomkvist into the visitors' room at the end of the corridor. Salander was wearing her worn and washed-out prison uniform, which was always ridiculously loose on her. Normally she would stand up when he came in. Now she just sat there, tense and apprehensive. With her head tilted slightly to one side, she was staring past him. She was uncharacteristically still, and answered his questions in monosyllables, never once meeting his eye. In the end he had to ask her if something had happened.

"That depends on how you look at it," she said. It was a start, at least.

"Do you want to tell me more?"

She did not—"not now, and not in here"—and there was silence. The rain was hammering down on the exercise yard and the wall beyond the barred window. Blomkvist gazed blankly around the room.

"Do I need to worry?" he said.

"You certainly do," she said with a grin. It was hardly the joke he had been hoping for. But it did relieve the tension and he smiled a little too and asked if there was anything he could help with. For a while neither spoke, and then she said, "Maybe," which surprised him. Salander never asked for help unless she badly needed it.

"Great. I'll do whatever you want—within reason," he said.

"Within reason?"

She was smirking again.

"I prefer to avoid criminal activity," he said. "It would be a shame for both of us to end up in here."

"You'd have to settle for a men's prison, Mikael."

"Unless my devastating charm gives me special dispensation to come here. What's going on?"

"I have some old lists of names," she said, "and something isn't right about them. For example, there's this guy called Leo Mannheimer."

"Leo Mannheimer."

"Right, he's thirty-six. It'll take you no time to find him online."

"That's a start. What should I be looking for?"

Salander glanced around the visitors' room, as if Blomkvist might find there what he was meant to be looking for. Then she turned and, with an absent look, said:

"I don't honestly know."

"Am I supposed to believe that?"

"Broadly, yes."

"Broadly?" He felt a stab of irritation. "OK, so you don't know. But you want him checked out. Has he done anything in particular? Or does he just seem shady?"

"You probably know the securities firm he works for. But I'd prefer your investigation to be unbiased."

"Come on," he said. "I need more than that. What are those lists you mentioned?"

"Lists of names."

She was being so cryptic and vague that for a moment he imagined she was simply winding him up, and they would soon go back to chatting, as they had the previous Friday. Instead, Salander stood up and called for the guard and said that she wanted to be taken back to her unit.

"You've got to be joking."

"I don't joke," she said.

He wanted to curse and shout and tell her how many hours it takes him to travel to Flodberga and back, and that he could easily find better things to do with himself on a Friday evening. But he knew it was pointless. So he stood and hugged her, and with a little fatherly authority told her to take care of herself. "Maybe," she said, and with any luck she was being ironic. Already she seemed lost in other thoughts.

He watched as she was led away by Olsen. He did not like the quiet determination in her step. Reluctantly, he let himself be escorted in the other direction, back to the security gates, where he opened the locker and retrieved his mobile and keys. He decided to treat himself to a taxi to Örebro Central Station, and on the train to Stockholm he read a novel by Peter May, a Scottish crime writer. As a sort of protest he put off checking up on Leo Mannheimer.

Olsen was relieved that Blomkvist's visit had been so short. He had worried that Salander was giving the journalist a story about Benito's domination of the unit, but there hadn't been time for that, which was the only good news. Olsen had worked damned hard to try to get Benito transferred. But nothing had come of it yet, and it didn't help that several of his colleagues had stood up for her and assured the prison management that no new measures were necessary. The outrage was allowed to continue.

For the time being all Salander had done was watch and wait. In fact, she had given him five days in which to straighten things out by himself and to protect Faria Kazi. Then Salander would step in—that at least was what she threatened. Five days had now passed without Olsen having managed to effect a single change. On the contrary, the atmosphere in the unit had become even more tense and unpleasant. Something ugly was brewing.

It seemed as if Benito was preparing for a fight. She was building fresh alliances and getting an unusual number of visitors. This likely meant that she was getting an unusual amount of information. Worst of all, she was stepping up the intimidation and violence against Faria Kazi. It was true that Salander was never far away, and that helped. But it annoyed Benito. She hissed and threatened Salander, and once in the gym Olsen overheard what she said.

"Kazi is my whore," she spat. "Nobody but me forces that brown tart to arch her back!"

Salander gritted her teeth and looked at the floor. Olsen had no idea if it was because of her deadline, or whether she felt powerless. He suspected the latter. However gutsy the girl might be, she did not have anything she could use against Benito. Benito was on a life sentence—she had nothing to lose—and her gorillas, Tine and Greta and Josefin, were behind her. Lately Olsen had been afraid that he would see the glint of steel in Benito's hands.

He was always getting on the staff who worked the metal detectors, and he had her cell searched over and over again. Still he worried that this was not enough. He imagined he could see Benito and her sidekicks passing things between them, drugs or glinting objects. Or maybe it was just his mind playing tricks. His life was made no easier by the fact that there had been a threat against Salander from the outset. Every time the alarm went off or he took a call on his radio, he feared that something had happened to her. He had even tried to persuade her to agree to solitary confinement, but she had refused. He was not strong enough to insist. He was not strong enough for anything.

He was cut through by guilt and by worry and kept looking over his shoulder. On top of which he was doing a crazy amount of overtime, and that upset Vilda and put a strain on his relations with his aunt and the neighbours. The unit was unbearably airless and hot. He was sweating like a pig. He felt mentally worn out and kept looking at his watch, waiting for a call from Fager to tell him that Benito was to be moved. But no call came. Olsen had for the first time been entirely open with Fager about the situation, so either the prison governor was an even bigger fool than Olsen had believed or he too was corrupt. It was hard to know which.

After the cell doors were locked on Friday evening Olsen went back to his office to gather his thoughts. But he was not left in peace for long. Salander called on the intercom. She wanted to use his computer again. She said very little and her look was dark. He did not get home until late that night either, and more than ever before he felt they were on a countdown to disaster.

On Saturday morning at Bellmansgatan, Blomkvist was reading a paper copy of *Dagens Nyheter* as usual, and on his iPad the *Guardian,* the *New York Times,* the *Washington Post* and the *New Yorker.* He was downing cappuccinos and espressos, eating yoghurt with muesli along with cheese and liver paté sandwiches, and he let time drift, as he always did when he and Erika had sent off the final proof of *Millennium* magazine.

Eventually he sat down at his computer and began a search on Leo Mannheimer. The name seemed to crop up in the business pages, though not often. Leo had a Ph.D. from the Stockholm School of Economics and was currently a partner and head of research at Alfred Ögren Securities, a company which Blomkvist—as Salander had guessed— knew well. They were reputable fund managers to the wealthy, even though managing director Ivar Ögren's loud-mouthed, flamboyant style did not sit happily with the firm's desire to be discreet.

Leo Mannheimer, in photos, appeared to be a slight man with alert, large blue eyes, curly hair and thick feminine lips. According to his latest tax return, he was worth eighty-three million kronor. Not bad, but modest alongside the biggest beasts. The most noteworthy hit—at least so far—was an article in *Dagens Nyheter* from four years earlier that mentioned his remarkably high I.Q. He had been tested as a small boy and it had caused quite a stir at the time. Engagingly enough, he played it down.

"I.Q. doesn't mean a thing," he said in the interview. "Göring had a high I.Q. You can still be an idiot." He spoke about the importance of empathy and sensitivity and all the things intelligence tests don't measure, and he pointed out that it was unworthy, almost dishonest, to put a number on somebody's capacities.

He did not come across as a crook. But then crooks are often very good at presenting themselves as the saintliest of saints, and Blomkvist was not going to let himself be impressed by the large amounts of money Mannheimer apparently gave to charity, or the fact that he seemed bright and modest.

Blomkvist supposed that the reason Salander had given him Mannheimer's name was not to have him held up as a shining example for all mankind. But he had no way of knowing. He was meant to search with an open mind; prejudices should not intrude. Why was she being so unhelpful? He stared out towards Riddarfjärden and retreated into his thoughts. For once it was not raining. The sky was clearing, and it looked as if it was going to turn into a beautiful morning. He considered going out for one more cappuccino down at Kaffebar, to finish his detective novel and forget all about Mannheimer, at least for the weekend. The Saturdays after they sent the magazine to press were the best days of the month, the only time he allowed himself the whole day off. On the other hand . . . he had promised.

Not only had Salander given him the scoop of the decade and helped restore *Millennium* to its previous pedestal in the public eye, she had saved the life of a child and unraveled an international criminal conspiracy. If anything was certain, it was that prosecutor Richard Ekström and the district court who convicted her were a bunch of idiots. Blomkvist was deluged with praise and admiration from all quarters, while the real hero was locked up inside a prison cell. So he kept reading up on Mannheimer, just as Salander had asked him to.

He did not turn up anything interesting, but he did soon discover that he and Mannheimer had something in common. Both had tried to get to the bottom of the hacker attack on Finance Security in Brussels. Admittedly half the journalists in Sweden and the entire financial market had been digging into it too, so the coincidence was not sensational, but still, perhaps this was a clue. Who knows, Mannheimer might have some insight of his own, some insider information about the attack.

Blomkvist had discussed the extraordinary events with Salander. She had been looking after her assets in Gibraltar at the time. It was on April 9 that year, just before she was due to go to prison, and she seemed strangely unconcerned. Blomkvist thought maybe she wanted to enjoy her last moments of freedom and not bother with the news, even if hacking was involved. But she might have been expected to show some interest, and just possibly—he did not rule this out—she knew something about it.

He had been in the editorial offices on Götgatan that day when his colleague Sofie Melker told him that the banks were having problems with their websites. Blomkvist didn't give it a second thought. The stock exchange was not responding to the news either. But then people began to notice that the domestic trading volume was low. Soon after that it dried up altogether, and thousands of customers discovered they could no longer access their holdings online. There were simply no assets in the securities accounts. A whole series of press releases went out:

```
We are experiencing technical difficulties
and we are working to correct them. The
situation is under control and will be
resolved soon.
```

And yet the concerns grew. The krona exchange rate dropped, and suddenly there came a tsunami of rumours that the damage was so extensive it would not be possible to reconstruct the securities accounts in full: significant blocks of assets had simply gone up in smoke. No matter that the various authorities dismissed this as nonsense, the financial markets plummeted. All trading stopped and there was much high-pitched shouting into phones and crashing of mail servers. A bomb threat was made against the Swedish

National Bank. Windows were smashed. Among other incidents, the financier Carl af Trolle kicked a bronze sculpture
so hard that he broke eight bones in his right foot.

And just as the situation seemed about to get out of control, it was over. The assets reappeared in everyone's accounts
and the head of the central bank, Lena Duncker herself,
announced that there had never been anything to worry
about. That may have been correct. But the most interesting
aspect of the scare was not I.T. security itself, it was the illu-
sion and the panic.

What had triggered it?

It became clear that the central register of Swedish securities, called Värdepapperscentralen before it was sold to the
Belgian company Finance Security (a sign of the times), had
been the target of a "denial of service" attack, which revealed
how vulnerable the financial system was. But that was not
the whole picture. There was also the merry-go-round of
imputations, warnings and plain lies which flooded social
media, and which caused Blomkvist to exclaim that day:

"Is some bastard trying to make the market crash?"

He did get support for his theory during the days and
weeks that followed. But like everyone else, he was unable to
get to the root of the events. No suspects were ever identified, so after a while he let it go. The whole country let it go.
The stock market went up once more. The economy blos-
somed. The markets became bullish again, and Blomkvist
turned to more pressing topics—the refugee catastrophe, the
terrorist attacks, the rise of right-wing populism and fascism
across Europe and the U.S. But now . . .

He remembered the dark look on Salander's face in the

visitors' room and thought about the threats against her, about her sister, Camilla, and her circle of hackers and bandits. So he started searching again and came across an essay Leo Mannheimer had written for *Fokus* magazine. Blomkvist was not impressed. Mannheimer had no new information. But parts of the article gave a good description of the psychological aspects of the incident. Blomkvist noted that Mannheimer would soon be giving a series of talks on the subject, under the heading "The Market's Hidden Worry." He was due to deliver a speech on the topic the following day, Sunday, at an event organized by the Swedish Shareholders' Association, on Stadsgårdskajen.

For a minute or two Blomkvist studied the photos of Mannheimer online and tried to get beyond his first impression. He saw a handsome man with clean-cut features, but he thought he could also detect a melancholy streak in his eyes, which not even the stylized portrait on the company's home page could conceal. Mannheimer never made any categorical statements. There was no sell, buy, act now! There was always doubt, a question. He was said to be analytical, and musical, interested in jazz, above all in older, so-called hot jazz.

He was thirty-six years old, the only child in a well-off family from Nockeby, west of Stockholm. His father, Herman, who was fifty-four when Leo was born, had been C.E.O. of Rosvik Industrial Group, and later in life sat on a number of boards. Herman owned 40 percent of the share capital of no less a company than Alfred Ögren Securities.

His mother, Viveka, née Hamilton, had been a housewife and active in the Red Cross. She seemed to have devoted much of her life to her son and to his talent. The few interviews she had granted betrayed a streak of elitism. In the *Dagens Nyheter* article about his high I.Q., Leo even hinted that she had been coaching him behind the scenes.

"I was probably a little unfairly well prepared for those tests," he said, and described himself as an unruly pupil during his early years in school, which, according to the author of the article, was typical for highly gifted and understimulated children.

Leo Mannheimer had a tendency to play down the complimentary and flattering things said about him, which could be seen as coy. But the impression Blomkvist got was rather that Mannheimer was burdened with guilt and anguish, as though he felt he had failed to live up to the expectations invested in him as a child. Yet he had nothing to be ashamed of. His doctoral thesis had been on the 1999 I.T. bubble and, like his father, he had become a partner at Alfred Ögren Securities. Most of his fortune looked to have been inherited and he had never stood out, in either a positive or negative way, at least not as far as Blomkvist could see.

The only remotely mysterious piece of information Blomkvist had unearthed was that Mannheimer had taken six months' leave of absence as of January the previous year, to "travel." Afterwards he had resumed his work and started to give lectures and sometimes even appeared on television—not as a traditional financial analyst, more as a philosopher, an old-fashioned sceptic unwilling to pronounce on something so uncertain as the future. In his latest contribution to *Dagens Industri*'s webcast, on the rise of market prices during the month of May, he said:

"The stock exchange is like someone who just came out of a depression. Everything that hurt so badly before suddenly seems far away. I can only wish the market the best of luck."

Obviously he was being sarcastic. For some reason Blomkvist watched the piece twice. Surely there was something interesting there. He thought so. It wasn't just the way in which Mannheimer expressed himself. It was his eyes. Their sparkle was mournful and mocking, as if Mannheimer was musing over something quite different. Maybe that was one aspect of his intelligence—the ability to pursue many lines of thought at the same time—but he looked almost like an actor wanting to break out of his role.

That did not necessarily make Leo Mannheimer a good story. Even so, Blomkvist abandoned his plans to take time off and enjoy the summer, if only to show Salander that he would not give in so easily. He got up from his computer, paced about and then sat down again, like a restless spirit, and he surfed the net and rearranged his bookshelf and rummaged around in the kitchen. But the subject of Mannheimer never left him. At 1:00 p.m., as he was about to shave and grumpily weigh himself—one of his new habits—he burst out:

"Malin, for heaven's sake."

How could he have missed it? That was why Alfred Ögren Securities had seemed familiar. Malin Frode used to work there. She was one of his exes. A firebrand feminist and altogether passionate person—now press secretary at the Foreign Ministry—she and Blomkvist had loved and fought with equal intensity in the days after she had given up her job as director of communications at Alfred Ögren. Malin had long legs, beautiful dark eyes, and a remarkable ability to get under people's skin. Blomkvist dialled her number and realized only afterwards that, faced with the temptation of the summer sun, he had missed Malin more than he cared to admit.

Malin Frode would have liked to do without her mobile on weekends. She wanted it to keep quiet and give her room to breathe; but it was a part of her job to be permanently accessible, so she always managed to sound pleasant and professional. One fine day she would explode.

These days she was a single mother, for all intents and purposes. Niclas, her ex-husband, wanted to be treated like a hero when he looked after his own son for the occasional weekend. He had just come to pick up the boy and threw out the comment:

"Go on then, have a good time, as usual!"

Presumably he was referring to the liaisons she had had when their marriage was irreparably over. She had smiled stiffly at him, hugged her six-year-old son, Linus, and said goodbye. But later she felt angry. She kicked a tin can in the street and swore to herself. And now her mobile was ringing, some global crisis no doubt. These days there was a never-ending stream of crises. But no—this time it was something much better.

It was Mikael Blomkvist, and on top of relief she felt a rush of longing. She looked over towards Djurgården at a lone sailing boat crossing the inlet. She had just emerged onto Strandvägen.

"What an honour," she said.

"Hardly," Blomkvist said.

"If only you knew. What have you been up to?"

"Working."

"Isn't that what you always do? Slave away?"

"Yes, unfortunately."

"I like you better when you're on your back."

"I probably prefer that too."

"Lie down, then."

"OK."

She waited a second or two.

"Are you lying down now?"

"Of course."

"What are you wearing?"

"Very little."

"Liar. So, to what do I owe this honour?"

"It's a business call."

"What a fucking bore."

"I know," he said. "But I can't stop thinking about that hacker attack on Finance Security."

"Of course you can't. You never let go of anything, apart from the women whose paths happen to cross yours . . ."

"I don't let go of the women so easily either."

"Apparently not, when you need them as sources. What can I do for you?"

"I've been reading that one of your old colleagues was trying to analyze that data breach too."

"Who was that?"

"Leo Mannheimer."

"Leo," she said.

"What's he like?"

"A cool customer—and unlike you in other ways too."

"Lucky man."

"Very lucky."

"In what ways is he different from me?"

"Leo, he's . . ." She paused.

"He's what?"

"For starters, he's not a leech like you, always sucking information from the people around you. He's a thinker, a philosopher."

"We leeches have always been a little primitive."

"You're a catch, Mikael. You know that," she said. "But you're more of a cowboy. You don't have time to stand around and dither like some Hamlet."

"So Mannheimer's a Hamlet."

"He should never have ended up in the finance industry, that's for sure."

"Where should he be instead?"

"In music. He plays the piano like a god. He's got perfect pitch; he's incredibly gifted. Plus, he's just not that into money."

"Not a great quality in a finance guy."

"No indeed. Must have had it too good when he was a kid. He's not hungry enough. Why are you interested in him?"

"He has some pretty exciting ideas about the hacker attack."

"That could be. But you won't find any dirt on him, if that's what you're looking for."

"Why do you say that?"

"Because it was my job to keep tabs on those guys, and to be totally straight with you . . ."

"Yes?"

". . . I doubt that Leo's capable of real deceit. Instead of making shady investments or generally misbehaving, he sits at home playing his grand piano and feeling miserable."

"So why's he in the business?"

"Because of his dad."

"Who was a big shot."

"Definitely a big shot. Best friends with old Alfred Ögren himself, and totally self-obsessed. He was determined that Leo should become a financial genius, take over his interest in Alfred's company, and go on to build a power base for himself in the Swedish economy. And Leo . . . What can I say . . . ?"

"Tell me."

"He doesn't have much backbone. He let himself be talked into it, and in fact he didn't do a bad job. He never does anything badly. But he wasn't that brilliant either, not in the way he could have been. He lacks the drive. One day he told me he felt like something vital had been taken away from him. He carries a wound."

"A wound?"

"Something bad from his childhood. I never got close enough to understand it, even though, briefly . . ."

"Briefly what?"

"Nothing, we were just playing around, I guess."

Blomkvist decided not to pursue it.

"I read that he took time off to travel," he said.

"After his mother's death."

"How did she die?"

"Oh, it was grim. Pancreatic cancer."

"Poor guy."

"I actually thought it would do him some good."

"Oh?"

"His parents were always on his case. I hoped he might have a chance to tear himself away from the world of finance and seriously start to play the piano or whatever. You know, right before I quit Alfred Ögren, Leo was on top of the world. I never found out why. For a brief moment he seemed to escape the cloud hanging over him. But then he was worse than ever. It was heartbreaking."

"Was his mother still alive then?"

"Yes, but not for much longer."

"Where did he go, on his travels?"

"No idea. I'd left the company by then."

"And in the end he returned to Alfred Ögren."

"I suppose he didn't have the courage to break free."

"He's giving lectures now."

"Maybe that's a step in the right direction," she said. "Why does he interest you?"

"He compares the attacks in Brussels to other known disinformation campaigns."

"Russian campaigns, right?"

"He describes it as a modern form of warfare, which intrigues me."

"Lies as weapons."

"Lies as a way of creating chaos and confusion. Lies as an alternative to violence."

"Isn't there evidence that the hacker attack was directed from Russia?" she said.

"Yes, but no-one knows who in Russia is behind it. The gentlemen in the Kremlin claim to have nothing to do with it, of course."

"Do you suspect that gang you've been chasing, the Spiders?"

"The thought had occurred to me."

"I doubt Leo could help you there."

"Maybe not, but I'd like . . ."

He seemed to have lost his train of thought.

". . . to buy me a drink?" she suggested. "Shower me with flattery and praise and expensive presents? Take me to Paris?"

"What?"

"Paris. A city in Europe. Said to have a conspicuous tower."

"Leo's being interviewed live on stage at the Fotografiska Museum tomorrow," he said, as if he hadn't been listening. "Why don't you tag along? We might learn something."

"Learn something? For Christ's sake, Mikael, is that all you've got to offer a damsel in distress?"

"For the moment, yes," he said, and sounded distracted again, which upset her even more.

"You're an idiot, Blomkvist!" she spat and hung up. She stood there on the pavement, seething with an old familiar rage that went hand in hand with talking to him.

But soon she calmed down. A memory which had nothing to do with Blomkvist rose slowly to the surface. In her mind's eye she could see Mannheimer in his office at Alfred Ögren late one night, writing on a sheet of sand-coloured paper. There was something about the scene which seemed to carry a message, spreading like mist over Strandvägen. For a little while Malin Frode stood lost in her thoughts. Then she wandered down towards Dramaten and Berns Hotel, cursing at ex-husbands, former lovers and other representatives of the male species.

Blomkvist realized that he had put his foot in it and was considering calling back and apologizing, maybe even asking her to dinner. But then a thousand and one thoughts crowded in and instead he called Annika. Annika Giannini was not only his sister, she was also Salander's lawyer. Maybe she would have an idea of what Salander was searching for. She was scrupulous about client confidentiality, but she could be forthcoming if sharing the information was helpful to her client.

There was no answer at first, but she rang back half an hour later and confirmed at once that Salander seemed changed. Annika thought Salander's eyes had been opened to what was going on in the maximum security unit and could now see that it was unsafe. That's why Giannini had been pushing for Salander to be transferred. But Salander had refused to go. She had things to do, she said. And, so she insisted, she was not in any danger. But there were others, especially a young woman called Faria Kazi, who had been the victim of honour-related violence at home and was being abused in jail too.

"That's an interesting case," Giannini said. "I'm thinking of taking it on. We may well have a common interest here, Mikael."

"What do you mean?"

"You land a good story, and I might get some help with my research. Something about it doesn't feel quite right."

Blomkvist did not take the bait. Instead he said:

"Have you heard any more about the threats against Lisbeth?"

"Not really, except that there's a frightening number of sources. All the talk is about her sister, those criminals in Russia and the Svavelsjö M.C."

"What are you doing about it?"

"Everything I can, Mikael. What do you think? I've put pressure on the prison to ramp up their efforts to guard her. Right now I don't see any acute danger. But there's something else that may have affected her."

"What's that?"

"Holger Palmgren went to see her."

"You're kidding."

"No, no, it was apparently a sight to see. But he insisted. I think it was important to him to go."

"I can't even imagine how he managed to make it to Flodberga."

"I helped him with the red tape and Lisbeth paid for the transport there and back. And there was a nurse in the car. He rolled into the jail in his wheelchair."

"Did the visit upset her?"

"She doesn't get upset easily, of course. But she and Holger are close, we both know that."

"Could Holger have said something to get her going?"

"Like what?"

"Something about her past, maybe. Nobody knows what went on there better than he does."

"She hasn't said so. The only thing she feels strongly about at the moment is that woman Faria Kazi."

"Have you heard of someone called Leo Mannheimer?"

"Sounds familiar. Why do you ask?"

"Just thinking."

"Did Lisbeth mention him?"

"I'll tell you later."

"Fine, but if you want to know what she and Holger talked about, it's probably best if you contact him yourself," Giannini said. "I think Lisbeth would appreciate it if you kept an extra eye on him just now."

"I will," he said.

They hung up and he called Palmgren at once. The line was busy, again and again for ages, and then suddenly there was no answer. Blomkvist considered going straight out to Liljeholmen. Then he thought about Palmgren's health. He was old and sick, in considerable pain. He needed his rest. Blomkvist decided to wait and instead kept going with his research into the Mannheimer family and Alfred Ögren.

He turned up a lot. He always found stuff when he dug deep. But there was nothing that stood out or seemed to be linked to Salander or the hacker attack. So he changed his strategy, precisely because of Palmgren and the old man's

knowledge about Salander's childhood. Blomkvist thought
it by no means impossible that Mannheimer belonged to her
past in some way; she had, after all, been talking about old
lists of names. He therefore decided to go way back in time,
at least as far back as the Internet and databases would allow.
An article in *Uppsala Nya Tidning* caught his eye. For a short
while the story had attracted a certain amount of attention
because it had been picked up in a T.T. telegramme which
went out the same day. As far as he could tell, the incident
had not been mentioned again, probably out of consideration for the people involved and because of the more indulgent approach of the media at that time—especially when it
came to the elite.

The dramatic event had taken place during an elk hunt in
Östhammar twenty-five years earlier. The Alfred Ögren hunting party, which Mannheimer's father, Herman, belonged to,
had headed back out to the woods after an extended lunch.
Wine had no doubt been consumed. It seems that there was
bright sunlight and for various reasons the group had dis-
persed. After two elk had been sighted among the trees, shots
were fired. An older man by the name of Per Fält, who at the
time was C.F.O. of Rosvik Group, said that he had become
disoriented by the excitement and confused by the animals'
rapid movements. He fired a shot and heard a scream and a
cry for help. A young psychologist named Carl Seger, one of
the hunting party, had been hit in the stomach, just below
the chest. He died not long after, beside a small brook.

Nothing in the ensuing police investigation suggested
that it had been anything other than an accident, still less
that either Alfred Ögren or Herman Mannheimer had been

involved. But Blomkvist thought he might be onto something, especially after he learned that Per Fält, the man who
fired the fatal shot, had died a year later, without leaving
a wife or children. In an inconsequential obituary he was
described as a "steadfast friend" and a dedicated and loyal
colleague in Rosvik Group.

Blomkvist looked out the window, lost in thought. The
sky had darkened over Riddarfjärden. A shift in the weather
had come and once more the damned rain had started to fall.
He stretched his back and massaged his shoulders. Could the
psychologist who had been shot have had any connection to
Leo Mannheimer?

There was no way of knowing. This could be a dead end,
a meaningless tragedy. Even so, Blomkvist tried to find as
much information as he could about the psychologist. There
was not much. When Carl Seger died, he was thirty-two and
had just gotten engaged. He had completed his doctorate at
Stockholm University the year before, with a dissertation
on the impact of hearing on self-perception. An "empirical
study," it was called.

It was not available online and he could not discover
exactly what the findings were, even though Seger had
touched briefly on the same topic in other essays Blomkvist
managed to find on Google Scholar. In one, the psychologist described a classic experiment which demonstrated
how subjects identify a picture of themselves more quickly,
among hundreds of others, if the picture has been embellished to make them appear more attractive. It is an evolutionary advantage to over-estimate ourselves when we need

to mate or seek leadership in our group, but this also entails a risk:

"Having too much faith in our capabilities can hinder development. Self-doubt plays a decisive role in our intellectual maturity," Seger wrote. Not exactly ground-breaking, but it was interesting at least that he referred to studies of children and the importance of self-confidence.

Blomkvist went into the kitchen to clear the table and tidy up around the sink. He resolved that he would hear Mannheimer's talk at the Fotografiska Museum, even without Malin. He was going to get to the bottom of this story. But before he could take his thoughts further, there was a ring at the door. He was annoyed—people should really phone ahead. He went to open the door anyway.

CHAPTER 5

June 18

Faria Kazi sat huddled on the bed in her cell, arms clasped around her knees. She was nothing more than a pale, vanishing shadow; that is how she thought of herself. But nearly everyone who met her was enchanted. It had been that way ever since she came to Sweden from Bangladesh at the age of four—and now she was twenty.

Faria grew up in a tower block in the Stockholm suburb of Vallholmen with four brothers, one younger and three older. Her childhood was uneventful. Her father, Karim, set up a chain of dry cleaners, became relatively prosperous, and later bought an apartment with large picture windows in Sickla.

Faria played basketball and did well at school, especially in languages, and she loved to sew and draw manga comic strips. But in her teenage years her freedom was gradually taken away from her. She knew it was a direct result of the wolf whistles she attracted in the neighbourhood once she hit puberty. Yet she was convinced that the change came from the world beyond, like a cold wind from the east. The situation worsened when her mother, Aisha, died of a massive stroke. The family lost not only a mother, but also a window on the world and a force for reason.

As she sat in her prison cell, Faria remembered the evening Hassan Ferdousi, the imam from Botkyrka, had paid an unexpected visit to their home. Faria was fond of the imam and she had been longing to talk to him. But Ferdousi had not come on a social call. From the kitchen she heard him say in an angry voice:

"You misunderstand Islam. If you go on like this, things will end badly—very badly."

After that evening, she believed so herself. Her two oldest brothers, Ahmed and Bashir, exuded a grim hatred that seemed increasingly unhealthy. They, and not her father, insisted she wear her niqab even to go round the corner to buy milk. If they had their way she would sit at home and rot. Her brother Razan was not as categorical, nor was he particularly involved. He had other interests. But that did not make him an ally. He tended to follow Ahmed and Bashir's lead; he too kept an eye on her.

Despite the supervision, Faria managed to find occasional windows of freedom, though it involved lying and being inventive. She was able to keep her laptop, and one day she saw online that Hassan Ferdousi himself would be taking part in a debate at Kulturhuset with a rabbi called Goldman on the religious oppression of women. It was the end of June. She had just graduated from Kungsholmen high school and she had not been outside for ten days. She was so longing to get away it almost killed her. Her aunt Fatima was a cartologist and single, and she was Faria's last ally in the family. It was not easy to convince her. But Fatima could tell how desperate Faria was, and eventually she agreed to say that she and Fazi would be meeting for a simple dinner. The brothers believed the story.

Fatima greeted Faria at her apartment in Tensta, but she allowed her to head straight into town. Faria had to be back at 8:30 p.m., when Bashir would come to collect her, but she had a bit of time. Her aunt had lent her a black dress and a pair of high-heeled shoes. That was perhaps overdoing it a little—she wasn't going to a party, she was attending a debate on religion. But being nicely dressed gave her a sense of occasion. In fact, she hardly remembered the discussion, she was far too caught up by just being there and seeing all the people in the audience, and once or twice she even found herself moved for no apparent reason.

After the debate there were questions, and somebody in the auditorium asked why it was that, whenever men establish a religion, it is always the women who end up suffering. Hassan Ferdousi answered rather darkly:

"It is deeply sad when we use the greatest being of all as an instrument for our own smallness."

She was reflecting on those words as people around her got to their feet. A young man in jeans and a white shirt came towards her. She was so unused to meeting a boy her own age without wearing a niqab or hijab that she felt naked and exposed. But she did not run away. She remained seated and observed him discreetly. He was around twenty-five years old and not especially tall, and although he did not look confident, his eyes shone. There was a lightness in his step which contrasted with the serious, even sombre look about him, and he also seemed shy, which she found reassuring. He addressed her in Bengali.

"You're from Bangladesh, aren't you?" he said.

"How can you tell?"

"I just know. From where?"

"Dhaka."

"Me too."

He smiled so warmly that she could not help smiling back. Their eyes met and her heart leaped. Afterwards all that Faria could recall was how they strolled out onto Sergels torg, talking quite openly from the outset. Before they had properly introduced themselves he was telling her about the blog he had contributed to in Dhaka which promoted free speech and human rights. The bloggers had ended up on Islamists' hit lists and had been targeted for murder, one after the other. They were butchered with cleavers, and the police and the government did nothing, "absolutely nothing," he said. And so he had been forced to leave Bangladesh and his family to seek asylum in Sweden.

"Once when it happened, I was right there. My best friend's blood was all over my sweater," he said. Even though she did not fully understand, at least not then, still she sensed a sorrow in him which was greater than her own, and she felt a closeness which she should not reasonably have been able to feel on such brief acquaintance.

His name was Jamal Chowdhury. She took his hand and they wandered towards Riksdagshuset. She was having difficulty swallowing. It was the first time in ages that she had felt completely alive. But the feeling did not last long. She became anxious and imagined Bashir's black eyes. When they reached Gamla Stan she went her own way. But during the days and weeks that followed she sought comfort in the memory of their meeting. It was like a secret treasure chamber.

Hardly surprising then that she clung to it in prison, especially on this evening just before the freight train came thundering by. With Benito's footsteps approaching, Faria knew in her whole body that this time would be worse than ever.

Olsen was in his office, still waiting for a call from Fager. But time passed and no call came. He swore under his breath and thought about his daughter. Olsen was scheduled to be off today with Vilda at a football tournament in Västerås, but he had cancelled everything because he did not dare to be away from the unit. When he asked his aunt to babysit for the umpteenth time, he felt like the worst father ever, but what was he to do?

His efforts to have Benito transferred had backfired. Benito knew all about it and glared threateningly at him. The whole place was seething. Everywhere the prisoners were whispering to each other as if there was about to be a major clash or breakout, and he, in turn, looked pleadingly at Salander. She had promised to deal with the situation, which worried him as much as the problem itself, and he had insisted that he would attempt to resolve it first. Five

days had now passed and he had achieved nothing. He was
scared to death.

Still, there was one positive outcome. He had believed he
would have to face an internal investigation because he was
caught on camera going into his office with Salander after
lockup, and staying until the small hours. In the days that
followed, he fully expected at any moment to be summoned
before the management and made to face the most awkward
questions. But it didn't happen. In the end he could stand it
no longer, and on the pretext of needing to check some incidents involving Beatrice Andersson, he took himself off to
the monitoring centre in B Unit. Apprehensively he located
footage from the evening of June 12 to the early hours of
June 13.

At first he could not take it in. He played the video over
and over, but all he saw was a quiet, deserted corridor with
no trace of either him or Salander. He was safe. Although he
would have loved to believe that, miraculously, the cameras
happened not to be working at that precise time, he knew
better. He had witnessed Salander hacking into the institution's server. She must have replaced some of the surveillance footage. It was a huge relief, but it also terrified him.
He swore and once again checked his e-mail. Not one word.
Was it really so damned difficult for someone to come and
take Benito away?

It was 7:15 p.m. Outside, the rain was cascading down,
and he ought to be checking that nothing unpleasant was
happening in Kazi's cell. He should be out there man-
marking Benito and making her life a misery. But he stayed
where he was, paralyzed. He looked around his office and

felt queasy. What could Salander have done yesterday when she was in here? Those hours had been weird. She had gone through those old registers again, this time searching for a Daniel Brolin. That much he knew, but otherwise Olsen had tried to avoid looking. He did not want to get involved. But then he had become involved, after all, whether he liked it or not. Salander had made a phone call via his computer. The strange thing was that she had sounded like a different person, friendly and thoughtful. During the conversation she asked if any new documents had turned up. And then, immediately afterwards, she had asked to be taken back to her cell.

Twenty-four hours later, Olsen was becoming increasingly uncomfortable, and resolved to go out into the unit. He jumped up from his office chair, but got no further. The internal telephone buzzed. It was Fager, finally calling back. Hammerfors Prison in Härnösand could take Benito the next morning. It was excellent news but Olsen was not as relieved as he thought he would be. At first he did not understand why. Then he heard the freight train passing. He hung up without another word and hurried to the cells.

Blomkvist would later say he had been assaulted. But it was one of the more agreeable assaults he had been subjected to in a long time. Malin Frode was in the doorway, soaked from the rain, make-up running down her cheeks, with a wild and determined look in her eyes. Blomkvist was not sure if she was there to punch him or tear his clothes off.

The result was somewhere in between. She pushed him against the wall, grabbed his hips and told him he was going to be punished for being all work and no play, and at the same time sexy as hell. And before he knew it she was straddling him on the bed. She came not once but twice.

Afterwards they lay close to each other, breathing heavily. He stroked her hair and said affectionate things to her. He realized he had really missed her. Sailing boats were crisscrossing on Riddarfjärden. Raindrops drummed on the rooftops. It was a good moment. But his thoughts drifted, and Malin was immediately aware of it.

"Am I boring you already?" she said.

"What? No, no, I've been longing for you," he said, and he meant it. But he was also feeling guilty. Moments after making love with a woman he hadn't been with for a long time, he shouldn't be thinking about work.

"When did you last utter an honest word?"

"I do try to, and quite often, actually."

"Is it Erika again?"

"Well, no. It's what we talked about on the phone."

"The hacker attack?"

"And other things."

"And Leo?"

"Him too."

"Then tell me, for God's sake. Why the hell are you so interested in him?"

"I'm not sure I *am*. I'm just trying to piece together some things."

"That's clear as mud, Kalle Blomkvist."

"Oh?"

"So there's something you're not telling me. Maybe you're trying to protect your source?" she said.

"Maybe."

"Bastard!"

"Sorry."

Her face softened and she brushed back a lock of her hair.

"I did actually think about Leo for a long time after we spoke," she said.

She drew the duvet closer around her. She was irresistible.

"Did you come up with anything?" he asked her.

"I remembered him promising to tell me what had made him so happy. But then when he was no longer happy it seemed heartless to press him."

"What made you think of that?"

She hesitated and looked out the window.

"Probably because I was glad of his happiness, but I worried about it too. It was excessive."

"Perhaps he was in love."

"I asked him exactly that and he flatly denied it. We were in the bar at Riche, and that in itself was unusual. Leo hated crowds. But he had agreed to come and we were supposed to be discussing who would be taking over from me. Leo was impossible. As soon as I mentioned some names, he changed the subject; he wanted to talk about love and life, and he went into a monologue about his music. It was incomprehensible and pretty dull, frankly. Something about being born to like certain harmonies and scales. I wasn't really listening. He was on such a high that I was offended, and like a fool I went at him. 'What's going on? You've got to tell me.'

But he refused to say anything else. He couldn't tell me, not yet. All he would say was that he had finally discovered where he belonged."

"He'd seen the light?"

"Leo hated religion."

"So what was it?"

"No idea. All I know is that it ended as quickly as it started, a few days later. He totally fell apart."

"How do you mean?"

"It was just before Christmas a year and a half ago, my last day at Alfred Ögren. I'd had a farewell party at home and Leo hadn't turned up, and that upset me. After all, we had been close." She shot Blomkvist a look. "No need to be jealous."

"It takes more than that to make me jealous."

"I know. And I hate you for it. You could at least humour me by pretending. Anyway, we had a harmless flirtation, Leo and I, around the time I met you. My life was a disaster, what with the divorce and everything, and that's probably why I was so struck by the immense happiness he had suddenly found. Plus it was at odds with his character. After the party, I called him in the middle of the night and he was still in the office, which only upset me more. But he apologized so profusely that I forgave him, and when he asked me to come up for a nightcap I ran over right away. I had no idea what to expect. Leo wasn't exactly a workaholic, and there was no reason for him to be there that late. That room used to be his father's office. There's a Dardel hanging on the wall. A Haupt chest of drawers standing in the corner. Mind-boggling. Sometimes Leo would say he was embarrassed by it, by the obscene luxury. But that evening when I went up there . . . I can hardly describe it. His eyes glowed, and there was something new, something broken in his voice. He was trying his best to smile and look happy, but his eyes looked lost and sad. There was an empty bottle of Burgundy and two used glasses on the chest of drawers. He had obviously had a visitor. We embraced and exchanged pleasantries, drank half a bottle of Champagne and promised to stay in touch. But it was obvious his mind was elsewhere. In the end I said: 'You don't seem happy anymore.' 'I am happy,' he said. 'I've just . . .' He didn't finish the sentence. He was quiet for a long time. Drained his glass of Champagne. Looked upset. Said he was going to make a large donation."

"To whom?"

"I have no idea, and I wondered if it was a spur of the moment decision. He immediately seemed embarrassed by what he had said, and I decided not to pursue it. It felt too private, and afterwards we just sat there awkwardly. In the end I got up, and he jumped up too, and we hugged again and kissed a little half-heartedly. I told him to take care and went out into the corridor to wait for the lift. A minute later I was getting annoyed and decided to go back. Why was he being secretive? What was he playing at? I wanted to understand. But when I reached his room—I mean, even before I could open my mouth—I realized I was disturbing him. He was sitting, writing on a distinctive-looking sheet of paper, and you could tell that he was taking extra care with each word. His shoulders were tense. He seemed to have tears in his eyes. I didn't have the heart to interrupt, and he never even noticed me."

"You have no idea what it was all about?"

"I guessed afterwards that it had something to do with his mother. She died a few days later, and Leo took a leave of absence as you know and disappeared on those extended travels. I should probably have gotten in touch and expressed my condolences. But, as you know, my own life then turned into a nightmare. I was working day and night at my new job, and having spectacular fights with my ex-husband in between. And on top of all that I was sleeping with you."

"Must have been the worst part."

"Probably was."

"And you haven't seen Leo since?"

"Not in the flesh, just in a short clip on T.V. I think I'd forgotten about him, or more likely pushed him from my mind. But when you called today"—Malin hesitated, as if she was searching for words—"I remembered that scene from the office, and it felt somehow wrong. I couldn't put my finger on it. It just bothered me. In the end I got so irritated that I tried to call him, but he's changed his number."

"Did I mention the psychologist who was killed at an Alfred Ögren hunting party? It happened when Leo was a child," Blomkvist said.

"Er, no, why?"

"His name was Carl Seger."

"The name doesn't ring a bell. What happened?"

"Seger was shot in the stomach twenty-five years ago during an elk hunt, in the forests around Östhammar—probably by accident. The person who fired the gun was Rosvik's C.F.O., Per Fält."

"Do you suspect foul play?"

"Not really, at least not yet. But I thought Seger and Leo may have had a close relationship. Leo's parents were prepared to invest a lot in the boy, weren't they? Practising for I.Q. tests and so forth. I read that Seger wrote about the importance of self-confidence for young people's development, so I was wondering—"

"Leo probably had more self-doubt than self-confidence," Malin said.

"Seger wrote about that too. Did Leo talk often about his parents?"

"Sometimes, but only reluctantly."

"Doesn't sound good."

"I'm sure Herman and Viveka had their qualities, but I believe one of Leo's tragedies was that he never managed to stand up to them. He was never allowed to go his own way."

"His becoming a reluctant financier, in other words."

"Some part of him must have wanted that too. Things are never straightforward. But I'm pretty sure his dream was to break free. Maybe that's why that scene at his desk troubles me. He almost seemed to be saying farewell—not just to his mother but also to something else, something bigger."

"You called him a Hamlet."

"Mainly as a contrast to you, I think. But it's true that he dithered about everything."

"Hamlet turned violent in the end."

"Ha, yes, but Leo would never . . ."

"Never what?"

A shadow flitted over Malin's face, and Blomkvist put a hand on her shoulder.

"What is it?"

"Nothing."

"Oh, come on."

"Well, I did once see Leo lose it completely," she said.

At 7:29 p.m. Faria felt the first shuddering of the freight train like a fierce pain shooting through her body. Only sixteen minutes to go before locking up. But a lot could happen in that time, she knew that better than anyone. The guards were rattling their keys out in the corridor, voices were raised, and even though she did not catch what was said, she could sense agitation in the hubbub. She had no idea what it was about, only that there was an urgency. And she had heard a rumour that Benito might be leaving. An hour ago it had felt like thunder was on its way. Now the shaking of the train was all that reached them from the outside world.

The walls appeared to be quaking, the inmates were walking back and forth, yet nothing serious seemed to be happening. Perhaps she would be left in peace tonight after all. The guards looked more watchful. The warden, Olsen, had been keeping a close eye on her, and he seemed to be working all hours. Maybe he would protect her, finally. Maybe it would be alright, whatever was being whispered out there. She thought about her brothers and her mother, and how once upon a time the sun had shone over the lawns in Vall-holmen.

But her dreaming was cut short. The sound of shuffling sandals could be heard from some distance, a sound she recognized with fear, and now there could be no doubt. Faria found it hard to breathe. She wished she could smash a hole in the wall and escape along the railway line, or vanish as if by magic, but she was at the mercy of her cell and her bed. She was as vulnerable as she had ever been in Sickla, and she tried to think about Jamal again. But that did not help; there was no solace to be found anywhere. The freight train rumbled past, the footsteps got closer and soon she would smell that sweet perfume again. Within a few seconds she would be slung into the same bottomless pit as ever, and it did not matter how many times she told herself that her life was already ruined, that she had nothing more to lose. She was petrified every time Benito appeared in her doorway and with a winning smile told her that her brothers sent their regards.

It was not clear whether Benito had ever met Bashir and Ahmed or was even in touch with them. The greeting was like a deadly threat, and it was always followed by Benito slapping and caressing her, touching her breasts and between her legs, calling her a slut and a whore. But the fondling and the insults weren't the worst of it. It was the feeling that this was all a preparation for something far more terrible. Sometimes she expected to see a glint of steel in Benito's hand.

Benito owed her notoriety to a pair of Indonesian knives she was rumoured to have forged herself while uttering a stream of oaths. It was said that just having the knives pointed at a person was a death sentence. The myths accompanied Benito along the prison corridors like an evil aura that mingled with her perfume. Faria had often imagined what would happen if Benito came at her with knives. Some days she thought she would welcome it.

She listened for sounds in the unit, and for a moment her

hopes lifted. There was no longer shuffling. Had Benito been stopped? No, the feet were on the move again, and Benito had company. Now the smell of perfume was mixed with an acrid stench of sweat, and peppermints. Tine Grönlund, Benito's stooge and bodyguard. Faria knew that this was no reprieve, but rather an escalation. It was going to be bad.

Benito's painted toenails were now visible in the door-way, her pale feet sticking out of standard-issue plastic sandals. She had rolled up her shirtsleeves to expose her snake tattoos. She was sweaty, and made up, and cold-eyed. Yet she was smiling. Nobody had as unpleasant a smile as Benito. She was followed by Grönlund, who closed the cell door behind them—even though only the guards were allowed to close doors.

"Greta and Lauren are right outside. So we don't need to worry about being disturbed," Grönlund said.

Benito took a step towards Faria, fingering something in her trouser pocket. Her smile narrowed to a thin line, a mere suggestion. New furrows formed on her pale forehead. A drop of sweat appeared on her lip.

"We're in kind of a hurry," she said. "The screws want to send me away, have you heard? So we have to come to a decision right now. We like you, Faria. You're a looker, and we like beautiful girls. But we like your brothers too. They've made a very generous offer, and now we'd like to know . . ."

"I don't have any money," Faria said.

"A girl can pay in other ways, and we have our preferences, our own currency, don't we, Tine? I've got something for you, Faria, which might make you a little more cooperative."

Again Benito's hand went to her pocket and she gave a broad smile. A smile that contained an icy certainty of victory.

"What do you think I've got here?" she said. "What could it be? It's not my Keris, so you don't need to worry about that. But it's still something valuable to me."

She pulled a black object from her pocket with a metallic click. Faria could not breathe. It was a stiletto knife. She went so rigid with terror that she had no time to react when Benito grabbed her by the hair and forced her head back.

Slowly the blade came closer to her throat until it was pointed at her carotid artery, as if Benito was demonstrating where to make the deadliest cut. Benito hissed and spat about atoning for one's sins in blood and making the family happy again. Faria felt the sweet perfume in her nostrils and inhaled a breath which was sour with tobacco, as well as something stale, sickly. She was incapable of any further thought and shut her eyes, and so did not understand why a sudden flutter of alarm had spread through the cell. But then she realized that the door behind her had opened and closed again.

Someone else was in the room. At first, Faria could not make out who. But from the corner of her eye she saw Salander. She looked strange, vacant and lost in thought, as if she didn't know where she was. She didn't even flinch when Benito came towards her.

"I'm not interrupting anything, am I?" she said.

"Goddamn right you are. Who the hell let you in?"

"The girls you left out there. They didn't make much of a fuss."

"Idiots! Can't you see what I have here," Benito hissed, brandishing her stiletto.

Salander glanced at the knife but did not react to that either. She looked absently at Benito.

"Fuck off, you slut, or I'll cut you up like a pig."

"I'm afraid you won't have time for that," Salander said.

"You don't think so?"

A wave of hatred rippled through the cell and Benito lunged towards Salander, knife raised. Faria never understood what happened next. A punch was thrown, an elbow jabbed, and it was as if Benito had run into a wall. Paralyzed, she fell onto her face on the concrete floor, not even breaking her fall with her hands. And then there was silence; only the freight train clattering by outside.

CHAPTER 6

June 18

Malin Frode and Blomkvist were leaning against the headboard. Blomkvist ran his fingertips across her shoulders and said:

"What happened to send Leo into such a state?"

"Have you got any decent red wine? I could use it."

"I've got some Barolo, I think," he said, and dragged himself off to the kitchen.

When he came back with the bottle and two glasses, Malin was gazing out the window. Rain was still falling over Riddarfjärden. A light mist lay over the water and there were sirens in the distance. Blomkvist poured the wine and kissed Malin on the cheek and mouth. As she began to talk, he pulled the duvet over them again.

"You know that Alfred Ögren's son Ivar is now the C.E.O., even though he's the youngest of the children. He's only three years older than Leo and the two of them have known each other since they were small. But they're not exactly friends. In fact, they hate each other."

"How come?"

"Rivalry, insecurity, you name it. Ivar knows Leo is cleverer and can see right through his blustering and lies, and he's got a complex, not just an intellectual one. Ivar spends his time eating out at expensive restaurants, and even though he's not yet forty he already looks like a bloated old man, whereas Leo's a runner and on a good day could pass for twenty-five. On the other hand, Ivar's more enterprising and forceful, and then . . ."

Malin pulled a face and drank some wine.

"And then what?"

"I'm embarrassed about this: that I was a part of it. Ivar could be a decent enough guy, maybe a bit full of himself, but OK. Other times he was a nightmare and it was terrible to witness. I think he was afraid that Leo would take over. Many people, even some on the board, wanted that. During my last week at the company—it was before I saw Leo that night—the three of us had a meeting. We were supposed to be discussing my successor, but inevitably we got onto other topics and, you know, Ivar was irritated right from the word go. I'm sure he picked up on the same thing I did. Leo was ridiculously happy, as if he were floating above everything. Besides, he had hardly been in to work all week and Ivar ripped into him, calling Leo a moralizing idler and a wimp. At first Leo took it well. He just smiled. That drove Ivar crazy and he started saying the most terrible things: racist slurs, like Leo was a gyppo. It was so absurd that I thought Leo would ignore the idiot. But he leaped up from his chair and grabbed Ivar by the throat. It was crazy. I threw myself at Leo and pulled him to the floor. I remember him muttering, 'We're better, we're better,' until finally he calmed down."

"What did Ivar do?"

"He didn't move from his chair, just stared at us in shock. Then he leaned forward, looking shamefaced, and apologized. After that he left and there I was on the floor with Leo."

"And what did Leo say?"

"Nothing, as far as I remember. It was a pretty fucked-up way to behave."

"But wasn't it fucked-up to call him a gyppo?"

"That's Ivar for you. When he gets upset, he becomes a monster. He could just as well have called him a creep or a pig. I think he's inherited that narrow-mindedness from his father. There's a whole lot of prejudiced crap in that family, and that's what I mean when I say I'm embarrassed. I should never have been working at Alfred Ögren."

Blomkvist nodded and drained his glass. Probably he should have asked a few more questions, or said something to comfort Malin, but he said nothing. Something was weighing on his mind, and at first he could not grasp it. Then it came to him that Salander's mother, Agneta, had come from a family of Gypsies on her father's side. Blomkvist seemed to recall that Salander's name had been listed in registers which had later been made illegal.

"You don't suppose . . ." he said at last.

"What?"

". . . that Ivar actually sees himself as superior?"

"I'm sure he does."

"I mean racially superior."

"That would be odd. Mannheimer's as blue-blooded as they come. What are you suggesting?"

"I'm not sure."

Malin looked wistful, and Blomkvist kissed her shoulder. He knew exactly what he needed to check. He would have to go a long way back in time, to the old church records if necessary.

Salander had landed quite a punch—possibly it was *too* hard. She knew it before Benito collapsed, even before she hit her, by the ease of her movements, by the unopposed force. By the way anyone who does explosive sports knows that the more effortless the action, the closer it comes to perfection.

She had swung a right at Benito's windpipe with surprising precision, and in rapid succession elbowed her twice in the jaw. Then she took a step to one side, and not only to make room for the fall. She needed to size up the situation. So she watched as Benito collapsed without protecting herself with her hands and smacked into the floor, chin first. Salander heard the crunch of breaking bones. It was better than she had hoped for.

Benito lay motionless on her stomach, her face twisted stiffly into a grimace. She gave no sound, not even of breathing. Nobody would shed fewer tears for Benito than Salander, but her death would be an unlooked-for complication. Besides which, Tine Grönlund was standing there right next to her.

Grönlund was no Benito. She seemed more of a natural follower, someone who needed to be told what to do. But she was tall and sinewy and fast, and her punch had a long reach which was hard to handle, especially when it came from the side, as now. Salander only half parried it. Her ears rang and her cheek burned and she readied herself for another round. But there wasn't one. Instead of launching an assault, Grönlund simply stared at Benito lying on the floor. Things were not looking good down there.

It was not only the blood coming out of her mouth and running into red, claw-like trickles along the concrete floor, it was her whole twisted body and face. Benito looked like a case for long-term care—if not worse.

"Benito, are you alive?" Tine croaked.

"She's alive," Salander said, without being entirely sure.

She had knocked out people before, both in the ring and outside it, and there had almost always been some whimpering or movement pretty much straightaway. Now there was nothing, only a silence which seemed amplified by the quivering nervousness in the air.

"What the fuck—she's completely lifeless," Tine hissed.

"You're right, she's not looking too good," Salander said.

Tine muttered a threat and looked ready to launch an attack. Then she stormed out, arms flailing. Salander remained impassive and stood her ground, her eyes on Faria. Faria sat on the bed in a blue shirt which was too big for her, arms clasped around her knees, and looked at Salander in bewilderment.

"I'm going to get you out of here," Salander said.

. . .

Palmgren was at home in Liljeholmen in his medical bed. He was thinking about his conversation with Salander. He was sorry that he still couldn't answer her question. He was feeling too wretched and unwell to find the documents himself. He had pain in his hips and legs and was quite unable to walk, even with his walker. He needed help with almost everything and aides came to his home. Most treated him like a five-year-old and did not seem to like their work, or even old people in general. Sometimes, but not often—he had his pride—he regretted having so flatly turned down Salander's offer to pay for qualified private care. Only the other day he had asked one of them, Marita—who was young and stern and always looked disgusted when she had to get him out of bed—whether she had any children.

"I don't want to talk about my personal life," she snapped at him.

So he was suspected of prying when he was only trying to be polite! Old age was degrading, an attack on one's integrity. That is how he saw it, and just a moment ago, when he needed to be changed, he had been reminded of Gunnar Ekelöf's poem "Waterlilies."

He had not read it since he was a young man. But still he remembered it well, maybe not word for word, but most of it. The poem was about a man—presumably the poet's alter ego—who wrote what he called a preface to his own death. He wanted his last trace to be a clenched fist rising through a pond of water lilies, words bubbling to the surface.

Palmgren had been feeling so miserable that this poem seemed to offer the only hope left to him—defiance! His condition would undoubtedly worsen, and soon Palmgren would be lying in bed like a cabbage, and probably lose his mind as well. All he had to look forward to was death. But that did not mean he had to accept it—that was the message and consolation offered by the poem. He could clench his fist in protest. He could sink to the bottom, proud and rebellious, raging against the pain, the incontinence, the immobility, all the humiliation.

His life was not exclusively misery. He still had friends and above all he had Salander. And Lulu, who would soon arrive to help him find the documents. Lulu was from Somalia. She was tall and beautiful, with long plaited hair. Her expression was so sincere that it gave him back some measure of self-esteem. It was Lulu who had the last shift at night, putting on his morphine patches and then his nightshirt and bedding him down. Even though she still made mistakes in Swedish, her questions were genuine. And they were not fatuous platitudes in the plural such as: "Are we feeling a little better now?" She asked him for suggestions on what she should study and learn, for stories about what Palmgren himself had done in his life, for his thoughts. She saw him as a human being, not some old carcass with no history.

These days Lulu was one of the highlights in his life, and the only person he had told about Salander and his visit to Flodberga. It had been a nightmare. Just seeing that high prison wall started him trembling. How could they put Salander in a place like that? She had done something fantastic, after all. She had saved a child's life. Yet she found herself among the worst female offenders in the country. It was plain wrong. And when he saw her in the visitors' room, he was so upset that he had not watched his words as he usually did.

He asked about her dragon tattoo. He had always wondered about it, and indeed he belonged to a generation that had no understanding of tattooing as an art form. Why embellish yourself with something that never goes away, when we constantly change and evolve?

Salander's answer was short and concise, and yet more than enough. He felt touched by it, and kept babbling on nervously and randomly. He must have gotten her thinking about her childhood, which was idiotic, especially since he himself hardly knew what he was talking about. What was the matter with him? It was not just down to his age and poor judgment. A few weeks earlier he had had an unexpected visit from a woman called Maj-Britt Torell, a bird-like elderly lady who had once been a secretary to Dr. Johannes Caldin, the head of St. Stefan's psychiatric clinic in Uppsala at the time when Salander had been a patient there. Torell had read newspaper articles about Salander and had decided to go through the boxes of case notes she had taken responsibility for when Caldin died. She was careful to point out that she had never before breached doctor-patient confidentiality. But in this case there were special circumstances, "as you know. It was dreadful how that girl was treated, wasn't it?" Torell was anxious to hand over the papers, to make the truth known.

Once Palmgren had thanked Torell, said goodbye and read through the notes, despair came over him. It was the same sorry old tale: psychiatrist Peter Teleborian had strapped Salander down in his treatment room and subjected her to serious abuse. There was nothing new in the documents, as far as he could tell, but he might be mistaken. It had taken only a few careless words at the prison to get Salander going. Now she knew that she had been part of a government-sponsored study. She said other children had been involved, both in the generation before her and later. But she had not managed to find the names of the people behind it all. Great efforts appeared to have been made to keep them off the Internet and out of all archives.

"Could you take another look and see if you can find anything?" she had said on the phone. He certainly would, as soon as Lulu came to help him.

A burst of spluttering and spitting could be heard coming from the floor, and even before Faria could make out any sounds she recognized them as curses and threats. She looked down at Benito. The woman lay with her arms spread wide. No part of her body was moving, not even a finger, nothing apart from her head which she raised a couple of inches off the ground, and her eyes, which stared sideways up at Salander.

"My Keris is pointed at you!"

The voice was so muffled and hoarse that it was barely human. In Faria's mind, the words flowed together with the blood that trickled from Benito's mouth.

"The dagger's pointed at you. You're dead."

This was nothing short of a death sentence. For a moment Benito seemed to be recovering some ground, but Salander did not look at all concerned. She said, as if she had hardly been listening, "You're the one who looks dead."

Then, Salander was listening out for noises in the corridor and it was as if Benito was no longer a factor. Faria heard heavy, quick steps approaching. Somebody was rushing towards her cell, and the next moment voices and swearing could be heard outside, and then: "Out of the fucking way!" The door flew open and Warden Olsen stood on the threshold. He was in his usual blue guard's shirt, short of breath. He had obviously been running.

"My God, what the hell's happened here?"

He looked from Benito on the floor to Salander, and then to Faria Kazi on the bed.

"What the *hell* has happened?" he said again.

"Look there on the floor," Salander said.

Olsen looked down and spotted the stiletto lying in a runnel of blood just by Benito's right hand.

"What the fuck . . . ?"

"Exactly. Someone got a knife past your metal detector. So what happened is that the staff at a major prison lost control and failed to protect a prisoner under threat."

"But that . . . that . . ." Olsen muttered, beside himself now and pointing at Benito's jaw.

"It's what you should have done a long time ago, Alvar."

Olsen stared at Benito's smashed-up face.

"My Keris is pointed at you. You're going to die, Salander, die," Benito spat, and at that Olsen felt true panic set in. He pressed the alarm on his belt and shouted for backup, then turned to Salander.

"She's going to kill you."

"That's my problem," Salander said. "I've had worse jerks threaten me."

"There *is* nobody worse."

Footsteps could be heard in the corridor. Had those shit-heads been nearby all along? It would not surprise him in the least. He felt a violent rage bubble up within him, and he thought about Vilda and the threats; in fact the entire unit, which was a disgrace. He looked at Salander again and remembered her words: what he should have done a long time ago. He knew he needed to do something. He had to recover his dignity. But there was no time. His colleagues, Harriet and Fred, crashed into the cell and stood as if paralyzed. They too saw Benito lying on the floor and heard the oaths being uttered, but now it was impossible to make sense of what she was trying to say. Fragments of words, only Ke or Kri, in Benito's evil rant.

"Oh, shit!" Fred shouted. "Oh, shit!"

Olsen took a step forward and cleared his throat. Only then did Fred look at him. There was fear in Fred's eyes, sweat was beading on his forehead and cheeks.

"Harriet, call the medic," Olsen said. "Quick, *quick*! And you, Fred . . ."

He did not know what to say. He wanted to play for time, to assert some authority, but clearly it wasn't working for him, because Fred interrupted in the same agitated tone:

"What a fucking *disaster*! What happened?"

"Things got very ugly," Olsen said.

"Did *you* hit her?"

Olsen did not answer, not at first. But then he remembered the chillingly accurate description of the route to Vilda's classroom. He remembered that Benito had told him the colour of his daughter's gum boots.

"I . . ." he said.

He hesitated. Yet he sensed that there was something both terrifying and appealing about the word "I." He shot a look at Salander. She shook her head, as if she knew exactly what was going through his mind. But no . . . it was make or break. It felt right.

"I had no choice."

"For Christ's sake, this looks horrible. Benito, Benito, are you OK?" Fred said. And that was the final straw after months of turning a blind eye.

"Instead of worrying about Benito, why don't you look after Faria," Olsen yelled. "We've let the whole unit go to shit. Look at the stiletto on the floor! See it? Benito's smuggled in a goddamn murder weapon, and she was about to attack Faria when I . . ."

He was groping for words. It was as if all of a sudden he realized the enormity of his lie, and almost in desperation he looked again at Salander, hoping to be rescued. But she was not about to spare him.

"She was going to kill me," Faria Kazi said from the bed. She pointed to a small cut on her throat and that gave Olsen renewed courage.

"So what was I supposed to do? Just wait and see if it all turned out OK?" he growled at Fred. And that felt better, though he was increasingly aware of the risk he was taking.

But it was too late to back out now. Other inmates were gathering in the doorway, some even pushing to get into the cell. The situation was going to get out of hand and there were agitated voices in the corridor. A few were also clapping. A great sense of relief began to spread. One woman shouted for joy, and the voices became a buzz, a wall of sound which grew in strength, something like the aftermath of a blood-thirsty boxing match or bullfight.

Yet not all the commotion was joyful. There were also threatening noises, threats to Salander rather than to him, as if a rumour about what had really happened had already gotten out. He knew he had to act with determination. In a loud voice he announced that the police were to be informed at once. He knew more guards would be on their way from other units, that was standard procedure when the alarm went off, and he wondered whether to lock the prisoners into their cells or if he should wait for reinforcements. He looked at Kazi and told Harriet and Fred that she should be seen by the medical orderlies and a psychologist too. Then he turned to Salander and instructed her to follow him.

They went into the corridor, elbowing past a crowd of prisoners and guards, and for a moment he thought the situation might boil over. People were shouting and pulling at them. The unit was on the verge of a riot. It was as if all the tension and exasperation which had been simmering beneath the surface for so long was about to explode. Only with the greatest effort did he manage to escort Salander into her cell and shut the door behind them. Someone started banging on it. His colleagues were shouting for order. His heart was pounding, his mouth was dry and he could not think what to say. Salander was not even looking at him. She just glanced at her desk and ran her fingers through her hair.

"I like to take responsibility for my actions," she said.

"I was trying to protect you."

"Bullshit. You wanted to feel a little better about yourself. But that's OK, Alvar. You can go now."

He wanted to say something more. He wanted to explain himself, but he could tell it would only sound ridiculous. He turned away and heard her mumble behind his back:

"I hit her in the windpipe."

The windpipe? he thought, as he locked the door. Then he fought his way through the mayhem in the corridor.

As Palmgren waited for Lulu, he tried to remember what the documents had actually said. Could there be something new and important buried in them? He found it hard to believe he would uncover more than he already knew: that there had been plans for Salander to be put up for adoption when things were really bad with her father, including his sexual assaults against Agneta.

Well, he would find out soon enough. On the four days of the week she worked, Lulu always arrived punctually at 9:00 p.m. He longed to see her. She would help with his bedtime routine, put on the morphine patch and make him comfortable, and then retrieve the papers from the bottom drawer in the chest in the living room where she had put them the last time, after Maj-Britt Torell's visit.

Palmgren vowed to devote his utmost attention to them.

This might give him the pleasure of helping Salander one last time. He groaned and felt a sharp pain in his hips. This was the worst time of day and he said a small prayer: "Dear, wonderful Lulu. I need you. Come now." And indeed he lay there for five, perhaps ten minutes, drumming his good hand against the bed cover, when steps he thought he recognized echoed in the hallway.

The door opened. Was she twenty minutes early? How wonderful! But there was no cheerful greeting from the front door, no "Good evening, my old friend," only footsteps stealing into the apartment and coming towards his bedroom. This scared him, and he was not easily scared. One of the advantages of age was that he no longer had much to lose. But now he was anxious, perhaps because of those papers. He wanted to read them properly, to use them to help Salander. All of a sudden he had something to live for.

"Hello," he called out. "Hel*lo*?"

"Oh—are you awake? I thought you would be asleep."

"But I'm never asleep when you arrive," he said, perceptibly relieved.

"I don't think you realize how exhausted and run-down you've been these last days. I thought that visit to the prison might be the end of you," Lulu said as she came through the doorway.

She was wearing eye make-up and lipstick and a brightly coloured African dress.

"Has it been that bad?"

"You have been almost impossible to talk to."

"I'm sorry. I'll try and do better."

"You're my number one, you know that. Your only flaw is that you keep saying sorry."

"Sorry."

"You see?"

"What's with you today, Lulu? You're looking particularly lovely."

"I'm going out with a Swedish guy from Västerhaninge. Can you imagine? He's an engineer and owns a house and a new Volvo."

"He's smitten with you, of course?"

"I hope so," she said. She straightened out his legs and hips, making sure he was lying properly on the pillow, and raised the backrest into a sitting position. As the bed moved with a soft buzzing sound she chattered on about the man from Västerhaninge who was called Robert, or possibly Rolf. Palmgren was not listening, and Lulu laid a hand on his forehead.

"You're in a cold sweat, silly. I should shower you."

No-one could call him silly with as much tenderness as Lulu. Usually he enjoyed this banter, but today he was impatient. He looked down at his lifeless left hand, which seemed more pitiful than ever.

"I'm sorry, Lulu. Could you do something for me first?"

"Always your service."

"Always *at* your service," he corrected her. "You know those papers you put away in the chest last time? Can you fetch them? I need to read them again."

"But you said it was awful to read them."

"It was. But I have to take another look."

She hurried off and reappeared a minute or two later with a larger sheaf than he remembered having looked through in the first place. Maybe she had grabbed more than one file. He began to fret. Either there would be nothing of significance in the papers, or else there would be, in which case who could predict what Lisbeth would get up to.

"You seem chirpier today. But you're not a hundred percent, are you? Is it that Salander woman you're thinking about?" Lulu said, setting down the bundle of papers on the bedside table next to his pill boxes and books.

"I'm afraid so. It was awful to see her in that prison. Can you fetch my toothbrush and put on my morphine patches? Move my legs a little bit over to the left, please. It feels as if the whole lower part of my body has—"

"—knives sticking in it?" she said.

"Exactly, knives. Do I say that all the time?"

"Yes, all the time."

"You see, I'm going senile. But I'll read these papers, and you can disappear off to see your Roger."

"Rolf," she corrected him.

"Right, Rolf. I hope he's nice. Being nice is the most important thing."

"Is it really? Did you choose your lovers based on their niceness?"

"I certainly should have."

"That's what all men say, and then they go chasing after the first beautiful woman they see."

"What? No, I never did."

His mind was drifting. He asked Lulu to put the files on

the bed beside him, but he barely managed to lift one even with his good arm. As Lulu unbuttoned his shirt, he began to read. Every now and then as Lulu got on with her work, he broke off to say something kind and encouraging. He wished her an especially fond farewell and good luck with her Rolf or Roger.

Just as he had recalled, the papers mostly consisted of observations by the psychiatrist Peter Teleborian: medication protocols, notes on pills the patient had refused to take and accounts of treatment regimens during which she silently dug in her heels, decisions to use coercive measures, re-evaluations, second opinions, decisions to use even more coercive measures, clear indications of sadism, even if expressed in dry, clinical terms—all the things which had so tormented Palmgren.

But he could find none of the information Salander was looking for even though he had read very carefully. He began to go through it all once more, and to be on the safe side he would use his magnifying glass this time. He studied each page closely, and eventually he did pick up something, though not much: two minor confidential notes made by Teleborian soon after Salander had been admitted to the clinic in Uppsala. But they gave Palmgren precisely what he had been asked to find—names.

The first note read:

Already known from the Registry for the Study of Genetics and Social Environment (R.G.S.E.). Took part in Project 9. (Finding: Unsatisfactory.)

Placement in foster home decided by Professor of Sociology Martin Steinberg. Impossible to enforce. Liable to run away.

Fertile imagination. Serious incident with G. in apartment on Lundagatan—ran away at the age of six.

Ran away at the age of six? Was that the incident Salander had referred to during his visit to the prison? It must have been, which might make G. the woman with the birthmark on her throat. But there was nothing more about it in the documents and so he could not be sure. Palmgren thought hard. Then he had another look at Teleborian's note and smiled a little. "Fertile imagination," the man had written. It was the only positive comment that bastard had ever made about Salander. Even a donkey can sometimes . . . But this was no joke. The note confirmed that Salander had been on the verge of being sent away as a child. Palmgren read on:

Mother, Agneta Salander, severely brain-damaged by blow to the head. Admitted to Äppelviken nursing home. Had previously been seen by psychologist Hilda von Kanterborg— who is believed to have broken confidentiality and disclosed information about the Registry. Should not be given any opportunity to contact the patient. Further measures planned by Professor Steinberg and G.

Professor Steinberg, he thought. Martin Steinberg. Somehow the name seemed familiar. With difficulty—it was the same with everything these days—Palmgren Googled the man on his mobile, and he recognized him at once. How could he have missed it? Not that he and Martin had been close. But they had met about twenty-five years ago. Steinberg was an expert witness at a trial in which Palmgren had defended an underprivileged young man who had been charged with assaulting his father.

He recalled his delight at having a resource like Steinberg on his side. Steinberg served on a number of prestigious committees and inquiries. His views tended to be antiquated, even rigid, but he had been a useful person to have on the case and his client had been acquitted. They had a drink together after the trial, and had met several times since. Palmgren could perhaps get something out of him.

Palmgren lay in bed, the large stack of papers resting on his chest and stomach. He tried to think clearly. Would it be rash to attempt to contact Steinberg? He spent ten or fifteen minutes mulling it over while the morphine did its work and the pain in his hips began to feel more like needle pricks than knives. In the end, he dismissed the concern. Salander had asked for his help and he owed it to her to make an effort. So he worked out a strategy and then made the call. While the number was ringing he glanced at the clock. It was now 10:20 p.m. A little late, but not too late. He would be careful. But as soon as Steinberg came on the line, Palmgren almost lost his nerve and he had to pull himself together to sound convincing.

"I hope I'm not intruding, calling at this hour," he said. "But I have a question for you."

Martin Steinberg was not unfriendly but he did sound apprehensive, and he didn't brighten up even when Palmgren congratulated him on all the grand appointments and assignments he had read about online. The professor dutifully enquired about Palmgren's health.

"What can I say, at my age? I have to be thankful that my body hurts and reminds me that it exists," Palmgren said, and tried to laugh. Steinberg laughed with him and they exchanged a few words about the old days.

Then Palmgren told him the reason for his call. He said he had been contacted by a client and would be grateful to know a little about the work Steinberg had been doing at the so-called Registry. Immediately he sensed that this was a mistake. Steinberg did not lose his cool, but he sounded distinctly nervous.

"I have no idea what you're talking about," the professor said.

"Is that right? How strange. It says here that you made decisions on behalf of the authority."

"It says that where?"

"In the papers I've got," Palmgren said, vaguer now and more defensive.

"I do need to know exactly where, because this sounds absolutely wrong," Steinberg said, in a surprisingly sharp tone.

"Very well. I suppose I had better have another look."

"Yes, you really should."

"Or perhaps I've got it all mixed up. At my age, you know . . ." Palmgren said.

"Ah well, that happens," Steinberg said, trying to strike a friendly or even a casual note. But he could not hide the fact that he was shaken, and he knew it. He added an unnecessary caution:

"There's also the possibility that something in your papers is inaccurate. Who is the client who contacted you?"

Palmgren mumbled that Steinberg would understand, would he not, being a medical man, that he could not disclose a name and ended the call as quickly as possible. But even before he had hung up, he realized that this call would have consequences. How could he have been such an idiot? He had wanted to help, but instead he had made things worse. As the hours passed and night fell over Liljeholmen, his anxiety and misgivings only grew and converged with the pain in his back and hips. Again and again he cursed himself for his stupidity and lack of judgment.

One had to feel sorry for poor old Holger Palmgren.

CHAPTER 7

June 19

Blomkvist woke early on Sunday morning and stole out of bed so as not to disturb Malin. He pulled on some jeans and a grey cotton shirt and made a strong cappuccino and a sandwich while he had a quick flick through the morning newspaper.

Then he settled down at his computer and wondered where to begin. He had dug into just about everything over the years: archives, diaries, databases, court proceedings, microfilms, stacks and stacks of paper, inventories of estates, tax returns, financial statements, wills, public tax returns. He had challenged confidentiality decisions, invoked the principles of public access to official records and the protection of whistle-blowers, found back doors and loopholes. He had pored over old photographs, unravelled contradictory witness statements, stumbled upon material in cellars and cold storage rooms, and—quite literally—burrowed through

trash cans. But he had never before tried to find out if someone had been adopted or born out of wedlock. He had
never thought that was any of his business, and he wasn't
sure it was this time either. But he followed his instincts.
Ivar Ögren had called Leo a gyppo and that was not just an
old, unpleasant racist insult. If that blockhead was questioning Leo's "Swedishness," it was plain incomprehensible. The
Mannheimer family had more noble lineage than the Ögrens
by any reckoning, with a family tree and ancestors stretching
back to the 1600s. But he had a feeling it might be worth
looking into the past.

Blomkvist began a search that soon brought a smile to
his face. Genealogy had become a popular pastime. There
were innumerable archives, and an extraordinary number
of church records, censuses and registers of emigrants and
immigrants had been scanned and digitized. This was nothing short of a goldmine. Anyone with enough money and
patience could go as far back as they wanted, tracing their
forefathers' meanderings across the steppes and continents
through the millennia, even to our ancestral mothers in
Africa.

Recent adoptions, however, were a problem. There was a
seventy-year confidentiality period for those. Requests could
be referred to the Administrative Court of Appeal, but was
possible only under particular conditions. Prying journalists
who had no idea what they were looking for were unlikely
to qualify. By the rules, this was the end of the road, but he
knew better than anyone that there was always a way. He
only had to work out how to go about it.

It was 7:30 a.m. Malin was still asleep, and out on Riddarfjärden it looked as if it was going to be a nice day. In a few hours they would be off to listen to Mannheimer at the Fotografiska Museum on Stadsgårdskajen. But first Blomkvist wanted to check out Mannheimer's past. It did not help that it was Sunday, when help desks and other friendly souls would be off work. And furthermore, after his conversations with Malin, he had begun to feel some sympathy for the man. But he was not going to give up. If he had understood correctly, he would first have to request Mannheimer's birth record from the Stockholm City Archives. If he was not allowed access, that would confirm his suspicions, but it would not be enough. The birth record could have been stamped confidential for all kinds of reasons, not necessarily adoption. Blomkvist would then have to get hold of the parents' personal files as well as Mannheimer's and compare them. The personal files—kept confidential only in exceptional cases—would contain information about where they had lived at various stages. If Leo Mannheimer and his parents were not registered in the same parish—presumably Västerled parish in Nockeby—at the time of Leo's birth, that would be a clear sign: Herman and Viveka could not be his biological parents.

Blomkvist therefore drafted an e-mail request for Mannheimer's birth record from the Stockholm City Archives as well as his and his parents' personal files. Yet he never sent it. Blomkvist's name was like a warning bell. People were always interested in why he wanted this or that information. The rumour mill would begin to turn—Mikael Blomkvist is snooping around again—and news of his application would almost certainly spread, which would be counterproductive if there really was something to the story. He decided instead to phone the archive the next day, Monday, using his right to access public documents while remaining anonymous.

Then it occurred to him that Holger Palmgren might already know the answer. Against all odds and probably in defiance of his doctors' recommendations, Palmgren had been to see Salander at Flodberga. It would be nice to talk to him anyway, to hear how he was. Blomkvist picked up his mobile and checked the time. Was it too early? No, no, Palmgren woke at the crack of dawn and never distinguished between weekends and weekdays. But Blomkvist could not get through; there seemed to be something wrong with the old man's mobile. The number was not currently in use, a voice said. Blomkvist tried his landline. No answer there either. He was about to try again when he heard the sound of bare feet behind him. He turned around with a smile.

Palmgren had also discovered that his mobile had stopped working. Typical, he thought, nothing worked, least of all himself. He was in pitiful shape. He had been lying awake ever since the small hours, suffering appalling pain. What on earth had gotten into him?

He was by now convinced that the conversation yesterday had been a big mistake. Sitting on grand committees and commissions did not prevent Steinberg from being a crook. It was damning enough that the man had signed the document that sent Salander to a foster home against her and her mother's wishes.

Lord in heaven, what an idiot he was! What should he do? First of all, he had to reach Salander and talk it through with her. But his telephone was not working. Palmgren had stopped using his landline because all he got these days were sales pitches and calls from people he wanted nothing to do with. With great effort he turned in his bed and could see that the telephone was no longer even plugged in. He reached past the mattress, his chest leaning over the bed rail, and finally succeeded in pushing the plug back in. Then he lay back for a while, panting, before he picked up the old handset on the bedside table. There was a dial tone. That was already an improvement: he was operational again. He dialled Information and asked to be put through to Flod-berga Prison. He wasn't expecting anyone especially friendly to come on the line, but he was nonetheless shaken by the arrogance and rudeness of the voice on the prison's switch-board.

"My name is Holger Palmgren," he said with all the authority he could muster. "I'm a lawyer. Please put me through to whoever is in charge of the maximum security unit. It's a matter of the utmost importance."

"Hold the line."

"There's no time for that," he said, but he was kept waiting all the same and only after endless delays was he connected to some guard in the unit, a Harriet Lindfors. Lindfors was abrupt but he told her how urgent the matter was. He needed to speak to Lisbeth Salander without delay. Her answer put a chill through him:

"You can't. Not the way things are right now."

"Did something happen?"

"Are you working on her case?"

"No. Or rather yes, I am."

"Which is it?"

"I'm not directly involved, but—"

"Then you'll have to call back later," Lindfors said, and hung up. Palmgren was furious. He pounded on the bed with his good hand. He worried that the worst had happened, and that it was all his fault. Though he tried to pull himself together, his mind raced in wild speculation. He wanted to stand up and take control of the situation. But his fingers were twisted and stiff, his body was crooked and half lame. He could not even get into his wheelchair without help. Oh, the indignity of it. If the night had been his Calvary, he now felt nailed to his cross, his wretched mattress. Not even good old Ekelöf and his clenched fist among the water lilies could comfort him any longer.

He looked at the base unit of the telephone. The light was flashing. Someone must have tried to call while he was holding for Flodberga's switchboard, and sure enough it was Mikael Blomkvist's voice that played back. Good news— Blomkvist would be able to help, he would know what to do with the information. Palmgren dialled his number. At first there was no reply, so he rang again, and again, until Blomkvist came on the line. He was breathing heavily and Palmgren recognized at once that it was a better sort of breathlessness than the one which afflicted him.

"Is this a bad time?"

"Not at all," Blomkvist answered, still short of breath.

"Do you have female company?"

"No, no."

"He certainly does," said a woman's voice in the background.

"Now don't you upset the lady, Mikael."

Even in the midst of a crisis, Palmgren could be scrupulously polite.

"Wise advice," Blomkvist said.

"Well, you look after her then. I'll ring your sister instead."

"Wait!" Blomkvist must have picked up the worried tone in his voice. "I've been trying to reach you. You've been to see Lisbeth, haven't you?"

"Yes, and I'm worried about her," Palmgren said hesitantly.

"Me too. What have you heard?"

"I've . . ." He remembered Blomkvist's old advice not to disclose sensitive information on the telephone.

"Yes?"

"She seems to be trying to look into things again," he said.

"What things?"

"From her childhood. But I feel awful, Mikael. I think I've put my foot in it. I wanted to help her, I really did. But instead I've messed everything up. If you come out here I can tell you."

"Of course, I'm on my way."

"Oh no you're not!" the woman could be heard to say.

Palmgren thought about the woman, whoever she might be. And he thought about Marita, who would soon be stomping in to begin the whole laborious, degrading process which would result in him sitting in his wheelchair, freshly changed and drinking his watery coffee which tasted like tea. The most important thing right now was to reach Salander.

Somehow he had to get the message to her that Professor Martin Steinberg was most likely the man in charge of the Registry for the Study of Genetics and Social Environment.

"Maybe it's better if you come over later, this evening after nine," he said. "Then we can have a drink too. I could really use one."

"OK, great, see you this evening," Blomkvist said.

Palmgren ended the call and picked up the old documents about Salander from his bedside table. Then he tried calling first Giannini, and then Rikard Fager, Flodberga's governor. He did not get through to either of them. A few hours later he realized that his landline was now not working either, and that the meddlesome Marita seemed not to be coming.

Leo Mannheimer often thought of that October afternoon. He was eleven then. It was a Saturday. His mother was having lunch with the Catholic bishop and his father was away on an elk hunt in the forests of Uppland. The house stood silent and Leo was alone. Not even Vendela, the housekeeper, was there to keep an eye on him, so he had abandoned all the extra homework his private tutors had given him. He sat at the grand piano, not to play any sonatas or études, but to compose.

He had only just begun to write music and his pieces had so far been received with little enthusiasm. His mother had referred to them as "snippets of musical nonsense, darling." But he loved to compose. He longed for it during the hours of classes and study. That afternoon he was working on a melancholy, melodic song which he would go on to play throughout his life, despite its disturbing similarity to "Ballade pour Adeline" and despite his having grasped perfectly well what his mother had said. It did not strike him as strange that she could say such a thing to her eleven-year-old son; all he could see was that she had a point.

His first compositions were too pompous. He was not yet sophisticated, and he still had to discover jazz, which would make his harmonies grittier and more spiky. Above all, he had not yet learned to handle the amplified sound of insects, rustling bushes, footsteps, distant engines, voices, fans—all those things which only he could hear.

However, he was happy at the grand piano that day, as happy as a boy like him could be. Despite the fact that somebody was always keeping an eye on him, he was a solitary child, and he loved only one person—his psychologist Carl Seger. Leo had a session with him every Tuesday at 4:00 p.m. at his practice in Bromma, and he often rang him in the evenings without his parents knowing. Seger understood him. Seger fought Leo's battles with his parents for him:

"The boy must be allowed to breathe! You have to let him be a child."

It did no good, of course, but Seger was the only person who stood up for him, Seger and his fiancée, Ellenor.

Seger and Leo's father were like night and day. Yet there was a bond between them which Leo did not understand. Seger had even agreed to go hunting, though he did not like killing animals. In Leo's eyes, Seger was a different kind of person from his father and Alfred Ögren. He was no player of power games. He did not laugh loudly and condescendingly around the dinner table. He was not interested in life's winners, and talked instead about the outsiders of the world. Seger read poetry, preferably French. He liked Stendhal and Camus, and Romain Gary; he loved Edith Piaf and played the flute, and he dressed simply, if in a deliberately bohemian style. Most important of all, he listened to Leo's concerns; only he had the true measure of the boy's talent—or curse, depending on your point of view.

"Be proud of your sensitivity, Leo. You've got so much strength in you. Things will get better, you'll see."

Leo took comfort in Seger's words, and their meetings were the high point of his week. Seger's practice was in his house on Grönviksvägen. There were black-and-white photographs on the walls of a mist-shrouded 1950s Paris, and a soft, worn-leather armchair in which Leo sat for an hour or sometimes two, talking about all those things his parents and friends could not understand. Seger was the best part of his childhood, although Leo was aware even then that he idealized him.

From that October afternoon onwards, Leo would spend the rest of his life idealizing him, and would return over and again to those last hours by the grand piano.

Leo was lingering over every note, each change in melody and harmony. He stopped abruptly when he heard his father's Mercedes drive up to the garage. His father was not expected back before the following day, so the fact of his early return was already alarming. But that was not all. There was a peculiar kind of stillness in the air in the driveway, a hesitation as the car door opened, and then—like a contradiction—a fury as it was slammed shut. The footsteps crunching on the gravel were heavy and slow, the breathing rapid, and sighs could be heard from the entrance hall, mingling with the sounds of a suitcase being put down and things being put away, guns, no doubt.

The curved wooden staircase to the upper floor creaked. Leo sensed the impending darkness even before his father's figure appeared in the doorway. That is how he would remember it. His father was dressed in green hunting breeches and a black waxed jacket and the sweat shone on his bald pate. He looked fretful. Normally he reacted with arrogance when he was in a tight spot. Now he seemed frightened, and he took a few unsteady steps forward. Uncertainly, Leo stood up from the piano and received an awkward hug.

"I'm sorry, my boy. So terribly sorry."

Though Leo never doubted the sincerity of the words, his father's account of what had happened and his inability to look Leo in the eye, while difficult to interpret, suggested that there was something more, something dreadful and unspoken. But just then, that did not matter.

Carl Seger was dead and Leo's life would never be the same again.

In spite of the warm weather, an unusually large crowd had turned up for the Shareholders' Association event at the Fotografiska Museum. It was in keeping with the times. Anything to do with stocks and shares drew crowds, and on this occasion the organizers had spiced up these dreams of wealth with a small measure of uncertainty. "Rising Index or Bursting Bubble? An Afternoon on the Theme of the Galloping Markets" was the title of the seminar and a great many well-known figures in the industry had been invited.

Leo Mannheimer was not the headline act, but he was the first to speak and Blomkvist and Malin Frode arrived just as he was about to go on stage. They had hurried through the hot, wind-still city and managed to find seats at the back of the auditorium. Malin was nervous about seeing Mannheimer again, whereas Blomkvist was full of misgivings after his conversation with Palmgren. He scarcely listened to Karin Laestander, the young chief executive of the Shareholders' Association, as she made her introductory remarks up on the podium.

"We have an exciting day ahead of us," she said. "We're going to be listening to a whole range of expert analyses of the current market. But first we thought we'd take a look at the stock exchange from a more philosophical point of view. Please give a big hand to Leo Mannheimer, who has a Ph.D. in economics and is head of research at Alfred Ögren Securities."

A tall, slender man with curly hair, in a light-blue suit, stood up in the front row and went up on stage. His step was firm and light and he looked as one would expect: rich and self-assured. But then a screeching sound cut through the crowded auditorium as a chair was dragged clumsily across the floor, and at that Mannheimer staggered. His face went ashen, and he looked like he might collapse. Malin grabbed Blomkvist's hand and whispered, "Oh no."

"Leo! Are you OK?" Laestander stammered.

"It's fine."

"Are you sure?"

Mannheimer grasped the edge of the round table in front of him and fumbled with a bottle of water.

"Just a bit keyed up," he said. He tried to smile.

"Well, a warm welcome to you," Laestander said, apparently not sure if she should keep going.

"Thank you, that's kind."

"Normally, Leo—"

"—I'm a bit steadier on my feet."

Nervous laughter rippled through the hall.

Laestander brightened. "Right. Rock solid. Normally you generate factual analyses of the economy for Alfred Ögren, but lately you've begun to describe the markets more philosophically. You call the stock exchange a temple for believers."

"Well, yes," he said. "I'm not the first to say this. It's obvious that both the financial markets and religion rely on faith. If we begin to doubt, they collapse," he said, squaring his shoulders. Some of the colour returned to his face.

"But surely we all doubt, all the time," Laestander said. "In fact it's the reason we're all here today—we're asking ourselves whether we're in a bubble or in the last phase of a boom economy."

"Doubt on a small scale is what makes the stock market possible," Mannheimer replied. "Every day, millions of people out there doubt and hope and analyze. That's what sets share prices. What I'm talking about is deep, existential doubt—lack of faith in growth and future returns. Nothing is more dangerous for a highly valued market. That level of fear can cause a crash and plunge the world into a depression. We could even start to question the whole idea, the imaginary construct. This will sound like a provocation to some of you, and I apologize for that. But the financial market is not something that exists like you or I, Karin, or this bottle of water on the table. The moment we stop believing in it, it ceases to exist."

"Isn't that a bit of an exaggeration?"

"No, no, just think about it. What is the market? It's a convention. We've decided to let our anxieties and dreams and thoughts about the future set the price of currencies, companies and raw materials. Much of what matters in our lives—like our cultural heritage and our institutions, for example—are mere creations of human imagination."

"And our money too, of course."

"Absolutely, now more than ever. We don't dive into piles of gold the way Scrooge McDuck used to in the comic books, nor do we keep cash under our mattresses. These days our savings are numbers on a computer screen, constantly shifting with movement in the market. And we rely completely on them. But imagine if we start to worry that those quotations not only bounce up and down with the markets, but also could quite simply be erased, like numbers on a slate, what happens then?"

"Our society would be shaken to its foundations."

"Exactly, and that's what happened to some extent a few months ago."

"You mean the hacker attack on Finance Security? The old Värdepapperscentralen?"

"Correct. We had a situation there in which our invest-ments ceased to exist for a short time. They couldn't be found anywhere in cyberspace and the market reeled. The krona fell by 46 percent."

"Yet the Stockholm Exchange reacted prodigiously quickly and closed all trading platforms."

"Indeed, we have to hand it to the people in charge there, Karin. But the collapse was limited by the fact that nobody in Sweden could keep dealing. There were no longer any assets. But believe you me, some people grew richer on the back of it. It's enough to make your head spin. You cannot imagine what they made, those who created the crash and then took positions in the market. You would have to rob innumerable banks to amass that sort of money."

"Absolutely," Laestander said. "There was a great deal written about it, not least in *Millennium* by Mikael Blomkvist. In fact I can see him sitting there at the back. But in truth, Leo, how serious was it, really?"

"In actual fact there was no major danger. Both Finance Security and the Swedish banks have extensive backup systems. Still, for a time we came to doubt the very existence of capital in a digital world."

"The hacker attacks were also accompanied by a massive disinformation campaign on social media."

"Very much so. There was an avalanche of fake tweets about how our assets could never be reconstructed, so it was an attack on our faith as much as on our money—to the extent, that is, that you can distinguish between the two."

"It seems there is conclusive evidence that both the hacker attack and the accompanying disinformation campaign on social media originated in Russia."

"We should be careful about accusations like that, but

it's still an eye-opener. Perhaps that is exactly how a war of aggression in the future will begin. Few things would create as much chaos as a complete loss of faith in our money. You have to keep in mind that it's not even necessary for us to doubt. It's enough if we think that others do."

"Could you elaborate on that, Leo?"

"Picture a large crowd. We ourselves may know that the situation is under control and nothing dangerous has happened. But if other people begin to run in panic, we have to run too. Good old Keynes, legendary economist, once compared the stock market to a beauty contest—one in which we, the jury, do not select the person we think is the most beautiful, but the one we think is going to win."

"Meaning?"

"That we have to forget our own preferences and instead think about other people's tastes and opinions. In fact, not even that: we should be thinking about who people think *other* people think is the most beautiful. Which is no more involved than what happens every second of the day in the financial markets. The stock market is not just the result of analyses of the values of companies and the world around us. Psychological factors play an equal role, real psychological mechanisms, and guessing about them. Guessing about other people's guesses. Everything is twisted and turned around because everybody wants to be one step ahead, to be able, so to speak, to start running before anyone else does, and this is no different than in Keynes' day. Actually, increased automated trading is making markets even more self-reflective. Algorithms act on people's buy and sell orders, so that patterns are reinforced. There's a significant

risk with this. A quick movement in the market can acceler-
ate out of control. In such a situation it becomes rational to
act irrationally—to rush even though you know it's lunacy
to do so. It's no good standing there shouting 'Dimwits,
there's no danger,' when everyone else is running for their
lives."

"But surely if the panic is unjustified, the market will correct itself, will it not?" Laestander said.

"It can take time, though, and then it doesn't matter how
right you are. You can be right all the way to the bankruptcy
courts, to paraphrase Keynes again. But there is hope, and
that's because the market is able to reflect on itself. When a
meteorologist analyzes the weather, that doesn't change the
weather. But when we study the economy, our guesses and
analyses become a part of the economic organism. That's
why the market is like any self-respecting neurotic—it's
capable of evolving and becoming a little bit wiser."

"That makes it impossible to predict, doesn't it?"

"A bit like me on stage. We never really know when there's
going to be a wobble."

Genuine laughter could be heard now, and in it a kind
of relief. Mannheimer gave a careful smile and took a step
towards the edge of the stage.

"In that respect, the stock market is a paradox," he said.
"We all want to understand it and make money from it. But
if we really understood it, our very understanding would
transform it, and then it would become something else, a
mutated virus. The one thing we can predict with certainty
is that it's unpredictable."

"And our disparity is its very soul," Laestander said.

"Quite so. You need both buyers and sellers, believers and doubters, and that's the beauty of it. The chorus of dissonant voices often makes it astonishingly wise, shrewder than any of us here who like to play the armchair guru. If people all over the world separately ask themselves: 'How can we make as much money as possible?' and when there is a perfect balance between guesswork and knowledge, between the buyer's hope and the seller's doubt, then an almost prophetic insight can appear. The problem is: When does the market know what it's doing? And when has it gone mad and run off like a crazy mob?"

"How are we supposed to know?"

"That's the point," Mannheimer said. "When I'm feeling full of myself, I like to say that I now know enough about the financial markets to realize that I don't understand them."

Malin whispered in Blomkvist's ear:

"He's certainly no fool, is he?"

Blomkvist was about to reply when his mobile buzzed in his pocket. It was his sister, Annika. He thought about his conversation with Palmgren, whispered an apology and, deep in thought, left the auditorium without noticing that his departure brought a flicker of alarm to Mannheimer's face. But Malin did not fail to see it, and she studied Mannheimer intently. She had another vision of him sitting in his office, writing on that sand-coloured paper. There was something significant and strange about the scene. She felt it more clearly now, and she decided to buttonhole Mannheimer after the presentation to ask him about it.

Blomkvist stood on the wharf, looking out across the water towards Gamla Stan and the Royal Palace. The sea was calm and in the distance a cruise ship was coming in to dock. He decided to use his Android mobile and his encrypted Signal app to call Giannini back. She answered after one ring, sounding slightly out of breath, so he asked if anything had happened. She was on her way home from Flodberga, she said. Salander had been questioned by the police.

"Is she accused of something?"

"Not yet, and with any luck she won't be. But it's serious, Mikael."

"Well, let's have it!"

"Easy, easy. That woman I was telling you about, Benito Andersson, the one who's been threatening and exploiting both the staff and fellow prisoners—an unimaginably sadistic person—well, she's been taken to Örebro University Hospital with severe injuries to her jaw and skull after a violent attack in the maximum security unit."

"And what's that got to do with Lisbeth?"

"Let me put it like this: The head of the unit, Alvar Olsen, claims he did it. He says he had to knock Benito out. Because she went for someone with a stiletto."

"Inside the prison?"

"It's a huge scandal, of course, and there's a parallel investigation going on to find out how the knife could have been smuggled in. So I'd say that the attack in itself shouldn't be a problem. Getting it adjudged as self-defence shouldn't be too difficult, especially since Olsen's version is backed up by

Faria Kazi, the woman from Bangladesh I told you about. Faria is adamant that Olsen saved her life."

"So what's the problem for Lisbeth?"

"Her own witness statement, for a start."

"She was a witness?"

"Let's deal with one thing at a time. There are contradictions between Faria's witness statement and Olsen's. Olsen claims that he punched Benito twice on the windpipe while Faria says that he elbowed her, and Benito then fell badly onto the concrete floor. But that may not be a problem. All experienced criminal investigators know that people's memories of traumatic incidents can be surprisingly inconsistent. What the C.C.T.V. shows is more problematic."

"Which is . . . ?"

"The whole drama happened just after 7:30 in the evening. It's the worst time in the maximum security unit. Most of the violence there occurs just before the cell doors are locked and, as Olsen knows perfectly well, no-one has been more exposed to it than Faria. He's been aware, but hasn't dared to do anything about it. He says so himself. He's good in that way, very frank—I've seen a copy of his interview notes. At 7:32 last night he's sitting in his office, and finally gets the call he's been waiting on for so long: he learns that Benito's going to be transferred to another prison. Yet he says nothing, apparently, he just puts down the receiver."

"Why?"

"Because at exactly that moment he realizes that it's 7:30, he says. He's worried, he rushes off to open the sally port gates with his code and runs along the corridor of the maximum security unit. The strange thing is . . . just then another inmate, Tine Grönlund, bursts out of Faria's cell. People in the maximum security unit call Grönlund Benito's lapdog, so that raises the question: Why does she come rushing out? Because she hears Olsen coming, or for some entirely different reason? Olsen says he never even sees her. He's busy barging past all the inmates gathered outside Faria's door, and once he's in the cell he discovers Benito with the knife in her hand. He hits her as hard as he can on the windpipe. For reasons of privacy there are no cameras in the cells, so we can't check his story. To me he seemed like a man of principle and integrity. But Lisbeth is already in the cell at that stage."

"And Lisbeth isn't the sort to stand idle while abuse happens in front of her eyes."

"Especially not when the victim is a woman like Faria. But that's not all."

"OK, go on."

"The mood in the unit, Mikael. As usual in prison, no-one wants to talk. But even at a distance you can tell that the atmosphere is seething. When I was just passing through the dining hall with Lisbeth the inmates started rattling their mugs on the tables. They see her as a hero, but also . . . as someone with a death sentence. I heard the words 'dead woman walking.' Even though it only adds to her reputation, it's critical, not just because of the unpleasant message in the words. It will also get the police thinking: If it really was Olsen who smashed Benito's jaw, how come Lisbeth is the one being threatened?"

"I get it," Blomkvist said reflectively.

"Lisbeth is now in isolation and she's being treated with

deep suspicion. Of course, there are many points in her favour. No-one seems to believe that someone so slight could have delivered such a devastating punch. And no-one can understand why Olsen would take the blame—and be backed by Faria—if he wasn't the one who hit Benito. But Mikael, for such an intelligent woman, Lisbeth is being exasperatingly dumb."

"What do you mean?"

"She won't say a word about what happened. She has only two things to communicate, she says."

"And what are they?"

"One, that Benito got what she deserved. And two, that Benito got what she deserved."

Blomkvist laughed. He had no idea why. He knew the situation was serious.

"So what do you believe *really* happened?" he asked.

"My job isn't to believe, it's to defend my client," Giannini said. "But purely as a hypothesis: Benito is exactly the type of person Lisbeth can't tolerate."

"Is there anything I can do?"

"That's why I'm calling. You can help me with Faria. I'm going to represent her too—on the issues which led to her imprisonment, that is—at Lisbeth's request. Lisbeth seems to have carried out some research into her background while in prison, and it might make a compelling major story for you and the magazine. Faria's boyfriend Jamal Chowdhury was killed by falling in front of a tunnelbana train. Could we meet up this evening?"

"I'm supposed to see Holger Palmgren at 9:00."

"Say hi from me, please. He seems to have been trying to

get in touch with me today. On second thought, why don't we have dinner together before? Shall we say 6:00 at Pane Vino?"

"OK," Blomkvist said. "Good."

He rang off and looked over towards the Grand Hôtel and Kungsträdgården, wondering whether to go back to the seminar. Instead he Googled a few things on his mobile, and it was nearly twenty minutes before he headed back in.

As he hurried past the table in the entrance with its display of books, something peculiar happened. He ran straight into Mannheimer. Blomkvist wanted to shake his hand and compliment him on the discussion on stage. But Mannheimer looked so nervous and unhappy that Blomkvist said nothing and watched him disappear out into the sunlight.

Blomkvist stood there for a minute, thinking. Then he went into the auditorium and looked for Malin. She was no longer in her seat. He could have kicked himself for having taken so long. Did she lose patience and head off? He scanned the room. An older man was now talking up on the podium, pointing at curves and lines on a white screen. Blomkvist ignored him. Eventually he spotted Malin standing at the bar over to the right. Glasses of red and white wine had been lined up as refreshment during the break. Malin, glass in hand, looked crestfallen.

CHAPTER 8

June 19

Faria Kazi leaned against the cell wall and closed her eyes. For the first time in ages she longed to see herself in a mirror. She felt a glimmer of hope, even though there was still fear in her body. She thought about the fact that the prison warden had apologized, and about her new lawyer, Annika Giannini, and the policemen who had questioned her. And of course she thought about Jamal.

In the pocket of her trousers was a brown-leather holder containing the business card Jamal had given her after the debate at Kulturhuset. JAMAL CHOWDHURY, it read, BLOG-GER, WRITER, PH.D. BIOLOGY (UNIVERSITY OF DHAKA), and then his e-mail address and mobile number. Underneath it in a different font was a web address: www.mukto-mona .com. The card was crumpled and the lettering was rubbing off. Jamal must have printed it himself. She never asked and why would she have? She had no way of knowing that this card would become her dearest possession. The night after they first met she had studied it under her blanket while she recalled their conversation and remembered every crease and line in his face. She should have called him right away. She should have gotten in touch that very evening. But she was young and innocent, and she did not want to appear too eager. Above all, how was she to know that soon everything would be taken away from her: her mobile, the computer, even the freedom to walk in the neighbourhood in her niqab?

Sitting in her cell now, with the faint first light stealing into her life, she remembered again the summer's day when her aunt Fatima admitted that she had lied for her sake, and Faria had found herself a prisoner in her own home. She was locked in and told that she was to be married off to a second cousin she had never met who owned three textile factories in Dhaka. Three! She had lost track of the number of times she had heard that number.

"Just imagine, Faria. Three factories!"

It would have made no difference to her if they had said three hundred and thirty-three. She found the cousin, whose name was Qamar Fatali, repulsive. In photographs he looked arrogant and mean, and it was no surprise that he was a Salafist and an outspoken opponent of the secular movement in Bangladesh. Nor was she amazed to learn that it was a matter of life and death to Qamar that she remain a virgin and be a good Sunni Muslim woman until the moment he arrived to save her from the West.

At that time nobody in the family knew about Jamal, but there were other factors being held against her, not just suspicions about what she had really been up to while she was not at Fatima's. There were also old, innocent Facebook pictures, gossip which was supposed to confirm that she had "made a whore" of herself.

The front door was security-locked from the inside and since two of the brothers, Ahmed and Bashir, were out of work, there was always somebody at home to keep an eye on her. She did not have much to do other than clean and cook and serve the household, or lie in her room and read whatever she could get her hands on: the Koran, Tagore's poetry and novels, biographies of Muhammad and the first caliphs. But most of all she liked to daydream. Just thinking about Jamal made her blush. She knew she was being pathetic, but that was her family's gift to her—because all joy had been taken from her, the mere memory of a walk along Drottninggatan could make the world quake.

She was already living in a prison then, but she never allowed herself to give in to feelings of resignation or hopelessness. Instead she became furious, and gradually she drew less and less comfort from her memories of Jamal. Just thinking of a conversation where words had flown free made every exchange at home feel inhibited and stiff, and not even God was compensation for that. There was nothing spiritual or generous about God, not in her family. He was little more than a hammer with which to beat people over the head, an instrument for small-mindedness and oppression, exactly as Imam Ferdousi had said. She began to suffer from shortness of breath and palpitations, and in the end she could stand it no longer. She had to escape this life, come what may.

It was already September. The weather was getting cooler and her eyes gained a new sharpness, constantly on the lookout for possible escape routes. That was just about all she thought of. At night she dreamed of running away, and in the morning she would wake up still fantasizing about it. Often she would steal a look at Khalil, her youngest brother. He too was affected: he was no longer allowed to watch his American or English T.V. series, or even see his best friend, Babak, because he was a Shia. Sometimes Khalil looked at her with such pain, as if he perfectly understood what she was going through. Could he help her?

She became obsessed by the idea, and also by phones. She began to follow her older brothers around the apartment, keeping her distance. Her eyes were fixed on their hands as they fiddled with their mobiles and keyed in security codes. But above all she noticed how sometimes they forgot their phones on tables and chests of drawers, and in less conspicuous places like the top of the television or next to the toaster or the electric kettle in the kitchen. Occasionally there would be a comic interlude when the brothers could not find their mobiles and argued and rang each other, and then swore even more when the mobiles were set to silent and they had to track down the muted buzzing.

She was beginning to realize that these farces were a big chance for her. She had to seize opportunities when they arose, though she knew how much was at stake. It was not only a matter of the family's honour. She was also putting her father's and her brothers' financial futures at risk. Those three bloody factories would be a heaven-sent windfall and make them all prosperous. If she thwarted that, the consequences would be dire, and it did not surprise her that the snare was being pulled tighter.

A poison spread throughout the apartment, and now it was no longer just self-righteousness and greed that shone in her older brothers' eyes. They were beginning to be afraid of her. Sometimes they forced more food on her because Qamar, it was said, liked his women to have curves, and it would not do for her to become too thin. She was not allowed to become impure, and definitely not free. They watched over her like hawks.

She might have resigned herself to the situation and given up. But then things came to a head one morning in the middle of that September two years ago. She was eating her breakfast and Bashir, the oldest brother, was fiddling with his mobile.

Malin took a sip of her red wine at the makeshift bar in the Fotografiska Museum. Blomkvist had left her happy and upbeat, yet now she was looking like a withered flower, her fingers buried in her long hair.

"Hello there," he said quietly. The presentation was still going on.

"Who was calling?" she asked.

"Just my sister."

"The lawyer?"

Blomkvist nodded. "Did something happen?"

"No, not really. I just had a word with Leo."

"It didn't go well?"

"It was great."

"So why are you looking so glum?"

"We said all sorts of nice things. How wonderful I was

looking, how fantastic he'd been on stage, how much we'd missed each other—blah, blah, blah. But I could tell right away that something was different."

"In what way different?"

Malin hesitated. She looked right and left, as if to be sure that Mannheimer was not within earshot.

"It felt . . . empty," she said. "As if they were all empty words. He seemed troubled to see me here."

"Friends come, friends go," Blomkvist said in a kind tone.

"I know, and I can survive without Leo, for heaven's sake. But still, it bothered me. We were, after all . . . for a while we were really . . ."

Blomkvist chose his words carefully. "You were close."

"We were. But it wasn't just that we've grown apart. It felt weird somehow. For instance, he says he got engaged to Julia Damberg."

"Who?"

"She used to be an analyst at Alfred Ögren. She's pretty, gorgeous even, but not the sharpest pencil in the box. Leo never liked her that much. He used to say she was childish. I can't get my head around them suddenly getting engaged."

"Tragic."

"Stop that!" she spat. "I'm not jealous, if that's what you think. I'm . . ."

"Yes?"

"Puzzled. Confused, to be honest. Something strange is going on."

"You mean something more than his planning to marry the wrong woman?"

"You're not right in the head, Blomkvist. You do know that, don't you?"

"I'm only trying to understand."

"Well, you can't understand," she said.

"Why not?"

"Because"—she hesitated, fumbling for words—"because I'm not there myself yet. There's something I have to check first."

"I wish you'd stop being so goddamn enigmatic!"

Malin looked at him in alarm.

"Sorry," he said.

"*I'm* the one who should be sorry," she said. "I'm making a bit of a meal of it."

Blomkvist made an effort to sound sympathetic. "So, tell me, what's going on?"

"I keep coming back to that time he was sitting in his office, in the middle of the night. Something doesn't add up. To begin with, Leo must have heard me when I came back from the lift, because he suffers from hyperacusis."

"From *what*?"

"Extreme sensitivity to sound. He hears incredibly well, the softest footstep, a butterfly fluttering by. I can't imagine how I forgot about it. But when that chair squeaked before he started speaking today and he had that agitated reaction, it all came back to me. What do you think, Mikael, shall we push off? I can't stand all this buy-and-sell talk," she said, and drained her glass of wine.

. . .

Faria Kazi was waiting to be called for questioning again, but she was not dreading it as much as she thought she would. Twice already she had not only told them about the bullying and abuse in the maximum security unit, but she had also managed to lie. It wasn't easy. The police kept pushing her about Lisbeth Salander.

Why had Salander been in her cell? What part had Salander played in the drama? Faria wanted to shout out: *It was Salander and not Alvar Olsen who saved me!* But she kept her promise. She thought it would be best for Salander. When was the last time anyone had stood up for her? She could not remember.

Once again she recalled the breakfast at home in Sickla when her brother Bashir had been sitting next to her, tapping on his mobile and drinking tea. It was a beautiful day. The sun was shining out there in a world which was off-limits to her. The days when the family had subscribed to a morning newspaper were long gone, and it was even longer ago that their father would have the P1 morning news programme on the radio. The family had cut itself off from society.

Bashir looked up from his tea.

"You know why Qamar's taking his time, don't you?"

She looked out at the street.

"He's wondering if you're a whore. Are you a whore, Faria?"

She didn't answer. She never replied to questions like that.

"This little shit of a heretic has been looking for you."

Now she could not help herself. "Who would that be?"

"Some traitor from Dhaka," Bashir said.

Maybe that should have made her angry. Jamal was no

traitor. He was a hero, a man who had risked his life for a better, more democratic Bangladesh. But she felt nothing but elation. It was hardly surprising that she had thought about Jamal night and day—she was locked up with nothing to do. But he was free and no doubt going to seminars and receptions all the time. He could easily have met another woman who was far more interesting than she was. Now, with Bashir spitting out his insults, she knew that Jamal wanted to see her again, and in her barricaded world this was greater than anything.

She wished she could be alone with her joy, but she did not let down her guard. The merest hint of a blush might be fatal. A stammer or a nervous look might betray her. So she kept her mask in place:

"A traitor?" she said. "Who cares about a traitor?"

She got up from the table. Only later did she realize her mistake. In trying to pretend that she was uninterested she had over-played her hand. But in the moment it felt like a victory, and once she had recovered from the shock she became more focused than ever.

She was obsessed with getting hold of a phone. Her determination must have shown—Bashir and Ahmed watched her every move, and no mobiles or keys were now left lying around. The days passed and October came. One Saturday evening their home filled with visitors and noise and movement. It took her a while to understand what was happening. No-one had bothered to tell her that the family was celebrating her engagement. Nobody seemed especially happy. But at least her prospective husband was not present—Qamar was having problems with his visa. There seemed to be others missing too, people who had fallen out of favour or who had distanced themselves from the brothers' beliefs. All of this highlighted the family's growing isolation. But Faria was concentrating instead on the faces of the guests. Could anyone help her?

As always, the likeliest person was Khalil. He was sixteen years old now and spent most of his time sitting around, looking nervously at her. Before, when they had lived in Vallholmen and shared a room, they often lay awake late at night talking, to the extent that it was possible to talk with him. In those days, soon after their mother had died, he had not yet started running around the city for hours on end. But already he was different. He was taciturn and what he liked most of all was to sew and draw. Often he said that he longed to go back home—to a country he had no memory of.

She considered asking him to help her run away there and then, under the cover of the party. But her nerves failed her and so she went to the toilet. It was while she was sitting there, by now used to being constantly on the lookout, that she spotted a mobile high up on the dark-blue towel cupboard. At first she could not believe her luck. It was Ahmed's—she recognized the photo on the lock screen, Ahmed showing off with a huge grin on his face, sitting on a motorbike which did not even belong to him. Her heart pounded and she tried to remember—she had watched him so carefully—how Ahmed had keyed in his code. It was like an L-shape, maybe one, seven, eight, nine? Wrong. She tried a new combination. That didn't work either and suddenly she became afraid. What if she locked it? She heard footsteps and voices outside. Were they waiting for her? Her father and brothers had been keeping an eye on her throughout the party, and really she should go out now, leaving the phone where she had found it. But she gave it one more try and—it ran through her like a shock—she got in. Terrified, she stepped into the bathtub, it was the place furthest from the door. Then she dialled Jamal's number, which by now she knew as well as her own name.

The ring tone was like a foghorn in the mist, distress signals on a dark sea, and suddenly there was a rustling in the receiver. Somebody was picking up. She closed her eyes and listened anxiously for sounds from the hall, ready to hang up at any second. But then she heard his voice and his name and she whispered:

"It's me. Faria Kazi."

"Oh, Faria!"

"I have to be quick."

"I'm listening," he said.

The very sound of his voice made her throat catch. She thought of asking him to call the police, but no, she did not dare. She said simply:

"I need to see you."

"That would make me very happy," he said.

All she wanted to do was shout: *Happy? I'm in heaven!* "But I don't know when I can," she said.

"I'm always at home. I'm renting a small apartment on Upplandsgatan. I spend most of my time reading and writing. Come whenever you can," he said, and then he gave her an address and a door code.

She deleted the number from Ahmed's call history, placed the phone back on the cupboard, and walked out past all the relatives and family friends and into her room. There were people standing in there too. She asked them to leave and they did so with embarrassed smiles. Then she lay down under the covers and made up her mind to run away, whatever the cost. That is how it started, both the happiest and the worst time in her life.

Malin Frode and Mikael Blomkvist walked behind the audience, past the display table in the entrance, and out into the sunshine. They passed the ships moored at the wharf and looked up at the massive rock on the other side of the roadway running behind the museum and the quayside. For a long time they did not speak. It was roasting hot. Blomkvist had shaken off his irritation, but Malin again seemed to have other things on her mind.

"Interesting, what you said about his hearing."

"Yes?" She sounded distracted.

"Seger, the psychologist who was shot on that hunt all those years ago, wrote his thesis on the impact of our hearing on our self-esteem," Blomkvist said.

"Was that because of Leo, do you think?"

"No idea. But it doesn't sound like your average research topic. How did Leo's extreme sensitivity to sound manifest itself?"

"We might be in a meeting and I'd see him suddenly sit up and cock his head for no apparent reason. Soon afterwards someone would come into the room. He always picked up on that before the rest of us. Once I asked him about it and he dismissed it. But later, at the end of my time at the firm, he told me that his hearing had been a burden all his life. He said he'd been useless at school."

"I thought he was top of his class," Blomkvist said.

"So did I. But during his first school years he couldn't sit still. If he'd been from a more ordinary family he probably would have been moved into a class for special needs. But he was a Mannheimer and all sorts of resources were thrown at the problem. They discovered that his hearing was exceptional and that was why he couldn't bear to be in a classroom; the slightest buzzing or rustling disturbed him. It was decided that he should be privately educated, and that would have helped him develop into the boy with the sky-high I.Q. you read about."

"So he was never proud of his good hearing?"

"I don't know . . . maybe he was ashamed of it on the one hand, but also used it to his advantage."

"He must have been good at eavesdropping."

"Did that psychologist write anything about exceptionally sensitive hearing?"

"I haven't gotten hold of his thesis yet," Blomkvist said. "But he did write somewhere that an evolutionary asset during one particular era can become a liability during another. In a forest in the age of hunting and gathering, someone with good hearing would be the most alert and therefore the most likely to find food. In a major city full of noise, that same person would risk confusion and overload. More recipient than participant."

"Is that what he wrote: more recipient than participant?"

"As far as I remember."

"How sad."

"Why do you say that?"

"That's Leo in a nutshell. He was always the onlooker."

"Apart from that week in December."

"Apart from that. But you think there's something dodgy about that shooting in the forest, don't you?"

He detected a new curiosity in her voice and took it as a good sign. Perhaps she would tell him more about what was so strange that time she saw Mannheimer late at night in his office.

"It's beginning to interest me," he said.

Leo Mannheimer never forgot Carl Seger. Even as an adult, he could still feel a sudden, sharp sense of loss at 4:00 on a Tuesday afternoon, the time he always went to Seger's consulting rooms, and he sometimes had conversations with him in his head, as if he were talking to an imaginary friend.

Yet Mannheimer did get better at coping with the world and its sounds, just as Seger had predicted. Often his hearing and his perfect pitch were an asset—certainly when he played music. For a long time he did little else but play his piano and dream of becoming a jazz pianist. In his late teens he even had a recording offer from Metronome. He turned it down because he didn't think the material he had was strong enough yet.

When he began his studies at the Stockholm School of Economics, he thought of them as no more than an interlude. As soon as he had put together some better pieces, he would make his record and become a new Keith Jarrett. But the interlude ended up being his life and he was never quite sure how. Was he afraid to fail and to disappoint his parents? Or was it the bouts of depression, which came as regularly as the seasons?

Mannheimer remained a bachelor, and that was no easier to understand. People were curious about him. Women were drawn to him. But he was not so easily drawn to them—in the company of others he yearned for the peace and quiet of home. However, he had genuinely loved Madeleine Bard.

And that was odd too, since they seemed not to have much in common. He did not think he had simply fallen for her looks, still less her wealth. She was different—that's how he would always see it—with her bright-blue eyes which seemed to harbour a secret, and the streak of nostalgia which sometimes flashed across her beautiful face.

They got engaged, and for a while lived together in his apartment on Floragatan. At the time, he had just inherited his father's shares in Alfred Ögren Securities and Madeleine's parents—who set store by such things—saw him as an excellent catch. The relationship was not without its complications. Madeleine wanted to give dinner parties, one after the other. Leo resisted as far as he could and they would fight for hours about it. Sometimes she even locked herself in the bedroom and cried. Nevertheless, it could have been a good marriage. He was convinced of that. He and Madeleine loved each other with fire and passion.

Yet disaster struck, and that probably only went to show that he had been deluding himself all along. It happened in August at a crayfish party at the Mörners' place out in the archipelago, on Värmdö. The atmosphere had been strained right from the start. He was feeling gloomy and found the

...ad and boring. He withdrew into himself, which ...ent Madeleine into social overdrive. She bounced around among the guests, gushing about how everything was "fantastic, really wonderful, it's amazing how beautifully you've decorated the place, and what a fabulous piece of property. I'm soooo impressed. We'd move out here in a second..." But it was nothing out of the ordinary that evening, just a part of the charade that is life.

At midnight he gave up and took himself off to a quiet room with a book, Mezz Mezzrow's *Really the Blues*. He was a little surprised to find it on the shelves, and it meant the party ended up being fun for him after all. He dreamed his way into the jazz clubs of New Orleans and Chicago in the 1930s, and scarcely paid any attention to the shrieking and *snaps*-drinking songs coming from next door.

Shortly after 1:00 a.m. Ivar Ögren stepped into the room, drunk as he always was at parties, dressed in a ridiculous black hat and a brown suit which strained across his midriff. Leo put his hands over his ears in case Ivar should shout or make some other foul racket, as he often did.

"I'm taking your fiancée out in a rowing boat," Ivar said.

Mannheimer protested: "You've got to be joking. You're drunk." It did no good, but Ivar did at least put a life vest on Madeleine, as a concession. Mannheimer went onto the veranda and stared at the red jacket as it vanished over the water.

The sea was calm. It was a clear summer's night and there were stars in the sky. Ivar and Madeleine talked softly in the boat. Not that it made any difference, Mannheimer could hear every word anyway. It was just silly chatter. A new, more vulgar Madeleine was emerging, and that hurt. Then the boat disappeared further out and not even he could hear what they were saying. They were away for a few hours.

By the time they returned, all the other guests had gone. It was beginning to get light and Mannheimer was standing on the shore with a lump in his throat. He could hear the boat being pulled up onto the shore and Madeleine coming unsteadily towards him. On the way home in a taxi, a wall seemed to rise between them and Mannheimer knew exactly what Ivar had said out there on the water. Nine days later, Madeleine packed her bags and left him. On November 21 that year, as snow fell over Stockholm and darkness settled over the country, she announced her engagement to Ivar Ögren.

Mannheimer came down with something that his doctor described as a partial paralysis.

Once he had recovered, he went back to the office and congratulated Ivar with a brotherly hug. He was at the engagement party and the wedding, and said a friendly hello to Madeleine whenever he bumped into her. He put on a cheerful face every damn day and gave the impression there was a lifelong bond of friendship between him and Ivar which could withstand any trials. But deep inside his thoughts were quite different. He was planning his revenge.

Ivar, for his part, knew that he had won only a partial victory. Mannheimer was still a threat and a rival for the top job at Alfred Ögren. He made plans to crush Mannheimer once and for all.

· · ·

Up on Hornsgatspuckeln Malin stopped for no apparent reason. It was far too hot to linger in the sunlight, but there they
stood, uncertain, while people passed them and a car hooted
in the distance. Malin said no more about her meeting with
Mannheimer. She looked down towards Mariatorget.

"Listen," she said. "I need to go."

She gave him a distracted kiss, dashed down the stone
steps to Hornsgatan and across to Mariatorget. Blomkvist
stood in the same spot, hesitating. Then he took out his
mobile and rang Erika Berger, his close friend and *Millennium*'s editor-in-chief.

He told her that he would not be coming to the office for
a few days. They had just put the July issue to bed. It would
soon be Midsummer, and for the first time in years they had
been able to afford two summer temps, which would help
reduce their workload.

"You sound miserable. Has anything happened?" Berger
said.

"There's been a serious assault in Lisbeth's unit at Flodberga."

"That's too bad. Who was the victim?"

"A gangster. It's a pretty ugly business, and Lisbeth witnessed it."

"She usually knows what to do."

"Let's hope so. But . . . could you help me with something
else? Can you ask someone at the office, ideally Sofie, to go
to the Stockholm City Archives tomorrow and get hold of
the personal files of three people? If anyone asks, she can say
we're entitled to them on the basis of rights of public access
to official records."

He gave Berger the names and national identity numbers, which he had made a note of on his phone.

"Old Mannheimer," Berger muttered. "Isn't he dead and buried?"

"Six years ago."

"I met him a couple of times when I was little. My father knew him vaguely. Has this got anything to do with Lisbeth?"

"Possibly."

"In what way?"

"I honestly don't know. What was the old man like?"

"Hard to say, given my age at the time, but he did have the reputation of being a bit of an old devil. Still, I remember him being quite nice. He asked me what kind of music I liked. He was good at whistling. Why are you interested in him?"

"I'll have to get back to you on that too," Blomkvist said.

"OK, suit yourself," Berger said and started to tell him something about the next issue and advertising sales.

He was not really listening. He ended the call abruptly and continued up Bellmansgatan. He passed the Bishops Arms and walked down the steep cobbled street to his front door and up to his attic apartment. There he sat down at his computer and resumed his search online while downing a couple of Pilsner Urquells.

His main focus was the accidental shooting in Östhammar, but he did not learn much more. He knew from experience that it was always difficult to find fresh information on old criminal cases. There were no digital archives that he could access—they were protected for public policy reasons—and, according to the record retention policy of the Swedish National Archives, files on preliminary court investigations were deleted after five years. He decided to go up to Uppsala district court the following day and have a hunt in their records. Afterwards, he could perhaps drop by the main police building there, or find some retired detective inspector who might remember the case. He would have to play it by ear.

He also called Ellenor Hjort, the woman who had been engaged to Carl Seger. He realized at once that this topic was closed as far as she was concerned. She did not want to talk about Seger. She remained polite and accommodating, but said she could not bring herself to look into it any further: "I hope you understand." Then she changed her mind and agreed to meet Blomkvist the following afternoon, not because of his old reporter's charm or even her curiosity as to what he was looking for, but rather because of his bold gamble in dropping Leo Mannheimer's name.

"Leo," she burst out. "My God! It's been far too long. How is he?"

Blomkvist said that he did not know. "Were you close to him?"

"Oh yes, Carl and I were very fond of that boy."

After ending the call, he tidied up the kitchen and wondered if he should call Malin to try to tease out what she was puzzling over. Instead, he showered and got changed. Just before six he left his apartment and walked down to Zinkensdamm to meet his sister at Pane Vino.

CHAPTER 9

June 19

She would deal with it. Martin did not need to worry, she said. It was their fourth phone conversation that day and she did not betray her impatience this time either. But as she hung up she muttered "wimp" and went through the kit that Benjamin, her loyal friend and assistant, had put together for her.

Rakel Greitz was a psychoanalyst and an associate professor of psychiatry, known for a number of things but primarily for her sense of order. She was massively efficient and that had not changed since she had been diagnosed with stomach cancer. Now she had to start taking clinical cleanliness very seriously indeed, and she was positively manic about it. Every speck of dust vanished as if by magic and no tables or sinks were as clean as the ones she had come into contact with. She was seventy years old and ill, yet she was permanently on the go.

Today the hours had flown by in a flurry of feverish activity. It was now 6:30 p.m. and much too late; she should have taken action right away. But it was always the same. Martin Steinberg was far too timid and she was glad she had ignored his advice. Already that morning she had gotten to work on her contacts with the telephone companies and the home care providers. Still, a great deal could have happened since then. That old fool could have had a visitor and disclosed whatever it was he knew or suspected. Although the operation was a risk, it was the only option. There was too much to lose. Too many things had gone wrong in the agency she had been running.

She squirted her hands with alcogel and went into the bathroom. She smiled into the mirror, if only to prove that she could still look happy. As Greitz saw it, what had happened had a silver lining. She had lived for so long in a tunnel of sickness and pain that what she now had to do gave her life an enhanced reality, a renewed sense of ceremony. Greitz had always enjoyed the feeling of vocation, of a higher purpose.

She lived alone in a 1,162-square-foot apartment on Karlbergsvägen, in the Vasastan district of Stockholm. She had just finished a cycle of chemotherapy and, all things considered, was not feeling too bad. Her hair was sparser and thinner, but most of it was still there. The cold cap she had worn had worked. She was still good-looking, tall, slim and upright, with clean features and a natural authority which had been hers since she had graduated in medicine from the Karolinska Institute.

She did have those flames on her throat, but although the birthmark had caused her all sorts of difficulties when she was young, she had come to appreciate it. She bore it with pride and even if nowadays she always wore a turtleneck, it was not because she felt shy or ashamed. It so happened that this style perfectly suited her reserved personality—dignified, never over-dressed. Greitz could still wear coats, skirts and trouser suits she had had made when she was young, and they had never needed altering. There was something cool and severe about her, and it was perhaps because of this that everybody made an extra effort in her presence. She was capable and quick, and she knew the value of loyalty to both ideas and people. She had never disclosed any professional secrets, not even to Erik, her late husband.

She went onto the balcony and looked towards Odenplan. Her right hand resting on the railing was steady. She turned back into the apartment and tidied up a little more. She took out a brown-leather doctor's bag from a cupboard in the hall and packed it with the items from Benjamin. Then she went back into the bathroom, this time to put on some make-up, and selected a cheap-looking black wig. She smiled again. Or perhaps it was a twitch. In spite of her experience, she suddenly felt nervous.

Blomkvist and his sister were at one of the outside tables at Pane Vino on Brännkyrkagatan. They had ordered truffle pasta and red wine, talked about the summer and the heat, and had shared their holiday plans. Giannini succinctly gave her brother some more information on the situation at Flodberga. And then at last she got on to the real reason for wanting to see him.

"Sometimes, Mikael, the police are such idiots," she said. "How familiar are you with the situation in Bangladesh?"

"I wouldn't say 'familiar,' but I do know a bit about it."

"Well, you'll be aware at least that the predominant religion is Islam. According to the constitution, however, it's a secular state which guarantees freedom of the press and freedom of speech. In theory that sounds perfectly feasible."

"But it isn't really working, that I know."

"The government is under pressure from Islamists and has enacted legislation which prohibits any statement liable to offend religious sensibilities. You can stretch 'liable' to cover pretty much anything if you try hard enough. The laws have also been interpreted strictly and a string of writers have been sentenced to long prison terms. But that's not the worst."

"The worst is surely that the law has legitimized the attacks on those writers."

"The law has put wind in the Islamists' sails. Jihadists and terrorists have begun systematically to threaten, harass and murder dissidents, and very few of the perpetrators are prosecuted. The website Mukto-Mona has been particularly hard hit. Their objective is to promote freedom of expression, enlightenment and an open secular society. Quite a number of bloggers have been murdered, around thirty I think, and others have been threatened and named on death lists. Jamal Chowdhury was one of them. He was a young biologist who on occasion wrote about the theory of evolution for Mukto-

Mona. Chowdhury was officially condemned to death by the country's Islamist movement and fled to Sweden with the help of Swedish PEN. For a long time it seemed as if he could breathe easy again. He was depressed, but slowly he got better, and then one day he went to a seminar about the religious oppression of women at Kulturhuset."

"And that's where he met Faria Kazi."

"Good, I see you've done your homework," Giannini said. "Faria was sitting at the back of the room and she is—one can safely say—a very beautiful woman. Jamal couldn't take his eyes off her and after the seminar he approached her. That was the start of not only a romance but also a tragedy, a modern *Romeo and Juliet*."

"In what sense?"

"Faria and Jamal's families are on opposite sides of the struggle. Jamal supported a free and open Bangladesh, while Faria's father and brothers lined up with the country's Islamists, especially once Faria had been promised against her will to Qamar Fatali."

"And who is that?"

"A fat gentleman of forty-five or so who lives in a large house in Dhaka with a lot of servants. He not only owns a small textile business, but he also finances a number of *qawmi* in the country."

"*Qawmi*?"

"Koranic schools which exist outside government control. There's evidence to suggest that young jihadists receive their ideological training in some of them. Qamar Fatali already has a wife his own age but this spring he became enthralled by photographs of Faria and wished to have her

as his second wife. As you can imagine, it wasn't straightforward for him to get an entry visa to come and visit his prospective bride, and he became increasingly frustrated."

"Besides which, Jamal came onto the scene."

"Indeed, and Qamar and the Kazi brothers found themselves with at least two reasons to kill him."

"So Jamal didn't take his own life, is that what you're saying?"

"I'm not saying anything yet, Mikael. I'm giving you some
background—a brief account of what Lisbeth and I talked
about. Jamal became the enemy, a Montague, if you like.
Jamal was also a practising Muslim, but more liberal, and
like his parents—both university professors—he believed
human rights should be fundamental in any society. That
was enough to make him an enemy of Qamar and the Kazi
family. His love for Faria made him a private threat too, not
only to the honour of her father and brothers but also to
their financial prospects. There were clear motives to have
him removed and Jamal realized early on that he was playing for high stakes. But he couldn't avoid the risk. He writes
about it in a diary found after the tragedy—which the police
have had translated from Bengali and is referred to in the
preliminary investigation into Jamal's death. Can I read you
a bit?"

"Please do."

Blomkvist drank his Chianti while Giannini got the
police report out of her briefcase and leafed through the
bundle of papers.

"Here," she said. "Listen to this."

Ever since I had to watch my friends die and was forced to leave my homeland, it was as if the world became shrouded in ashes. I could no longer see any colour. There was no point in living.

"That last sentence was later used to support the argument that he committed suicide in the tunnelbana," she said. "But there's more."

I still tried to find things to do and, one day in June, I went to listen to a debate in Stockholm on religious oppression. I wasn't expecting much. Everything meaningful from my past now seemed irrelevant, and I couldn't understand why the imam on stage still believed there was so much to fight for. I had given up. I'd plunged into a grave. I felt like I too had been killed.

"He's a bit melodramatic," Giannini said apologetically.

"Not at all. Jamal was young, wasn't he? We all write like that when we're young. He reminds me of our poor colleague Andrei. Go on."

I thought I was dead and lost to the world. But then I saw a young woman in a black dress at the back of the hall. She had tears in her eyes and was so beautiful that it hurt to look at her. Life awakened in me again. It came back like an electric shock and I knew I had to speak to her. In some way I knew that we belonged together and that it was I and no-one else who could comfort her. I walked over and said something banal. I thought I had messed it up, but she smiled. We went out onto the square—as if we'd always known we would go out onto the square—and then we walked down a long pedestrian street past the parliament.

"Well, I won't continue. Jamal never could bring himself to discuss with anyone what happened to his friends on Mukto-Mona. But with Faria the story came streaming out—he tells her everything, that's clear from the diary. After they've walked for a little more than half a mile, Faria says she has to rush off, takes his business card and promises to call soon. But she never does. Jamal waits and becomes desperate. He finds Faria's mobile number on the Internet and leaves a message. He leaves four, five, six messages. Still no response. Then, a man phones Jamal and snarls at him, tells him he should never get in touch again. 'Faria despises you, you shit,' the man says, and that breaks Jamal. But after a while he becomes suspicious and does some investigating. He doesn't grasp the full picture: that her father and brothers have taken Faria's mobile and computer and that they're checking her e-mails and calls and keeping her a prisoner in the apartment. But soon he understands that something is very wrong and he goes to see Imam Ferdousi, who says that he too is worried. Together they contact the authorities, but they don't get any help. Nothing happens, not one single thing. Ferdousi visits the family himself, but is shown the door. Jamal is ready to turn the world upside down. But then . . ."

"Keep going."

"Then Faria herself calls, from another number, and

wants to see him. At the time Jamal is secretly renting an apartment on Upplandsgatan, with the help of Norstedts publishing company. It's not clear what happens next. All we know is that the youngest brother in the family, Khalil, helps Faria to escape, and she goes straight to Upplandsgatan. Jamal and Faria's reunion is like something out of a movie or a dream. They make love and talk, day and night. Faria, who otherwise said nothing during the police interviews, confirmed that. They decide to contact the police and PEN, for help to go into hiding. But then . . . it's so sad. Faria wants to say goodbye to her youngest brother—and she's come to trust him. They agree to meet at a café on Norra Bantorget. It's a chilly autumn day. Faria heads out wearing Jamal's blue down jacket with a hood which she draws over her head. She never arrives."

"She was ambushed, right?"

"It was definitely an ambush—there were witnesses. But neither Lisbeth nor I believe that Khalil lured her there. Our suspicion is that the older brothers followed him. They were waiting for Faria in a red Honda Civic on Barnhusgatan and, with lightning speed as soon as they see her approach—drag her into the car and take her back to the family home in Sickla. It seems that the brothers contemplate packing Faria off to Dhaka. But unsurprisingly they see it as too risky. How would they prevent her from causing a scene at Arlanda, or on the flight? Would they have to drug her?"

"So they get her to write a letter to Jamal."

"Exactly. But the letter's not worth the paper it's written on, Mikael. The handwriting is Faria's, that much is clear. But it's obvious her brothers or her father dictated it—except for the clues Faria manages to slip into the text. 'I said all along that I have never loved you.' That was certainly a secret message. In his diary, Jamal describes how they told each other over and over again, every evening and every morning, how much they loved each other."

"Jamal must have raised the alarm when she didn't come back from the meeting with Khalil."

"Of course he did. Two police assistants dutifully visited Sickla, and when the father stood at the front door and assured them that all was well, except that Faria had the flu, they left. But Jamal would not be fobbed off. He called everybody he could think of, and the family must have realized they were running out of time. On Monday, October 23, Jamal writes in his account of events that he wakes up with a feeling of death in his body. The police made a big deal of this after it was all over, but I don't interpret that to mean he has given up. It's how Jamal expresses himself. He's been torn apart, and has started to bleed to death. He can't sleep, can't think, can hardly function as a human. He 'staggers on,' he writes. Cries out his 'despair.' The police investigators read too much into those words. That's my opinion. Between the lines he sounds much more like a man who wants to fight and to recover what he has lost. Above all he is worried. 'What's Faria doing now?' 'Are they hurting her?' He makes no reference to Faria's letter, even though it's lying open on his kitchen table. He probably sees right through it. We know that he tries again to get in touch with Ferdousi, who's at a conference in London. He rings Fredrik Lodalen, an associate professor of biology at Stockholm University with whom he's become friendly. They meet at 7:00 in the evening on

Hornsbruksgatan, where Lodalen lives with his wife and two children. Jamal stays for a long time. The children go to sleep. Lodalen's wife goes to sleep. Lodalen has tremendous sympathy, but he also has to get up early the next morning and, like many people facing a crisis, Jamal is going over things again and again and, come midnight, Lodalen asks him to go home. He promises to contact the police and the women's crisis centre in the morning. On the way to the tunnelbana, Jamal phones the author Klas Fröberg, whom he's gotten to know through PEN. There's no answer, and Jamal goes down into Hornstull station. It's 12:17 on Tuesday, October 24. A storm has just blown in. It's raining."

"So there aren't many people around."

"There's one woman on the platform, a librarian. The C.C.T.V. camera catches Jamal as he's walking by her, and he looks absolutely wretched. Understandably so. He has hardly slept since Faria disappeared, and he feels abandoned by everybody. But still, Mikael . . . Jamal would never abandon Faria when she needed him most. One of the C.C.T.V. cameras on the platform was broken, and that may have been an unfortunate coincidence. But I cannot believe it's a coincidence that a young man walks up to the librarian and talks to her in English just as the train rolls in to the station and Jamal falls onto the track. The woman doesn't see what happens. She has no idea whether Jamal jumped or was pushed and it hasn't been possible to identify the young man who spoke to her."

"What does the train driver say?"

"His name is Stefan Robertsson and it's basically because of him that the death was ruled a suicide. Robertsson says he's certain that Jamal jumped. But he was also traumatized by the incident and my guess is that he was asked some leading questions."

"In what way?"

"The person conducting the interview didn't seem to want to consider any other possibility. In his first account—before his brain pieced together a more comprehensive description—Robertsson says he saw some wild flailing, as if Jamal had had too many arms and legs. He doesn't refer to it again, and curiously enough his memory seems to get better as time goes by."

"What about the guard at the ticket gate? He or she surely must have seen the perpetrator."

"The guard was watching a film on his iPad and said that a number of people passed him. But he didn't take notice of anybody in particular. He thinks that most of them were passengers who had gotten off the train. He has no clear recollection."

"Aren't there cameras up there?"

"There are, and I've found something. Nothing significant, but most of the people who come up out of the station have been identified, apart from one man who looks young and lanky. He keeps his head down, and is wearing a hat and sunglasses so it's impossible to see his face. His attitude suggests that he's nervous and doesn't want to be recognized. It's a disgrace that he hasn't been followed up on, especially since he has a very distinctive, jerky way of moving."

"I agree. I'll give it a closer look," Blomkvist said.

"Then we've got Faria's own offence, the one she's been convicted of," Giannini said. She was about to go on when the food arrived and their concentration lapsed. Not just because of the waiter and his fussing with the plates and the grated Parmesan but also because a group of noisy youths came by on their way towards Yttersta Tvärgränd and Skinnarviksberget.

Palmgren was thinking about the war in Syria and all sorts of other miseries—including the pain which felt like knives in his hips—and about the idiotic call he had made to Martin Steinberg. He was also terribly thirsty. He had drunk very little, and he hadn't had anything to eat either. It would still be a while before Lulu arrived and took him through his evening ritual, if indeed Lulu was coming at all.

It seemed as if nothing was working. His phones certainly weren't, neither of them, and no help had come, not even Marita. He had spent all day lying in bed, getting more and more upset. He really should trigger his alarm. He wore it on a cord around his neck and although he was reluctant to use it, now seemed the right time. He was so thirsty he could hardly think straight. It was warm too. No-one had aired his room or opened a window all day. No-one had done anything. Almost in desperation he listened out for sounds in the stairwell. Was that the lift? You could hear the lift all the time. People came and went. But nobody stopped at his door. He swore and turned in his bed and felt terrible shooting pains. Instead of calling Professor Steinberg—who was probably a crook—he should have gotten in touch with the psychologist who was also mentioned in the confidential notes, the one named Hilda von Kanterborg, who was said to have breached her duty of confidence by talking to Lisbeth's mother about the Registry. If anyone could have helped him, surely it was she rather than the one who ran the whole project. What a prize donkey he had been, and how dreadfully thirsty he was! He considered shouting as loudly as he could in the direction of the stairwell. Perhaps one of the neighbours would hear him. But, wait . . . now he heard footsteps heading his way. A smile spread across his face. That must be Lulu, his wonderful Lulu.

As the door opened and closed and shoes were wiped on the doormat, he called out with his last reserves of strength, "Hello, hello, now tell me all about Haninge. What was his name again?" He got no answer, and now he could hear that the steps were lighter than Lulu's, more rhythmic and somehow harder. He looked around for something to defend himself with. Then he breathed out. A tall, slender woman in a black turtleneck appeared in the doorway and smiled at him. The woman was sixty, maybe seventy years old, and she had sharp features. There was a cautious warmth in her eyes. She was carrying a brown doctor's bag which seemed to belong to another era, and she held herself upright. There was a natural dignity about her. The smile was refined.

"Good afternoon, Herr Palmgren," she said. "Lulu is very sorry, but she can't come today."

"There's nothing wrong with her, I hope."

"No, no, it's just a personal matter, nothing serious," the woman said, and Palmgren felt a sting of disappointment.

He could sense something else, too, but he could not quite put his finger on it. He was far too dazed and thirsty.

"Could you please bring me a glass of water?"

"Oh my goodness, of course," the woman said, and she sounded just like his old mother all those years ago.

She put on a pair of latex gloves and went off, returning with two glasses. He drank with a shaky hand and felt that the world was getting its colour back. The water restored him to some sort of stability. Then he looked up at the woman. Her eyes seemed warm and affectionate, but he did not like the latex gloves or the hair, which was thick and did not suit her at all. Was she wearing a wig?

"Now that's better, isn't it?" she said.

"Much better. Are you temping for the care company?"

"I sometimes help out in an emergency. I'm seventy, so sadly they don't like to call on me too often," the woman answered and unbuttoned his nightshirt, which was damp with sweat after the long day in bed.

She took a morphine patch from the brown leather bag, raised his medical bed and swabbed a spot high up on his back with a cotton ball. Her movements were precise, her touch careful. She knew what she was doing, no question about it. He was in good hands. There was none of the clumsiness of some of the other helpers. But it also made Palmgren feel vulnerable—the woman's professionalism was almost too much.

"Not too fast," he said.

"I'll be careful. I read about your pain in the notes. It sounds very unpleasant."

"It's bearable."

"Bearable?" she repeated. "That's not good enough. Life should be better than that. I'll give you a slightly stronger dose today. I think they've been a bit stingy with you."

"Lulu—" he began.

"Lulu's wonderful. But she isn't the one who decides about the morphine. That's beyond her authority," the woman interrupted, and with her practised hands—her easy mastery—she applied the patch.

It felt as if the morphine was taking effect immediately.

"You're a doctor, aren't you?"

"No, no, I never got that far. For many years I was an ophthalmic nurse at Sophiahemmet."

"Is that so?" he said, and he seemed to detect something tense about the woman, a twitch around her mouth. But perhaps it was nothing.

Or so he tried to tell himself. Still, he could not help examining her face more closely now. She had a certain class, didn't she? But there was nothing classy about her hair. Or her eyebrows for that matter—they were the wrong colour and style, and they looked as if they'd been stuck on in a hurry. Palmgren thought how strange his day had been and recalled the conversation of the day before. He looked at the woman's turtleneck. What was it that bothered him about it? He could not think straight, the air was too close and hot. Without really being conscious of it, he moved his hand towards his personal alarm.

"Could you please open a window?" he asked.

She did not answer. She stroked his neck with soft, deliberate movements. Then she removed the cord with the alarm from around his neck and with a smile said:

"The windows will have to stay closed."

"Eh?"

Her response was so unpleasant in its austerity that he

could hardly take it in. He stared at her in astonishment and wondered what to do. His options were limited. She had taken away his alarm. He was lying down and she had her medical bag and all her professional efficiency. And it was odd, the woman looked blurred, as if she were moving in and out of focus. Suddenly he understood: everything in the room was becoming hazy. He was drifting away.

He slid into unconsciousness, fighting against it with all his strength. He shook his head, waved his good hand, gasped for air. All the woman did was smile, as if in triumph, and put another patch on his back. Then she put his night-shirt back on, straightened his pillow and lowered his bed. She gave him a few gentle pats, as if she wanted to be especially nice to him in some sort of perverse compensation.

"Now you're going to die, Holger Palmgren," she said. "It's about time, isn't it?"

Giannini and Blomkvist sipped their wine and were silent for a little while as they looked up towards Skinnarviksberget.

"Faria was probably more afraid for her own life than for Jamal's," Giannini said. "But the days passed and nothing happened. We don't know a great deal about what went on in the apartment in Sickla. Her father and brothers gave such a consistent and embellished account that it can only have been false. But we can be sure that they felt under pressure. There was talk in the neighbourhood and reports were made to the police. They may have been having a tough time keeping Faria under control.

"Two things we know for sure," Giannini went on. "We

know that just before 7:00 p.m. the day after Jamal has fallen in front of the tunnelbana, Ahmed, the oldest brother, is standing in the living room by the big windows four storeys up. Faria comes over to him. There's a brief exchange, according to the middle brother, and then, out of the blue, she goes crazy. She throws herself at Ahmed and pushes him out the window. Why? Because he tells her that Jamal is dead?"

"That sounds likely."

"I agree. But does she also discover something else— something that gets her to take out her rage and despair specifically on her brother? And above all: Why doesn't she talk to the police? She had everything to gain by telling them what happened. Yet she clams up throughout her questioning and during the trial."

"Like Lisbeth."

"A bit like Lisbeth, but different. Faria withdraws into her wordless grief. She refuses to take any notice of the world around her and answers her accusers with a stony silence."

"I can see why Lisbeth doesn't like people messing with that girl," Blomkvist said.

"I agree, and that worries me."

"Has Lisbeth had access to a computer at Flodberga?"

"No, absolutely not," Giannini said. "They're inflexible on that. No computers, no mobiles. All visitors are meticulously searched. Why do you ask?"

"I get the feeling that while she's been in there Lisbeth has discovered something more about her childhood. She might have heard it from Holger."

"You'll have to ask him. Remind me, when are you seeing him?"

"At 9:00."

"He's been trying to get in touch with me."

"So you said."

"I tried to call him today. But there was something wrong with his phones."

"His phones, plural?"

"I called both mobile and landline. Neither was working."

"What time did you call?" Blomkvist said.

"At about 1:00."

Blomkvist got to his feet and, with a distracted air, said:

"Will you pick up the tab, Annika? I think I need to go."

He vanished down into the Zinkensdamm tunnelbana station.

Through what seemed like a gathering fog, Palmgren saw how the woman picked up his mobile and the documents about Salander from the bedside table and put them in her doctor's bag. He could hear her rummaging around in his desk drawers. But he could not move.

He was falling through a black ocean and for a moment he thought he might be lucky enough to sink forever into oblivion. Instead he was shaken by a spasm of panic, as if the air around him had been poisoned. His body arched, he could not breathe. The ocean closed over him again. He drifted down towards the bottom and thought it was all over. Yet he became dimly aware of some presence. A man, somebody familiar, was pulling at his nightshirt and tearing the patches off his back, and then Palmgren forgot everything else. He concentrated as hard as he could and fought desperately, the way a deep-sea diver does when trying to reach the surface before it is too late. Considering all the poison in his body and his enfeebled breathing, that was an amazing achievement.

He opened his eyes and managed five words, which should ideally have been six, but were the start of an important message.

"Talk to . . ."

"Who? Who?" the man shouted.

"To Hilda von . . ."

Blomkvist had come running up the stairs to find the front door wide open. As soon as he set foot in the apartment and was hit by the stifling, stale air, he knew that something was badly wrong. He ignored the litter of documents scattered on the hall floor and burst into the bedroom. Palmgren lay on his bed in a contorted position. His right hand was close to his throat and his fingers were cramped and splayed. His face was ashen, his mouth fixed in a gaping, desperate grimace. The old man looked as though he had died a terrible death and Blomkvist stood there for an instant, bewildered and in shock. Then there was something; he thought he could see a gleam deep in the eyes, which galvanized him into calling the emergency services. He shook Palmgren and inspected his chest and mouth. Clearly the old man was having trouble breathing, so he at once pinched his nostrils tight and breathed heavily and steadily into his airways. Palmgren's lips were blue and cold, and for a long time Blomkvist thought he was doing no good. Even so he refused to give up. He would have kept going until the ambulance arrived if the old man had not suddenly given a start and waved one of his hands.

At first Blomkvist thought it was a spasm, an instinctive movement as life and strength returned, and he felt a glimmer of hope. Then he wondered, was the hand trying to tell him something? It was gesticulating towards Palmgren's back, and Blomkvist yanked off his nightshirt. He discovered two patches, which he tore off without hesitating. What was written on them? What the hell did it say? He tried to focus.

Active substance: fentanyl

What was that? He looked at Palmgren and wondered for a moment where to begin? He took out his mobile and Googled. It said,

Fentanyl is a powerful synthetic opioid analgesic that is similar to morphine but 50 to 100 times more potent . . . normal side-effects are respiratory depression, cramping in the muscles of the windpipe . . . naloxone is an antidote.

"Shit, shit!"

He rang emergency services again, gave his name and said he had called moments earlier. He almost shouted:

"You've got to bring naloxone, do you hear? He has to have naloxone injections. He's in deep respiratory distress."

He hung up and was about to go on with his artificial respiration when Palmgren tried to say something.

"Later," Blomkvist hushed him. "Save your strength."

Palmgren shook his head and gave a hoarse whisper. It was impossible to understand what he was saying. It was a low, almost soundless croaking, terrible to hear. Blomkvist bit his lip and was about to start breathing more air into the old man when he thought he could make out something he was saying, two words:

"Talk to . . ."

"Who? Who?" And then with his last reserves of strength Palmgren wheezed something which sounded like "Hilda from . . ."

"Hilda from what?"

"To Hilda von . . ."

It had to be something important, something crucial.

"Von *who*? Von Essen? Von Rosen?"

Palmgren gave him a desperate look. Then something happened to his eyes. The pupils widened. His jaw dropped open. He looked dramatically worse, and Blomkvist did everything in his power—artificial respiration, C.P.R., everything—and for a split second he thought it was working again. Palmgren raised his hand. There was something majestic about the movement, the crooked fingers clenched, a knotted fist held up as if in defiance a couple of inches above the bed. Then the hand fell back against the blanket. Palmgren's eyelids opened wide. His body convulsed, and then it was all over.

Blomkvist could tell; he knew in his heart of hearts. But he did not let up. He pressed down harder on Palmgren's chest and steadily blew air into his windpipe. He gently slapped his cheeks and yelled at him to live and breathe. Eventually he had to accept that it was to no avail. There was no pulse, no breathing, nothing. He banged his fist on the bedside table so hard that the pill box fell off and pills rolled all over the floor. He looked out towards Liljeholmen. It was 8:43 p.m. Outside in the square a couple of teenage girls were laughing. There was a faint smell of cooking in the air.

Blomkvist closed the old man's eyes, smoothed the covers and looked at his face. There was nothing positive you could say about any one of his features. They were crooked and twisted and withered. Yet there was a profound dignity there. That's how it seemed to him. It was as if the world had all of a sudden become a little poorer. Blomkvist felt his throat catch, and he thought about Salander and how Palmgren had gone all the way to visit her. He thought of everything and nothing.

And then the ambulance crew arrived, two men in their thirties. Blomkvist gave as factual an account of events as he could. He told them about the fentanyl. He said that Palmgren had probably had an overdose, that there could be suspicious circumstances and that the police should be called. He was met by a resigned indifference which made him want to scream. But he kept his mouth shut and only nodded stiffly when the men laid a sheet over Palmgren and left the body lying on the bed to wait for a doctor to come and issue a death certificate. Blomkvist stayed in the apartment. He picked the pills up off the floor, opened the windows and the balcony door, and sat down in the black armchair next to the bed and tried to think clearly. There was far too much buzzing around in his head. Then he remembered the documents which had been scattered in a mess on the hall floor when he rushed into the apartment.

He went to pick them up and read them while standing by the front door. At first he did not understand the context, but he did spot one name which he latched on to immediately. Peter Teleborian. Teleborian was the psychiatrist who had fabricated the report on Salander after she threw a fire-bomb at her father when she was twelve years old. It was he who had claimed to want to treat and cure Salander, to restore her to a normal life, but who had in fact systematically tormented her day in and day out, strapping her to her bed and subjecting her to extreme psychological torment. Why on earth were there papers about that man lying in Holger Palmgren's hall?

A quick look through the documents was enough to tell Blomkvist that there was nothing new. They looked like photocopies of the same grimly dry case notes which later led to Teleborian being found guilty of gross dereliction of duty and stripped of his right to practise medicine. But it was also clear that the pages of the documents, which were not numbered, were not in a complete sequence. Some pages ended in the middle of a sentence and others began in a different context. Were the missing papers in the apartment? Had they been taken away?

Blomkvist considered searching through the drawers and cupboards. He decided not to interfere in the police investigation which would no doubt ensue, and instead he called Chief Inspector Jan Bublanski to tell him what had happened. Then he rang the maximum security unit at Flodberga Prison. A man answered, identifying himself as Fred. He spoke in an arrogant drawl and Blomkvist almost lost his temper, especially as he looked over at the bed and saw the contours of Palmgren's body beneath the white sheet. But he mustered all his authority and explained that there had been a death in Salander's family, and at last he was allowed to talk to her.

It was a conversation he could have done without.

Salander hung up and was escorted by two guards down the long corridor back to her cell. She did not pick up on the deep hostility in the face of one of them, Fred Strömmer. She did not take in anything going on around her, and her face betrayed nothing of her emotions. She ignored the question "Has somebody died?" She didn't even look up. She just walked and heard her own footsteps and breathing and nothing else, and she had no idea why the guards followed her into her cell. Except that they wanted to mess with her. Since Benito had been floored, they took every opportunity to poison her life. Now it seemed they wanted to search her cell again, not because they thought they would find anything, but because it was an excellent excuse to turn the place upside down and throw her mattress onto the floor. Perhaps they were hoping for an outburst from her, so that they could have a proper fight. They almost succeeded. But Salander gritted her teeth and did not even look up at them as they left.

Afterwards she picked up the mattress, sat on the corner of the bed and focused on what Blomkvist had said.

She thought about the morphine patches he had ripped off Palmgren's back and the papers that had been lying about on the hall floor. And the words "Hilda von . . ." She concentrated especially hard on them, but it didn't make sense. She stood up and banged her fist on the desk, then kicked the clothes cupboard and the washbasin.

For one dizzying second she looked as if she could kill. But then she pulled herself together and tried to focus on one thing at a time. First you find out the truth. Then you take revenge.

CHAPTER 10

June 20

Chief Inspector Bublanski had a tendency to deliver lengthy philosophical discourses, but just now he said nothing.

It was 3:20 p.m. and his team, the murder squad of the Violent Crimes Division, had been working hard all day long. It was stuffy and hot in the meeting room on the fifth floor of police headquarters on Bergsgatan.

Given his age, Jan Bublanski was afraid of many things. But perhaps he feared the absence of doubt most of all. He was a man of faith who was uncomfortable in the face of convictions too strongly held or over-simplified explanations. He was forever producing counter-arguments and contrary hypotheses. Nothing was so certain that it could not be challenged one more time. While this behaviour slowed him down, it also prevented him from making too many mistakes. His goal right now was to persuade his colleagues to come to their senses. He did not know where to begin.

In many ways, Bublanski was a lucky man. He had a new woman in his life, Professor Farah Sharif, who—so he said—was more beautiful and intelligent than he deserved. The couple had just moved into a three-bedroom apartment near Nytorget and they had acquired a Labrador. They often ate out and went regularly to art exhibitions. But the world had gone mad, in his opinion. Lies and stupidity were more widespread than ever before. Demagogues and psychopaths dominated the political scene, and prejudice and intolerance were poisoning everything, sometimes even penetrating the discussions within his own, otherwise sensible team.

Sonja Modig, his closest colleague, was rumoured to be in love and radiated sunshine. But that simply annoyed Jerker Holmberg and Curt Svensson, who were constantly interrupting her and arguing with her. When Amanda Flod, the youngest member of the group, sided with Modig—and generally she had clever ideas to contribute—the situation was only exacerbated. Maybe Svensson and Holmberg felt that their positions as senior figures were under threat. Bublanski tried to give them an encouraging smile.

"Basically . . ." Holmberg began.

"Basically is a good start," Bublanski said.

"Basically, I can't see why anyone would go to that much trouble to kill a ninety-year-old man," Holmberg said.

"An eighty-nine-year-old man," Bublanski corrected him.

"Right. An eighty-nine-year-old man who hardly leaves his apartment and who seems to have been at death's door anyway."

"Yet that's what it looks like, doesn't it? Sonja, can you please sum up what we have so far?"

"There's Lulu Magoro," she said. She smiled and looked glowing, and even Bublanski wished that she would tone it down a little, if only to keep the peace.

"Haven't we talked enough about her?" Svensson asked.

"Not yet," Bublanski said rather sharply. "Right now we need to go over everything again, to get an overview."

"It's not just Lulu," Modig said. "It's the whole of Sofia Care, the company responsible for looking after Palmgren. Yesterday morning, the people there received a message that Palmgren had been admitted to the ER at Ersta hospital with acute hip pain. No-one thought to question it. The person who called claimed to be a senior doctor and orthopaedic specialist, and introduced herself as Mona Landin. It turns out to be a fake name but she seemed perfectly credible and was given information about Palmgren's medications and general condition. After that, all home visits to Palmgren were cancelled. Lulu, who was especially close to him, wanted to visit him in hospital. She tried the switchboard there, to find out which ward he was in, but because he wasn't actually there, she got no further. That same afternoon, however, she was contacted by this Mona Landin, who said Holger was in no danger but still under anaesthetic after some minor surgery and was not to be disturbed. Later that evening Lulu tried calling Palmgren's mobile and the service had been suspended. Nobody at his service provider Telia could explain how that happened. That morning his telephone had quite simply been disconnected, but they did not know who in the system had authorized or carried out the operation. Somebody with the necessary computer skills and the right connections seems to have wanted to isolate Palmgren."

"Why go to such lengths?" Holmberg said.

"Here's one factor worth bearing in mind," Bublanski said. "Remember that Palmgren visited Salander at Flodberga. Since we know there are threats against her, a reasonable hypothesis might be that Palmgren got drawn into her problems—maybe because he found out something, or because he wanted to help. Lulu Magoro told us that she dug out a stack of papers for him on Saturday, and Palmgren read them with great concentration. Apparently he had been given them a few weeks earlier by a woman who'd had some connection to Salander."

"What woman?"

"We don't know yet; Lulu didn't catch her name. And Salander's saying nothing, but we have a lead. As you know, Blomkvist found some papers lying in the hall, either because Palmgren or his attacker dropped them. They appear to be case notes from St. Stefan's psychiatric clinic for children, where Salander was admitted as a girl. Peter Teleborian's name comes up in them."

"That snake."

"That sly bastard, more like," Modig said.

"Has Teleborian been questioned?"

"Amanda spoke to him today. He's living with his wife and a German shepherd in high style on Amiralsgatan. He said he was sorry to hear about Palmgren but has no idea what might have happened. He doesn't know anyone called Hilda von something, and he didn't want to say anything more."

"We'll probably have to circle back to him," Bublanski

said. "In the meantime we'll go through the rest of Palmgren's papers and belongings. But go on with Lulu, Sonja."

"She looked after Palmgren's evening care four or five times a week," Modig said. "Each time she would apply a pain-killing patch, Norspan they're called, and the active ingredient is . . . What's it called again, Jerker?"

Nice move, Bublanski thought. *Involve them. Make them feel like they can contribute.*

"Buprenorphine," Holmberg said. "It's an opioid made from poppies, used as a painkiller in geriatric care. It's also present in a drug called Subutex, which is prescribed for heroin addicts."

"Right. Palmgren ordinarily got a modest dose," Modig said. "But what Blomkvist tore off his back yesterday was something entirely different: two prepared fentanyl Actavis patches. Together they add up to a lethal amount, isn't that right, Jerker?"

"Would have killed a horse."

"It's amazing Palmgren survived for as long as he did, and he even managed to get out a few words."

"Interesting words, too," Bublanski said.

"They certainly are. Though anything said by a heavily drugged man in a situation like that needs to be viewed with a degree of caution. The words were: 'Hilda von,' or rather, 'Talk to Hilda von.' According to Blomkvist, Palmgren seemed to want to tell him something important. One can speculate as to whether that is the perpetrator's name. As you know, we have a witness statement that yesterday evening a slim, black-haired woman of indeterminate age, wearing sunglasses, was seen hurrying down the stairs with a brown leather bag. Right now it's impossible to judge how much value we should be attaching to it. Besides, I rather doubt that Palmgren would say 'Talk to' if he was referring to the person who had just hurt him. It sounds more likely that this 'Hilda von' is somebody with important information. Or else it could be someone completely unconnected, but whose name came into his head at the moment he died."

"Could be, but still, what do we have on the actual name?"

"At first it looked promising," Modig said. "The 'von' prefix is associated with aristocracy in Sweden, and that gives us a pretty limited circle. But Hilda is a common name in Germany too, and there the 'von' can also be a preposition simply meaning 'from.' Therefore, if we include Germanic names, we're talking about a much larger group. Jan and I agree that we should get a little further in the investigation before we embark on questioning all the aristocratic Hildas from the grandest families in Sweden."

"And what are you getting out of Salander?" Svensson said.

"Not a lot, unfortunately."

"Bloody typical."

"Well, yes, I suppose that's fair," Modig said. "But we haven't yet spoken to her ourselves; we've relied on our colleagues in the Örebro force. She's a witness for them in a different case, a serious assault on Beatrice Andersson at Flodberga."

"Who the hell was brave enough to attack Benito?" Holmberg burst out.

"The warden in the maximum security unit, Alvar Olsen. He says he had no choice. I'll get to that."

"I hope he's got bodyguards," Holmberg said.

"Security in the unit has been stepped up and Benito's being transferred to another prison as soon as she's fit to be moved. Right now, she's in hospital in Örebro."

"That won't be enough, I can promise you that," Holmberg said. "Do you have the slightest idea what sort of person Benito is? Have you ever seen the state of her victims? Trust me, she won't give up until Olsen's had his throat cut—slowly."

"Both we and the prison management know the situation is serious," Modig said, slightly irritated. "But we see no acute danger for the time being. May I continue? Our colleagues in Örebro didn't get much out of Salander, as I said. We have to hope that you, Jan—she trusts you—will do better. All of us—that's right, isn't it?—have a feeling that Salander is a key person here. According to Blomkvist, Palmgren was worried about her and told Blomkvist on the phone a day or so ago that he'd done something rash or stupid because of it, and that's interesting. What did he mean? And how rash can an infirm eighty-nine-year-old possibly be?"

"I would suggest we're talking about a phone call, or an impetuous search on his computer," Flod said.

"I agree. But we're not finding anything helpful. Plus, his mobile seems to have vanished into thin air."

"That sounds suspicious," Flod said.

"Indeed. And there's something else I think we should talk about. It's better if you take over here, Jan," Modig said.

Bublanski squirmed as if he would rather not. Then he took them through the story of Faria Kazi, which he himself had learned that morning.

"As you've heard, Salander didn't want to talk to the Örebro police about her meeting with Palmgren," he said. "She didn't want to say much about the assault on Benito either. But there was one thing she did want to discuss, and that was the investigation into the death of Jamal Chowdhury, the refugee from Bangladesh. She thinks it was very badly handled, and I have to say I agree."

"What makes you say that?"

"The haste with which it was determined to be a suicide. If this had been just another case of some poor wretch jumping in front of a tunnelbana train, I might understand it. But this was no ordinary incident. There was a fatwa against Chowdhury, and you cannot make light of that. There's a small group in Stockholm which has been radicalized through the influence of extremist elements in Bangladesh, and which seems prepared to kill at the drop of a hat. Since Chowdhury first arrived in Sweden, we should have been suspicious if he'd so much as slipped on a banana skin. But then he falls in love with Faria Kazi—whose brothers want to marry her off to a rich Islamist in Dhaka. You can imagine how furious they must have been when Faria ran away, into the arms of Chowdhury, of all people. Not only is Chowdhury the man who destroys the family's honour; he's also a religious and political enemy. Then all of a sudden he goes and falls in front of a train, and what do our colleagues do? They write it

off as a suicide, as easily as they'd investigate a domestic bur-
glary in Vällingby, when in fact there's a long list of strange
circumstances surrounding the events. On top of that, what
happens the day after Chowdhury's death? Faria Kazi has a
fit of rage and shoves her brother Ahmed out through a window in Sickla. I find it very hard to believe that has nothing
to do with the incident in the tunnelbana."

"OK, I get that, and it doesn't sound too good. But in
what way is it connected to Palmgren's death?" Svensson said.

"Maybe it isn't, but still—Faria Kazi ends up in the maximum security unit at Flodberga with Salander and, like her,
is the target of serious threats. There are major concerns
that her brothers will want their revenge, and today we've
had confirmation from Säpo that they've been in touch with
none other than Benito. The brothers call themselves believers, but they have more in common with Benito than with
Muslims in general, and if it's revenge they're after, Benito is
the ideal weapon."

"I can imagine," Holmberg said.

"It also seems that Benito has taken an interest in both
Kazi and Salander."

"How do we know that?"

"From the investigation carried out by the prison into
how Benito got her stiletto into the unit. They went through
absolutely everything, including the trash in the visitors'
section in H Block. A crumpled note was found in one of
the wastepaper baskets there, with some very disturbing
information in Benito's handwriting. Not only the address
of the school to which Olsen's nine-year-old daughter was
moved some months ago, but also about the particulars of

Faria's aunt, Fatima, the only one in the family she's still close to. And, most noteworthy, details about people close to Salander: Mikael Blomkvist, a lawyer by the name of Jeremy MacMillan in Gibraltar—no, I still don't know who that is—and Holger Palmgren."

"Oh no, really?" Flod said.

"Unfortunately. It feels almost uncanny to see Palmgren's name there and to know it was written before he died. Not only his name, but his address, door code and telephone number."

"Not good," Holmberg said.

"No. It's not necessarily linked to his murder, or what we believe to be his murder. But it is striking, isn't it?"

Blomkvist was walking along Hantverkargatan on Kungsholmen when his mobile rang. It was Sofie Melker at the office. She wanted to know how he was. "So-so," he answered, and he thought that was the end of it. Melker was the eighth person that day to call and extend condolences. There was nothing wrong with that, but he would rather be left alone. He wanted to deal with the situation the way he normally dealt with death—through hard work.

He had been in Uppsala that morning and read the file for the investigation of the Rosvik finance director who had been involved in the accidental shooting of psychologist Carl Seger. Now he was on his way to meet Ellenor Hjort, the woman who had been engaged to Seger at the time.

"Thanks, Sofie," he said. "Speak later. I'm going into a meeting now."

"OK, we can deal with it later."

"Deal with what?"

"Erika asked me to check something for you."

"Oh yes. Did you find anything?"

"Depends."

"What do you mean, 'depends'?"

"There's nothing untoward in Herman and Viveka Mannheimer's personal files."

"I'd have been surprised if there had been. I'm more interested in Leo's file. He might have been adopted, or maybe there was something sensitive or out of the ordinary in his background."

"In fact his documents look neat and tidy. They state clearly that he was born in Västerled parish, where his parents lived at the time of his birth. Column 20, headed 'Adoptive parents or children etc.,' is blank. There's nothing redacted or declared confidential. Everything seems normal. Each parish he lived in while growing up is neatly listed. There's nothing that stands out at all."

"But didn't you say 'depends'?"

"Let me put it this way: I thought it could be fun to take a look at my own personal file, since I was down at the City Archives anyway, so I asked for it and paid the eight kronor, which I've decided not to claim back from *Millennium*."

"How very generous of you."

"The thing is, I'm only three years older than Leo. But my file looks totally different," she said.

"In what way?"

"It's not as tidy. Reading it made me feel really old. There's one column, column 19, where dates and other details have been recorded from whenever I moved and was transferred to another parish. I don't know who writes those entries, civil servants I would guess. But they're an absolute mess. Sometimes the notes are written by hand, sometimes they're typed. Some of the information has been stamped in, and then it's not always straight, as if they'd had difficulty lining it up properly. But in Leo's file it's all perfect, everything is consistent, filled in on the same kind of machine or computer."

"As if someone had reconstituted it?"

"Well . . ." Sofie said. "If someone else had asked me or if I'd just happened to see his file, the thought would never have occurred to me. But you make us all a bit paranoid, you know, Mikael. With you, we smell a rat. So yes, with all that in mind, I wouldn't rule out that the file was re-written after the fact. What's all this about?"

"I don't know yet. You didn't say who you were, did you, Sofie?"

"I took advantage of my right to remain anonymous, as Erika suggested, and fortunately I'm not a celebrity like you."

"Great. Take care now, and thanks!"

He ended the call and looked gloomily over Kungsholmstorg. It was a glorious day, which only made things worse. He carried on down to the address he had been given—Norr Mälarstrand 32—where Carl Seger's former fiancée Ellenor Hjort lived with her fifteen-year-old daughter. These days she was a manager at Bukowskis' auction rooms, fifty-two years old, divorced for three years and active in a number of non-profit organizations. She also coached her daughter's basketball team. Clearly an active woman.

Blomkvist looked down towards Lake Mälaren, which was lying wind-still, and across to his own apartment on the other side of the water. It was oppressively hot, and he felt sticky and heavy as he keyed in the code and took the lift to the top floor. He rang the doorbell and did not have to wait long.

Ellenor Hjort looked surprisingly young. She had short hair, beautiful dark-brown eyes and a small scar just below the hairline. She was dressed in a black jacket and grey trousers, and her home was filled with books and paintings. As she served Blomkvist tea and biscuits she seemed nervous. The cups and saucers rattled as she set them down on a table between a light-blue sofa and matching armchairs. Blomkvist made himself comfortable in one of them, beneath a rather garish oil painting of Venice.

"I must say, I'm surprised you should bring up this story again after all these years," she said.

"I do understand, and I'm sorry if I'm opening old wounds. But I would like to know a little bit more about Carl."

"Why is he of interest all of a sudden?"

Blomkvist hesitated and decided to be honest:

"I wish I could say. Perhaps there's more to his death than meets the eye. Something feels not quite right."

"What do you mean, more specifically?"

"It's still mostly a gut instinct. I went to Uppsala and read all the witness statements, and there's actually nothing inconsistent or odd about them except, well, precisely that there *is* nothing odd about them. If I've learned anything over the years, it's that the truth is generally a little unexpected, or even illogical, since we humans aren't entirely rational. Whereas lies, as a rule, tend to be consistent and comprehensive and often sound like a cliché—especially if the liars aren't very good."

"So the investigation into Carl's death is a cliché," she said. "Is that it?"

"The whole thing hangs together a little too well," Blomkvist said. "There aren't enough inconsistencies, and too few details that really stand out."

"Do you have anything to tell me that I don't already know?" Ellenor Hjort sounded almost sarcastic.

"I could add that the man who was supposed to have fired the shot, Per Fält—"

Hjort interrupted and assured him that she had every respect for his profession and his powers of observation. But when it came to this investigation, there was nothing he could teach her.

"I've read through it a hundred times," she said. "All the things you're talking about I've felt like stabs in the back. Don't you think I've shouted and screamed at Herman and at Alfred Ögren—'What are you bastards hiding!?' Of course I did!"

"And what answer did you get?"

"Indulgent smiles and kind words. 'We understand it can't be easy. We're so very sorry . . .' But after a while, when I wouldn't give up, they threatened me. They told me to watch my step. They were powerful men and my insinuations were lies and slander, and they knew good lawyers and all that. I was too weak and too grief-stricken to keep arguing. Carl had been my life. I was devastated and I couldn't study, or work or cope with the most day-to-day routines."

"I understand."

"But the strange thing was—and it's also the reason that I'm sitting here with you today, in spite of it all—who do you think comforted me more than anyone else, more than my father and mother and my sisters and friends?"

"Leo?"

"Exactly, lovely little Leo. He was as inconsolable as I was. We sat in the house Carl and I shared on Grönviksvägen and wept and ranted against the world and those bloody bastards in the forest, and when I screamed and sobbed, 'There's only half of me now,' he said the same thing. He was only a child. But we were united in our grief."

"Why did Carl matter so much to him?"

"They saw each other every week in Carl's consulting rooms. But there was more to it than that, of course. Leo looked upon Carl not just as a therapist, but also as a friend, maybe the only person in the whole world who understood him, and for his part Carl wanted to . . ." She trailed off.

"What?"

"To help Leo, and to get him to understand that he was an immensely gifted boy with extraordinary potential, and then of course . . . I'm not going to pretend this wasn't a factor too: Leo became important for Carl's research, for his doctoral thesis."

"Leo had hyperacusis."

Hjort looked at Blomkvist in surprise and said:

"Yes, that was part of it. Carl wanted to discover whether

that contributed to the boy's isolation, and whether Leo saw the world differently from the rest of us. But don't think that Carl was being cynical. There was a bond between them which not even I understood."

Blomkvist decided to take a chance.

"Leo was adopted, wasn't he?" he said.

Ellenor Hjort emptied her cup of tea and glanced out at the balcony to her left.

"Maybe," she said.

"Why do you say that?"

"Because sometimes I got the impression that there was something sensitive about his background."

Blomkvist decided to take another gamble:

"Did Leo have Gypsy heritage?"

Hjort looked up, her eyes fixed in concentration.

"Funny you should say that," she said.

"Why?"

"Because I remember . . . Carl invited Leo and me to lunch in Drottningholm."

"What happened?"

"Nothing much, but I remember it all the same. Carl and I were deeply in love. But sometimes it felt as if he was keeping secrets from me—not just professional ones from his therapy work—and that was probably one of the reasons I was so jealous. That lunch was one of those occasions."

"One of which occasions?"

"Leo was upset that someone had called him a 'gyppo,' and instead of just coming right out and saying 'What kind of idiot is calling you that?' Carl held forth like a school-teacher and explained that 'gyppo' was a racist term and a relic from dark times. Leo nodded as if he'd heard it all before. Even though he was a child, he already knew about the Romani community and about their oppression—forced sterilizations, lobotomizations and even ethnic cleansing in some parishes. It felt . . . somehow . . . surprising for a boy like him."

"And so what happened?"

"Nothing happened, not a single damn thing," she said. "Carl dismissed it when I asked afterwards. It might have been confidential because of a client-therapist relationship, but, given the broader context, I got the feeling he was hiding things from me. That episode still sometimes pricks me like a thorn."

"Was it one of Alfred Ögren's boys who called Leo a 'gyppo'?"

"It was Ivar, the youngest, the afterthought. The only one who followed in his father's footsteps. Do you know him?"

"A little," he said. "He was nasty, wasn't he?"

"Seriously nasty."

"How come?"

"I suppose one always wonders. There certainly was rivalry from the early days onwards, not only between the boys but also between their fathers. As a means to outdo each other, Herman and Alfred pitted their sons against each other to see whose was the cleverer, or the more enterprising. Ivar always came first whenever brawn counted. Leo was best at everything that involved the intellect, and that must have caused a lot of envy. Ivar knew about Leo's hyperacusis. But instead of being considerate about it, he would wake him during their summers in Falsterbo by turning up the stereo to insane levels. Once he bought a bag of balloons which he inflated and then burst one by one behind Leo's back when he was least expecting it. When Carl heard about it, he took Ivar aside and slapped him. Alfred Ögren went ballistic."

"So there was some aggression against Carl in the wider circle around the family?"

"For sure. But I will say that Leo's parents always stood up for Carl. They knew how important he was to their boy. That's why ultimately I came to terms with—or tried to come to terms with—the idea that the shooting was an accident. Herman Mannheimer would never have killed his son's best friend."

"How did Carl first come into contact with the family?"

"Through his university. The timing was perfect. Previously, schools had done nothing whatsoever for exceptionally gifted children. Singling them out was seen as being at odds with the Swedish ideal of equality. Schools also lacked the ability to identify and understand them. Many intelligent pupils were so under-stimulated that they became disruptive and were put in classes which catered to special educational needs. It seems that there was a disproportionately large number of gifted children in psychiatric care. Carl hated that, and he fought for those boys and girls. Just a few years earlier he'd been called an elitist. Then he started getting recruited onto government committees. He got to know Herman Mannheimer through his supervisor, Hilda von Kanterborg."

Blomkvist started.

"Who is Hilda von Kanterborg?"

"She was an associate professor on the faculty of psychology and academic supervisor to two or three doctoral students," Hjort said. "She was young, not much older than Carl, and was expected to have a great future ahead of her. That's why it's so tragic that she . . ."

"Is she dead?"

"Not that I know. But she ended up with a bad reputation. I heard that she became an alcoholic."

"Why the bad reputation?"

For a moment, Hjort seemed unfocused. Then she looked straight into Blomkvist's eyes.

"It was after Carl died, so I have no inside knowledge. But my feeling is that it was pretty unfair."

"In what way?"

"I'm sure Hilda was no worse than any male academic with a bit of swagger. I met her a few times with Carl, and she was incredibly charismatic; you just got drawn in by her eyes. Apparently she kept having all sorts of affairs, including with two or three of her students. That wasn't good, but they were all consenting adults and she was popular and clever and nobody much minded, not at first. Hilda was just ravenous. Ravenous for life, for new friendships—and for men. She was neither calculating nor evil, she was simply all over the place."

"So what happened?"

"I'm not altogether sure. All I know is that the university administration produced a couple of students who claimed—or rather hinted, somewhat vaguely—that Hilda had sold herself to them. It felt so cheap—as if they could think of nothing better than to make a whore of her. What are you doing?"

Without realizing it, Blomkvist had gotten to his feet and was searching on his mobile.

"I have a Hilda von Kanterborg living on Rutger Fuchsgatan. Do you think that's her?"

"There can't be many with that name. Why are you so interested in her all of a sudden?"

"Because . . ." Blomkvist trailed off. "It's complicated. But you've been very helpful."

"Does that mean you're off now?"

"Yes, I have to move quickly. I have a feeling that . . ."

He did not finish that sentence either. Malin called, sounding at least as agitated as he was. He said he would call her back. He shook Ellenor Hjort's hand, thanked her and ran down the stairs. Out on the street he called Hilda von Kanterborg.

DECEMBER, ONE AND A HALF YEARS EARLIER

What can be forgiven, and what cannot? Leo Mannheimer and Carl Seger had often discussed this. These were questions important to both of them, but in different ways. For the most part their position was generous: most things could be forgiven, even Ivar's bullying. For the time being, Leo was reconciled with him. Ivar didn't know any better; he was malicious in the same way that others are shy or unmusical. He had as little understanding of other people's feelings as someone with a tin ear has of tones and melodies. Leo indulged him, and occasionally he would be rewarded by a friendly pat on the shoulder, a look of complicity. Ivar often asked him for advice, maybe out of self-interest, but still . . . Sometimes he paid him a backhanded compliment: "You're not so stupid after all, Leo!"

Ivar's marriage to Madeleine Bard destroyed all that. It pitched Leo into a hatred which no amount of therapy could cure or check. Nor did he resist it. He welcomed it as a fever, a storm. It was worst at night or in the small hours. That was when a thirst for revenge pounded in his temples and his heart. He fantasized about shootings and other accidents, social humiliation, sicknesses, hideous skin rashes. He even pricked holes in photographs and used the power of thinking to try to get Ivar to fall from balconies and terraces. He teetered on the edge of madness. But nothing came of it, except that Ivar became vigilant and anxious and possibly started planning something himself. Time passed and the situation sometimes got better, sometimes worse.

It was snowing and exceptionally cold. His mother was on her deathbed. He sat with her three or four times a week and tried to be a good, comforting son. But it was not easy. Her illness had not made her any milder. The morphine had peeled off yet another layer of restraint, and on two separate occasions she called him weak:

"You have always been a disappointment, Leo," she said.

He did not answer his mother when she was like this, but he did dream of leaving the country for good. He was not seeing many people other than Malin Frode, who was getting a divorce and was about to leave the firm. Leo never believed that she loved him, but it was nice just to be with her. They helped each other through a difficult time and they laughed together, even if the anger and fantasies did not disappear even then. At times Leo became genuinely frightened of Ivar. He imagined that he was being followed, spied on. He no longer had any illusions. Ivar was capable of just about anything.

Leo felt that he too was capable of just about anything. Maybe one day he would hurl himself at Ivar and cause him a terrible injury. Either that or he would get ambushed. He tried to dismiss it all as paranoia and foolishness, but the feeling would not go away. He kept hearing foot-steps behind him, and felt eyes on his back. He imagined shadow-like figures in alleyways and on street corners, and a few times in Humlegården he found himself suddenly turning to look, but he never saw anything unusual.

On Friday, December 15, it was snowing harder than ever. The Christmas decorations were sparkling in the streets and he went home early. He changed into jeans and a woollen sweater and put a glass of red wine on the grand piano. It was a Bösendorfer Imperial with ninety-seven keys. He tuned it himself every Monday. The piano stool was a black-leather Jansen, and he sat down and played a new composition which he began in a Dorian flat mode. At the end of every phrase landed on the seventh tone, he produced a sound which was both ominous and mourn-ful. He played for a good while and heard nothing else, not even the footsteps in the stairwell. He was deep in concen-tration. But then he registered something so peculiar that for a while he thought it was a figment of his own heated imagination, the result of his hypersensitive hearing. Yet it really did sound as if someone was accompanying him on a guitar. He stopped playing and went to the front door. He thought about calling out through the mail slot.

Instead he unlocked and opened the door, and then it was as if he had cut himself loose from reality.

CHAPTER 11

June 20

In the maximum security unit, the prisoners had finished their supper and left the dining hall. Some had headed off to work out. Two or three were smoking and gossiping in the exercise yard. Others were glued to a film—*Ocean's Eleven*. The rest were wandering up and down the corridor and the recreation rooms, or talking in hushed voices in each other's cells with the doors wide open. It could have been almost any day. But nothing would ever be the same again.

Not only were there more guards than usual, but there was also a ban on visits and telephone calls, and it was hotter and stuffier than before. Rikard Fager, the prison governor, had been doing the rounds, and the guards, already affected by the atmosphere among the inmates, became even more apprehensive.

The air was vibrating with a feeling of liberation. People walked and smiled with a new sense of freedom. The general hubbub was now lighter and more lively, no longer fraught with fear and anxiety. On the other hand there was uncertainty, and evidence of a power vacuum. It was as if a tyrant had fallen. A few—and Tine Grönlund was one—seemed fearful of being attacked from behind. Everywhere people were discussing what had happened and what would happen next.

Even if much of it was myth and hearsay, the prisoners still had more information than the guards. Everyone knew that it was Salander who had smashed Benito's jaw, and they all knew that her life was very much in danger. There were rumours that relatives of Salander had already been murdered and that the revenge would be terrible, especially because Benito was said to have been disfigured for life. It was common knowledge that there was a price on Faria Kazi's head and there were whispers that the reward was being put up by rich Islamists, by sheiks even.

They all knew Benito was being transferred to a new prison straight from the hospital, as soon as she was fit to be moved, and that major changes were in store. The mere fact that the governor was on the scene suggested as much. Fager was the most detested person in the place—if you discounted the women in C Block who had murdered their own children. But for once the prisoners regarded him not only with hostility, but also with a degree of hope. Who knows, maybe things would ease up now that Benito was gone?

Fager looked at his watch and waved away one of the inmates who came to complain about the heat. Fager was forty-nine years old and good-looking, but with a blank expression. He was wearing a grey suit, red tie and polished

Alden shoes. Even though prison management tended to dress down to avoid provocation, he did the exact opposite so as to reinforce his authority. Today he regretted it. Sweat ran down his forehead and he was uncomfortable in his close-fitting jacket. His trousers were sticking to his thighs. He took a call on the intercom.

Afterwards, he gave a tight-lipped nod and went up to acting head guard Lindfors and whispered something in her ear. Then he walked off in the direction of cell number seven, where Salander had been in isolation since the previous evening.

Salander was at her desk doing some calculations on a particular aspect of so-called Wilson loops, which had become increasingly central to her efforts to formulate loop quantum gravity, when Fager and Lindfors walked into her cell. But she saw no reason to look up or interrupt her work. She did not notice that the governor prodded Lindfors, prompting her to announce his arrival.

"The governor is here to talk to you," Lindfors said in a stern voice and with a look of distaste. Only then did Salander turn. She noted that Fager was brushing at something on his jacket sleeves, as if fearing that he had already picked up some dirt in the cell.

His lips moved almost imperceptibly and he narrowed his eyes. It looked as if he was trying to suppress a grimace. Clearly he didn't like her, and that suited her just fine. She did not care for him either. She had read too many of his e-mails.

"I've got good news," he said.

Salander said nothing.

"Good news," he said again.

Still she said nothing, and that seemed to irritate Fager.

"Are you deaf or something?" he said.

"No."

She looked down at the floor.

"Ah, OK, well that's good," he said. "Listen, you've got another nine days to go. But we're going to release you tomorrow morning. You'll be questioned shortly by Chief Inspector Jan Bublanski from Stockholm police, and we'd like you to be cooperative."

"You don't want me in here anymore?"

"It's got nothing to do with what we do or don't want. We have our instructions, and also the staff have confirmed . . ."

Fager seemed to be having difficulty getting the words out.

". . . that you've conducted yourself well, and that's enough for an early release."

"I have not conducted myself well," she said.

"Haven't you? I've had reports . . ."

"Bullshit window dressing, I'm sure. Like your own reports."

"What do you know about *my* reports?"

Salander was still looking at the floor and her answer was matter-of-fact, as if she was reading it out:

"I know that they're badly written and wordy. You often use the wrong prepositions and your style is stilted. But above all they're ingratiating and ignorant, and sometimes untruthful. You withhold information which you've obviously received. You've persuaded the board of the prison service that the maximum security unit is a great place, and that's a serious matter, Rikard. It's one of the factors that's made Faria Kazi's time here a living hell. It just about cost her her life, and that makes me fucking angry."

Fager gaped and his mouth twitched. The blood drained from his face. But still he managed to clear his throat and said incoherently:

"What are you saying, girl? What do you mean? Did you see some official documents, then?"

"Some of them may have been official, yes."

Fager hardly seemed conscious of what he was saying:

"You're lying!"

"I'm not lying. I've read them and it's none of your business how."

His whole body was shaking.

"You are . . ."

"What?"

Fager did not seem able to come up with anything fitting.

"Just remember that the decision to release you can be revoked at any time," he barked instead.

"Go ahead then, revoke it. There's only one thing I care about."

Sweat broke out on Fager's upper lip.

"And what might that be?" he said guardedly.

"For Faria Kazi to get support and help and be kept in absolute safety until her lawyer, Annika Giannini, can get her out of here. After that she'll need witness protection."

Fager roared, "You're not in a position to ask for anything!"

"That's where you're wrong. You, on the other hand,

shouldn't be in any position at all," she said. "You're a liar and a hypocrite, and you've allowed a gangster to take over the most critical unit in your prison."

"I don't think you know what you're talking about," he spluttered.

"I couldn't care less what you think. I have the proof. All I need to know is what you're going to do about Faria Kazi."

His gaze was unsteady.

"Don't worry, we'll look after her," he said.

He seemed embarrassed, and added ominously:

"You know that Faria Kazi isn't the only person receiving serious threats."

"Get out," she said.

"I'm warning you. I will not tolerate—"

"Out!"

Fager's right hand shook. His lips twitched, and for a second or two he stood as if paralyzed. He clearly wanted to say something more, but instead he turned and ordered Lindfors to lock up. Then he slammed the door shut and his heavy footsteps resounded in the corridor.

Faria Kazi heard them and thought of Salander. In her mind's eye she kept seeing Salander going on the attack and Benito crashing to the concrete floor. She could hardly concentrate on anything else. The scene played over and again in her thoughts. Sometimes it triggered associations to the events that had led to her now sitting in prison.

She remembered how she had been lying in her room in Sickla a few days after the stolen phone conversation with

Jamal, reading poems by Tagore. Bashir had looked in at around 3:00 p.m. that day and had snarled that girls should not read because it only turns them into whores and heretics, and then he slapped her. But for once she felt neither angry nor humiliated. In fact she gained strength from that blow. She got up and paced around the apartment, seldom taking her eyes off her youngest brother, Khalil.

That afternoon she changed her plans minute by minute. She considered asking Khalil to let her out of the apartment when nobody was looking. She would get him to call the social services, the police, her old school. Or he could contact a journalist or Imam Ferdousi, or their aunt Fatima. She would tell him that if he did not help her, she would slit her wrists.

But she said none of those things. Just before 5:00 p.m. she looked in her wardrobe. There was nothing much there except for veils and casual wear. The dresses and skirts had long since been cut up or thrown away. But she still had a pair of jeans and a black blouse. She pulled them on with some sneakers and went into the kitchen, where Bashir was sitting with Ahmed. They glared suspiciously at her before turning away. She wanted to scream and smash every glass and plate in there. But she just stood still and listened as footsteps headed towards the front door. Khalil's footsteps. Then she acted with lightning speed, as if she could not quite believe what she was doing, and pulled a kitchen knife out of a drawer, hiding it under her blouse before hurrying out of the kitchen.

Khalil was standing at the front door in his blue tracksuit, looking miserable and lost. He must have heard her steps, because he was fumbling nervously with the key in the security lock. Faria was panting. She said:

"You have to let me out, Khalil. I can't live like this. I'd rather kill myself."

Khalil turned and gave her a look of such unhappiness that she recoiled. At the same moment, she heard Bashir and Ahmed pushing back their chairs in the kitchen. She drew her knife and said quietly:

"Pretend that I threatened you, Khalil. Do whatever you want. Just let me out!"

"They'll kill me," he said, and then she thought it was all over.

It was not going to work. That was too high a price to pay. Bashir and Ahmed came closer, and she could also hear voices coming up the stairs. That was it. She was sure she had failed. And yet . . . his face still a picture of sorrow, Khalil opened the door, and she dropped the knife on the floor and ran. She dodged past her father and Razan out in the corridor and raced down the stairs, and for a while she heard nothing, only her own breathing and her own steps. Then voices came rumbling from above. Heavy, angry feet pounded after her. Now she remembered how it had felt to be actually running away. It had felt so strange. She had not been outside for months. She had hardly moved and was obviously not in any sort of shape. But it felt as if she were being borne along by the autumn winds and the bracing cold.

She ran as she had never run before, this way and that among the houses, along the waterfront at Hammarbyhamnen and then up again along the streets over the bridge to Ringvägen. There she jumped on a bus which took her to

Vasastan, where she kept on running, and once or twice she lost her footing and fell. Her elbows were bleeding by the time she went in through the street entrance at Upplands-gatan and rushed up three flights of stairs.

She rang the bell and stood there, and she recalled hearing footsteps inside. She prayed and hoped and closed her eyes. Then the door opened and she was terrified. Jamal Chowdhury was wearing a dressing gown even though it was the middle of the day, and he was unshaven and tousle-haired and seemed disoriented, almost frightened. For a second she thought she had made a mistake. But Jamal was only shocked. He could hardly take it in.

"Thank God!" he said.

Shaking all over, she fell into his arms and would not let him go. He led her into the apartment and closed the door. He too had a heavy security lock, but here it made her feel safe. For a long time they did not utter a word. They just lay entwined on the narrow bed and the hours went by, and then they began to talk and kiss and cry, and in the end they made love. Slowly, the pressure in her chest eased, the fear ebbed away. She and Chowdhury became one in a way she had never experienced with anyone. But what she did not know—and would not have wanted to know—was that something was changing at the apartment in Sickla. The family had acquired a new enemy, and that enemy was her brother Khalil.

Blomkvist could not understand what Malin was telling him. He was so focused on trying to get hold of Hilda von Kanterborg that he was barely listening. He was in a taxi crossing Västerbron on his way to Rutger Fuchsgatan in Skanstull. People were sunbathing in the park below. Motorboats cruised out on Riddarfjärden.

"Now listen, Micke," she said. "Please concentrate. You're the one who dragged me into this whole mess."

"I know, I'm sorry. I have to pull myself together. Let's take it from the top. It's this thing about Leo sitting and writing something in his office, is that right?"

"Exactly, there was something odd about it."

"You thought he was writing a will."

"It wasn't *what* he was writing. It was *how*."

"What do you mean?"

"He was writing with his left hand, Mikael. Leo was always left-handed—suddenly I remembered it very clearly. He always wrote with his left hand. He caught apples, oranges, anything at all, with his left hand. But now he's right-handed."

"Sounds a bit weird."

"It's true all the same. Must have been already there in my subconscious, ever since I saw Leo on TV a while back. He was making a PowerPoint presentation and holding the remote in his right hand."

"Sorry Malin, but that's not enough to persuade me."

"I'm not done yet. I didn't attach too much importance to it either. I hadn't even really taken it on board. But there was something nagging at me and so I observed Leo very carefully at Fotografiska. We were quite close towards the end of my time at Alfred Ögren, so I was very familiar with his gestures."

"OK."

"The movements were exactly the same when he gave his talk at Fotografiska, only the opposite way round. Like all right-handers, he picked up the water bottle with his right hand, transferred it to his left and unscrewed the top with his right, and then also held the glass with his right hand. That was when I realized. Afterwards, I went to talk to him."

"Not a successful conversation."

"I could tell he just wanted to be rid of me, and then at the bar he was holding his wine glass with his right hand. It actually gave me the shivers."

"Could it be something neurological?"

"That's more or less what he said himself."

"What? You confronted him about it?"

"Not me, but afterwards I refused to believe my own eyes. I watched all the TV clips of Leo I could find online. I even called and spoke to my old colleagues, but none of them had noticed a thing. Nobody ever seems to notice anything. Then I spoke to Nina West. She's a Forex trader and pretty sharp, and she'd noticed the change. You can imagine how relieved I was to hear that. She's the one who asked him about it."

"And what did he say?"

"He was embarrassed and started muttering. He said he was ambidextrous, that he decided to change hands after his mother died, as a part of his liberation. That he was looking for a new way of living."

"Isn't that a good enough explanation?"

"Both hyperacoustic *and* ambidextrous? That seems a bit much to me."

Blomkvist looked out at Zinkensdamm.

"Maybe, but it's not impossible. But . . ." He reflected for a while longer. "You're right in saying something doesn't feel right about this story. Let's get together again soon."

"Absolutely," she said.

They ended the call and he continued in the direction of Skanstull and Hilda von Kanterborg.

Over the years, Bublanski had taken quite a liking to Salander, but he still did not feel at ease in her presence. He knew that she disliked authority, and even though he could sympathize, given her background, he hated generalizations.

"Eventually you'll have to start trusting people, Lisbeth, even the police. Otherwise you'll have a hard time of it," he said.

"I'll do my best," she said drily.

He was sitting facing her, fidgeting, in the visitors' section in H Block. She looked oddly young, he thought.

"Let me begin by expressing my deepest sympathies at the death of Holger Palmgren. It must have been a big blow. I remember when I lost my wife—"

"Skip it," she said.

"OK, let's get to the point. Do you have any idea why anyone would want to kill Palmgren?"

Salander raised her hand to her shoulder, just above the chest, where she had an old bullet wound. She started to speak with a strange coldness which made Bublanski feel quite uncomfortable, but what she said did at least have the advantage of being concise and accurate—an interrogator's dream, in a way.

"A few weeks ago, Holger had a visit from an elderly woman named Maj-Britt Torell, a former secretary to Professor Johannes Caldin, who was once head of St. Stefan's psychiatric clinic for children in Uppsala."

"Where you were a patient?"

"She had read about me in the newspapers and left him a bunch of documents. At first Holger didn't think they contained anything new, but in the end, they turned out to have serious implications. There had been plans to have me adopted when I was little and I'd always thought it was a misguided attempt to help deal with the problems linked to my bastard of a father. But these documents prove it was actually part of a scientific experiment set up by an authority called the Registry for the Study of Genetics and Social Environment. Its existence is a secret and I was annoyed that I couldn't find the names of the people in charge of it. So I called Holger and asked him to take a closer look at those documents. I have no idea what he found. All I know is that Mikael Blomkvist called to tell me that Holger was dead, that he might have been murdered. So my advice is that you contact Maj-Britt Torell. She lives in Aspudden. She may have copies of the documents or they may be backed up somewhere. It might also be a good idea to check that she's OK from time to time."

"Thanks," he said. "That is helpful. What exactly did this authority do?"

"The name ought to give you a clue."

"Names can be misleading."

"There's a creep called Teleborian."

"We've questioned him already."

"Do it again."

"What should we be looking for?"

"You could try grilling the heads of the genetics centre at Uppsala. But I doubt you'll get very far."

"Could you be a bit more specific, Lisbeth. What's all this about?"

"About science—or rather pseudo-science—and about some idiots who imagined you could study the impact of social environment and heredity by sending children away for adoption."

"Doesn't sound too good."

"Full marks for insight," she said.

"Any other clues?"

"No."

Bublanski did not believe her.

"I'm sure you know that Holger's last words were 'Talk to Hilda von . . .' Does that ring any bells?"

It certainly did. It had rung a bell when Blomkvist called the day before, too. But for the time being she kept that to herself. She had her reasons. Neither did she mention anything about Leo Mannheimer or the woman with the birthmark. She gave only brusque answers to the rest of Bublanski's questions. Then she said goodbye and was taken back to her cell. At 9:00 a.m. the following morning she would be leaving Flodberga. She supposed that Fager was eager to be rid of her.

CHAPTER 12

June 20

Rakel Greitz was, as usual, unhappy about the job the cleaners had done. She should have given firmer instructions. Now she had to do the mopping and drying herself, and water her house plants and tidy up the books, the glasses, the cups. No matter that she was feeling sick and that her hair was coming out in tufts. She gritted her teeth. She had a lot to do.

She read one more time through the documents she had taken from Holger Palmgren. It was not hard to see which were the references that had prompted his telephone call. The notes in themselves were not so much of a problem, especially since Teleborian had been good enough to refer to her using only her initial. There was no detailed description of the actual research being done, and no other children had been named. In any case, that is not what made her uncomfortable. What upset her was the fact that Palmgren had been reading them now, after all these years.

It could have been a coincidence. Martin Steinberg believed so. Maybe Palmgren had had the papers for ages and decided on a whim to look through them, which then got him thinking about the information without attaching too much importance to it. If that is how it was, then her recent actions would have been a disastrous mistake. But Greitz did not believe in coincidence, not now that so much was teetering on the brink of disaster.

Plus she knew that Palmgren had recently been to see Salander at Flodberga women's prison. Greitz was not going to underestimate Salander again, especially not with Hilda von Kanterborg's name in the documents. Hilda was the only connection Greitz could think of that might lead Salander to her. She was pretty certain that Hilda had not been indiscreet again, not since her unfortunate friendship with Agneta Salander. But you could never be sure about anything, and it was possible that there were copies of the documents out there, which was why it was crucial for Greitz to find out how Palmgren had gotten hold of them. Had it been in the context of the Teleborian investigation, or had he gotten them later—and, if so, from whom? Greitz had been convinced they had removed all the sensitive material from St. Stefan's, but maybe . . . she was deep in thought when an idea struck her: Johannes Caldin, the head of the clinic. He had always been a thorn in their side. Could he have handed over the papers before he died? Or had someone close to him done so—such as his . . . ?

Greitz swore to herself. "Of course, that bloody woman."

She went into the kitchen and swallowed two painkillers with a glass of lemonade. Then she called Steinberg—that

wimp could get off his backside and make himself useful—
and told him to get in touch with Maj-Britt Tourette, as
Greitz liked to call her.

"Right away," she said. "Now!"

Then she made herself an arugula salad with walnuts and
tomatoes and cleaned the bathroom. It was 5:30 p.m. She felt
warm, even though the balcony door was open. She longed
to be able to take off her turtleneck and put on a linen shirt
but resisted the temptation and again thought of Hilda. She
had nothing but contempt for the woman. Hilda was a lush
and a slut. Yet there had been a time when Greitz envied her.
Men flocked around her, women and children too, for that
matter. She had an open and generous mind in the good old
days, when they all had such high hopes.

Their project was not the only one of its kind. Their
source of inspiration had been in New York, though she and
Steinberg had driven their project further. Even though they
had sometimes been surprised, or disappointed, by their
findings, she had never thought the broader costs, taken as a
whole, were too high. Admittedly, some of the children were
worse off than others. But that was the lottery of life.

Project 9 was fundamentally worthy and important—that
was how she saw it. It would show the world how to produce
stronger and better-balanced individuals, and that is why it
was such a tragedy that two of their subjects had jeopardized
everything and forced her to take such extreme measures.
She was not particularly troubled by her transgressions—
and sometimes that surprised her. She did not, after all, lack
self-knowledge and she knew that she was not much inclined
to remorse. But she did worry about consequences.

Distant shouting and laughter could be heard out on Karlbergsvägen. Her apartment smelled of detergent and rubbing alcohol. She looked at her watch again, got up from her desk and took out another doctor's bag—this one was black and more modern—and a new discreet wig, new sunglasses, a few syringes and ampoules and a small bottle containing bright-blue liquid. Then she retrieved a walking stick with a silver handle from the closet and a grey hat from the shelf in the hall, and she went down to wait for Benjamin to pick her up and take her to Skanstull.

Hilda von Kanterborg poured herself a glass of white wine and drank it slowly. She was without question an alcoholic. Even if she did not drink as much as was widely believed, she did drink too much, just as she over-indulged in her other vices. Contrary to what people thought, Hilda was not some grand noblewoman fallen on hard times. Nor was she someone who just drifted around and got drunk. She was still publishing articles on psychology under the pseudonym Leonard Bark.

Her father, Wilmer Karlsson, had been a contractor and a conman until he was convicted of gross fraud by Sundsvall district court. Later, he came across the name of one Johan Fredrik Kanterberg, a young lieutenant in the Royal Life Guard Dragoons who died in a duel in 1787, the last of his line. Thanks to some negotiating and one or two tricks, and despite the strict rules of the Swedish House of Nobility, Wilmer Karlsson managed to change his name—not to Kanterberg but to Kanterborg—and on his own initiative he

added a "von," which in due course found its way into official records.

Hilda found the name clumsy and affected, particularly
after her father abandoned the family and moved into a dis-
mal two-room apartment in central Timrå. The name von
Kanterborg sounded as out of place in those surroundings as
she herself would have felt at the House of Nobility. Maybe a
part of her personality was shaped in defiance of the name.
During her teenage years she experimented with drugs and
hung out with greasers in the town centre.

But she did well at school and went on to study psychology at Stockholm University. She spent much of her early
years there partying, but the teachers began to take notice
of her. She was attractive and intelligent and an original
thinker. She also had high moral standards, though not in
the way that was expected of girls in those days. She was
no prude, nor some quiet, pretty little thing. She abhorred
injustice and she never let anyone down.

Just after she had defended her thesis, she happened to
see sociology professor Martin Steinberg in a restaurant on
Rörstrandsgatan in Vasastan. All doctoral students knew
Steinberg. He was tall and handsome with a well-groomed
moustache, and he looked a bit like David Niven. He was
married to a stocky woman called Gertrud, who was occasionally taken for his mother. She was fourteen years older
and quite plain beside her charismatic husband.

It was said that Steinberg saw other women, that he was
a real power player with more clout than even his impressive C.V. would seem to warrant. He had been head of the
Department of Social Work at Stockholm University and

had chaired a number of government inquiries. Hilda found him dogmatic and obtuse, but she was fascinated by him, and not just by his appearance and his aura. She saw him as a riddle to be solved.

She was intrigued when she saw him in that restaurant with a woman who was certainly not his wife. She had short ash-blond hair, beautiful, determined eyes and a regal presence. Hilda could not be sure that this was a lover's tryst, but Steinberg was obviously disturbed when he caught sight of her. There was in fact nothing out of the ordinary about the scene. Even so, it felt as if she had caught a glimpse of the secret life she had always imagined Steinberg to be living, and she quickly stole out again.

During the days and weeks that followed, Steinberg looked at her with curiosity, and one evening he invited her to take a walk with him along the forest paths around the university. The sky was dark that day. For a long time Steinberg stayed quiet, though it seemed he was on the verge of sharing something important with her. Then he broke the silence with a question which was so trite that it amazed her:

"Have you ever wondered, Hilda, why you are just as you are?"

She answered politely:

"Yes, Martin, I have."

"It's one of the big questions, not just for our own pasts but also for our future," he said.

That was how she was drawn into Project 9. For a long time it seemed harmless: a number of children from different social backgrounds, who had been placed in foster homes when they were small, were tested and assessed. Some were gifted, others not. But none of the results were made public. On the surface there was nothing at all exploitative about it. Quite the opposite. The children were treated with care and consideration, and in some areas the team was initiating new if not pioneering lines of research.

Yet with the benefit of hindsight she should have asked more questions: How had the children been selected and why had so many been placed in such widely different social circumstances? Gradually she came to understand the broader picture, but by then the door was closed. And in any case, she still thought the project was defensible, both as a whole and for each individual case.

Then came another autumn, and the news that Carl Seger had been accidentally killed during an elk hunt. That really frightened her. She decided to get out. Steinberg and Greitz noticed it right away. They gave her the chance to have a positive influence on the project, and that kept her involved for a little while longer. Her task was to save one particular girl who was living an absolute nightmare with her twin sister on Lundagatan in Stockholm. The authorities had been no help so Hilda was to find a solution and a foster family.

Nothing was as straightforward as she had been told. She found herself getting close to the mother and the girl. She stood up for them and it cost her her career; it almost cost her her life. Sometimes she regretted it, but more often she was proud, and she came to see it as the best thing she had done during her time at the Registry.

Now, as the evening drew in, Hilda drank her Chardonnay and looked out the window. People were strolling by

and looking happy. Did she feel like going down and settling with a book at some outdoor café? No sooner had the
thought occurred to her than she spotted a figure getting out
of a black Renault a little way down the street. It was Rakel
Greitz. There was nothing strange about that in itself. Greitz
came by every now and again and treated her to a flood of
friendly chatter and flattery. But lately things had not felt
quite right. Greitz had sounded tense on the phone and had
begun to utter threats again, just as she used to.

She was now standing on the pavement outside, wearing a disguise but nevertheless unmistakable, and she was
accompanied by Benjamin. Benjamin Fors was Greitz's factotum. He not only ran her errands, but he was also called in
when there was need for coercion. Or brute force. Hilda was
frightened by what she saw and made an instant and drastic
decision.

She quickly put on her coat and grabbed her wallet and
mobile which had been lying on silent on her desk. Then
she left the apartment and locked the door. Not quite quick
enough. Footsteps could be heard in the entrance hall below.
She was gripped by panic and rushed downstairs, knowing
that she might run straight into their grasp. As luck would
have it they were waiting for the lift. Hilda made it into
the backyard, her only escape route that avoided the street
entrance. She could climb over a yellow wall at the far end if
she moved the garden table a little closer. The table screeched
as she pushed it across the flagstones. She scrambled over the
wall like a clumsy child and dropped into the neighbouring
yard, and then made her way out onto Bohusgatan. There

she turned towards Eriksdalsbadet and the waterfront. She walked quickly, even though her left foot throbbed from the fall and she was not entirely sober.

Down near the outdoor gym by Årstaviken she reached for her mobile. There were a number of missed calls, and when she listened to the messages she realized that something was very wrong. The journalist Mikael Blomkvist had been trying to reach her and, even though he apologized profusely, his voice sounded agitated. In his second message he added that now that Holger Palmgren was dead, he was "particularly keen to have a word."

Holger Palmgren, she muttered to herself. *Holger Palmgren.* Why did that name sound familiar? She searched on her mobile and it came up immediately. Palmgren had been Lisbeth Salander's guardian. Of course. Some story was obviously about to break and that was not good. If the media were chasing after information, she could be the weak link.

As she walked faster she looked out towards the water and the trees, and all the people strolling or picnicking on the grass. Just beyond the outdoor gym, by the open space on the waterfront where the small boats were moored, she saw three surly-looking teenage boys sprawled on a blanket, drinking beer. She stopped and looked at her mobile again. Hilda was no expert in technology, but she did know that it could be used to track her. So she made a quick last call to her sister, which she immediately regretted—every one of their telephone conversations left an aftertaste of guilt and accusation. Then she walked over to the teenagers and chose one with long straggly hair and a frayed denim jacket. She held out her telephone.

"Here you go," she said. "An iPhone, brand-new. It's yours. Just change the SIM card or whatever."

"What? Why are you giving me this?"

"Because you seem like such a nice guy. Good luck, don't buy any drugs," she said and then she hurried away in the evening sun.

Thirty minutes later she was standing at an ATM in Hornstull, damp from the heat, and withdrew three thousand kronor in cash before heading for Stockholm Central Station. She would go to Nyköping, to a small out-of-the-way hotel where she had gone into hiding years ago when all her colleagues at the university had accused her of being a slut.

Blomkvist passed an older woman in the doorway. She was wearing a hat and carrying a walking stick, and she was followed by a powerfully built man of his own age who must have been six and a half feet tall with small eyes and a round face. But he didn't pay them much attention. He was just relieved to have managed to get into the building, and he ran up the stairs to Hilda von Kanterborg's apartment. There did not seem to be anyone at home.

He left and walked towards the Clarion Hotel in Skanstull, and there he tried to call her again. This time an arrogant voice answered. A son, perhaps?

"Hey!"

"Hello!" Blomkvist said. "Is Hilda there?"

"There's no fucking Hildas here. This is my mobile now."

"What do you mean?"

"Some crazy drunk woman gave it to me."

"When?"

"Just now."

"How did she seem?"

"Stressed and bonkers."

"Where are you?"

"None of your fucking business," the boy said, and hung up.

Blomkvist swore. For want of anything better to do, he went into the bar of the Clarion and ordered a Guinness.

He sat down in an armchair next to the windows over-looking Ringvägen. He needed to think. A bald man at the reception desk behind him was in a heated argument over his bill. Two young women were sitting not far from his window table and whispering.

Thoughts were chasing around in his head. Salander had mentioned lists of names and Leo Mannheimer. In view of Palmgren's death and the documents found in his hallway, it was probably safe to assume that whatever this was all about had happened a long time ago.

Talk to Hilda von . . .

Could he have meant somebody other than Hilda von Kanterborg? It was possible but unlikely. Plus there had been Hilda's erratic behaviour just now, giving her mobile away to a teenage boy. Blomkvist's Guinness arrived. He looked over at the young women sitting in the bar who now seemed to be whispering about him. He took out his mobile and searched for Hilda von Kanterborg. He did not expect to find what he was looking for so swiftly on Google, or for anything to be available online. But he might be able to read between the lines. Leads could sometimes be found in perfectly anodyne or evasive answers to interview questions, or in someone's choice of subjects or interests.

He found nothing. Hilda had been a reasonably prolific author of scientific articles until she lost her position at Stockholm University. Then there was silence. Blomkvist found no trail of clues to follow and, in the old material, nothing remotely confidential or shady, or to do with adopted children, and still less boys with hyperacusis who had gone from being left-handed to being right-handed. Her articles did muster clear and sound arguments against the hidden racist agenda, which at the time was still in evidence in research into the significance of nature over nurture. But that was it.

He ordered another Guinness. Maybe there was someone he could call. He searched the articles for names of co-authors and colleagues, and then he looked up "von Kanterborg" in the directory. He found only one other living person in the country with that name: a woman, six years younger, by the name of Charlotte. She lived a few blocks away on Renstiernas gata and was listed as a hairdresser, with a salon on Götgatan. Blomkvist looked at photographs of Hilda and Charlotte von Kanterborg and saw the resemblance. They were probably sisters. Without giving it much thought, he dialled Charlotte's number.

"Lotta," said the voice.

"Hello, my name is Mikael Blomkvist and I'm a journalist at *Millennium* magazine," he said, and he sensed at once that this worried her.

He was used to that and he often regretted it, and joked

that he should write more positive articles so that people would not get anxious when he called. But this time there seemed to be more to it.

"I'm so sorry to disturb you. I need to get hold of Hilda von Kanterborg," he said.

"What happened to her?"

Not "Has anything happened to her?" but "What happened . . ."

"When did you last hear from her?" he asked.

"Only an hour ago."

"And where was she at the time?"

"Can I ask why you're calling? I mean . . . well, it's not as though journalists come looking for her all the time these days."

She drew a deep breath.

"I don't mean to worry you," Blomkvist said.

"She sounded frightened. What's going on?"

"I honestly don't know," he said. "But a wonderful old man called Holger Palmgren has been murdered. I was there while he was fighting for his life, and the last thing he said was that I should talk to Hilda. I think she has some important information."

"About what?"

"That's what I'm trying to find out. I want to help her. I want us to help each other."

"How can I know whether to believe that?"

Blomkvist answered with surprising honesty:

"In my job, it's not that easy to promise anything. The truth—if I manage to find it, that is—can end up hurting even those to whom I wish no harm. But most of us tend to feel better once we've opened up about what's troubling us."

"She feels absolutely horrible," Lotta said.

"I understand."

"She's been feeling horrible for the last twenty years, in fact. But this time it seems worse than ever."

"Why's that, do you think?"

"I . . . I have no idea."

He heard the hesitation in her voice and struck like a cobra.

"Can I pop round for a moment? I see you live nearby."

That seemed to make the woman even more nervous, but he was almost certain she would say yes. So it surprised him when she answered with a sharp and uncompromising "No! I don't want to get involved."

"Involved in what?"

"Well . . ."

Blomkvist could hear her breathing hard on the other end of the line. He understood that this was one of those moments when things hang in the balance. He had experienced it many times as a journalist. When people get to the point of debating whether to speak out or not, they tend to freeze in concentration as they try to weigh the consequences. He knew that this often ended with them talking. But there were no guarantees, so he tried not to sound too eager.

"Is there something you want to say?"

"When Hilda writes, she sometimes uses the pseudonym Leonard Bark," Lotta said.

"Oh, wow, is that her?"

"So you've heard of Leonard Bark?"

"I may be just an old hack, but I do try to keep reasonably up to date with the culture pages. I like his—or rather her—stuff. But why is this important?"

"As Leonard Bark she wrote a feature article for *Svenska Dagbladet* under the title 'Born Together—Raised Apart.' This would have been about three years ago."

"OK."

"It was about a scientific investigation by some people at the University of Minnesota. Nothing out of the ordinary. But it was important to her, that was obvious from the way she talked about it."

"Right," he said. "What are you trying to say?"

"Nothing really. Except that she was clearly upset by it."

"Can you be a little more specific?"

"I don't actually know anything more. I've never been bothered to dig into it, and Hilda never said a word about it, however much I pressed her. But you can draw the same conclusions from the article as I did."

"Thanks. I'll follow it up."

"Promise not to write anything too nasty about her."

"I think there are bigger crooks than Hilda in this story," he said.

They said goodbye and Blomkvist paid for his drinks before leaving the hotel. He crossed over to Götgatan and then continued up towards Medborgarplatsen and St. Pauls-gatan. He waved aside both acquaintances and strangers who wanted to talk to him; the last thing he felt like was socializing. He only wanted to read the article, but he waited until he was home before looking it up on his computer.

He went through it three times, and afterwards read a number of other essays on the same topic and made a couple of calls. He kept going until 12:30 a.m. He then poured himself a glass of Barolo and speculated that he might be beginning to understand a little of what had happened, even if he had not yet worked out what part Salander had played in the story.

He had to speak to her, he thought, whatever the prison management might say.

PART II

TROUBLING TONES

JUNE 21

A minor sixth chord consists of a keynote, a third, a fifth and a sixth from the melodic minor scale.

In American jazz and pop music, the minor seventh is the most common minor chord. It is considered elegant and beautiful.

The minor sixth is rarely used. The tone may be regarded as harsh and ominous.

CHAPTER 13

June 21

Salander had left the maximum security unit for the last time. She was now standing in the guard box of Flodberga Prison, being scrutinized from head to toe by a crew-cut young man with angry red skin and small arrogant eyes.

"A Mikael Blomkvist called, looking for you," he said.

Salander ignored this information. She did not even look up. It was 9:30 in the morning and she just wanted to get out of there. She was irritated by the paperwork she still had to deal with and scribbled illegibly on the forms required to take receipt of her laptop and her mobile. Olsen had not needed much persuading to see to it that they were both fully charged. After that, they let her go.

She passed through the gates, walked the length of the wall and along the railway line, and sat by the main road on a bench with peeling red paint to wait for bus number 113 to Örebro. It was a hot morning, and the air was still. Flies were buzzing around her. Even though she turned her face to the sun and seemed to be enjoying the weather, she did not feel any particular joy at being out of prison.

But she was happy to have her laptop back. Sitting on the bench, her black jeans sticking to her legs, she opened it up and logged on. She checked that Giannini had sent her, as promised, the file on the police investigation into the death of Jamal Chowdhury. There it was in her inbox. Salander would be able to deal with it on the journey home.

Giannini had a theory, a suspicion based partly on the strange fact that Faria had refused to say a word during police questioning, and partly on a short C.C.T.V. sequence from the tunnelbana station at Hornstull. Giannini appeared to have discussed it with an imam in Botkyrka called Hassan Ferdousi, and he believed she might be on the right track. The thought now was that Salander, with her skills, should take a look as well, so she set about locating it in the file Giannini had sent her. Before examining the sequence, she looked out at the road and the yellowing fields and thought of Holger Palmgren. She had spent most of the night thinking about him. *Talk to Hilda von . . .*

Hilda von Kanterborg was the only "Hilda von" known to Salander; dear old Hilda with her sweeping gestures, who had often sat in their kitchen at home on Lundagatan when Salander was a child, and who was one of her mother's few friends when everything around her was falling apart. Hilda had been a rock, at least so Salander had believed. That was the reason Salander had looked her up one day, some ten years ago now. They spent a whole evening together drinking cheap rosé because Salander had wanted to find out more about her mother. Hilda told her quite a lot, and Salander told her one or two things as well; she shared confidences with Hilda which she had kept even from Palmgren. It had been a long evening and they had raised their glasses to Agneta, and to all women whose lives had been destroyed by shits and bastards.

But Hilda had not breathed a word about the Registry. Had she kept the most important thing to herself? Salander refused to believe it at first. She was usually good at detecting what might be hidden beneath the surface. But she might have been fooled by Hilda's whole damaged façade. She thought back to the files she had downloaded on Olsen's computer and remembered a pair of initials in those documents: H.K. Was it conceivable that they referred to Hilda von Kanterborg? Salander ran a search and discovered that Hilda had been a more influential psychologist than she had realized at the time. A flash of anger flared in her. But she decided to withhold judgment for the time being.

The number 113 to Örebro was approaching in a cloud of dust and spewing gravel. She paid the driver and sat down at the back, where she had a careful look at the C.C.T.V. sequence showing the ticket barrier at Hornstull station just after midnight on October 24 nearly two years ago. Gradually she focused in on one detail, an irregularity in the movement of the suspect's hand. Could it be relevant? She was not sure.

She knew that movement recognition as a technology was still in its infancy. She had no doubt that all human gestures carry a mathematical fingerprint. It is still difficult to read, however. Every little movement is made up of thousands of pieces of information and is in itself not wholly conclusive. Every time we scratch our heads there is a difference. Our gestures are always similar, but never exactly the same. One needs sensors, signal processors, gyroscopes, accelerometers, motion-plotting algorithms, Fourier analyses and frequency and distance gauges to be able to describe and compare movements with precision. There were some programmes available for download from the Internet. But that was not an option. It would take too long. She had another idea.

She thought of her friends in Hacker Republic and the deep neural network which Plague and Trinity had been working on for so long. Could that be optimized and used? It was not out of the question. It would require her to find a more comprehensive index of hand movements for the algo-rithms to study and learn from, but it would not be impos-sible.

She worked hard on the train from Örebro back to Stock-holm and in the end had a wild thought. The prison service would not think much of it, especially not on her first day of freedom. But that was irrelevant. She got off the train at Central Station and took a taxi home to Fiskargatan, where she continued to work.

Dan Brody laid his guitar—a newly purchased Ramirez—on the coffee table and went into the kitchen to make himself a double espresso, which he drank so quickly it burned his tongue. It was 9:10 a.m. He had not noticed the time go by. He had lost himself in "Recuerdos de la Alhambra" and was now late for work. Not that it mattered much to anyone, but he did not want to give the impression that he did not take his work seriously. So he went into his bedroom and picked out a white shirt, dark suit and black Church's shoes. Then he hurried down to the street to discover that it was already oppressively hot. Summer, to his dismay, was in full swing.

His suit felt wrong for the time of year—severe and inappropriate in the sunshine—and after only a few feet his back and armpits were damp with sweat. It only added to his sense of alienation. He looked at the gardeners working in Humlegården—the noise of the lawnmowers pained him. He continued at high speed towards Stureplan, and even though he still felt uncomfortable he noted with some satisfaction that other suited men also had sweaty, miserable faces. The heat had come suddenly, after a long period of rain. There was an ambulance standing further down on Birger Jarlsgatan and he thought about his mother.

She had died in childbirth. His father was a travelling musician who never paid any attention to him and had died young, from cirrhosis of the liver, after many years of heavy drinking. Dan—who was born Daniel Brolin—grew up in an orphanage in Gävle and later, from the age of six, as one of four foster children on a farm to the north of Hudiksvall. He had to work extremely hard there with the animals and the harvest, mucking out the stables and slaughtering and butchering the pigs. The farmer, his foster father, Sten, made no secret of the fact that he had taken on his foster children—all of them boys—because he needed extra hands. When the boys came to live with him, Sten was married to a red-haired thickset woman called Kristina. But she had pretty soon taken off and had not been heard of since.

She was said to have gone to Norway, and people who met Sten were hardly surprised that she had tired of him. He was tall and imposing and by no means ugly, with a carefully groomed beard which was beginning to turn grey, but there was something grim about his mouth and forehead which frightened people. He seldom smiled. He did not like socializing or small talk, and he hated pretension and refinement.

He was always saying: "Don't get ideas above your station. Don't think you're anything special." When the boys in their high spirits declared that they wanted to become professional footballers when they grew up, or lawyers or millionaires, he would always snap back: "One should know one's place!" He was stingy when it came to praise and encouragement, and certainly when it came to money. He distilled his own spirits, ate the meat of animals which he himself had shot or slaughtered, and the farm was as good as self-sufficient. Nothing was ever bought unless heavily discounted or in a clearance sale. He got his furniture at the flea market or it was passed on by neighbours and relatives. His house was painted a strident yellow, and nobody knew why until it transpired that Sten had gotten the paint free, from surplus stock.

Sten had no appreciation of beauty and he never read books or newspapers. That did not trouble Daniel since there was a library at the school. But he was bothered by the fact that Sten disliked all music unless it was jolly and Swedish. All Daniel had inherited from his biological father was his surname and a nylon-stringed Levin guitar, which had been abandoned in the attic of the farmhouse until Daniel picked it up one day, and which he came to love. It was not only that the instrument seemed to have been waiting for him. He felt that he was born to play it.

He soon learned the basic chords and harmonies and realized that he could copy tunes from the radio having heard them only once. For a long time, he played the usual repertoire of a boy of his generation: ZZ Top's "Tush," the Scorpions' ballad "Still Loving You," Dire Straits' "Money for Nothing" and several other rock classics. But then something happened.

One cold, autumn day he stole out of the cowshed. He was fourteen years old and school was a nightmare. He was quick to learn, but found it difficult to listen to the teachers. He was disturbed by the racket around him and yearned to get back to the silence and calm of the farm, even though he hated the work and the long days. He escaped whenever he could, to find time for himself.

On this particular day, just after 5:30 p.m., he came into the kitchen and turned on the radio, which was playing something corny and dull. He fiddled with the dial and tuned to P2. He knew very little about the station, he had thought it was mostly oldies, and what he heard only confirmed his prejudice. It was a clarinet solo and the sound jarred on his nerves, like the buzzing of a bee or an alarm going off.

But he kept listening, and then the sound of a guitar came in, a tentative, playful guitar. He shivered. There was a new feeling in the room, a sense of reverence and concentration, and he felt himself come alive. He heard nothing else, not the other boys swearing and arguing, or the birds or tractors or distant cars, or even the sound of approaching footsteps. He just stood there, cocooned in an unexpected joy, and tried to understand what made these notes different from everything he had ever heard before. Why did they affect him so much? Then suddenly he felt a sharp pain in his scalp and neck.

"You lazy little shit, you think I don't see how you're always sneaking off?"

Sten was pulling Daniel's hair, shouting and swearing. But Daniel barely noticed. He was focusing only on one thing: listening to the end of the tune. The music seemed to be showing him something unknown, something richer and greater than the life he had so far been living. Although he did not manage to hear who had been playing, he glanced up at the old kitchen clock above the tiled stove as Sten dragged him out of the room. He knew that the exact time was important.

The next day he used one of the school telephones to ring Radio Sweden. He had never done anything like it before. He did not possess that kind of resourcefulness and self-confidence. He never put his hand up in the classroom even when he knew the answer, and he had always felt inferior to city folk, especially if they worked in as glamorous a profession as radio or television. But he made the call anyway and was put through to Kjell Brander, in jazz programming. In a voice which almost failed him, he asked which tune had been playing at just after 5:30 p.m. the day before. To be on the safe side, he hummed a bit of the tune. Kjell Brander recognized it immediately.

"Cool! You like it? You've got good taste, young man. That was Django Reinhardt's 'Nuages.'"

No-one had ever called Daniel "young man" before. He

asked how to spell the name of the song and added, even more nervously:

"Who is he?"

"One of the best guitarists in the world, I'd say. And yet he played his solos with just two fingers."

Daniel could not subsequently remember what Kjell Brander had told him and what he later found out for himself. But gradually he learned that there was a story behind the man, and this made what he had heard only more precious. Django grew up in poverty in Liberchies in Belgium, sometimes stealing chickens just to survive. He began to play the guitar and violin at an early age and was considered very promising. But when he was eighteen, he knocked over a candle in his caravan, setting alight the paper flowers his wife sold to earn a living, and the blaze spread. Django suffered serious burns, and for a long time it was thought that he would never play again, especially not when it turned out that he had lost the use of two fingers of his left hand. Yet with the help of a new technique he was able to keep on developing his playing, and he soon became world famous and a cult figure.

But first and foremost, Django was a Gypsy—or Roma, as people now said. Daniel was also Roma. He had learned this the hard way—through the pain of being excluded, and being called a "gyppo" and worse. It had never crossed his mind that this was anything other than deeply shameful. Now Django allowed him to look upon his origins with a new pride. If Django could become the world's best with a severely damaged hand, Daniel too could become something special.

He borrowed some money from a girl in his class, bought a compilation record of Reinhardt's tunes and taught himself all the classics—"Minor Swing," "Daphne," "Belleville," "Djangology" and many more—and in no time at all he changed the way he played the guitar. He abandoned his blues scales and instead played minor sixth arpeggios and solos with diminished major and minor seventh scales, and with each day his passion grew. He practised until he had leathery calluses on his fingertips. His fervour never dimmed—not even when he slept. He played in his dreams. He thought of nothing else, and whenever he had the chance he would make for the forest, sit on a rock or tree stump and improvise for hours on end. Hungrily he absorbed new skills and new influences, not just from Django but also from John Scofield, Pat Metheny and Mike Stern, all the modern jazz guitar greats.

At the same time, his relationship with Sten deteriorated. "You think you're special, don't you? You're just a little shit," his foster father would often snarl, adding that Daniel always walked around with his nose in the air. Daniel could not understand it, he who had always felt inferior and inadequate. He tried his best to oblige, even though he neither wanted to, nor could, stop his playing. Before long Sten began to beat him around the ears and punch him, and sometimes his foster brothers joined in. They hit him in the stomach and on his arms, and punished him with loud noises, metal scraping against metal or saucepan lids clashed together. Daniel now hated the work in the fields, especially in summer when there was no escape from the muck-spreading, ploughing, harrowing and sowing.

During the summer months the boys would work from morning until late at night. Daniel tried hard to be liked and accepted again, and sometimes he succeeded. In the evenings he was happy to play requests for his brothers, and occasionally he won applause and a certain appreciation. Yet he knew that he was a burden and made himself scarce whenever he could.

One afternoon, as the sun beat down on the back of his neck, he heard a blackbird singing far away. He was sixteen and already dreaming of his eighteenth birthday, when he would come of age and could leave this place far behind. He was planning to apply to the Royal College of Music in Stockholm, or get a job as a jazz musician, putting so much effort and ambition into his work that one day he would get a record contract. Dreams spun around in his head day and night. At times, as happened now, nature fed him a sound which he developed into a riff.

He whistled back at the blackbird, a variation on its song which became a melody. His fingers moved as if over an imaginary guitar, and he shuddered. Later, as an adult, he would think back to those moments when he believed something would be irretrievably lost if he did not sit down straightaway to compose, and nothing in the world would stop him from sneaking off to get his guitar. Daniel could still recall the illicit thrill in his chest as he raced down to the water at Blackåstjärnen in his bare feet, overalls flapping and guitar in hand, and settled on the dilapidated jetty to pick out the melody he had been whistling and give it an accompaniment. It was a wonderful time, and that is how he would remember it.

But it did not last long. One of the other boys must have seen him go and ratted on him. Sten soon appeared bare-chested and in his shorts, and furious, and Daniel, who did not know whether to apologize or simply disappear, hesi-tated a second too long. Sten managed to grab hold of the guitar and yanked it away with such violence that he fell over backwards. It was not a bad fall; it just looked ridiculous. But something in Sten snapped. He got to his feet, his face puce, and smashed the guitar against the jetty. Afterwards he looked shocked—as if he did not quite understand what he had done. But it made no difference.

Daniel felt as if a vital organ had been torn from his body. He yelled "idiot" and "bastard," words he had never before uttered in front of Sten. He ran across the fields, burst into the house, stuffed his records and some clothes into a back-pack, and left the farm for good.

He made for the E4 motorway and walked for hours, until he picked up a lift in a tractor-trailer as far as Gävle. Then he continued south, sleeping in the forest, stealing apples and plums and eating berries he found along the way. An old lady who drove him to Södertälje gave him a ham sandwich. A young man who took him to Jönköping bought him lunch, and late in the evening on July 22 he arrived in Göteborg. Within a few days he had gotten himself some low-paid, cash-in-hand work down at the docks. Six weeks later, living on virtually nothing and having occasionally slept in stairwells, he bought himself a new guitar, not a Selmer Maccaferri—Django's guitar, which he dreamed of owning—but a second-hand Ibanez.

He decided to make his way to New York. But it was not

as easy as people said. He had neither a passport nor a visa and you could no longer earn passage on a ship, not even as a cleaner. Early one evening, when he had finished his work in the harbour, a woman was waiting for him at the dockside. Her name was Ann-Catrine Lidholm. She was overweight and dressed in pink, and she had kind eyes. She told him she was a social worker, and that someone had called her about him. That was when he found out that people were searching for him, that he had been reported as missing, and he followed her reluctantly to the social welfare agency on Järntorget.

Ann-Catrine explained that she had spoken to Sten on the telephone and had a positive impression of him, which made Daniel even more suspicious.

"He misses you," she said.

"Bullshit," he said, and told her that he could not go back. He would be beaten, his life would be hell. Ann-Catrine listened to his story and afterwards gave him a few options, none of which felt right. He said he could manage on his own, she didn't need to worry. Ann-Catrine replied that he was still a minor and that he needed support and guidance.

That was when he remembered the "Stockholm people," as he thought of them: psychologists and doctors who had visited him every year of his childhood. They had measured and weighed him, interviewed him and taken notes. And they had made him take tests, all kinds of tests. He never much liked them and sometimes he had cried afterwards. He felt lonely and exposed to scrutiny, and he had thought of his mother and the life he never had with her. On the other hand, he did not hate them either. They would give him encouraging smiles and praise, and they said what a good and clever boy he was. There had never been a single unkind word. Nor did he see the visits as anything out of the ordinary. He thought it perfectly normal that the authorities should want to see how he was getting along with his foster family, and the fact that people were writing about him in medical records and protocols did not bother him. To him, it was a sign that he counted for something. Depending on who came to see him, he sometimes even viewed the visits as a welcome relief from work on the farm, especially more recently when the Stockholm people had shown an interest in his music and filmed him as he played the guitar. A few times, they seemed impressed and whispered to each other, and he had gone on to dream of how those films might get around and end up in the hands of agents or record producers.

The psychologists and doctors never gave more than their first names, and he knew nothing about them—apart from one woman who shook his hand one day and introduced herself with her full name, presumably by mistake. But that was not the only reason he remembered her. He had been entranced by her figure and her long strawberry-blond hair, and the high heels which were so unsuited to the dirt paths around the farmhouse. The woman had smiled at him, as if she genuinely liked him. Her name was Hilda von Kanterborg and she wore low-cut blouses and dresses, and had full red lips which he dreamed of kissing.

This was the woman he thought of when he asked if he could make a call from the social welfare offices. He was given a telephone directory for the Stockholm area and nervously flicked through it. For a moment he was convinced that Hilda von Kanterborg had been a cover, and that was the first time it crossed his mind that the Stockholm people might not be regular officials of the social welfare system. But then he did find her name and dialled the number. There was no answer, so he left a message.

When he returned the next day, having spent the night at Göteborg City Mission, she had returned his call and left another number. This time she answered and seemed happy to hear his voice. Straightaway he realized that she knew he had run away. She told him that she was "terribly sorry" and said he was "exceptionally gifted." He felt unbearably lonely and stifled an impulse to cry.

"Well, help me, then," he said.

"My dear Daniel," she said, "I would do just about anything. But we're supposed to study, not to intervene."

Daniel would return to that, time and again, over the years; it was one of the factors that made him take on a new identity and guard it with all his might. But right then, gripping the receiver, he felt miserable and blurted: "What, what are you talking about?" Hilda became nervous, he could tell. She swiftly began to talk about other things, how he needed to finish school before he made any rash decisions. He said that all he wanted was to play the guitar. Hilda told him he could study music. He replied that he wanted to go to sea and make his way to New York to play in the jazz clubs there. She advised strongly against that: "Not at your age, and not with everything you've got going for you," she said.

They talked for so long that Ann-Catrine and the other

social workers were beginning to get impatient, and he promised to think about the options she had given him. He said he hoped to see her. She said she'd like that, but it did not come to pass. He was never to see her again.

People seemed to appear from nowhere to help him get a passport, a visa and a job as a kitchen worker and waiter on a Wallenius Lines freighter. He never understood how it all happened. The freighter would take him not to New York, but to Boston. He found a slip of paper stapled to his employment contract with the following words in blue ball-point pen: "Berklee College of Music, Boston, Massachusetts. Good luck! H."

His life would never be the same again. He became an American citizen and changed his name to Dan Brody, and the years that followed were full of wonderful, exciting experiences. And yet, deep down, he felt disillusioned and alone. He nearly had a breakthrough at the start of his career. One day, jamming at Ryles Jazz Club on Hampshire Street in Cambridge, he played a solo which was both in the spirit of Django and at the same time something else, something new, and a murmur went through the audience. People began to talk about him and he got to know the managers and scouts of record companies. But in the end they felt he was lacking something, courage perhaps—and self-confidence. Deals fell through at the last minute, and he was eclipsed by others who were less talented and yet somehow more enterprising. He would have to be satisfied with a life in the shadows; he would be the one sitting behind the star. He would always miss the fervour he had felt as he played on the jetty at Black-åstjärnen.

. . .

Salander had tracked down several larger hand-motion data sets—used for medical research and to develop robots—and had fed them into Hacker Republic's deep neural networks. She had been working so hard that she had forgotten to eat and drink, despite the heat. Finally she looked up from the computer and poured herself a glass, not of water, but of Tullamore Dew.

She had longed for alcohol. She had longed for sex, sunlight, junk food, the smell of the sea and the buzz of bars. And she had longed for the feeling of freedom. But for now she made do with Irish whisky. It might not be bad to end up reeking like a drunken bum, she thought. No-one expects much from a wino. She looked out over Riddarfjärden and closed her eyes for a few moments. She stretched her back and let the algorithms in the neural network do their job while she went into the kitchen and microwaved a pizza. Then she rang Annika Giannini.

Annika was not pleased to hear what she was planning. She advised strongly against it, but when that fell on deaf ears she told Salander that the most she could do was film the suspect, nothing more. She recommended that Salander get in touch with Hassan Ferdousi, the imam. He would help her with "the more human aspects." Salander ignored this advice, but that did not matter as Annika later contacted the imam herself, and sent him off to Vallholmen.

Salander dug into her pizza and drank whisky, and then hacked into Blomkvist's computer to type into the file he had called LISBETH STUFF:

```
<Back home. Got out today.
  Hilda is Hilda von Kanterborg. Find her.
  Also check out Daniel Brolin. He's a
guitarist, very talented. Am busy with
other things. Will be in touch.>
```

Blomkvist saw Salander's message and was thankful that she had been released. He tried to call her. When there was no answer, he cursed. So she too knew about Hilda von Kanterborg. What could that mean? Did she know her personally, or had she obtained the information by other means? He had no idea. But he needed no encouragement from Salander to go after von Kanterborg. He had already set his mind on that.

On the other hand, he had not been able to discover where this Daniel Brolin came into it. He found many different Daniel Brolins online, but none was a guitar player, or any kind of musician at all. Perhaps he was not trying as hard as he might have. He had gotten too involved following up other leads.

It had started the evening before, with the article Hilda's sister had told him about. When he first read it, it seemed unremarkable, too general to contain anything revelatory, let alone controversial. Hilda—under the pseudonym Leonard Bark—wrote about how the classic nature versus nurture debate had become politicized long ago. The Left would like us to believe that our prospects in life are primarily determined by social factors, while the Right argues for the influence of genetics.

Hilda observed that science always loses its way when

guided by ideology or wishful thinking. There was a note of anxiety in her introductory passage, as if she was about to propose something shocking. But the article was balanced: it held that we are affected by genetics and social environment to the same degree, which was more or less what Blomkvist had expected.

One thing did surprise him, however. The environmental factors said to be most influential in shaping us were not those he had predicted. The essay suggested that mothers and fathers are often convinced they have a decisive influence over their children's development, but they "flatter themselves."

Hilda argued that our fate is more likely determined by what she called our "unique environment"—the one we do not share with anyone, not even our siblings. It is the environment we seek out and create for ourselves, for example, when we find something which delights and fascinates us and drives us in a certain direction. Rather like Blomkvist's reaction as a young boy, perhaps, when he saw the film *All the President's Men* and was struck by a strong urge to become a journalist.

Heredity and environment interact constantly, Hilda wrote. We seek out occurrences and activities which stimulate our genes and make them flourish, and we avoid things which frighten us or make us uncomfortable.

She based her conclusions on a series of studies, among others MISTRA, the Minnesota Study of Twins Reared Apart, and investigations by the Swedish Twin Registry at the Karolinska Institute. Identical twins, or so-called monozygotic twins, with their essentially indistinguishable sets of genes, are ideal subjects. Thousands of twins, both identical and fraternal, grow up apart from each other, either because one or both have been adopted, or, more rarely, as the result of some unfortunate mix-up in a maternity ward. Many of these cases are heartrending, but they also provide scientists with crucial test cases. The studies come to more or less the same conclusion: hereditary factors in conjunction with our unique environment are the primary factors in shaping our personalities.

Blomkvist had no trouble coming up with hypotheses to challenge Hilda's findings, and he could also identify problems with how the research material was to be interpreted. Yet he found that the article made for interesting reading. He learned about some extraordinary cases of identical twins who had grown up in different families and only met as adults, but were strikingly similar, not just in appearance but also in behaviour. In the U.S., there were the so-called Jim Twins of Ohio: unaware of each other's existence, yet both became chain-smokers of Salem cigarettes, bit their fingernails, suffered from bad headaches, had carpentry workbenches in their garage, named their dogs Toy, got married twice to women with the same name, had sons they christened James Allan and James Alan, and God knows what else.

Blomkvist could see why the tabloids had become excited, but he himself was not all that impressed. He knew how easy it was to become fixated by similarities and coincidences—how the sensational always sticks in the mind and stands out at the expense of the ordinary, which—maybe precisely because it is so ordinary—tells us something more significant about the real world.

But Blomkvist did see that all these studies on twins resulted in a paradigm shift for epidemiological science. The research community began to believe more in the power that genes have over us, and in their intricate interplay with environmental factors. Earlier, especially in the 1960s and '70s, more weight had been given to the impact of social considerations. There was a prevailing notion that to grow up in a certain environment or to be raised in a particular way would inevitably produce a specific type of individual. Many scientists dreamed of being able to prove this, in order perhaps to determine how to produce better, happier people. It was one of the reasons why so many research projects with twins were initiated at that time, some of which Hilda, in evasive terms, described as "tendentious and radical."

It was there that Blomkvist suddenly sat up and continued his research with renewed energy. He had no idea whether he was on the right track, yet he kept digging, including by searching combinations of the words "tendentious and radical" in the context of twins research. That is how he came across the name Roger Stafford.

Stafford was an American psychoanalyst and psychiatrist who had been a professor at Yale. He had worked closely with Freud's daughter Anna and was said to be charismatic and charming. There were pictures of him with Jane Fonda, Henry Kissinger and Gerald Ford, and he looked a little like a film star himself.

But his main claim to fame was less flattering. "Tendentious and radical" was precisely the point. In September 1989 the *Washington Post* disclosed that, in the late 1960s, Stafford had established close relationships with the female

managers of five adoption agencies in New York and Boston. Two of the women had affairs with him, and there may
have been promises of marriage. Not that he was reliant on
that. Stafford was quite an authority at the time. In one of
his books, *The Egoistic Child,* he claimed that identical twins
thrive better and become more independent if they grow up
apart. This conclusion was later debunked, but by then it
had become established among therapists on the East Coast.

It was agreed that these women would contact Stafford
as soon as twins were referred to them for adoption. The
children were then placed in consultation with him. A total
of forty-six babies were involved, twenty-eight identical and
eighteen fraternal twins. None of the families was informed
that their adopted son or daughter was a twin, or even that
they had a sibling. The adoptive parents, on the other hand,
were required to allow Stafford and his team to examine the
children once a year and make them undertake a series of
personality tests.

Before long one of the managers—a woman by the name
of Rita Bernard—noticed that Stafford insisted on placing
twins with sets of parents who were utterly different from
each other in terms of status, education, religious affiliation,
temperament, personality, ethnicity and in their methods
of child-rearing. Instead of putting the twins' interests first,
Stafford seemed bent on pursuing research into heredity and
environment, she said.

Stafford did not deny that he was engaged in scientific
work. He saw it as an excellent opportunity to improve our
understanding of how we are formed as individuals. He said
that his research would become an "inestimable scientific

resource." He vehemently denied that he was not prioritiz-
ing the interests of the child, but for "reasons of integrity"
he refused to make his material public. He donated it to the
Yale Child Study Center, with the proviso that researchers
and the public should have access to it only in 2078, when all
those involved would be long dead. He did not, he said, want
to exploit the fate of those twins.

That sounded noble, but there were critics who claimed
that he declared the material confidential because it had
fallen short of his expectations. Most agreed that the experiment was deeply unethical, and that Stafford had deprived
siblings of the joy of growing up together. A fellow psychiatrist from Harvard even compared his activities with Josef
Mengele's experiments on twins at Auschwitz. Stafford retal-
iated, wildly and proudly, with two or three lawyers, and the
debate came to an end not long after. When Stafford died
in 2001, he was buried with a certain amount of pomp and
circumstance and in the presence of a number of celebrities.
Some fine obituaries were published in the specialist press
and newspapers. The experiment did not tarnish his memory to any significant extent, perhaps because the children
who had been so brutally separated from each other had all
come from the lower strata of society.

That was nothing unusual in those days, as Blomkvist
knew only too well. One could inflict abuses on ethnic and
other minorities in the name of science and for the good of
society and get away with it. For that reason Blomkvist was
unwilling to dismiss Stafford's experiment as an isolated episode and looked further into the history. He noted that Stafford had been to Sweden in the 1970s and '80s. There were

pictures of him with Lars Malm, Birgitta Edberg, Liselotte Ceder and Martin Steinberg, the leading psychoanalysts and sociologists of the day.

At the time, nothing was known about Stafford's experiments with twins, and he may have had other reasons for visiting Sweden. But Blomkvist kept digging, thinking of Salander all along. She too was a twin, a fraternal twin to a nightmare sister named Camilla. He knew the authorities had attempted to examine her when she was little and she had hated it. He also thought about Leo Mannheimer and his high I.Q. score, and about Ellenor Hjort's suggestion that he might have been born into the Gypsy community.

He became absorbed by an article in *Nature* magazine which explained how one fertilized egg splits in the womb and results in identical twins. Then he got up from his desk and stood motionless for a minute or two, muttering to himself. He rang Lotta von Kanterborg again and told her what he suspected. In fact he took a chance and presented his new, wild theory as fact.

"That sounds completely crazy," she said.

"I know. But will you tell Hilda, if she gets in touch? Tell her that the situation is critical."

"I will," Lotta said.

Blomkvist went to bed with his mobile next to him on the bedside table. But no-one called. Even so, he hardly slept, and now, he was back at his computer. He was looking into the people Stafford had met on his trips to Sweden, and to his surprise he came across Holger Palmgren's name. Palmgren

and sociology professor Martin Steinberg had been working together on a criminal case more than two decades ago.
Blomkvist hardly thought that this was significant. Stockholm is a small place, after all—people are always running
into each other.

Still, he made a note of Steinberg's telephone number
and address in Lidingö, and carried on searching into his
background. But his concentration was drifting. He was
of two minds: Should he send an encrypted message to
Salander and tell her what he had found? Should he confront Mannheimer, to see if he was on the right track? He
had another espresso and suddenly missed Malin. In no time
at all she had found her way back into his life, like a force of
nature.

He went into the bathroom and stepped on the scale.
He had gained weight, so he needed to do something about
that. And he should get his hair cut. It was sticking out in
all directions and he tried to smooth it down. But then he
said out loud, "To hell with it," and went back to his desk to
call, e-mail and text Salander. In the end he wrote into their
shared file on his computer:

<Get in touch! I think I've found some-
thing.>

Something about his message did not feel quite right: the
word "think." Salander was not keen on half measures. He
corrected it:

<I've found something.>

and hoped it was true. Then he went to his wardrobe, put on a newly ironed cotton shirt and went out, down Bellmansgatan to the tunnelbana station on Mariatorget.

On the platform he took out his notes from the night before and went through them one more time. He looked at his question marks and speculations. Was he going mad? He looked at the digital display above him and saw that a train was about to arrive. At that moment his mobile rang. It was Lotta von Kanterborg and she was breathing hard.

"She called," she said.

"Hilda?"

"She told me that what you said about Leo Mannheimer sounded crazy. That it couldn't possibly be right."

"I see."

"But she wants to meet you," she said. "She'd like to tell you what she *does* know. Right now she's—"

"Don't tell me over the phone."

Blomkvist suggested that they meet right away at Kaffebar on St. Paulsgatan, and hurried back up the station steps.

CHAPTER 14

June 21

Bublanski was in an apartment in Aspudden, surrounded by old-fashioned furniture and talking to Maj-Britt Torell, the woman who, according to Salander, had visited Palmgren a few weeks before. She was an old lady with probably the best intentions, Bublanski thought, but there was something odd about her. Not only was she fiddling nervously with the Danish pastries on the coffee table, she also seemed surprisingly forgetful and disorganized for someone who had spent so many years working as a medical secretary.

"I'm not quite sure what I gave him," she said. "I'd just heard so much about the girl, and thought it was time he got the full story—about how appallingly she was treated."

"So you gave Palmgren the original papers?"

"I suppose I did. The professor's practice has been closed for ages and I have no idea what became of all the medical records. But I had some papers given to me unofficially by Professor Caldin."

"Secretly, you mean?"

"You could put it like that."

"Important documents, then?"

"I suppose so."

"Wouldn't you have kept copies, or scanned them into a computer?"

"You would think so, but I . . ."

Bublanski said nothing. It seemed like the right moment to keep quiet. But Torell did not finish her sentence and went on picking even more nervously at her pastries.

"You haven't by any chance . . ." Bublanski said.

"What?"

". . . had a visit from someone, or a phone call about these papers? Is that maybe what's making you a bit anxious right now?"

"Absolutely not," Torell said a little too fast and a little too nervously.

Bublanski got to his feet. It was high time now. He looked at her with his most wistful smile, which he was well aware could make a deep impression on people who were wrestling with their conscience.

"In that case I'll leave you in peace," he said.

"Oh, really?"

"Just to be on the safe side, I'll call a taxi and have you taken to a nice café in town. This is so important and serious that I believe you need a bit of time to think, don't you agree, Fru Torell?"

Then he handed her his business card and went out to his car.

DECEMBER, ONE AND A HALF YEARS EARLIER

On this particular day, Dan Brody was playing with the Klaus Ganz Quintet at the A-Trane Jazz Club in Berlin. Years had gone by. He was thirty-five years old, had cut off his long hair and no longer wore an earring. He had started to wear grey suits. He could be mistaken for an office worker, and he liked it that way. It was some sort of early midlife crisis, he supposed.

He was fed up with touring, but he had no choice. He had not managed to put away any savings and he owned nothing of value, no apartment, no car, nothing. Any likelihood of a breakthrough—of becoming rich and famous—was long gone. He was never the star, even if he was invariably the most talented musician on stage. And he always had work, albeit for less and less money. It was ever harder to make a living as a jazz musician, and maybe he was no longer playing with the same passion as once he did.

He no longer worked at his music all that often. He managed fine without it. During the downtime when he was travelling, instead of practising for hours each day as he used to, he now read. He devoured books and did not tend to socialize. He could not stand idle chatter or the bawling and buzz in bars and clubs, and he felt far better when he drank less. All in all, he was cleaning himself up, and increasingly he yearned for a normal life: a wife and a home, a steady job, a measure of security.

Over the years he had tried just about every drug, and had had plenty of love affairs and casual relationships. But there always seemed to be something missing. Music had been his solace, though when this no longer revived his spirits, he began to wonder if he had taken the wrong path in life. Maybe he should have become a teacher. He had recently had an overwhelming experience at his old music college in Boston.

He had been asked to lead a workshop on Django Reinhardt, and the prospect had scared him half to death. He was sure that speaking in public was beyond him, that his lack of stage presence was one of the reasons the record companies had not wanted to invest in him. But he agreed to do it anyway and set about preparing down to the last detail. He told himself he just needed to stick to his script, a lot of music and little talk. But when he stood up there in front of two hundred students, he went weak at the knees. He was shaking all over, incapable of uttering a single word, and only after what seemed like an eternity did he manage to say:

"And there I was, thinking I'd be the cool guy coming back to my alma mater—instead I'm standing here like a complete idiot!"

It was not even meant as a joke, more like the desperate truth. But the students laughed, so he told them about Django and Stéphane Grappelli and the Quintette du Hot Club de France. He talked about club life and its ups and downs, and about how there were so few written sources. He played "Minor Swing" and "Nuages" and variations on solos and riffs, and became bolder and bolder. All sorts of ideas came to him, some comical, some serious. He found himself saying that Django had been doomed to ruin. During the Hitler years he was at risk of being deported to a death camp for being Roma, but he was saved by a Nazi, of all people, an officer in the Luftwaffe who loved his music. He ultimately died in France on May 16, 1953, after a brain haemorrhage while walking from the railway station in Avon to his house. "He was a great man," Dan said. "He changed my life."

Silence. He was in limbo.

But then, seconds later, there was thunderous applause. The students stood up and whooped, and Dan went home astonished and happy.

He had carried the memory with him and sometimes, even now on tour in Germany, he would make a few comments between numbers, or tell an anecdote which made the audience laugh, though it was not he who was centre stage. That often gave him more pleasure than his solos, perhaps because it was something new.

When he did not hear from the school again, he was disappointed. He had imagined how the teachers and professors would be talking about him, saying: "Now *there's* someone who can really fire up our students." But no further invitations came and he was too proud—and

too timid—to get in touch to say how happy he would be
to return. He failed to grasp that this was one of his problems: that he lacked get-up-and-go. The school's silence was
painful, and afterwards he became withdrawn and per-
formed with little enthusiasm.

It was 9:20 p.m. on Friday, December 8, and the bar
was full. The audience was better dressed and classier than
usual, perhaps also less engaged. *Probably finance people,* he
thought. He had met Wall Street types who treated him like
a servant. There seemed to be a lot of wealth in the room
and that depressed him. Sure, there were times when he
did pretty well for himself. After the first few lean years in
America, he had never gone hungry. But even when he *had*
money, it simply ran through his fingers.

He decided to ignore the audience and focus on the
music, even though the first set felt routine. Then came
"Stella by Starlight," a tune he had played a thousand times
and where he knew he could shine. He took the second-
to-last solo, just before Klaus Ganz himself, and closed his
eyes. The piece was in B-flat, but instead of following the
two-five-one progression, he played almost entirely outside
the key. By his own standards it was not the most dazzling
solo. But it was not bad, and he heard someone applaud
spontaneously as he began to play. When he looked up to
show his appreciation, he met the eye of a young woman
in an elegant red dress, wearing a sparkling green necklace.
She was blond and slender, and there was something fox-
like about her beautiful features. She was probably one of
the money people, he thought, but there was nothing blasé
or disinterested about her. In fact she was rapt, and gazing

intently at him. He could not recall any woman ever having looked at him like that before, not a stranger, and certainly not an upper-class beauty. But more extraordinary was the sense of intimacy. It was as if the woman was watching a dear friend. She appeared dazed and enchanted, and towards the end of his solo she mouthed something effusive, as if she knew him. Her face was wreathed in smiles and she shook her head. There were even tears in her eyes.

After the set she approached the stage, more reserved now. Perhaps he had hurt her feelings by not acknowledging her enthusiasm. Nervously she fingered her necklace as she looked at his hands and his guitar. She gave the impression of being puzzled, and he felt a sudden affection for her, a protective instinct. He climbed down from the stage and smiled at her. She laid a hand on his shoulder and said to him in Swedish:

"You were incredible. I knew you played the piano, but this . . . this was magical. It was insanely good, Leo."

"My name isn't Leo," he said.

Salander knew that she and her sister had figured on a list kept by the Registry for the Study of Genetics and Social Environment. The organization's existence was known to only a few, but it was part of the State Institute for Human Genetics in Uppsala, which until 1958 had been known as the State Institute for Racial Biology.

There were sixteen other people on the list, the majority older than Lisbeth and Camilla. They had the letters M.z.A. or D.z.A. next to their names. Salander understood that M.z.

stood for "monozygotic," in other words, identical twins; D.z. stood for fraternal twins; and the letter A referred to "apart," as in "raised apart."

She soon worked out that they were twins who had grown up separately in accordance with a carefully devised plan. She and Camilla, unlike the others, were labeled "D.z.—failed A." All the rest of the twins had been separated at an early age. The results of a series of intelligence and personality tests were recorded beneath their names.

Two names stood out: Leo Mannheimer and Daniel Brolin. They were described as mirror-image twins and quite exceptional. Their test results were consistent, and on a number of counts they were outstanding. They were said to have been born into the Gypsy community. One note, initialled M.S., said:

Highly intelligent and extremely musical. To some extent child prodigies. But lacking initiative. Inclined to doubt and depression, possibly also psychoses. Both have suffered from paracusis, auditory hallucinations. Loners, but with an ambivalent attitude to their isolation. Perhaps drawn to it. Both speak of a strong sense of "missing something" and "an intense loneliness." Both show empathy, neither shows signs of aggression—apart from the occasional fit of anger triggered by loud noises. Remarkable scores, even for creativity. Excellent verbal skills, yet low self-esteem, somewhat better in L., for obvious reasons, but not by as much as one would expect. Perhaps due to difficult relationship with mother, who has not bonded as we had hoped.

That last sentence made Salander feel sick. She was not impressed by their other character assessments either, especially not the rubbish written about her and Camilla. Camilla was "very beautiful, if somewhat cold and narcissistic." *Somewhat?* She remembered how Camilla had gazed at the psychologists with her doe-like eyes. It obviously turned their heads.

Nonetheless . . . there were a few details in the material which could be useful and might provide her with a lead. Among other things, there was a line about "unfortunate circumstances" having required the authorities to "inform Leo's parents in the strictest confidence." No indication was given as to what information they had passed on. But it might have been about the project itself. That would be interesting.

Salander had gotten hold of the documents by hacking into the computer system of the State Institute for Human Genetics and creating a bridge between the network and the intranet of the Registry for the Study of Genetics and Social Environment. It was an advanced exercise, which had taken hours of work. She knew full well that there were not many others who could have managed to pull off that sort of hack, especially with so little preparation time.

She had hoped to strike gold. But the parties involved must have been extremely cautious. She did not find a single name for those responsible, only initials, including H.K. and M.S. She decided that the files about Daniel and Leo were her best hope. They were incomplete—most of the material was missing or had been archived in a different way—but she was keen to study what remained.

Someone had put a question mark next to Mannheimer's name and then done a not very good job of erasing it.

Daniel Brolin appeared to have emigrated, with the ambition of becoming a guitarist. He had taken a one-year course at the Berklee College of Music in Boston, financed by a scholarship, since which all contact with him was lost. He had probably changed his name.

Mannheimer had studied at the Stockholm School of Economics. There was a later note on him: "Very bitter after breaking up with a woman of his own social class. First dreams of violence. A risk? Renewed attack of paracusis?"

Then there was a decision—again initialled M.S.—which looked recent, announcing that the Registry was to be officially closed.

Project 9 to be terminated. Mannheimer a cause for concern,

it said.

Since Salander had been in prison, unable to research Mannheimer or those around him, she had asked Blomkvist to take a closer look. He'd been hopeless lately, fussing about her like some sort of father figure. Sometimes all she'd wanted to do was tear his clothes off and pull him onto her prison mattress, just to shut him up. But as a journalist he was indefatigable and sometimes—she reluctantly admitted—he did spot things she herself had missed. Which is why she had deliberately not told him everything; Blomkvist would see more clearly if she let him investigate without his mind already being made up. She would ring him shortly and come to grips with the whole situation.

She was sitting on a bench on Flöjtvägen in Vallholmen, her laptop connected to her mobile, and looked up at the grey-green tower blocks whose colour was changing in the sunlight. She was wearing a leather jacket and black jeans, not the right clothes for a muggy day.

Vallholmen was often described as a ghetto. Cars burned at night. Gangs of youths roamed about and mugged people. A rapist was said to be at large, and there was often chatter in the press about a community in which nobody dared to talk to the police. But right now the place seemed idyllic. A small group of women in veils were sitting with a picnic basket on the lawn in front of the tower blocks. A couple of small boys played football. Two men stood by the front entrance, spraying water with a hose and laughing like children.

Salander wiped a drop of sweat from her forehead and kept on working with her deep neural network. It was tough, just as she had anticipated. The video sequence from the ticket gate at Hornstull tunnelbana station was too short and too blurred, and the body was masked by other passengers coming up from the platform. And the face was at no point visible. He—it was evidently a young man—had been wearing a baseball cap and sunglasses. His head was bent forward. Salander could not even measure how broad his shoulders were.

All she had was the distinctive splayed movement of his fingers and a jerky, dysmetric gesture of his right hand. She had no way of knowing how characteristic they were. It might have been a nervous reaction, an anomaly in his usual pattern of movement. But there was a striking spasmodic irregularity which was now being analyzed in the nodes in her network and compared to a sequence she had uploaded of a young man jogging past her on a training circuit forty minutes earlier.

There were correlations between the patterns of movement, and that was encouraging. But it was not enough. She needed to capture the runner in a situation more comparable to the one in the tunnelbana station. Every so often, therefore, she looked up at the lawn and the paved path along which the young man had disappeared. There was no sign of him for the time being, so she scrolled through her e-mails and messages.

Blomkvist had written to say that he had found something. She was tempted to call him, but it would be disastrous to lose her concentration now. She needed to be prepared. Occasionally she glanced over towards the path. After fifteen minutes, the young man reappeared in the distance. He was tall, had a professional runner's gait, and was also extremely thin. But that was irrelevant to her. All she was interested in was his right arm—the irregular jerk in the upward drive and the splayed movement of the fingers. She filmed him with her mobile and got instant feedback. The correlation was less pronounced, maybe because the runner was beginning to feel fatigue, or because it had not been adequate in the first place.

It might be a long shot, but it was still a reasonable supposition. The man in the video sequence was one of the few who were impossible to identify after Jamal Chowdhury's death. There were obvious similarities to the young man now approaching. If her suspicions were confirmed, this would also account for Faria's silence during questioning.

Salander needed more video material. She stuffed her

laptop into her bag, got up from the bench and called out. The runner slowed his steps and squinted at her in the sunlight. She pulled a hip flask of whisky from an inside pocket of her jacket, took a slug and staggered sideways. The young man seemed unconcerned, but he stopped and stood there panting.

"Jesus, you can run," Salander said, her speech slurred.

He did not answer. He looked as though he wanted to be rid of her and get in the entrance door, but she was not going to give up so easily.

"Can you do this?" she said, making a movement with her hand.

"Why?"

She had no good answer to that, so she took a step towards him:

"Because I want you to?"

"Are you stupid or something?"

She said nothing. She just glared at him with dark eyes. That seemed to scare him, so she decided to press her advantage. She lurched towards him with a threatening swagger and growled, "What was that?"

Then the man did move his hand as she wanted, either because he was scared or because he thought it was the quickest way to extricate himself. He ran off into his building without noticing that she had filmed him on her mobile.

She stood there and looked at her laptop and watched as the nodes in her network were activated. Everything became clear. She had scored a hit, a correlation in the asymmetry of the fingers. Nothing which would stand up in court, but enough to convince her that she was right.

She walked towards the front entrance of the building. She did not know how she would gain access, but it turned out to be easy. The door gave way with a firm shove of her shoulder and she found herself in a shabby stairwell where everything looked either broken or dilapidated. It reeked of urine and cigarette smoke and the lift was out of order. The walls were grey and covered with graffiti, visible, thanks to the dim sunlight shining into the ground floor. But there were no windows in the stairwell and few functioning lights. It was stuffy and close and the steps were covered in litter.

Salander climbed the stairs slowly, focusing intently on the laptop balanced on her left arm. She paused on the third floor and sent the analysis of the hand motion to Bublanski and his fiancée Farah Sharif, who was a professor of computer sciences, and also to Giannini. On the fourth floor she put the laptop into her bag and looked at the nameplates. Furthest to the left was K. Kazi—Khalil Kazi. She straightened up and took a deep breath. Khalil was nothing much to worry about, but Giannini had heard that his older brothers came regularly to see him. Salander knocked at the door and heard footsteps. The door opened and Khalil stared at her, apparently no longer frightened.

"Hi," she said.

"*Now* what?"

"I want to show you something. A film."

"What kind of film?"

"You'll see," she said. He let her in. It seemed a little too easy, and soon she realized why.

Khalil was not alone. Bashir Kazi—she recognized him

from her research—stared at her disdainfully. This was going to be as much of an aggravation as she had feared.

DECEMBER, ONE AND A HALF YEARS EARLIER

Dan Brody was baffled. The woman simply refused to believe that he was not that Leo guy. She fiddled with her necklace and played with her hair, and said she would understand if he wanted to keep a low profile. She reminded him that she had always said he deserved better.

"You don't seem to understand how amazing you are, Leo," she said. "You never have. No-one at Alfred Ögren does. And certainly not Madeleine."

"Madeleine?"

"Madeleine's a total fool. To choose Ivar over you. That's just *soooo* dumb. Ivar's a fat dickhead and a loser."

He thought she had a child-like way of speaking. But perhaps he was out of touch with modern Swedish. She was also nervous. There was quite a commotion around them, people pushing past to buy drinks at the bar. Klaus and the other band members came to ask if Dan wanted to tag along for dinner. He shook his head and looked again at the woman. She was standing strangely close to him. Her breasts were heaving, and he caught a whiff of her perfume.

She was very beautiful. It was like a dream. *A nice dream,* he thought, although he was not entirely sure. He was bewildered.

At the back of the club a glass broke. A man started shouting, and that made Dan grimace.

"I'm sorry," the woman said. "Maybe you and Ivar are still buddies."

"I don't know an Ivar," he said sharply.

The woman looked at him in such despair that he regretted it. He felt that he would say anything she wanted—that he was called Leo and knew Madeleine, and that Ivar was a dickhead. He did not want to disappoint her. He wanted her to be as happy and excited as she had been during his solo.

"I'm sorry," he said.

"That's OK."

He stroked her hair. He was shy and reserved by nature, but tonight he wanted to pretend, if only for a short while. So he went along with it. He was Leo. Or rather, he no longer denied it. He packed his guitar in its case and suggested they go for a drink somewhere quieter.

They walked down Pestalozzistrasse. He had to be careful what he said; every word was a potential trap. Sometimes he thought she had found him out. At others, he thought she was playing along too. Was she not looking critically at his suit and shoes? His clothes, which until recently had seemed elegant, now felt cheap and ill-fitting. Was she toying with him? And yet she had known that he was Swedish. These days almost no-one knew about his origins.

They went into a small bar along the street and ordered margaritas. He let her talk and that gave him some clues. He still did not know her name, and he dared not ask. But she was apparently running—or helping to run—a pharmaceutical fund at Deutsche Bank.

"Can you imagine what a step-up that is, after all the crappy jobs Ivar gave me?"

He made a note of Ivar, Ivar who might have been called Ögren, as in Alfred Ögren Securities, where the woman had been working until recently, and where there was also someone named Malin Frode whom she regarded as a rival.

"I heard that you and Malin have been seeing a bit of each other?" she said.

He answered: "Not really. In fact not at all."

He gave evasive answers to almost every question, although he was quite open about how he came to be playing with Klaus Ganz. Through contacts, he said. He'd been recommended by Till Brönner and Chet Harold.

"I played with them in New York. Klaus took a chance on me."

The truth was, it was no gamble for any jazz band to hire him. He knew that much at least about his talents.

"But the *guitar,* Leo? You're incredible. You must have been playing for years. When did you start?"

"In my teens," he said.

"I thought only the grand piano and violin were good enough for Viveka."

"I played on the sly."

"The piano must have been useful, though. I recognized the harmonies when you played your solo, not that I'm an

expert. But I remember hearing you at Thomas and Irene's.
It was the same feeling. The same vibe."

The same feeling on a piano? What on earth did she
mean? He wanted to ask, to have more clues. But he did not
dare. He mostly kept quiet or simply smiled and nodded.
Occasionally he would make a harmless remark, or tell her
about something he had read somewhere. Such as—he had
no idea how this came up—that the sleeper shark can live
to the age of four hundred years, because it exists in slow
motion.

"That's dreary," she said.

"And *loooong*," he said in a protracted drawl, and that
made her laugh. It did not take much to make her laugh,
and he became more and more confident. He even dared to
answer a question about where he thought the market was
heading "now that valuations are so full and with interest
rates low."

"Up," he said. "Or down."

She found that funny too, and he felt he was discover-
ing something new: that he enjoyed playing a role, that it
added something to his personality and helped him to enter
a world which had until now been closed to him, a world
of money and opportunity. It may have been the drinks. It
may have been the way she was looking at him. He talked
and talked and was pleased with what emerged.

More than anything, he was glad to be seen with her.
He loved her refinement, which was impossible to describe
and was so much more than just clothes, jewelry and shoes.
It came out in small expressions and gestures: her slight
lisp, her ease in talking to the barman. Her poise seemed to

give him status. He looked at her hips and legs and breasts
and knew he wanted her. He kissed her in the middle of a
sentence. He was more forward than he would ever have
been as Dan Brody. Outside the bar he pressed his groin
against her.

At her hotel—the Adlon Kempinski next to the Bran-
denburg Gate—he took her hard and confidently. He was
no longer an inhibited lover. She said wonderful things
about him afterwards, and he said wonderful things about
her too. He felt happy—happy like a fraudster who has
pulled off a scam, but happy all the same. Maybe also a
little bit in love, not only with her but with his new self too.
He couldn't sleep. He wanted to Google the names she had
given him, to try to understand. But he resisted the temptation. He wanted to experience that on his own. He thought
of sneaking off at first light, but she looked so lovely in her
sleep, clean and clear, as if she were a superior being even in
her dreams. She had a red mark on her shoulder. He liked
every little blemish.

Just before 6:00 a.m. he wrapped his arms around her,
whispered a thank-you in her ear, and said that he had to
go. To a meeting. She mumbled that she understood and
gave him her business card. Her name was Julia Damberg.
He promised to call "soon, very soon." He dressed, took his
guitar and left the hotel.

He started looking up Alfred Ögren Securities on his
mobile during the taxi ride back to his own hotel. The
C.E.O. of the company was indeed Ivar Ögren. He really did
look like a dickhead. A smug creep with double chins and
small, watery eyes. But that was immaterial. Right under-

neath his picture was one of Leo Mannheimer, head of research and partner . . .

He could not believe it. It was insane. It was *his* picture. The man in the photograph was so like him that it made his head spin. He took off his seatbelt and leaned forward to catch a glimpse of his own face in the rear-view mirror.

That only made things worse. He smiled exactly like Alfred Ögren's head of research. He recognized the folds around the mouth and the furrows in the forehead and also the nose, curly hair, everything, even the posture, although the man in the picture was better groomed. The suit was certainly in a different class.

Back in his hotel room, Dan kept Googling. He lost track of time and swore and shook his head. He was beside himself. They were devastatingly alike, only the context was different. Leo Mannheimer belonged to another world, another order. He was light-years away from Dan, and yet not. It was incomprehensible. Most shattering of all was the music. Dan found an old recording from the Stockholm Concert Hall. Leo was probably twenty, perhaps twenty-one, and he looked tense and solemn. The auditorium was full; it was a semi-official performance in which Leo was a guest artist.

In those days no-one would have mistaken the one for the other. Dan was a long-haired bohemian in jeans and sweatshirts, while Leo was already the well-turned-out young man in the Alfred Ögren portrait, just a bit younger, with the same hairstyle and a similar tailor-made suit. Only the tie was missing. But none of that mattered.

When Dan saw the video, his eyes filled with tears. He

cried not only because he realized that he had an identical twin, but also for the whole of his lonely life—his childhood on the farm, Sten's beatings and his bullying demands, the work in the fields, the guitar smashed against the jetty, and his escape and journey to Boston and the first months of destitution. He cried for what he had never known and for everything he had had to do without. But most of all he cried for what he was hearing. In the end he took out his guitar and played along—fifteen years later and a world away.

It was not only the melancholy piece—apparently composed by Leo himself—but also the melodic base and harmony. Leo played with the same three-tone arpeggios as Dan did at the time. Just like Dan, he used diminished chords without the flattened fifth, or the minor seventh without the flat ninth as most of the others did, and he often landed on the seventh tone in the Dorian minor scale.

Dan had believed himself to be unique when he came across Django and found his own path, so remote from all the rock and pop and hip-hop his generation was absorbed in. But now there was a guy in Stockholm, someone who looked exactly like him, who had found the same harmonies and scales in an entirely different kind of world. It was impossible to fathom, and there was so much else bubbling to the surface—longing and hope, maybe love, but above all, sheer wonder. He had a brother.

And that brother had grown up with a wealthy family in Stockholm. It was not only extraordinary, it was also deeply unjust. As he recalled later, the anger and the rage set in early, like a pounding force in the midst of everything else. At the time, Dan could not know how this had come about. But he thought about the Stockholm people with their tests, their questions and films. Had they known?

Of course they had. He smashed a glass against the wall. Then he looked up Hilda von Kanterborg's number. It was only mid-morning, but Hilda did not sound sober and that annoyed him.

"It's Daniel Brolin," he said. "Do you remember me?"

"What did you say your name was?" she slurred.

"Daniel Brolin."

He could hear laboured breathing on the other end of the line and also, he was not sure, he thought he could detect fear.

"Dear Daniel," she said. "Of course. How are you? We were so worried when we didn't hear from you."

"Did you know I had an identical twin? Did you?"

His voice broke. There was silence on the line. Then she poured something into a glass. He understood that she must have known—that this was the whole reason behind the visits to the farm and her strange words: "We're supposed to study, not to intervene."

"Why didn't you say anything?"

Still she did not answer, and he repeated his question, more aggressively this time.

"I wasn't allowed to," she managed to whisper. "I had signed confidentiality agreements."

"So some bits of paper were more important than my life?"

"It was wrong, Daniel. Plain wrong! I'm no longer part

of the authority. They kicked me out. They didn't like me making objections."

"So it was some fucking authority."

His mind was spinning. He had no idea what he was saying. He only remembered her question.

"Have you and Leo found each other?"

Then he lost it completely. It was a while before he realized why. It was the natural tone in which she had referred to him and Leo, as if it was an old, familiar notion to her. For him it was earth-shattering.

"Does he know about this?"

"Leo?"

"Yes, Leo!"

"I don't think so, Daniel. I can't say any more. I really can't. I've already said too much."

"Too *much*? I called you in the middle of a crisis, when I had nothing, and what did you say then? Not one word. You let me grow up without knowing the most important thing in my life. You've robbed me . . ."

He struggled for words, but found nothing which would do his feelings justice.

"I'm sorry, Daniel, I'm sorry," she stammered.

He yelled abuse at her, then hung up. He ordered some beer. A whole load of beer. He had to get his nerves under control, because already then it was clear to him that he must get in touch with Leo. But how? Should he write, call? Simply show up? Leo Mannheimer was different, rich and probably happier and much more sophisticated, and perhaps—Hilda had hinted at the possibility—Leo already knew about him and had chosen not to get in touch.

Perhaps he was ashamed of his poor, downtrodden twin brother.

Dan went back to the Alfred Ögren home page and looked again at the picture of Leo. Did those eyes betray a hint of insecurity? That was a small boost. Perhaps Leo was not so cocky, after all. He remembered how easy it had been to talk to Julia the night before, and he lapsed into dreams and implausible hopes. He could feel his anger ebbing away and the tears welling up again.

What should he do? He Googled himself, looking for recordings of his own performances. He came across something from six months earlier, when he had just cut his hair and was sitting in a jazz club in San Francisco, playing the solo from Sinatra's "All the Things You Are" and using the same sort of melodic base that Leo had at the Stockholm Concert Hall. He set up the recording as an attachment and wrote a long e-mail:

```
Dear Leo, Dear Twin Brother,
    My name is Dan Brody and I'm a jazz
guitarist. I was completely unaware of
your existence until this morning, and I
feel so emotional and shaken that I can
hardly write.
    I don't want to bother you or cause
you any inconvenience. I'm not asking for
anything, not even a reply. I only want to
say: knowing you exist, and knowing that
you play the same kind of music as I do,
```

will remain the greatest thing that has
ever happened to me.

I have no idea if you're interested in
my life, in the way that I'm burning with
desire to hear about yours. But I want to
tell you all the same. Did you ever meet
our father? He was a good-for-nothing and
a drunk, but he was exceptionally musical. Our mother died giving birth to us.
I never found out much about it . . .

Dan wrote twenty-two pages. But he never sent them. He
didn't have the nerve. Instead he rang Klaus Ganz and told
him there had been a death in the family. Then he booked a
flight to Stockholm for the following morning.

It was the first time in eighteen years that he had set foot
in Sweden. A cold, piercing wind was blowing. It was snowing. As always at that time in December, the Nobel Prize
celebrations were under way. In the streets, the Christmas
lights had been switched on, and he looked around in wonder. Stockholm was the great city of his distant childhood
memories. He was nervous and feverish, but he was also as
eagerly expectant as a little boy. Yet it would still be five days
before he mustered the courage to take action. Until then,
he lived as Leo Mannheimer's invisible shadow, his stalker.

CHAPTER 15

June 21

Bashir Kazi's beard was long and untidy. He wore khaki trousers and a multipocket vest. His arms were thick and muscular. In purely physical terms, he was impressive, but he was slumped on the leather sofa watching television, and having appraised Salander with a condescending look, he ignored her. With any luck he would be high. She pretended to lurch sideways, steadied herself and took a slug from her hip flask. Bashir smirked and said to Khalil, "Who's this whore you've dragged home?"

"I've never seen her before. She was just standing outside. She said something about a film we had to see. Get her out of here!"

Khalil was frightened of her, it was obvious, but he was more frightened of his brother. That should serve her purpose. She put her bag with the laptop on a chest of drawers by the door.

"And who are you, little girl?" Bashir said.

"No-one special," she said. This did not provoke much of a reaction, but Bashir did at least get to his feet and yawn, presumably to show how bored he was of girls being fresh with him.

"Why did you move back to this part of town?" he said to Khalil. "There's nothing but hookers and crazies here."

Salander looked around. It was a single-room apartment with a small kitchen, sparsely furnished. Apart from the sofa and chest of drawers, there was a loft bed and a low table. Clothes were strewn everywhere. A hockey stick was propped against the wall next to the chest.

"That's a pretty sweeping generalization," she said.

"What's that?"

"That's a rather broad generalization, Bashir, wouldn't you say?"

"How come you know my name?"

"I'm just out of prison. Your buddy Benito says hi."

It was a shot in the dark. Or not. She was fairly sure they were in touch with each other, and she saw a spark of recognition in Bashir's watery eyes.

"What's she got to say?"

"It's actually a video clip. Do you want to see?"

"Depends."

"I think you'll enjoy it." She took out her mobile and fiddled about as if trying to switch it on, but in fact she keyed in some commands and connected to the infrastructure run by Hacker Republic. She took a step forward and looked Bashir in the eye.

"Benito likes to do her friends favours, as you know. But there are a few things that need to be discussed."

"Such as?"

"It's a prison, and that in itself presents a problem. Oh, by the way, it was pretty clever of you to get a knife into the secure unit. Congratulations."

"Get to the point."

"The point is Faria."

"What about her?"

"How could you have treated her so badly? You behaved like pigs."

Bashir looked stunned.

"What the hell are you saying?"

"Pigs. Creeps. Bastards. There are many different ways of putting it, all understatements in the circumstances. Don't you think you should be punished?"

Salander had expected a reaction, but she had underestimated how violent it would be, the sudden burst of fury after the initial confusion. Without a second's warning Bashir punched her hard, right on the chin. She only just managed to keep her balance, while the rest of her was focused on holding her mobile steady down by her right hip, the screen directed at his face.

"You seem upset," she said.

"Damn fucking right I am!"

Bashir threw another punch and this time too she staggered, but made no effort to defend herself, she didn't even raise her hand. Bashir was staring at her, a combination of rage and astonishment in his eyes. Salander tasted blood. She took a chance.

"Was it really such a good idea to murder Jamal?" she said.

Bashir hit her again and this time it was harder to stay upright. She felt groggy and shook her head, hoping it would clear her vision, and then she caught sight of Khalil's terrified eyes. Would he attack her too? She could not be sure; it was hard to read him. But more likely he would stay out of it. There was something pathetic about his scrawny figure.

"Not a good idea after all?" she said, and looked at Bashir as provocatively as she could.

He lost control, just as she had hoped.

"You have no idea what a fucking brilliant idea it was, you slut."

"Oh yeah?"

"He made a whore of Faria," Bashir screamed. "A whore! They dishonoured all of us."

Another blow to the head and Salander fumbled to keep hold of her mobile.

"So Faria has to die too, doesn't she?" she stammered.

"Like a rat, a little pig. We won't stop till she's burning in hell."

"OK, now things are becoming clearer," Salander said. "Do you want to see my film?"

"Why the fuck would I?"

"You don't want Benito to be disappointed. That's not a good idea. Surely you know that by now."

Bashir was hesitating, she could tell from his eyes and his twitching arm. But that changed little. He was beside himself with fury, and Salander could not take many more punches. She swiftly measured the distance with her eyes, made a calculation, ran through a chain of consequences. Should she brain him? Knee him in the groin? Strike back? She decided to hold out a little longer, to appear broken, defeated. She did not have to try hard. The next punch came from the side and was heavier than the others. Her upper lip split open and her head boomed. She staggered, almost to her knees.

"Show me now," he growled.

She licked her lips, coughed, spat blood and collapsed on the leather sofa.

"It's on my mobile," she said.

"Show me." Bashir sat next to her. Khalil came closer too, a good thing, she thought. Deliberately, without being too slick, she keyed in the commands and soon the coding appeared on the screen. The brothers became visibly nervous.

"What the hell's happening?" Bashir said. "Is it broken? Is this some sort of crap phone?"

"Oh no," she said. "This is normal. The film's being loaded into a botnet, and look, now I'm naming the file and using Command and Control to distribute it."

"What the hell do you mean?"

She could smell rancid sweat.

"Let me explain," she said. "A botnet is a network of hacked computers which have been infected with a virus—a Trojan horse. It's a little bit illegal, but convenient. Before I say more, we should look at the film. I haven't even seen it myself; it's completely unedited. Hold on . . . here it is."

Bashir's face appeared on the screen. He looked confused, like a child who doesn't understand a difficult question.

"What the hell's that?"

"You. Unshaven, and a bit out of focus. It's hard to film from the hip. But it gets better. More lively. Look, here you pack a real punch, and now, just listen: Sounds like you're confessing to Jamal Chowdhury's murder."

"What the fuck? What the *fuck*?"

In the film Bashir was screaming about how Faria would die like a rat, how she would burn in hell. Then it got shaky, and there were more words and punches which were hard to see. A confused sequence of walls and the ceiling.

"What the fuck have you done?" he yelled, banging his fist on the low table in front of them.

"Just calm down, take it easy," Salander said. "There's no need to panic."

"What do you mean? Answer me, you bitch!" Bashir's voice cracked.

"A significant majority of the world's population hasn't yet gotten the film," Salander said. "I'd say barely more than a hundred million people have received it, and I'll bet most of them will think it's spam and delete it right away. But I did have time to name it. I called it 'Bashir Kazi.' Your friends will probably want to have a look, and the police of course, and Säpo, and your friends' friends, and so on. It might even go viral, you never know. The net's such a crazy place. I've never really gotten my head around it."

Bashir looked deranged. His head jerked this way and that.

"I can see this is tough for you," Salander said. "Publicity's never easy to handle. I can remember the first time I had my name all over the papers. I still haven't gotten over it, to be honest. But the good news is, there's a way out."

"How . . . ?"

"I'll tell you. I just have to—"

Lightning quick and taking advantage of his bewilderment and desperation, she grabbed hold of his head and smashed it twice onto the tabletop in front of them. Then she stood up.

"You can run, Bashir," she said. "You can run so fast that your disgrace won't catch up with you."

Bashir stared at her, rooted to the spot. His right arm shook. He put his hands to his forehead.

"It might work," she went on. "Not for long, but for a little while. If you run and run, like your brother, maybe not as fast—you're getting flabby, aren't you?—I'm sure you'll be able to stagger on, somehow or other."

"I'm going to kill you," Bashir said. He leaped up and made as if to throw himself at her, but then hesitated and looked nervously at the front door and windows.

"What are you waiting for," Salander said. "You need to get going."

"I will find you," he hissed.

"I'll be seeing you again, then," she said in a cold monotone. She turned and took a step towards the chest of drawers, giving him every chance to attack her from behind. But he was as dumbfounded and helpless as she had anticipated.

At that moment his mobile rang.

"Maybe it's someone who saw the film. But it's all cool, right? Just don't pick up, and keep your head down when you're out," she said.

Bashir cursed and came at her, but Salander grabbed the hockey stick from against the wall and hit him as hard as she could in the throat, face and stomach.

"This is from Faria," she said.

Bashir doubled over and took another hit, but managed to straighten up. With unsteady steps he stumbled through the door, down the dark stairwell, out into the afternoon sun.

Salander stood holding the hockey stick. Khalil Kazi was behind her by the sofa, his eyes flitting back and forth, his mouth hanging open. A teenager still, with a wiry, slight body, he looked terrified. He was hardly a threat to anyone, but he might flee and begin to unravel. Giannini had mentioned a risk of suicide. Salander kept her eye on the door and glanced at her watch.

It was 4:20 in the afternoon. She checked her e-mails. Neither Bublanski nor Farah Sharif had answered. Giannini had written:

<Excellent, looks promising. Go home right now!>

She looked at Khalil, who was breathing heavily. He seemed to want to say something.

"It's you, isn't it?" he said.

"Who?"

"The woman in the papers."

She nodded. "You and I have another film to look at. This one's less exciting; it's mostly hand movements."

She propped the hockey stick against the wall, took the bag with her laptop from the chest of drawers and motioned to Khalil to sit on the sofa. He was pale and looked as if his legs might give way. But he did as he was told.

She gave him a brief factual account of movement recognition and deep neural networks. She told him she had filmed his run earlier, and about the C.C.T.V. in the tunnelbana. He muttered something inaudible and she knew at once by the way his body stiffened that he had understood. She sat down next to him and opened the files on her laptop. As they watched she tried to explain, but he did not seem to be taking any of it in. For a long time he stared blankly at the screen, and then his mobile rang. He looked at her.

"Go ahead and answer it," she said.

Khalil picked up and it was obvious from the formality in his voice that he was speaking to someone for whom he had the greatest respect. His imam was in the neighbourhood— that must have been Annika Giannini's doing—and he was asking if he could join them. Salander nodded; that might be a good idea. Confessions were more the imam's province anyway.

A short while later there was a knock at the door. A tall, elegant man stepped into the apartment. He was in his fifties and had a long beard and a red turban. He nodded to Salander and then turned to Khalil with a melancholy smile.

"Hello, my boy," he said. "You and I can talk in peace now."

His voice was heavy with sorrow and for a moment there was silence. Salander felt uncomfortable, all of a sudden unsure what she should do.

"I don't think it's safe here," she said. "I suggest you leave, get yourselves to the mosque."

She took her laptop and bag and left them without saying goodbye, disappearing into the dark stairwell.

DECEMBER, ONE AND A HALF YEARS EARLIER

Dan Brody sat on a bench in Norrmalmstorg. It was his first day back in Stockholm. The sky was clear, the air cold, and he was wearing a scruffy black coat with a white fake-fur collar, sunglasses and a grey woollen hat pulled down over his forehead. On his lap was a book on the Lehman Brothers collapse. He wanted to learn about his brother's world.

He had checked into the af Chapman youth hostel on Skeppsholmen, an old converted ship where the cabins cost 690 kronor per night. This was just within his means. A few people in the neighbourhood had seemed to recognize him, and that hurt—as if he were no longer himself but a poorer copy of somebody else. Having only recently been the urbane musician, now once again he was the farm boy from Hälsingland province who had always thought he wasn't good enough for Stockholmers. On Birger Jarlsgatan he had slipped into a clothes shop where he bought the sunglasses and woollen hat and tried to hide behind them.

He never stopped thinking about contacting his

brother. Should he e-mail after all, send a video link or simply call? He did not have the courage. First he wanted to observe Leo from a distance, and that is why he was sitting outside Alfred Ögren Securities on Norrmalmstorg, waiting.

Ivar Ögren emerged with a determined, impatient stride and was picked up by a black BMW with tinted windows and driven off like a statesman.

But no sign of Leo. He was up there in the red-brick building. Dan had called and asked for him in English, and had been told he was in a meeting. He would be free soon, they said. Every time the entrance door opened Dan sat up, but he was still waiting. Darkness had long since fallen over Stockholm. An icy wind was blowing up from the water's edge and it was getting too cold to sit and read.

He stood up and walked back and forth across the square, rubbing his fingertips through his leather gloves. Still no sign. The rush-hour traffic was easing, and he looked over at the restaurant in the square with its large glass windows. The guests inside were smiling and talking, and he felt excluded. Life always seemed to be happening elsewhere, a party to which he had not been invited. It occurred to him that he was a perpetual outsider.

And then Leo appeared. Dan would never forget it. Time seemed to stand still and his field of vision narrowed; all sound died away. But the experience was not purely joyful, not there in the cold and the glow of light from the restaurant. The sight of his twin only intensified his pain. Leo was heartbreakingly like him. He had the same walk, the same smile, the same hand movements and the same lines on his cheeks and around his eyes. Everything was the same, and yet: It was as if Dan were seeing himself in a gilded mirror. The man over there was him, but was not him.

Leo Mannheimer was the man Dan could have been, and the more he looked, the more dissimilarities he noticed. Not just the coat and the expensive suit and shoes. It was the spring in his step and the bright look in his eyes. Leo seemed to radiate the kind of self-confidence Dan had never possessed, and when he thought of this he found it hard to breathe.

His heart pounded as he looked at the woman walking beside Leo with her arm around his waist. She had an intelligent, sophisticated air about her and seemed very attached to Leo. They were both laughing, and Dan realized that she must be Malin Frode, the woman Julia had spoken about with a certain note of jealousy. He dared not approach them. Instead he watched as they strolled up towards Biblioteksgatan. He followed without really knowing why, walking slowly and keeping his distance.

Not that they were likely to notice him. They were absorbed in each other. They disappeared in the direction of Humlegården, their laughter floating in the air. He felt heavy, as if their carefree ease were dragging his body to the ground. He tore himself away and walked back to his youth hostel, alone, not considering for a moment that appearances can be deceptive, that others might regard Dan as the one who had had all the luck.

Life often looks its best from a distance. He was yet to understand that.

Blomkvist was on his way to Nyköping. He carried a shoulder bag with a notebook and tape recorder, as well as three bottles of rosé. Lotta von Kanterborg had suggested them. Her sister, Hilda, was staying at Hotel Forsen near the river under the name Fredrika Nord. She was prepared to talk, apparently, as long as certain conditions were met. One of these was the bottles of rosé.

Another was extreme discretion. Hilda was certain that someone was after her, and what Blomkvist had said only made her anxiety worse. According to Lotta, the information had derailed her. Accordingly, Blomkvist had not told anyone where he was going, not even Erika.

Now he was sitting at a café by the main meeting point in Stockholm Central Station, waiting for Malin. He needed to talk to her—he must leave no stone unturned. He wanted to test his theories to see if they held water. Malin arrived ten minutes late. She looked gorgeous in jeans and a blue blouse, even though, like half of Stockholm, she was flustered and sweating.

"Really sorry," she said. "I had to drop off Linus at my mother's."

"You could have brought him along. I only have a few questions."

"I know. But I'm on my way somewhere."

He gave her a quick kiss and got straight to the point.

"When you met Leo at the Fotografiska Museum, did you

notice any differences beyond the fact that he seemed to be right-handed?"

"Such as?"

Blomkvist glanced up at the station clock.

"Well, a birthmark, for example, on one side rather than the other. Or a cowlick pointing in a new direction. His hair's pretty curly, isn't it?"

"You're scaring me, Mikael. What do you mean?"

"I'm working on a story about identical twins separated at birth. Can't say more than that for the moment. Please don't tell anyone, OK?"

All of a sudden Malin looked terrified and grabbed him by the arm.

"So you're saying . . ."

"I'm not saying anything, not yet. But I do wonder . . ." He paused. "Identical twins have identical genes, pretty much," he said. "Certain genetic changes, small mutations, take place in all of us."

"What are you trying to say?"

"I'm giving you some simple facts—otherwise the whole thing's incomprehensible. Identical twins are formed from a single egg which splits relatively quickly in the uterus. The question here is how soon that split takes place. If it's more than four days after fertilization, the twins share a placenta, and that increases the risk to the foetuses. And if the split occurs even later, between seven and twelve days, say, the babies can turn out to be mirror-image twins. Twenty percent of all identical twins are mirror-image twins."

"Meaning what?"

"That they're identical, except they're each other's mirror

image. One becomes left-handed, the other right-handed. In rare cases their hearts can be on opposite sides of their bodies."

"So you're saying that . . ." She stuttered over the words and Blomkvist laid his hand on her cheek to reassure her.

"The whole idea may be off the wall," he said. "And even if it isn't, even if the person you met at Fotografiska really was Leo's mirror-image twin, that doesn't necessarily mean a crime has been committed. It's not identity theft like in *The Talented Mr. Ripley*. Maybe they've just swapped roles, they've been having a bit of fun, trying something new. Can you walk with me towards the train? I'm going to run out of time."

Malin sat there as if turned to stone. Then they stood up and took the escalator to the level below and walked past the shops to platform 11. He told her that he was off to Linköping on an assignment. He wanted to leave as few leads as possible.

"I've been reading about identical twins who met only as adults and had been unaware of each other's existence until then," he went on. "They almost always describe this first meeting as fantastic, Malin. Apparently it's the most earth-shattering experience ever. Imagine: You think you're one of a kind, unique—and then another one pops up. They say that identical twins who meet late in life can't get enough of each other. They run through everything: talents, shortcomings, habits, gestures, memories—the works. They become whole, they grow. They're happier than ever before. Some of these stories really moved me, Malin. You yourself said that Leo had been euphoric for a while."

"That's right—but then after a while he wasn't."

"True."

"He left the country and we lost contact."

"Exactly," Blomkvist said. "I've thought about that too. Is there anything—either in his appearance or elsewhere—that could help me understand what's been going on?"

They had reached the platform. The train was already there.

"I don't know," she said.

"Think!"

"Well, maybe one thing. Do you remember I told you he'd gotten engaged to Julia Damberg?"

"That upset you, didn't it?"

"Not really."

He did not entirely believe her.

"More than anything I was surprised," she said. "Julia used to work for us. Then she moved to Frankfurt and none of us heard from her for a few years. But towards the end of my time at the firm she called and wanted to speak to Leo. I'm not sure he ever called her back, in fact. Julia said something odd."

"What?"

"She asked me if I knew that Leo played the guitar even better than the piano. He was a virtuoso, she said. I'd never heard Leo mention it, so I asked him."

"What did he say?"

"Nothing. He just blushed and laughed. It was during that time when he was deliriously happy."

Blomkvist was no longer paying attention. The words "guitar" and "virtuoso" had struck a troubling note. He was deep in thought as he said goodbye to Malin and got on the train.

DECEMBER, ONE AND A HALF YEARS EARLIER

For a few days Dan stayed away. It was a worrying time. He either read in his cabin on the hostel ship or took nervous walks on Skeppsholmen and Djurgården. Sometimes he went for a run. In the evenings, in the bar on board, he drank more than he normally would. When he could not sleep at night he wrote about his life in red, leather-bound notebooks. On Wednesday, December 13, he headed back to Norrmalmstorg, but he could not bring himself to approach Leo then either.

Then, on Friday, December 15, he took along his guitar and sat on the bench next to the restaurant in the middle of the square. It was snowing again, the temperature had dropped and his coat was no longer adequate to keep out the cold, but he couldn't afford anything warmer. He was running out of money, and he could not bear the idea of playing for random jazz groups just to make a living. He could think only of Leo. Nothing else was important.

That day, Leo emerged from the office early. Dressed in a dark-blue cashmere coat and a white scarf, he set off at a brisk pace. Dan followed, keeping closer this time, which was a mistake. Outside the Park cinema Leo turned suddenly and looked around, as if he had sensed that there was someone on his tail. But he did not see Dan. The street was full of people and Dan, wearing his woollen hat and sunglasses, turned away and looked in the direction of Stureplan. Leo kept walking and crossed Karlavägen.

Dan stopped outside the Malaysian embassy on Floragatan and watched as Leo went into his apartment building. The door closed behind him with a bang, and Dan stood in the cold and waited, just as he had waited before. He knew it would be a while. Lights came on in the top apartment after a few minutes. They shone like the aura of a more beautiful world. Occasional notes could be heard from a grand piano, and when Dan recognized the harmonies his eyes filled with tears. But he was also freezing, and he swore under his breath. Sirens wailed in the distance. A bitter wind was blowing.

As he approached the building and took off his sunglasses, he heard footsteps behind him. An elderly lady in a black hat and bright-green coat came past him with a pug on a lead. She smiled.

"Don't you feel like going home today, Leo?"

For a second, no more, he looked at her in panic. Then he smiled back, as if he found her question witty and appropriate in the circumstance.

"Sometimes you just don't know what you want," he said.

"How true. But come on in now. It's much too cold to be standing around outside, philosophizing."

She punched in the door code and they went in together and stood waiting for the lift. She smiled at him again and said, "What's that old coat you're wearing?"

He felt a stab of nerves.

"This old thing?"

The woman laughed.

"'This old thing?' That's what I say when I've put on my very best party frock, fishing for compliments."

He tried to laugh at that too, but he was clearly not convincing and the woman bit her lip and looked serious. He was sure that she had seen through his deception; not only his clothes but his clumsy way with words must have betrayed his lack of style.

"I'm sorry, Leo. I know it must be hard for you right now. How is Viveka?"

He could tell by her tone that "Fine" would not be an appropriate answer.

"So-so," he said.

"Let's hope she won't have to suffer too long."

"Let's hope," he said, and realized that he would not be able to handle a ride in the lift with her. "You know what? I need some exercise. I'll take the stairs."

"Nonsense, Leo. You're as slender as a gazelle. Give Viveka a hug from me. Tell her I'm thinking of her."

"I certainly will," Dan said, and he bounded up the stairs with his guitar.

As he approached Leo's apartment he slowed. If Leo's hearing was even half as good as his own, he would have to be as quiet as a mouse. He tiptoed the last few feet. It was the only apartment on the top floor, which was good—it was set apart. Making as little noise as possible, he sat on the floor with his back against the wall. What should he do now? His heart pounded. His mouth was dry.

The hallway smelled of polish and cleaning products. His eyes fixed on the ceiling, painted as a blue sky. Who would think to paint a fresco onto the ceiling of a stairwell? From downstairs came the sound of footsteps, the shuffling of feet, television sets, a chair being moved, a door being unlocked. A note on the piano from inside the apartment. It was an A.

There were some tentative bass notes, as if Leo had not quite made up his mind to play. Then he got started. He was improvising—or perhaps not. It was a dark, disquieting loop, with Leo always ending on the seventh tone in the minor key, just as he had done in the recording at the Stockholm Concert Hall. There was something almost ritual and obsessive about it, but also sophisticated, mature. Somehow he managed to conjure up a feeling of being broken and lost, at least that's how it seemed to Dan. He shuddered.

He could not quite explain it, and all of a sudden it hit him. Tears welled up and he trembled, not only because of the music. It was the kinship in the harmonies, the very fact that when Leo played he conveyed such pain, as if he, not even a professional musician, was better than Dan at expressing their sorrow.

Their sorrow?

It was a strange thought, and yet just then it appeared true. A moment before, Leo had seemed like a stranger, like someone very different, and more fortunate. Now Dan recognized himself in his twin. He got unsteadily to his feet. He had intended to ring the doorbell, but instead he took his guitar from its case, swiftly tuned it and joined in. It was not hard to find the chords and follow the notes in the loop. The way Leo dwelled on the beat in the syncopation and changed the triple phrasing for straight eighths was similar to his own. He felt . . . at home. That was the only way he could explain it. It was as if he had played with Leo many times before. He played for several minutes, expecting Leo to notice the accompaniment. But perhaps Leo did not hear as well as Dan did. Perhaps he was entirely absorbed in his playing. Dan couldn't say.

Then Leo fell silent in the middle of the motif, on an F-sharp. But there were no footsteps, no movement. Leo must have sat stock-still, and Dan too fell silent, and waited. What was going on? He could hear loud breathing from deep inside the apartment and he played the loop again, a little quicker now and with a flourish of his own, a new variation. At that, the piano stool scraped against the floor and he heard steps approaching the door. He stood with his guitar and felt like a beggar, a street musician who had strayed into an elegant drawing room and was hoping to be accepted. But he was also burning with hope and longing. He closed his eyes and heard the security chain being unhooked by what sounded like fumbling fingers.

The door opened and Leo looked at him. He was dumbfounded. His mouth fell open. He looked shocked, terrified.

"Who are you?"

Those were his first words, and how was Dan to answer him? What should he say?

"My name is . . ."

Silence.

". . . Dan Brody," he said. "I'm a jazz guitarist. I must be your twin brother."

Leo said nothing. He seemed on the verge of sinking to his knees. His face was white.

"I . . ."

That was all he managed, and Dan could not speak either. His heart pounded and the words would not come. He too tried to speak:

"I . . ."

"*What?*"

There was a desperation in Leo's voice that was almost too much for Dan to bear. He resisted an impulse to turn and run, and instead said:

"When I heard you playing the piano . . . I was thinking that all my life I've felt like half a person. As if I've been missing something. And now at last . . ."

He got no further. He didn't know if the words were true, or even half true—or whether he was simply spouting set phrases without thinking.

"I can't get my head around this," Leo said. "How long have you known?" His hands were shaking now.

"Only a few days."

"I just can't get my head around this."

"I know, it's unreal."

Leo held out his hand. It seemed strangely formal in the circumstances.

"I've always . . ." he said. He bit his lip. His hands would not stop shaking. "I've always felt the same. Will you come in?"

Dan nodded and stepped into an apartment which was grander than anything he had ever seen.

PART III

THE VANISHING TWIN

JUNE 21–30

As many as one pregnancy in eight may begin as a twin pregnancy, although sometimes one of the embryos does not thrive and is reabsorbed into the gestational sac. This is known as Vanishing Twin Syndrome, or V.T.S.

Some twins lose a sibling after birth because of adoption, or, more rarely, a mix-up in the maternity ward. Some meet for the first time only as adults; others never meet at all. Identical twins Jack Yufe and Oskar Stöhr first encountered each other at a railway station in West Germany in 1954. Jack Yufe had lived on a kibbutz and been a soldier in the Israeli army. Oskar Stöhr had been active in the Hitler Youth.

Many people feel they are missing someone.

CHAPTER 16

June 21

Blomkvist walked along the river in Nyköping to Hotel Forsen. It was a simple brown wooden building with a red-tile roof, more of a hostel than a hotel. But it was in a beautiful location, right next to the water. It was 8:30 p.m. by the time he got there. In the entrance was a miniature watermill and photographs of fishermen in gum boots.

A young blond woman sat behind the reception desk, possibly a summer temp. She could not have been more than seventeen. She was wearing jeans and a red shirt and was busy with her mobile. Blomkvist worried that she might recognize him and post something on social media, but he was reassured by her disinterested expression. He went up two floors and knocked on the grey door of room number 214. He heard a cracked voice from inside.

"Who is it?"

He gave his name, and Hilda von Kanterborg opened the

door. For a moment he caught his breath. She looked wild. Her hair was unkempt, her eyes darting about nervously, like a frightened animal's. Her skin was covered in pigment spots. She was busty, with broad shoulders and hips—her light-blue dress seemed barely big enough for her.

"It's good of you to see me," he said.

"Good? It's terrifying. What you told Lotta seemed crazy."

He did not ask her to be more specific. First he wanted to calm her, allow her to get her breathing under control. He took the bottles of rosé out of his bag and put them on the round oak table next to the open window.

"I'm afraid they're not so chilled now," he said.

"I've survived worse."

She went to the bathroom and came back with two Dura-lex glasses.

"Are you going to stay sober and sensible or will you join me?"

"Whatever makes you feel comfortable," he said.

"All drunks want company, so you'll have to drink. Look at it as a professional strategy."

She filled Blomkvist's glass to the brim and he swallowed a large mouthful to show that he meant business. He looked out at the river and the subtly shifting daylight of the evening sky.

"Let me just assure you—"

"Don't try to assure me of anything," she said. "You can't. I don't need any sententious bullshit about protection of sources. I'm telling you what I'm telling you because I don't want to keep quiet any longer."

She knocked back her glass and looked him in the eye. There was something appealing and easygoing about her.

"OK, I understand. Forgive me for worrying you. Shall we get to it?"

She nodded. He got out his voice recorder and switched it on.

"I assume you've heard about the State Institute for Racial Biology," she said.

"Oh God yes," he said. "What an appalling outfit."

"Indeed, but don't get yourself too worked up, you star reporter. This is not half as exciting as it sounds. The institute was closed down in 1958, as you may know, and you'd have a hard time finding anyone in the whole of Sweden these days who's into race biology. I'm only saying this because there's a connection. When I started my work at the Registry, I had no idea; I thought I was only going to be working with gifted children. As it turned out"—she drank some more wine—"I don't know where to start."

"Take your time," Blomkvist said. "We'll find a way in."

She emptied her glass and lit a cigarette, a Gauloise, looking at it with a grin.

"Smoking's not allowed here," she said. "Actually, the story could begin right there, with smoking—and the suspicion that it might be harmful. In the 1950s, some researchers claimed that smoking could cause lung cancer. Imagine that!"

"Unbelievable!"

"I know, right? As you know, the theory met with massive resistance. One line of thought said: Maybe a lot of smokers do get lung cancer, but that isn't necessarily because of the tobacco. It could just as easily be because they eat too many vegetables. Nothing could be proven. 'More Doctors smoke Camels than any other cigarette' was a well-known slogan at the time. Humphrey Bogart and Lauren Bacall were held up as examples of how sophisticated smoking was. And yet the suspicion stuck, and it was no small matter. The British Ministry of Health discovered that deaths due to lung cancer had increased by a factor of fifteen in two decades, and a group of doctors at the Karolinska Institute here decided to test the theory by using twins. Twins are ideal research subjects, and a register of more than eleven thousand of them was established over a period of two years. They were questioned about their smoking and drinking habits and their responses made an important contribution to the sorrowful discovery that ciggies and booze aren't all that great for you after all."

She gave a mournful laugh, took a deep drag on her cigarette and poured herself yet another glass of rosé.

"It didn't stop there," she said. "The register grew and new twins were added, including many who did not grow up together. In Sweden in the 1930s, several hundred twins had been separated at birth, mostly for reasons of poverty. Many of them didn't meet until they were adults. This provided a wealth of valuable scientific material used by researchers not only to investigate new illnesses and their causes, but to also address the classic question: How do heredity and environment shape an individual?"

"I've read about that," Blomkvist said, "and I know about the Swedish Twin Registry. But surely the work done is aboveboard?"

"Absolutely, it's valuable and important research. All I'm trying to do is give you some background. While the Twin Registry was being constituted, the State Institute for Racial Biology changed its name to the State Institute for Human Genetics and was integrated into Uppsala University. It wasn't just semantics. These gentlemen gradually began to devote themselves to something which at least vaguely resembled scientific work. The old business of measuring heads and crap theories about the purity of the Swedo-Germanic race were finally abandoned."

"But they still had all the registers of Roma and other minorities?"

"Yes, also something more important, and much worse." Blomkvist raised his eyebrows.

"Their outlook on mankind. Maybe they no longer thought that one race was better than another. Maybe there was no such thing as 'different races.' But still, some purebred Swedes were arguably more diligent and hardworking than others of their countrymen. Why was that? Because they'd been given a good, solid Swedish upbringing, perhaps? Maybe we can find a way to create a real, honest-to-goodness Swede, they thought—someone who doesn't smoke Gauloises and get drunk on lukewarm rosé."

"Doesn't sound so good."

"No. Times had changed, but people on one extreme can easily start heading towards a different one, don't you think? Before long this group at Uppsala began to believe in Freud and Marx in the same way they'd once believed in racial biology. Their organization was called the Institute for Human Genetics so they didn't dismiss the significance of heredity.

Far from it. But they believed that social and material factors played by far the greater role. Nothing wrong with that, especially not these days when class barriers can be such impenetrable walls.

"But this group—whose leading figure was sociology professor Martin Steinberg—took the view that we were inevitably conditioned by our circumstances. A certain type of mother and certain types of social and cultural factors would more or less automatically produce a certain type of person. That's not the way it is, not by a long shot. A human being is infinitely more complex than that. But our friends wanted to experiment; they wanted to establish what sort of upbringing and background would create a solid Swede. They had close contacts with the Twin Registry and kept abreast of the research there, and then they came across Roger Stafford, an American psychoanalyst."

"I read about him."

"But you haven't met him, have you? He's incredibly charismatic. He would light up any elegant gathering, and he made a deep impression on one woman in this group in particular. Her name is Rakel Greitz. She's a psychiatrist and psychoanalyst, and she ... Oh, I could say a lot about Greitz. She not only fell head over heels for Stafford, she became obsessed by his work. She wanted to push it further. At some stage—I don't know exactly when—she and the group decided that they would deliberately separate twins, both identical and fraternal, and place them with families in diametrically opposite circumstances. Because the objective was elitist—to produce fine, outstanding Swedes—the group was very particular about their research subjects. They left no stone unturned. Among other things, they looked through the old registers of Roma and other Gypsies, and Sami and so on, searching for people who had escaped even the race biologists' pool of candidates for forced sterilization. They were looking for highly gifted parents of twins. To be cynical, what they wanted was first-class research material."

Blomkvist thought back to the guitar virtuoso Salander had mentioned in her message. "And one of these pairs of twins was Leo Mannheimer and Daniel Brolin?"

Hilda was quiet and looked out the window.

"Yes, and that's why we're here today, right?" she said. "What you said to Lotta—that Leo isn't Leo any longer?— that sounded insane. To be honest I don't believe it. I just don't. Anders and Daniel Brolin, as they were then called, belonged to the Gypsy community and were from an extremely musical family. Their mother, Rosanna, was a fabulous singer. There's an old recording of her singing Billie Holiday's version of 'Strange Fruit' that tears your heart out. But she died days after the twins were born, of puerperal fever. She had never been to secondary school, but they dug up her reports from her last years in primary school. Top of the class in every subject. The boys' father was named Kenneth and he was manic-depressive but an absolute genius on the guitar. He wasn't an evil or callous man, just mentally unstable, and he couldn't cope with the twins. They were put in a children's home in Gävle, and that's where Greitz found them and separated them almost immediately. I'd rather not know how she and Martin Steinberg went about finding families for all those twins. But when it came to Daniel and Anders, or 'Leo,' as he was renamed, it was especially awful."

"In what way?"

"It was just so unfair. Daniel stayed on at the orphan-age for a few years and then ended up with a mean, narrow-minded farmer outside Hudiksvall who was only interested in more hands on his farm. At first there was a wife but she soon disappeared, and what came after that can unquestion-ably be described as child labour. Daniel and his foster broth-ers worked their fingers to the bone from early morning till late at night. Often they weren't allowed to go to school. Leo, on the other hand . . . Leo had been taken in by a prosperous and influential family in Nockeby."

"By Herman and Viveka Mannheimer."

"Exactly. It was crucial to the project that the adoptive parents should not learn anything about the children's ori-gins, and above all the fact that they were twins. But Herman was a hotshot, and he managed to wear down Martin Stein-berg. Steinberg caved in, he cracked. That was bad enough. But it got worse. Herman began to have second thoughts. He had always disliked Gypsies and 'loose people,' as he called them, and without Greitz or Steinberg knowing, he asked his business partner, Alfred Ögren, for advice."

"I see," Blomkvist said. "And his son Ivar found out about it too."

"Yes, but that was later. By which time Ivar had long been envious of Leo; people considered Leo much more prom-ising and bright. Ivar would do whatever he could to gain the upper hand, to get Leo into trouble. It was a minefield between the families, and so my colleague Carl Seger was called in to help."

"But if Herman Mannheimer was such a prejudiced old fart, why had he agreed to take the boy in the first place?"

"Herman was probably a run-of-the-mill reactionary, not fundamentally a heartless person, in spite of what happened to Carl. But Alfred Ögren ... he was a swine and a true racist and strongly advised against the idea. It would probably have come to nothing except there were reports that the boy had highly developed motor skills and all sorts of other advanced abilities, and that tipped the scales. And Viveka fell in love with him."

"So they took him into the family because he was precocious?"

"Probably. He was only seven months old but there were high expectations of him from an early age."

"His personal file says that he's the Mannheimers' biological son. How did they pull that one off, considering the baby was adopted so late?"

"Their closest friends and neighbours knew the truth, but it became a matter of honour. They all knew how much it pained Viveka that she hadn't been able to have children of her own."

"Did Leo know he was adopted?"

"He found out at the age of seven or eight, when Ögren's sons started teasing him. Viveka felt she had to tell him. But she asked him to keep it a secret—for the sake of the family's honour."

"I understand."

"It wasn't an easy time for the family."

"Leo suffered from hyperacusis."

"He suffered from that, and from what today we would call hypersensitivity. The world was too harsh for him, and he withdrew and became a very solitary child. Sometimes I think Carl Seger was his only real friend. At first, Carl and I and all the younger psychologists were not fully in the picture. We thought we were investigating a group of gifted children. We didn't even know we were working with twins. We were split up so that we only ever met one sibling. But in time we came to understand and slowly we accepted it—more or less. Carl was the one who had the greatest difficulty coming to terms with the deliberate separation of the twins, probably because he was so close to Leo. The other children did not have the feeling that they had been separated from someone. But Leo was different. He didn't know that he was an identical twin, only that he'd been adopted. He must have had an inkling, though, as he often said he felt as if he were missing one half of himself. Carl found that increasingly hard to bear. He was forever asking me about Daniel: 'Does he feel the same way?' 'He's lonely,' I said, and I mentioned that Daniel had sometimes shown signs of depression. 'We've got to tell them,' Carl insisted. I told him we couldn't, it would only make all of us unhappy. But Carl kept on, and in the end he made the biggest mistake of his life. He went to Rakel, and you know . . ."

Hilda opened the second bottle, even though the first was not empty.

"Rakel may give the impression of being business-like and upstanding. She's completely fooled Leo. They've been in touch all these years, get together for Christmas lunch and so on. But in point of fact she's ice cold. It's because of her that I'm here under a false name, shaking with fear and getting drunk. She's kept a close watch over me all these years, and when she wasn't buttering me up, she was threatening me. She was coming over to my apartment as I was making my escape. I saw her in the street."

"So Carl went to her," Blomkvist said.

"He marshalled his courage and announced that he was going to tell the full story, whatever the cost. A few days later he was dead, shot in the woods like a hunted animal."

"Do you think it was murder?"

"I have no proof. I've always refused to believe it, not wanting to accept that I might have been part of something that was capable of killing."

"But in fact you've suspected it all along, right?" Blomkvist said.

Hilda was silent. She drank her rosé and stared at the floor.

"I read the police report," Blomkvist said. "It felt dodgy even then, and now you've provided a motive. I can see no explanation other than that they were all in on it—Mannheimer, Ögren, Greitz, the lot of them. They risked being identified and associated with an operation which had separated children who belonged together. They needed to eliminate the threat before their names were dragged through the mud."

Hilda looked frightened and said nothing.

"It was a high price to pay, though," she said at length. "Despite all his money and privilege, Leo was never happy.

He never recovered his self-confidence. He joined the family business reluctantly, only to be given a rough ride by cretins like Ivar."

"What about Daniel, his brother?"

"In some ways he was stronger, perhaps because he had no choice. All the things Leo was encouraged to be—a literate, educated, musical boy—Daniel had to become in secret, and independently, alone against the odds. But he too felt terrible. He was bullied by his foster brothers and beaten by his father. He was always made to feel like a misfit and an outsider."

"What became of him?"

"He ran away from the farm and vanished off the Registry's radar. I was fired soon afterwards, so I'm not altogether sure. The last thing I did for him was to recommend a music school in Boston. Then I heard nothing more until . . ."

Blomkvist could tell from the atmosphere in the room and the way she handled her glass that something had changed.

"Until when?"

"One morning in December a year and a half ago. I was reading the morning paper and having a glass. The telephone rang. The Registry had given us strict instructions never to give the children our real names. But I . . . I suppose I was already drinking, and in any case I must have let it slip a few times, because Daniel had managed to track me down before. And here he was, calling out of the blue. He said that he had worked it all out."

"Worked what out?"

"That Leo existed, that they were identical twins."

"Mirror-image twins, right?"

"Yes, but I don't think he was aware of that yet. Anyway, it didn't make a difference, at least not at the time. He was in a terrible rage, asking if I had known. I hesitated for a long time. When I finally told him yes, he was silent. Then he said he would never forgive me and hung up. I wanted to die. I phoned the number back and got through to a hotel in Berlin, but no-one there had heard of a Daniel Brolin. I did everything I could to find him. But it was hopeless."

"Do you think he and Leo have met?"

"No, I don't believe so."

"Why do you say that?"

"Because that sort of thing always gets out. Several of our identical twins have met as adults. Nowadays, in the world of social media, someone sees a picture on Facebook or Instagram, says it looks just like so-and-so, and then the story spreads and sometimes it gets into the newspapers. It's the sort of story journalists thrive on. But none of our twins has ever managed to piece it all together. There were always explanations at the ready and the newspapers only empha-sized the sensational aspects of the meetings. No-one has looked into the whole thing properly. In fact, I can't imagine how *you* got onto it. Everybody's been scrupulously careful about confidentiality."

Blomkvist helped himself to some more rosé, though he did not much care for it, and wondered how to express what he wanted to say. His tone remained sympathetic.

"I think that's wishful thinking, Hilda. There's reason to believe that Daniel and Leo *have* met. I have a friend who knows Leo well and something doesn't add up. He"—he

opted, for safety's sake, to refer to Malin Frode as a "he"—
"has studied Leo closely and is convinced that Leo has
become right-handed, as I told your sister. On top of which
he's become a very proficient guitar player, apparently from
one day to the next."

"So he's also changed instruments!" Hilda shrank into
her chair. "Are you suggesting . . ."

"I'm only asking what conclusions you would draw, if
you were being honest with yourself."

"If what you say is true, I would think that Leo and Daniel had swapped identities."

"But why would they?"

"Because . . ." She was searching for words. "Because they
both have a strong melancholy streak and are highly gifted.
They would be able to move into a completely new context
without much difficulty, and maybe they'd see it as a novel
and exciting experience. Carl used to tell me that Leo often
felt imprisoned in a role he did not enjoy."

"And Daniel?"

"For Daniel . . . I don't know, it must be fantastic to be
able to step into Leo's world."

"You said that Daniel was furious on the telephone,
didn't you? It must have been painful for him to realize that
his twin brother grew up in affluent circumstances, while he
had to work long days on a farm."

"Yes, but . . ."

Hilda studied the bottles of rosé, as if worried that they
might soon run out.

"You have to understand how exceptionally sensitive and

empathic these boys are. Carl and I often talked about it. They were lonely. But the two of them are a perfect match and my guess, if they have met, is that it was a fantastic meeting. It may have been the best, the very happiest thing that's ever happened to them."

"So you don't think it's likely that something went wrong?"

Hilda shook her head. Rather too emphatically, Blomkvist thought.

"Did you ever tell anybody that Daniel had called you?"

Hilda hesitated maybe a little too long. She lit a cigarette from the butt of the previous one.

"No," she said. "I no longer have any contact with the Registry. Who would I have told?"

"You said that Greitz came to see you quite regularly."

"I haven't told her a thing. I've always been wary of her."

Blomkvist pondered a while, then went on in a sterner tone than he had intended.

"There's one more thing you have to tell me about."

"Is it about Lisbeth Salander?"

"How did you guess?"

"It's hardly a secret that the two of you are close."

"Was she a part of the project?"

"She caused Rakel more trouble than all the others put together."

DECEMBER, ONE AND A HALF YEARS EARLIER

Leo stepped into his apartment alongside the man who looked like him. The man wore a tatty black coat with a white fake-fur collar, grey suit trousers and reddish-brown boots which looked like they had done a lot of walking. He took off his woollen hat and coat and set down his guitar. His hair was more untidy than Leo's, the sideburns longer and his cheeks more chapped. But that only made the similarity more chilling.

It was like seeing oneself in a new guise. Leo broke into a cold sweat. He realized that he was scared to death. He felt the floor opening up in front of him. But it above all was puzzling. He looked at the man's hands and fingers and then at his own, and he longed for a mirror. He wanted to compare every crease and wrinkle in their faces. More than anything, he had questions, and he wanted to ask and ask and never stop. He thought about the music he had heard coming from the stairwell, and the man describing himself as only half a person—it was just as he himself had always felt. There was a lump in his throat.

"How is this possible?" he asked.

"I believe . . ." the other man said.

"What?"

". . . that we were part of an experiment."

Leo could hardly take it in. He remembered Carl, and his father coming up the stairs that autumn day, and he faltered. He collapsed onto the red sofa beneath the Bror Hjorth painting. The man sat in the armchair beside it.

There was even something eerily familiar about that movement, the body sinking into the chair.

"I always knew something was wrong," Leo said.

"Did you know you were adopted?"

"My mother told me."

"But you had no idea I existed?"

"Absolutely not. Or rather . . ."

"What?"

"I've thought. I've dreamed. I've imagined all kinds of things. Where did you grow up?"

"On a farm outside Hudiksvall. Then I moved to Boston."

"Boston . . ." Leo muttered.

He heard a heart beating. He thought it was his own, but it was the other man's, his twin brother's.

"Would you like a drink?" he asked.

"I sure could use one."

"Champagne? It goes straight into your bloodstream."

"Sounds perfect."

Leo got up and went towards the kitchen, but stopped without really knowing why. He was too confused, too agitated to understand what he was doing.

"I'm sorry," he said.

"Sorry? Why?"

"I had such a shock at the door, I can't even remember your name."

"Dan," the man said. "Dan Brody."

"Dan?" Leo said. "Dan."

Then he went to fetch a bottle of Dom Perignon and

two glasses. Perhaps that was not the exact moment it began. Their conversation must have been surreal and incomprehensible for a while longer. But it was snowing outside and the sounds of a Friday evening could be heard: laughter, voices, music from cars outside and from the other apartments. They smiled and raised their glasses and opened up more and more. Soon they were talking as they never had to anyone before.

Later, neither was capable of describing the conversation and its meanderings. Every thread, every topic was interrupted by more questions and digressions. It was as if there were not enough words—as if they could not talk fast enough. Night came, and then a new day, and only rarely did they stop to eat or sleep, or to play music.

They played for hours on end, and for Leo this was the best thing of all. He was a loner. He had played every day of his life, but almost always alone. Dan had played with hundreds of other musicians—amateurs, professionals, virtuosos, some of whom were hopeless, some with a keen ear, some who could only play in one genre, some who could play them all, people capable of shifting into another key mid-phrase and picking up every shift in rhythm. Yet never before had he played with anyone who understood him so intuitively, so immediately. They not only jammed together, they spoke about their music and shared ideas, and sometimes Leo would climb onto a table or chair and propose a toast:

"I'm so proud! You're so good, so phenomenally good."

It was such an overwhelming joy to play with his twin brother that he raised the level of his own playing and became more adventurous, more creative with his solos. Even though Dan was the more skilled musician, Leo rediscovered the fire in his music too.

Sometimes they talked and played at the same time. They told each other every detail of their lives, and discovered connections and coincidences of which they had been unaware. They let their stories run together and each added a touch of colour to the other.

However, even though Dan did not say so at the time, the feelings were not always mutual. At times he found himself consumed by envy when he remembered how, as a child, he had gone hungry or how he had run away from the farm. How he had been betrayed by Hilda. *We're supposed to study, not to intervene.* He felt flashes of anger, and when Leo complained that he had lacked the courage to devote himself fully to his music and was instead forced to become a partner in Alfred Ögren—forced to become a partner!—the injustice was almost more than Dan could bear. Yet that moment was an exception. Their first weekend that December was a time of great, all-enveloping joy for him too.

It was a miracle to meet not just a twin brother, but also someone who thought and felt and heard as he did. And how much time they spent discussing the things they could hear! They became totally engrossed, two nerds enjoying the mind-boggling experience of at last being able to discuss a subject no-one else understood. Sometimes Dan too climbed onto a chair to propose a toast.

They promised to stick together. They swore to be as one. They vowed many magnificent and beautiful things—

but also they vowed to work out what had happened, and why. They spoke about the people who had examined them when they were young, and about the tests and filming and questions. Dan told Leo about Hilda, and Leo told Dan about Carl Seger and Rakel Greitz, with whom he had stayed in touch over the years.

"Rakel Greitz," Dan said. "What does she look like?"

Leo described the birthmark on her throat, and at that Dan stiffened. He knew that he too had met Greitz. That realization was a decisive moment. Eleven p.m. on Sunday, December 17. The street was dark and silent, and it was no longer snowing. Snowploughs could be heard in the distance.

"Isn't Greitz kind of wicked?"

"She comes across as pretty cold," Leo said.

"She gave me the creeps."

"I didn't care much for her either."

"But you went on seeing her?"

"I never stood up to her as much as I perhaps should have."

"We're both feeble, aren't we?" Dan said, gently.

"I suppose we are. But Rakel was also my link to Carl. She always told me nice stories about him, all the things I wanted to hear, I suppose. I'm having Christmas lunch with her next week."

"Have you ever asked her about your background?"

"Thousands of times, and every time she's said . . ."

". . . that you were left at an orphanage in Gävle, but they never managed to trace your biological parents."

"I've also called that bloody orphanage," fumed Leo, "and they confirmed the information."

"Well, what about the whole Gypsy thing, then?"

"That's just a rumour, she says."

"She's lying."

"Clearly."

A grim look came over Leo's face.

"Rakel seems to be the spider at the centre of the web, don't you think?" Dan said.

"It would seem so."

"We should nail them all!"

A wild thirst for revenge flared in the apartment on Floragatan, and as Sunday night turned into Monday morning, they agreed to lie low and not tell a soul about their meeting. Leo would cancel the reservation for Christmas lunch, call Greitz and invite her to the apartment instead, catching her with her guard down while Dan hid in an adjoining room. Greitz needed to suffer. The brothers concocted a plan.

Hilda had downed one glass after another, and although she did not seem drunk, she was shaky and sweating so profusely that her throat and chest were glistening.

"Lisbeth and her sister, Camilla, were included in one of the registers from the Institute of Human Genetics and were regarded as ideal candidates. No-one had much respect for Agneta, but their father was—"

"A monster."

"A highly gifted monster, and that's what made the children so very interesting. Rakel wanted to separate them. She became obsessed with the idea."

"Even though the girls already had a home and a mother."

"Please don't think I'm trying to defend Rakel, not for one second. But . . . at the time she had strong arguments, even from a purely human point of view. The father, Zalachenko, was both violently abusive and an alcoholic."

"I know about that."

"I know you do. But I want to say it in our defence. It was a hellish home environment, Mikael. It wasn't just the father's rapes and assaults. The fact is, he clearly favoured Camilla, which made for a disastrous relationship between the daughters from the outset. It was as if they were born to be enemies."

Blomkvist thought about Camilla and the murder of his colleague Andrei Zander. He gripped his glass firmly but said nothing.

"There were compelling reasons—I even thought so myself—to place Lisbeth with another family," Hilda said.

"But she adored her mother."

"Believe me, I know. I learned a lot about that family. Agneta may have seemed a broken woman when Zalachenko beat her black-and-blue, but when it came to her children, she was a fighter. She was offered money. She was threatened. She was sent nasty letters with all sorts of official stamps on them. But she refused to give up her child. 'Lisbeth stays with me,' she said. 'I will never abandon her.' She fought tooth and nail, and the process went on for so long that eventually it became too late to separate the girls. But for Rakel it had become a matter of principle, an obsession. I was called in to mediate."

"What happened?"

"To begin with, I was more and more impressed with Agneta. We saw a lot of each other at the time. You could almost say that we became friends. I took up her case. I really did fight to help her keep Lisbeth. But Rakel would not let herself be beaten so easily, and one evening she showed up with Benjamin Fors, her flunky."

"Who?"

"He's basically a social worker, but he's done Rakel's dirty work for ages. Martin Steinberg arranged for him to work with her. Benjamin is more brawn than brain and he's unswervingly loyal. Rakel has helped him through some difficult times, including when he lost his son in a car accident, and in return he'll do anything for her. I should think he's almost sixty by now. He's six and a half feet tall and super-fit, and has this slightly comical, good-natured look about him, complete with bushy eyebrows. But he can turn rough, if Rakel wants, and this particular evening on Lundagatan . . ."

Hilda paused and swallowed some more rosé.

"Yes?"

"It was in October, and cold," she said. "Carl Seger had just been killed, and I was away attending a memorial service, which was probably no coincidence. The operation had been carefully planned. Camilla was sleeping over at a friend's; only Agneta and Lisbeth were at home. Lisbeth must have been six. Their birthday's in April, right? She and Agneta were in the kitchen, having tea and toast. There was a storm blowing outside on Skinnarviksberget."

"How do you know all these details?"

"I've heard it from three different sources: our own official report—which is no doubt the least reliable—and also Agneta's version. We talked for hours after it happened."

"And the third?"

"Lisbeth herself."

Blomkvist looked at her in surprise. He knew how secretive Salander was about her own life. He had certainly never heard a word about the episode, not even from Holger Palmgren.

"When was that?" he said.

"About ten years ago now," she said. "It was a time in Lisbeth's life when she wanted to know more about her mother, and I told her what I knew. I told her that Agneta had been strong and intelligent, and I saw that made Lisbeth happy. We spent a long time chatting at my place in Skanstull, and in the end she told me this story. It was like a punch to the gut."

"Did Lisbeth know you belonged to the Registry?"

Hilda reached for the third bottle of rosé.

"No. She didn't even know Rakel's name. She thought it was just some compulsory measure imposed by the social services. She had no idea about the twins project, and I . . ."

Hilda fingered her glass.

"You held back the truth."

"There were people watching me, Mikael. I was bound by professional secrecy; I knew what had happened to Carl."

"I understand," he said, and to a degree he really did. It could not have been easy for Hilda, and it was brave of her to be sitting there talking openly with him. There was no cause for him to judge her.

"Please go on," he said.

"That evening on Lundagatan, there was a storm, as I said. Zalachenko had been there the previous day and Agneta was covered in bruises and had pains in her stomach and between her legs. She was in the kitchen drinking tea with Lisbeth. They were enjoying a quiet moment together. Then the doorbell rang, and as you can imagine they were terrified. They thought the father was back."

"But it was Rakel."

"It was Rakel and Benjamin, which was not much better. They solemnly announced that under the terms of such and such a law, they had come to fetch Lisbeth, for her own protection. Then things turned nasty."

"In what way?"

"Lisbeth must have felt terribly betrayed. She was only a little girl, after all, and when Rakel had first come and given her different tests to do, she had also given her hope. Say what you will about Rakel, but she does have an aura of authority about her. She's even a bit regal, with her straight back and that fiery birthmark on her throat. I think Lisbeth had dreamed that she would be able to help them keep her father away from their home. But that evening she realized that Rakel was like all the rest—"

"Another person who did nothing to stop the abuse and the violence."

"And now on top of it all Rakel was going to take Lisbeth away for *her* own safety. *Her* safety! Rakel even had a syringe filled with Stesolid. She meant to sedate the girl and carry her off. Lisbeth went crazy. She bit Rakel's finger, climbed on a table in the living room, managed to open the window and just threw herself out. They were only one floor up, but it was still an eight-foot drop to the ground and Lisbeth was a skinny little thing. She had no shoes, just socks, jeans and some sort of sweater, and there was a full-blown storm raging outside. She landed in a crouch, fell forward and banged her head, but she jumped to her feet and ran off into the darkness. She ran and ran, all the way down towards Slussen and into Gamla Stan, until she got to Mynttorget and the Royal Palace, frozen and soaked through. I think she slept in a stairwell that night. She stayed away for two days." Hilda fell silent. "Could I ask you . . ."

"What?"

"I'm feeling so miserable today. Could you run down to reception and bring back some cold beers? I need something cooler than this dishwater," she said, pointing at the bottles.

Blomkvist looked at her with concern. But he nodded and went down to reception. To his surprise, he not only bought six cold bottles of Carlsberg, he also sent off an encrypted message, which may not have been such a good idea. But he felt that he owed it to her.

```
<The woman with the birthmark on her
throat who wanted to send you away when
you were small is named Rakel Greitz. She
was a psychoanalyst and psychiatrist and
one of the people in charge of the Reg-
istry.>
```

Then he carried the beers up to Hilda and listened to the rest of the story.

CHAPTER 17

June 21–22

Salander was in the Opera Bar, trying to celebrate her release from prison. It was not going well. A group of silly, giggling girls with wreaths in their hair, probably a bachelorette party, were at a table behind her. Their laughter cut right through her as she looked out at Kungsträdgården. A man walked by outside with a black dog.

She had chosen the place because of its cocktails, and maybe also for the atmosphere and bustle, but it was not really doing it for her. Occasionally her eyes scanned the faces in the room; she could bring someone back to her place—maybe a man, possibly a woman.

All sorts of things went through her mind, and she kept looking at her mobile. She had had an e-mail from Hanna Balder, August's mother. August, the autistic boy with the photographic memory who had witnessed the murder of his father, was now back in the country after a long stay abroad,

and according to Hanna was "doing well, all things considered." That sounded promising, although Salander could not
help thinking about his gaze, those glazed eyes which had
not only seen much more than they should, but also seemed
to be retreating into a shell. She reflected, not without pain,
that certain things are seared into your brain. You can never
shake them off, you have to live with them. She remembered
how, when they were hiding in that small house on Ingarö,
the boy had banged his head over and over on the kitchen
table in a fit of wild frustration. For a fleeting moment she
felt like doing the same: smashing her head against the bar
counter. But all she did was clench her jaw.

She noticed a man coming her way. Dressed in a blue suit
and with slicked-back dark-blond hair, he sat down next to
her and looked with exaggerated concern at her split lip and
bruised face: "My God, who did you manage to upset?" He
would have received a withering look at the least, but at that
moment her mobile buzzed. It was an encrypted message
from Blomkvist which set her even more on edge. She got
up, tossed some hundred-kronor notes onto the bar and
gave the man a shove on her way out.

The city was shimmering and music was playing in the
distance. It was a glorious summer evening for anyone in the
mood for it. Salander noticed none of that. She looked ready
to kill. She searched on her mobile for the name she had been
given and soon realized that Rakel Greitz had protected-
identity status. That in itself was not a problem. We all
leave traces, for example when we buy things online and are
careless about giving out our addresses. But as she crossed
Strömbron on her way to Gamla Stan, she was unable to do

anything, not even hack a site where Rakel Greitz might have bought a book. Instead, she thought about dragons.

She thought about how, as a little girl, she had run shoeless through Stockholm until she got to the Royal Palace and hurried past a tall pillar towards a cathedral which was lit up in the darkness. That was Storkyrkan. She knew nothing about it then, she was simply drawn to it. She was freezing cold, her socks were soaked through and she needed to get some rest and warmth. She ran into an inner courtyard and walked through the side doors of the cathedral. The ceiling was so high that it seemed to reach to the sky. She remembered how she had gone further in so that people would stop staring at her. And that's when she saw the statue. Only later did she realize that it was famous, said to represent Saint George killing a dragon and rescuing a damsel in distress. But that was not something Salander knew then or would even have cared about. She saw something entirely different in the statue that evening: an assault.

The dragon—she still remembered it clearly—was on its back with a spear through its body, while a man with an indifferent, blank expression struck the animal with his sword. The dragon was defenceless and alone, and that had made Salander think of her mother. With every muscle in her body she felt that she wanted to save her. Or better still, she wanted to be the dragon herself and fight back, and breathe fire, and pull the rider down from his horse and kill him. Because the knight was clearly none other than Zala, her father. He was the evil destroying their lives.

But that was not all. There was another figure depicted in the statue, a woman one could easily miss because she was standing to one side. She wore a crown on her head and was holding out her hands, as if reading a book. The strangest thing was that she was so calm, as if she was looking out over a meadow or an ocean rather than a slaughter. At the time, Salander could not recognize the woman as the maiden being rescued. In her eyes, the woman was ice cold and indifferent. She looked exactly like the woman with the birthmark from whom she had just escaped and who, like all the others, was allowing the violence and the abuse to continue at her home.

That was how she saw it. Not only were her mother and the dragon being tormented, but the world was looking on heartlessly. Salander felt a deep revulsion for the knight and the woman in the statue, and she had run back out into the rain and the storm, shaking with cold and fury. It was all so long ago and yet remarkably present.

Now, many years later, as she crossed the bridge to Gamla Stan on her way home, she muttered the name to herself: *Rakel Greitz*. This was her link to the Registry. She had been looking for it ever since Palmgren came to visit her at Flod-berga.

Hilda opened a beer. By now her left eye was wandering a little. At times she lost her train of thought and seemed gripped by remorse, at others she was astonishingly focused, as if the alcohol had merely sharpened her wits.

"I don't know what Lisbeth did after she ran out of Storkyrkan, only that she managed to beg some money at Central Station the next day and pinched a pair of over-sized shoes and a down jacket at Åhléns. Agneta was beside herself with worry, of course, and I . . . I was furious and told Rakel that she would jeopardize the whole project if she went through with her plan. In the end, she gave in. She left Lisbeth alone. But she never stopped hating her. I think she was involved when Lisbeth was locked up at St. Stefan's."

"Why do you say that?"

"Because her good friend Peter Teleborian worked at the clinic."

"They were *friends*?"

"Rakel was Teleborian's psychoanalyst. They shared a belief in repressed memory and other similarly ridiculous theories, and he was very loyal to her. But the interesting thing is that Rakel not only hated Lisbeth, she also became more and more frightened of her. I believe she recognized, long before anyone else did, just what Lisbeth was capable of."

"Do you think Rakel had anything to do with Holger Palmgren's death?"

Hilda glanced down at her shoes. Voices could be heard outside on the quay.

"She's merciless. I can vouch for that more than anyone. The rumour mill she set in motion when I decided to leave the Registry just about did me in. But murder? I'm not sure. I would find that hard to believe. At least I'd rather not believe it, still less . . ."

Hilda pulled a face. Blomkvist waited for her to continue.

". . . still less can I believe it about Daniel Brolin. He's such a vulnerable, gifted boy. He would never harm anyone, least of all his twin brother. They were made to be together."

Blomkvist was about to answer that this is exactly what

people say when their friends or acquaintances commit the most heinous crimes. "We just don't understand." "It's not possible." "Not him/not her, surely?" And yet it happens. We have the highest opinion of someone and then that person is blinded by rage and the unthinkable happens.

But he said nothing and tried not to jump to conclusions. There were any number of possible scenarios. They talked for a while longer and then ran through a few practical details, including how they would communicate over the coming days. He urged her to take every care and to look after herself, and then he checked his mobile to see if there was a late train back to Stockholm. He had fifteen minutes. He packed away his voice recorder, gave her a hug and rushed off. On his way to the station he tried once more to reach Salander. He both needed and wanted to see her. It had been too long.

On the train he watched a shaky video his sister had sent him in which a furious Bashir Kazi appeared to confess to being behind the murder of Jamal Chowdhury.

Not only had the video gone viral, it had also triggered a flurry of activity in police headquarters on Bergsgatan. This was intensified when, soon after, two sophisticated hand-movement analyses were sent to Bublanski of the murder squad. Those analyses were also the reason a young man with a runner's physique and a lost look in his eyes was slumped in one of the interview rooms on the seventh floor, together with his imam, Hassan Ferdousi.

Bublanski had known Ferdousi reasonably well for some time now. Ferdousi and Bublanski's fiancée, Farah Sharif, had been students together. He was also one of those leaders who worked to encourage closer interaction between the various religious communities in the face of the country's rising anti-Semitism and Islamophobia. Bublanski did not always see eye to eye with Ferdousi, especially over the question of Israel, but he had great respect for him, and he had greeted the imam with a reverential bow.

He heard that Ferdousi had helped to bring about a breakthrough in the investigation into Jamal Chowdhury's death, and he was grateful but also dejected. It revealed the extent of his colleagues' incompetence and Bublanski was overloaded with work as it was.

Fru Torell had at last gotten in touch to say that someone had indeed come to see her in connection with the papers she had handed over to Holger Palmgren. A certain Professor Martin Steinberg—a respected citizen, apparently, who had worked for both the social services and the government. Steinberg told her that some individuals had already gotten themselves into difficulties because of those papers, and made her swear before God and the late Professor Caldin that she would never again talk about them, nor should she mention Steinberg's visit, "for the safety and well-being of our former patients." Steinberg then took away her backup, a USB stick. Torell did not remember what had been on it, other than the medical notes on Salander. But Bublanski was uneasy, especially since he had not been able to get in touch with Steinberg.

Bublanski wanted to spend more time trying to unravel the mystery, but he would have to forget about it all for a while. He had been asked to handle this interview, even though he hardly had the time for it. He looked at his watch. It was 8:45 a.m. Another glorious day that would pass him by. He looked at the young man sitting quietly next to the imam, waiting for his court-appointed defence lawyer. His name was Khalil Kazi and he had apparently confessed to murdering Jamal Chowdhury out of love for his sister. Out of *love*? It was incomprehensible. But that was Bublanski's unhappy lot in life. People did terrible things and it was his responsibility to understand why and to bring them to justice. He looked at the imam and the young man, and for some reason he thought of the ocean.

Blomkvist woke up in Salander's double bed on Fiskargatan. It had not exactly been his plan, but it was his own fault.

He had turned up on her doorstep and been let in with a silent nod. Admittedly, at first they just worked and shared information. But it had been an eventful day for both of them, and in the end Blomkvist could no longer keep his mind on what they were doing. He wiped the dried blood from her lip and asked about the dragon in Storkyrkan. It was 1:30 in the morning and the summer sky was already brightening as they sat on her sofa.

"Was that the reason you had the dragon tattooed on your back?"

"No," she said.

Clearly she did not want to talk about it and he had no wish to press her. He was tired and was getting up to go home when Salander pulled him onto the sofa again and placed a hand on his chest.

"I had it done because it helped me," she said.

"Helped you? How?"

"I thought about the dragon when I was strapped to the bed at St. Stefan's."

"What were you thinking?"

"That it looked helpless with the spear stuck in its body, but that one day it would rise up, breathe fire and destroy its enemies. That's what kept me going." Her eyes were dark and apprehensive.

She and Blomkvist looked at each other, and they might have been about to kiss. But Salander seemed miles away and she turned to gaze out over the city and at a train which was rolling into Central Station. She said that she had tracked down Rakel Greitz via an online store in Sollentuna which sold disinfectants. Blomkvist murmured his appreciation, although it worried him. Soon afterwards, the heat having gone out of the moment, his head started to droop and he asked if he could lie down for a while on her bed. Salander had no objection. She went to bed herself a little while later and fell asleep.

Now, in the morning, Blomkvist heard sounds from the kitchen. He dragged himself out of bed and turned on the coffee machine. He watched Salander retrieve a Hawaiian pizza from the microwave and sit at the kitchen table. He rummaged around in her refrigerator, and swore because there was nothing else to eat. Then he remembered that she had just gotten out of prison, and there had been more than enough for her to do on her first day of freedom. He contented himself with coffee and tuned in to P1 on the kitchen radio. He caught the end of the daily news bulletin and listened to the forecast of record temperatures for the Stockholm area. He said good morning to Salander, who muttered something in return. She was wearing jeans and a black T-shirt, no make-up, and her swollen lip and the bruises on her face looked excruciatingly painful. Shortly afterwards they went down to the street together. They went their separate ways at Slussen. He told her to take it easy and she nodded.

He was on his way to Alfred Ögren Securities.

She was going to track down Rakel Greitz.

While Khalil Kazi was being questioned in the interview room, his defence lawyer, Harald Nilsson, sat poking nervously at the table with his pen. There were moments when Bublanski could hardly bear to listen. Khalil should have had a bright future; instead he had ruined everything.

It had been at the beginning of October, almost two years before.

After Faria had run away from the apartment in Sickla, she managed secretly to keep in touch with Khalil and told him that she intended to sever all links with the family. They arranged to meet at a café on Norra Bantorget so that she could say goodbye to her youngest brother. Khalil swore that he had not said a word to anybody, but the brothers must have tailed him. They dragged their sister into a car and took her back to Sickla. Faria spent the first few days tied up. They put duct tape over her mouth and a piece of cardboard across her chest saying "WHORE." Bashir and Ahmed beat her. They spat on her and let other men who came to the apartment do the same.

Khalil realized that Faria was no longer regarded as a sister, even a human being. Her body was no longer hers, and he was afraid he could guess what was in store for her. She would be taken to some remote place, beyond the reach of the police, where her blood would be shed to cleanse the family's honour. Occasionally they talked about how she might be saved through marriage to Qamar, but Khalil did not believe that. She had already been defiled. And how would they get her out of the country while keeping her under control?

Khalil was sure that Faria was facing certain death. He too had had his telephone taken away and was effectively a prisoner, so there was no way he could raise the alarm. In his despair he could only hope for a miracle. A small miracle did occur, or at least a measure of relief: They untied Faria's hands and got rid of the sign, and she was allowed to shower, eat in the kitchen and move around in the apartment without a veil. Presents were handed out, and it seemed as if Faria were to be given compensation for her suffering instead of harsher punishment.

The brothers gave her a radio and for Khalil they found a second-hand StairMaster, brought over by an acquaintance in Huddinge. That built up his strength. He had been missing his running—his freedom of movement, the power of his stride—and now he trained for hours on end. He began to see light at the end of the tunnel, even though he still expected the worst. Some days later Bashir and Ahmed came into his room and sat on the bed. Bashir was holding a pistol, but even so, the brothers did not appear angry. Both were wearing freshly ironed shirts in the same shade of blue. They smiled at him.

"We've got good news!" Bashir said.

Faria would be allowed to live, or rather she would be allowed to live as long as someone paid the price. Anything else would bring down the wrath of Allah, their honour would not be avenged and the stain would spread and poison them all. Khalil was given a choice: he could either die, together with his sister—or he must murder Jamal and thereby save the two of them. Khalil did not understand at first. He did not want to understand, he said. He just kept up his stepping on his StairMaster. So they put the choice to him again.

"But why me?" Khalil said. "I could never hurt anybody." He was utterly distraught.

Bashir explained that, of all the brothers, only Khalil was not known to the police. He had a good reputation. Above all, by doing this Khalil could atone for having failed the family.

At some point he must have answered yes, he would kill Jamal. He was desperate, caught in an impossible situation. He loved his sister, and his life was threatened.

But there was one detail Bublanski did not understand: Why had Khalil not called the police when he was let out of the apartment to carry out the murder? Khalil claimed he had planned to do exactly that. He was going to reveal everything and seek protection. But then he was bewildered and paralyzed, he said, by the precision with which the operation had been prepared. Others were also involved, Islamists who never let him out of their sight, and who missed no opportunity to tell him what a despicable person Jamal was. Jamal had a fatwa against him. He had been condemned to death by devout people in Bangladesh. He was worse than swine, and Jews and rats that spread the plague. He had besmirched the family's honour and that of his sister. Slowly but surely, Khalil was drawn into the darkness and driven to do the unthinkable. He pushed Jamal in front of the train. He was certainly not alone, but it was he who had run onto the platform and pushed him.

"I killed him," he said.

Faria Kazi was in the visitors' room in H Block of Flodberga. Inspector Sonja Modig and Annika Giannini were sitting facing her. The proceedings were tense and halting as Giannini replayed the poor-quality video in which Bashir appeared to confess to having been involved in Jamal Chowdhury's murder. Giannini explained hand-movement analyses and told her that Khalil had made a detailed statement confessing that he pushed Jamal under the train.

"He thought it was the only way to save you, Faria—and to save himself. He says he loves you."

Faria did not respond. She knew all of this already and she wanted to scream "*Loves* me? I *hate* him." She really did hate him. But Khalil was the reason she had kept her mouth shut for so long. However much Khalil may have hurt her, she still felt protective towards him. Mostly for their mother's sake, she thought. Once upon a time Faria had promised her that she would look after Khalil. But now there wasn't any family left to protect, was there? She steeled herself, then looked at the women and said:

"Is that Lisbeth Salander's voice in the film?"

"It is, yes."

"Is she OK?"

"She's OK. She's been fighting in your corner."

Faria swallowed. She drew herself up and began to talk. The atmosphere in the room was one of solemn anticipation, as always when, after a long silence, a witness or suspect decides to speak. Giannini and Modig were concentrating so hard that they did not hear the intercoms going off in the corridor and the rising agitation in the voices of the guards.

It was unbearably hot in the visitors' room. Modig mopped the sweat from her forehead and repeated what Faria had said, twice now, in two versions which were similar and yet not quite the same. Something still seemed to be missing.

"So you had the sense that your situation was improving. You thought your brothers were relenting, that you might be given some sort of freedom after all."

"I'm not sure what I thought," Faria said. "I was a wreck. But they did apologize. Bashir and Ahmed had never treated me like that before. They said they had gone too far. That they were ashamed. That all they wanted was for me to live a respectable life and that I had been punished enough. They gave me a radio."

"Did it occur to you at any stage that it might be a trap?"

"I thought that constantly. I'd read about other girls

who'd let themselves be lulled into a sense of security and then . . ."

"And then killed?"

"I realized that there was a real risk, not least because of Bashir's body language, which scared me. I hardly slept. I had a knot in my stomach. But I was also guilty of wishful thinking. You have to understand, it was the only way for me to bear it. I missed Jamal so much I was going crazy. More than anything I hoped, I believed Jamal was out there somewhere, fighting for me. I bided my time and told myself that things were improving. Khalil meanwhile kept working out on his StairMaster like an insane person. I heard that step machine thumping away all night long. *Swoosh, swoosh.* It was driving me mad. I have no idea how he could do it. He just wouldn't stop, and occasionally he'd come out of his room and hug me and say, 'I'm sorry, I'm sorry,' a hundred times over. I said I would look after him and make sure that Jamal and his friends protected us both, and maybe, I don't know . . . It's hard to say now, looking back."

"Try to be clear. It's important," Modig said, more sharply than usual.

Giannini looked at her watch and patted down her hair, and said angrily:

"Enough of that! If Faria's being unclear, it's because the situation itself was unclear. Under the circumstances I think she's being admirably clear."

"I'm simply trying to understand," Modig said. "Faria, you must have realized that something was about to happen. You say that Khalil was in a state of high tension. That he was exercising so hard there was nothing left of him."

"He was in a really bad way. He was a prisoner too. But I had the impression that he was beginning to feel better, and it was only afterwards that I remembered the look in his eye."

"And how *did* he look?"

"Desperate. Like a hunted animal. But at the time I didn't see it."

"You didn't hear your other brothers leave the apartment on the evening of October 23?"

"I was asleep, or at least trying to sleep. But I do remember that they came back in the middle of the night and were whispering in the kitchen. I couldn't hear what they were saying. The next day they gave me odd looks, and I took that as a good sign. It seemed to me that Jamal was somewhere nearby. I felt his presence. But as the hours passed this weird, tense atmosphere was building up. Evening came and then I saw Ahmed, just as I told you."

"You said he was by the window."

"There was something angry, something menacing about the way he stood there, and he was breathing heavily. I felt a weight on my chest. Ahmed said, 'He's dead.' I didn't understand who he was talking about. He tried again. 'Jamal's dead,' he said more loudly. I think I sank to my knees. I blacked out for a moment. I hadn't really taken it in."

"You were in shock," Giannini said.

"And yet an instant later, you found this incredible strength," Modig said.

"I've already explained that."

"She has, you know," Giannini said.

"I'd like to hear it again."

"Khalil was there all of a sudden," Faria said. "Or maybe

he'd been there all along. He cried out that he was the one who had killed Jamal, and that made even less sense. But he went on saying he'd done it for my sake, that they would have murdered *me* otherwise; he'd had to choose between me and Jamal. And that's when the strength came to me, that fury. I just lost it, and I went for Ahmed."

"Why not Khalil?"

"Because I . . ."

"Because you . . . ?"

"Because I must have understood, in spite of it all."

"What? That they'd used Khalil's love for you as a means of pressuring him into this terrible act?"

"That they'd driven him to it, that they'd destroyed his life along with mine and Jamal's, and that's why I flew into a blind rage. I went crazy. Can't you get that?"

"I can," Modig said. "Honestly I can. But there are other things I find more difficult to understand—for example, the fact that you refused to answer any questions during your police interviews. You said you wanted revenge. But you could have struck back also against Bashir, the biggest criminal of them all. With our help you could have had him put away for conspiracy to murder."

"But don't you understand?" Faria's voice broke.

"Don't we understand what?"

"My life ended with Jamal's. What would I gain by having Bashir or Khalil locked up as well? Khalil was the only one in the family who . . ."

"Go on."

"He was the only one I loved."

"But he killed the love of your life."

"I hated him. I loved him. I hated him. Is that so hard to understand?"

Giannini was just about to interrupt to say that Faria needed a break from the interview when there was a knock at the door. Rikard Fager wanted to have a word with Modig.

It was immediately clear that something serious had happened, that whatever it was had shaken the governor's confidence. Modig was irritated that he was being so long-winded. He would not get to the point, as if he intended to find excuses rather than to explain. He said there had been security guards and surveillance and even metal detectors. He said not to forget that Benito had been in a serious condition, having sustained injuries to her skull, a concussion, and a smashed jaw.

"She's escaped from the hospital, is that what you're trying to say?"

Fager was not to be put off: "No-one expected she would be able to leave the place." All visitors had been searched. Or at least should have been searched. But then something happened to the hospital's computer system. It crashed, and some of the medical equipment stopped working. The situation became serious. Doctors and nurses were running around all over the place, and just then three men in suits turned up. They told reception that they were there to visit another patient, an engineer from ABB apparently, who was on the same ward. Then things happened quickly. The men were armed with nunchakus. Fager, that idiot, started to explain that nunchakus were wooden sticks used in martial arts.

Modig waved it all away.

"What actually happened, for heaven's sake?"

"These men overpowered the security, hustled Benito out of the hospital and disappeared in a grey van with what turned out to be fake number plates. One of the men has been identified as Esbjörn Falk, of Svavelsjö M.C., the criminal motorcycle gang."

"I know what Svavelsjö M.C. is," Modig said. "So what's been done so far?"

"There's a nationwide alert issued on Benito. We've told the media. Alvar Olsen's under protection."

"And Lisbeth Salander?"

"What about her?"

"Idiot," she muttered, then said she had to leave right away because the situation required immediate action.

On her way out through prison security, she called Bublanski and told him about Benito and about Faria Kazi's interview. He quoted an ancient Jewish saying back to her: "One can see into a man's eyes, but not into his heart."

CHAPTER 18

June 22

Dan Brody was late for work again today. He was agitated and listless, haunted by dark thoughts. But he was better dressed for the weather in a light-blue linen suit, a T-shirt and sneakers. The sun beat down as he walked along Birger Jarlsgatan thinking about Leo. All of a sudden he heard a car's screeching halt, and he staggered, just as he had at the Fotografiska Museum.

For a moment he struggled for breath. Yet he kept walking and became reimmersed in his thoughts. Those days in December, after their first weekend together, were still the happiest of his life, in spite of moments of pain and resentment. He and Leo had talked and played music without interruption. But they never left the building together, only ever one at a time. For they had devised a plan. They were going to confront Greitz and she must not suspect anything.

DECEMBER, ONE AND A HALF YEARS EARLIER

Leo cancelled his Christmas lunch at a restaurant with Greitz and invited her over to his place at 1:00 p.m. on December 23 instead. In the meantime, the brothers enjoyed playing games with their identities. Out and about in town they were both Leo, and that amused them enormously. Dan borrowed Leo's suits, shirts and shoes. He had his hair cut like Leo's and practised being Leo with role-play. Leo kept saying that Dan was the more convincing of the two of them. "You're more Leo than I am!"

Leo did only short days at the office. One evening he went out with his colleagues to Riche but even then he was back early to tell Dan that he'd come *this close*—he showed Dan with a thumb and forefinger—to revealing their secret to Malin.

"But you didn't say anything?"

"Oh, no. She seems to think I'm in love."

"Is she upset?"

"No, not really."

Dan knew that Leo had a flirtation going with Malin Frode, who was getting divorced and would soon be leaving Alfred Ögren. But Leo always claimed it wasn't serious. He thought she had her eye on Blomkvist, the journalist. And anyway, Leo didn't think he loved her either. They were just fooling around, he said. Mostly.

He and Leo were always swapping ideas and memories and gossip. They made a pact which seemed unbreakable, and rehearsed in detail what they would do when Greitz arrived, how Dan would hide himself and Leo would question her, cautiously at first, and then more aggressively.

The day before the lunch, December 22, a Friday, Malin was giving a farewell party at her home on Bondegatan. Just like Dan, Leo disliked parties in small spaces. There was too much noise. He could not bring himself to go, he said. He had another idea. He would show Dan his office at Alfred Ögren. The building would probably be deserted because most of the staff would be at Malin's, and no-one worked late on a Friday evening, especially one so close to Christmas. Dan thought it sounded like a good idea. He was curious about Leo's work.

At around 8:00 p.m. they left the apartment ten minutes apart. Leo first with one bottle of good Burgundy and another of Champagne in his briefcase. Dan left ten minutes later, also dressed in Leo's clothes, but in a paler suit and a darker overcoat. It was cold. It was snowing. They were going to celebrate.

They planned to go public with their story the day after their meeting with Greitz and, even though Dan was against it, Leo had promised him a substantial sum of money. There would be no more inequality between them, he said. And no more boring investment banking. He would leave his job and the gloominess at Alfred Ögren so that they could begin playing music together. The evening got off to a wonderful start. They drank and toasted each other, and the air was full of promise. "Tomorrow," they said. "Tomorrow!"

But something went wrong. Dan thought it was because of Leo's office. There were Renaissance angels on the ceiling, turn-of-the-century art on the walls, and gilt handles on the chests of drawers. It was so opulent and vulgar that Dan became provocative. He needled his brother:

"Looks like you have it made," he said.

Leo agreed. "I know. I feel ashamed. I've never liked this room, it was my father's."

Dan pushed things a step further. "You were hell-bent on bringing me here though, weren't you? You wanted to show off and ram all this down my throat."

"Oh, no, I'm sorry," Leo said. "I just wanted you to see my life. I know it's unfair."

"*Unfair*?" Dan raised his voice.

The word was no longer enough. It was obscene. It was beyond belief. They argued back and forth, Dan accusing Leo, then calming down and apologizing, before going on the offensive again. And then—it was hard to know at what point—Dan had gone too far. The resentment that had been lying beneath the surface, causing tension from the beginning but kept in check by the delirious joy of their meeting, now broke out. Not only did it tear open a wound between them, it seemed to cast the whole situation in a new light.

"You've had all of this, yet all you do is complain. 'Mamma doesn't understand me, Pappa didn't have a clue. I wasn't allowed to play music. It was so tough, poor little rich me.' I don't want to hear another word. Don't you get that? I was beaten and I went hungry. I had nothing, absolutely nothing, and you . . ."

Dan was shaking all over, he had no idea what had come over him. Perhaps they were both drunk. He accused Leo of being a shit and an insincere bastard, a show-off who flaunted his depressions. He was about to smash a pair of Chinese vases, but instead he walked out, slamming the door behind him.

He spent hours wandering the streets, freezing cold and crying. Eventually he ended up back at the af Chapman youth hostel at Skeppsholmen and spent the night there. But at 11:00 the next morning he went back to Leo's apartment on Floragatan and hugged him and they both apologized. They turned their attentions to preparing themselves for the meeting with Greitz. Still, something unresolved hung in the air which would affect what was about to happen.

A year and a half later Dan was thinking of that time as he turned into Smålandsgatan, and his face showed it. He passed the Konstnärsbaren restaurant and emerged on Norrmalmstorg. The weather was hot for ten in the morning. He was not feeling all that well, and was certainly not looking forward to meeting Sweden's most famous investigative journalist.

Rakel Greitz and Benito Andersson, who had nothing in common save their sadism and the fact that neither was currently in good physical health, were both looking forward to meeting Lisbeth Salander. Neither knew who the other was, and if they should have happened to meet they would have regarded each other with contempt. But they were equally single-minded and equally determined to get Salander out of the picture. And they each had their networks. Benito was associated with that particular chapter of Svavelsjö M.C., which from time to time received information from Salander's sister, Camilla, and her group of hackers. Greitz could rely on backup from her organization, which had its own technologically savvy resources as well.

Above all, Greitz had her willpower and her vigilance, despite the cancer. She had for the time being taken up residence in a hotel on Kungsholmen to keep anyone from following her home. She was well aware that things were going badly. She had foreseen it, in fact. Ever since December 23, two Christmases ago, when everything had fallen apart. At the time, she had done what she had done because she saw no choice. It had been a bold gamble on her part, and now she stood ready once more.

She would have preferred to start with Salander and von Kanterborg. But the two women were impossible to track down, so she decided to deal first with Daniel Brolin. He was the weak link. She came walking along Hamngatan, past NK department store, dressed in a thin grey coat and skirt and a black cotton turtleneck. Despite the nausea and pain, she felt strong. But the heat was getting to her. What had *happened* to Sweden? When she was young there had never been a summer like this one. This was tropical. It was insane. She felt hot and sticky, but she pulled herself together and drew her shoulders back. Further down the street, as she passed two men in blue overalls digging a hole at the edge of the pavement, she caught the smell of drains in the stifling, stagnant air. She thought the men looked overweight and ugly. She walked on to Norrmalmstorg and was about to reach

Alfred Ögren's building when she made a deeply troubling discovery: Mikael Blomkvist the journalist, whom she had already encountered on the stairs at Hilda's place in Skanstull, now on his way into the firm's offices.

Greitz took a step into the shadows and called Benjamin.

Dan Brody, or Leo Mannheimer, as he called himself nowadays, was sitting in his far-too-elegant office and felt his pulse pounding and the walls closing in on him. What was he to do? His "junior adviser"—as his male secretary liked to style himself—had informed him that Mikael Blomkvist was in reception. Dan had said that he would be ready for him in twenty minutes.

Even as he said it he knew it sounded impolite. But—as so often in the past—he needed time to think. Who knows, maybe Blomkvist would help him get even with Greitz. Whatever the cost might be.

DECEMBER, ONE AND A HALF YEARS EARLIER

It was snowing that day at Floragatan as they waited for Rakel Greitz. Dan apologized again and again.

"It's OK," Leo said. "I had a visitor at the office yesterday after you left."

"Who was that?"

"Malin. We finished the Champagne. It wasn't a great success. I wasn't at my best. I was in the middle of writing something. Would you like to see?"

Dan nodded. Leo got up from the piano and left the room. He came back a minute later with a sheet of paper inside a plastic folder. He looked solemn and burdened by guilt. With a slow, deliberate gesture he handed over the document, which was sand-coloured and lightly textured with a watermark at the top.

"I think it needs to be witnessed," he said.

The handwriting was neat and full of flourishes. The document stated that Leo was hereby giving half of all his assets to Dan.

"Jesus!" Dan said.

"I'm seeing my lawyer after Christmas," Leo said. "Given the circumstances, it should all go smoothly. I don't even see it as a gift. You're getting what should have been yours a long time ago."

Dan was silent. He knew he should be throwing his arms around his brother and saying, "It's too much, it's crazy, you're being far too generous." But what was written on the document did not make him feel any better, or the situation any clearer, and initially he could not understand why. He felt oversensitive and ungrateful. Then he decided there was something passive-aggressive about the gift. The money was being given to him from a position of overwhelming advantage, and however grand the gesture, it was also diminishing.

So he said in a resolute voice: "I can't accept it."

He saw despair in Leo's eyes.

"But why not?"

"It doesn't work like that. You can't fix it that easily."

"I didn't think I needed to fix anything. I just want to do the right thing. I'm not interested in the damn money anyway."

"Not *interested*?"

Dan went crazy, even though some part of him must have realized how absurd it was. He had been handed tens of millions of kronor, which would fundamentally change his life. Yet he felt offended and angry. It could have been because of their argument the day before, or because he had been drinking and had hardly slept. It could have been because of any number of things.

"You just don't get it," he yelled. "You can't say that to someone who's always lived a marginal existence. It's too late, Leo. Too late!"

"No, it's not! We can begin again."

"It's just too late."

"Stop!" Leo shouted back. "You're being unfair."

"I feel like I'm being bought. Do you understand that? Bought!"

He was going too far and he knew it, and it hurt when Leo did not come back at him with the same fury. Instead Leo simply answered sadly:

"I know."

"What do you know?"

"Those people destroyed almost everything. I hate them for it. But still, we found each other. That's what's important, isn't it?"

There was such despair in his voice that Dan muttered:

"I'm grateful of course, but . . ."

He got no further. He regretted the "but" and was about to say something else, like "Sorry, I'm an idiot." He remembered it so well afterwards. They were on the verge of a reconciliation, and would no doubt have found each other again, given time. Instead they heard sounds in the hallway, footsteps, and then silence. It was a minute before midday. Rakel Greitz was not due for an hour and Leo had not even set the table.

"Hide," he whispered.

Leo put away the document, and Dan went into one of the bedrooms and closed the door.

Leo had always been a source of worry, and not only because of the business with Carl Seger. He had been unpredictable of late. She thought it might have something to do with Madeleine Bard. Losing Madeleine had made him suspicious. So Greitz wondered what was up when he cancelled their Christmas lunch and invited her instead to his apartment.

She knew everything about Leo. She knew, for example, that like many bachelors he did not like to cook or invite anyone over, especially not anyone with whom he did not feel entirely comfortable. Greitz had therefore decided to show up early, with the excuse that she wanted to help in the kitchen. But in fact what she wanted to know was whether something had happened, or if he had discovered anything about his adoption.

As she stepped out of the lift into the hallway with its painted blue ceiling, she heard agitated voices coming from inside the apartment, and they were strangely alike. Suddenly the voices stopped and she knew that whoever they belonged to was aware of her presence. Leo's hearing was quite exceptional. She was shaken to realize that something really was amiss. She texted Benjamin:

```
<At Leo's at Floragatan. Need your
help.>
```

She added:

```
<Bring my doctor's bag, with everything
in it!>
```

Then she drew herself up and knocked, ready with her warmest Christmas smile. But she didn't need it. Leo was already beaming in the doorway and, as always, he kissed her on both cheeks and helped her off with her coat, as he had been brought up to do. He was far too tactful to point out that she was an hour early.

"You're looking as elegant as ever, Rakel. What a Christmas this is going to be!" he said.

He's playing his part well, she thought. She only detected traces of tension in his face after studying him very carefully. He might have been able to deceive her, had things been different. But she had keen eyes. He had been careless,

which no doubt he knew himself: A moment before there
had been voices, and now he was on his own. And there was
a guitar lying on the sofa.

"How's Viveka?" she said.

"I don't think she's got much longer."

"Poor thing."

"It's just awful."

Bullshit, she thought. *I bet you're glad the bitch is finally
on her way out.*

"When both parents are gone, there's only you left," she
said, touching his arm. She wanted to reassure him, to show
her sympathy, and at the same time hide her suspicion. But
that was a miscalculation. Leo shuddered, evidently affected
by the physical contact, and there was a flash of anger in
his eyes. For a moment she felt frightened and looked again
at the guitar. She decided to let things rest for a while. She
wanted to give Benjamin time to pack her doctor's bag and
make his way over, so she kept the conversation going for
another ten minutes, but then she could stand it no longer.

"Who's here?"

"Who do you think?" Leo said.

She had no idea, she told him. But that was a lie. Things
were beginning to fall into place, and she could see how
tense Leo now was, how he was looking at her as he never
had before. She realized she would have to strike hard, and
mercilessly, before Daniel Brolin appeared from wherever
he was hiding.

CHAPTER 19

June 22

Rakel Greitz was not at home on Karlbergsvägen and
Salander decided to bide her time. She took the tunnelbana
back to Slussen and then walked along Götgatan. She had
heard from Giannini that Benito had been sprung from Örebro hospital, and so she was on her guard. She was always
on her guard. Life in prison had made her, if anything, more
careful, but even so she might be underestimating the danger she was in. There were more alliances after her than she
realized. Sinister forces from the past were mustering their
followers, exchanging information and perhaps agreeing to
work together.

It was a scalding June day and life in the city seemed to
have slowed down. People were mooching about, window-
shopping or sitting out on the terraces of cafés and restaurants. Salander went on up towards Fiskargatan. There was
a buzzing in her pocket. An encrypted text from Blomkvist.

```
<Leo is Daniel. I'm as good as certain.>
```

She wrote:

```
<Is he talking?>
```

He answered:

```
<Don't know yet. Will get back to you.>
```

She considered making her way to Alfred Ögren's offices on Norrmalmstorg to see how Blomkvist was getting on there but decided against it. She wanted first to get hold of Rakel Greitz, or to see if she could trace her to another address. Her watchfulness remained high as she walked up Fiskar- gatan towards her apartment building, and she wondered if it really was such a good idea to go home. There was no official record of her living there—the apartment was regis- tered to Irene Nesser, an identity she occasionally assumed. She had put up a number of smokescreens, but the net was closing in. People were beginning to recognize her. She was something of a celebrity these days, and she hated that. Also, two people—Kalle Fucking Blomkvist and the N.S.A. agent Ed the Ned—had tracked her down here before, and word does tend to get out. She should sell the damn place. It was too big for her anyway. She should move far away, maybe even take off right now.

But it was too late. She realized it the moment she saw a grey van facing in her direction further up the street. There was nothing outwardly remarkable about it. It was an old model, parked perfectly normally by the curb. Still, it made her suspicious. And now it was rolling towards her. She turned back down the hill, but she had gone only a few paces when a bearded man suddenly appeared from a doorway and put a wet rag over her face. She felt sick, but above all she felt stupid and careless. And now she was just about to pass out. The street and the buildings danced around her, she had no strength to resist. She managed only to pull out her mobile and whisper the codeword—"Harpy"—before she felt herself falling and was lifted in through the back doors of the van. Her vision was blurred, but she detected a sweet perfume which was only too familiar.

DECEMBER, ONE AND A HALF YEARS EARLIER

Dan heard the voices in the drawing room and realized that nothing was going as planned. Greitz seemed to have seen straight through them and the element of surprise that they had hoped for was no longer an option. He decided to go in and confront her.

But Dan had underestimated the effect that Greitz would have on him. Her physical presence cast him right back to his childhood self. He remembered her standing on the upper floor of the farm all those years ago, observing him coldly as he played his guitar. She must have been comparing him to Leo even then, studying their similarities, and at this realization he lost his composure.

"You know who I am, I guess," he said, wild with rage. He took a step forward, but he could not help still feeling small.

Greitz stood her ground, astonishingly composed.

"Of course I do," she said. "How are you?"

"We want to know exactly what happened to us," Dan shouted at her, and only then did she back away. But she remained calm as she adjusted her collar and looked at her watch. Even though she was nervous—the twitch around her mouth made that evident—she had a stature and an icy cool about her, like a schoolmistress, and this made Dan feel that it was he rather than she who was about to be castigated.

"You need to calm down," she said.

"No way," Dan said. "You've got a lot of explaining to do."

"And I will explain. I will. But first I need to know if you've gone to the press." When there was no response, Greitz went on: "I do understand that you're upset. But it would be dangerous for the story to get out now, before you know the full picture. It's not what you imagine."

"We haven't gone public—yet," Dan said, and wondered straight-away if that was a mistake, the more so when he saw a hint of satisfaction in Greitz's face. He looked at Leo.

Leo was standing there, silent, feet planted, giving him no clue as to how he should act. How could he stop Greitz taking the initiative?

"I'm an old woman now," she said, "and I'm having terrible stomach pains. Forgive me for being so frank. Is it OK if I sit down? Then I'll tell you whatever you want to know."

"Go ahead," Leo said eventually. "Make yourself comfortable. We want answers to all our questions."

Greitz began hesitantly, hoping that Benjamin would show up before she had to give away anything that really mattered, or was forced to tell any ill-considered lies. Leo and Daniel sat opposite her, each in his own armchair, and glared at her, wanting answers. Despite the tension and the air of crisis, she was amazed at how astoundingly alike the brothers were, more than was common in identical twins of their age. The fact that they had the same haircut and wore the same kind of clothes made the similarity yet more striking.

"Here's how it was," she said. "We found ourselves in an extremely difficult situation. We had reports from several children's homes and hospitals about identical twins whose parents were not able to take care of them."

"Who's 'we'?" Daniel broke in, and even though his voice was angry and full of hate, she welcomed any interruption. She said—on a sudden inspiration—that she had been given something, she had it in her coat, which would perhaps help them to understand the situation. Should she

fetch it? She wondered if she was being even remotely credible. But they let her go, and that filled her with contempt.
Daniel and Leo were weak and pathetic, weren't they?
When she got to the hall, she coughed to cover the sound
of her unlocking the front door. She then made a pretence
of looking for something in her coat pocket, and exclaimed:
"Hopeless!"

She came back to the sofa, shaking her head, and went
on talking in vague terms. This exasperated Leo, and when
she casually mentioned Carl Seger his blood rose, and
he looked almost unhinged. He called her a monster and
demanded that she explain what had happened to Carl.
That really frightened her, because she remembered the fits
of rage which both boys had manifested when they were
young. In the end, Leo's outburst turned out to be a good
thing because at that moment Benjamin appeared. The
shouting must have stiffened his resolve, because he strode
in without knocking and grabbed hold of Leo from behind.
Meanwhile, Greitz bent to dig around in the doctor's bag
which Benjamin had dropped at her feet. Leo cried out
for help and Daniel made a rush for Benjamin. She knew
she needed to be resolute. Quickly, quickly, she rummaged
through the medication in the bag—Stesolid, opiates, morphine, the lot—and then . . . a chill ran through her: pan-
curonium bromide, a synthetic curare to mimic the extract
used on poison arrows. That would be too brutal. But
wait . . . there was also physostigmine, an antidote which
could either wholly or partly neutralize its effect. She had
an idea, inspired by an accusation Daniel had spat out during their conversation, which suggested that he harbored a

deep bitterness. It was a bold and wild idea. She pulled on her latex gloves.

Benjamin was immovable as ever and had a firm hold on Leo, who was screaming as Daniel tried to tear him free. She prepared a syringe. It took an extra moment to get the dose right. She realized she would have to inject straight into the muscle—there was no time to find a vein—but perhaps there was an advantage in that. At least, that's what she told herself as she jabbed the needle through Leo's sweater. He looked at her in shock while Daniel bawled: "What are you doing? What the *fuck* are you doing?"

She grimaced. The neighbours below must be wondering about the racket, and if they came up Leo might already be convulsing; he would begin to suffocate as soon as his respiratory muscles ceased to function. The situation was critical and she was in danger. She had crossed yet another line, and more than ever she needed to keep her wits about her. In her most authoritative doctor's voice she said:

"Calm down now, both of you. I've only given him a sedative, nothing more. Breathe, Leo, breathe. Good! You'll soon feel better. We've got to talk like sensible people. You've got to stop yelling like that. This is . . . John, he works with me, he's medically trained. I'm quite sure we can work this out and it's high time I told you the rest of this sad story. I'm so glad you've found each other at last."

"You're lying," Daniel hissed.

Things were getting out of hand. There was far too much noise and by now she was terrified that the neighbours would be on their way. She kept talking, trying to defuse the situation, all the while counting down the seconds to the inevitable consequence of her injection—the poison penetrating Leo's blood and acting on the nicotinic acetylcholine receptors to inhibit his muscles. The building was still quiet. No-one had called the police. Now Leo was beginning to stiffen, as she knew he would, and spasmodic movements sent him crashing to the red Persian rug. This was an extreme step even for her, but Greitz savoured the dizzying feeling of power. She could save his life at any moment. Or she could let him die. The circumstances would dictate. Her mind needed to be clear, sharp and convincing, so that she could work on Daniel's evident bitterness and sense of inferiority.

She would get him to play the role of his life.

As Leo fell to the ground, Dan realized that something was terribly wrong. His brother had collapsed as if his body had simply stopped functioning. Leo was grabbing at his throat and seemed paralyzed. Dan forgot everything else and crouched next to his brother, screaming and shaking him. When Greitz began to speak he was barely listening. He was wholly concentrated on trying to restore life to Leo, and anyway, she was saying something far too outlandish for him to take in.

"Daniel," she said. "We can make this work. We'll see to

it that you're better off than you could ever have imagined. From now on you'll have an incredible life with unlimited resources."

It was nonsense, of course, empty words, and all the while Leo was getting worse. He was whimpering and convulsing. His face was ash grey and his lips blue, and he was fighting for breath. He seemed to be suffocating, his eyes were watery and panic-stricken. The blueish tinge spread from his lips out to his cheeks, and Dan prepared to give him artificial respiration. But Greitz stopped him and was saying something, and he could not help but listen—by now he was willing to grasp at straws. Greitz's tone seemed different now, not as impassioned as before, more like a soothing doctor. She took Leo's pulse and smiled reassuringly at Dan.

"There's nothing to worry about," she said. "He's just suffering some cramps. He'll be fine soon. The dose I gave him was powerful, but not dangerous. See for yourself!"

She handed Dan the syringe and he looked at it in his hand, at a loss as to what it could prove or tell him.

"Why are you giving me this?"

He looked at her as she stood next to the big man who was still wearing his jacket and winter boots.

A terrifying thought struck him.

"You want my fingerprints on this, don't you?"

He dropped the syringe.

"Calm down, Daniel. Listen to me."

"Why the hell should I listen to you?"

He pulled out his mobile; he had to call an ambulance. But a threatening, lurching movement from the man stopped him. His panic intensified. Were they trying to kill Leo? Was that even imaginable? He was terror-stricken, and next to him Leo gasped and looked as if he was about to die. Dan yelled straight into Leo's hypersensitive ear, "Fight! You can do it!" Leo's forehead furrowed. He gritted his teeth. A patch of colour returned to his face. But it soon drained away, and again he seemed to be fighting for air. Dan turned to Greitz.

"Save him, for God's sake! You're a doctor. You're not trying to kill him, are you?"

"What are you *talking* about? Of course not. He'll soon be back on his feet, you'll see. Move away so I can assist him," she said. When he saw how smoothly and professionally she handled the contents of her bag, he felt he had no alternative but to trust her.

It was as good a measure as any of the extent of his desperation. He held his twin brother's hand, hoping that the person who had injected him with poison would also be the one to save him.

That was precisely what Greitz was thinking: how critical it was for her to behave like a doctor and inspire confidence. She resisted the urge to block Leo's airways and make short work of the whole process, and instead prepared a syringe with physostigmine before pushing up the sleeve of Leo's sweater to inject the substance into a vein. He improved rapidly, although he was still dazed. She felt—and this is what mattered most—that she had regained some of Daniel's trust.

"Will he be OK?" he asked.

"He'll be fine," she said, and kept on talking.

She was improvising, but she could draw on the emergency plan which had been in place for some time. Years ago, Ivar Ögren had gotten hold of Leo's log-in details at the firm and in Leo's name—or rather using various names, dummy companies and other fronts—had made a series of illegal transactions in the share and derivatives markets. Details of these had been collected in a file which could not only spell Leo's social and professional ruin, but also put him in prison. Ivar had already used the information to get his hands on Madeleine Bard—and Greitz did not approve. Her private opinion was that Ivar was stupid. But in the end she had acquiesced. After all, she needed the information he had gathered in order to put pressure on Leo if ever he found out anything and tried to expose her.

"Listen to me, Daniel," she said. "I have to tell you something. It may be the most important thing you'll have heard in your whole life."

There was such a pleading look on his face that she was filled with confidence. She spoke in a voice that was both soothing and business-like, like a doctor conveying a diagnosis.

"Leo's a bad apple, Daniel. It hurts me to say it, but that's how it is. He's been involved in insider dealing and illegal transactions. He's going to end up in prison."

"What? What are you saying?"

She could tell that he wasn't taking it in. He just kept stroking his brother's hair, telling him that everything was going to be alright. What bullshit. That aggravated Greitz, and she took on a sharper tone:

"*Listen,* I said. Leo's not what you think. We have proof, and he's going to end up in prison. He's a crook and a swindler."

Daniel looked at her in confusion.

"Why the hell would he do that? He isn't even interested in money."

"That's what you think."

"Is it? Before you arrived he tried to give me half of everything he owns—just like that." He gestured with his hand, and she bit her lip. It was not what she wanted to hear.

"Why should you make do with only half?"

"I don't want anything at all. I want . . ."

He fell silent, as if he had understood. Certainly he sensed something. Seeing the panic in his eyes, Greitz expected an outburst, perhaps even a violent one. She glanced at Benjamin; he had to be ready. But Daniel only looked intently at Leo.

"What did you really give him? It wasn't a sedative, was it?"

She did not answer. She was unsure now how best to play her cards. She knew that every word, every nuance in her voice, could be decisive.

"Curare," she said eventually.

"And what's that?"

"A plant-based poison."

"Why the hell did you give him poison?" Dan was shouting again.

"Because I thought it necessary," she said.

Like a desperate animal caught in a trap, Daniel looked up at Benjamin.

"But then . . . then you gave him something else."

"Physostigmine. It's an antidote," she said.

"OK, so now let's take him to the hospital."

Greitz said nothing and so he picked up his mobile. She considered telling Benjamin to take it from him, but as long as he made no calls, there was no danger. She guessed he was Googling information on curare, and she let him search for a while. But when she saw fear in his eyes she snatched the phone from him. He went crazy. He yelled and flailed about, and even Benjamin had difficulty restraining him.

"Calm *down*, Daniel."

"Never!"

"But don't you understand that I'm giving you a fantastic gift?" she said.

"I don't want to hear it!" he screamed.

She told him that physostigmine would suspend the effect of the curare for only a short time.

"So you can't save him?" His voice was barely human.

"I'm so sorry," she lied, and Benjamin had no choice but to silence him.

As he taped Daniel's mouth shut, Greitz voiced her regret at having to go through all this and explained in more detail that Leo's respiratory muscles would soon be blocked again, that he would suffocate and die. She looked at him. "We have a difficult situation on our hands, Daniel. Leo is near death and we not only have your fingerprints on the syringe, we also have a clear motive, don't we? I see in your eyes just how envious you are of everything he has. But there's a plus side . . ."

Daniel was struggling to hit out left and right, trying to tear himself free.

"The plus side is that Leo can go on living—but in a different way, Daniel. Through you."

She gestured around the apartment.

"You can have his life, his money and opportunities, an existence you could only have dreamed of before. You can take over, Daniel. You can have it, and I promise you, all the terrible things Leo's done, his despicable greed, will never come to light. We'll see to it, we'll back you up in every way. The fact that you're mirror-image twins could present some difficulties, admittedly. But you're so extraordinarily alike. Everything will be fine, I just know it."

At that very moment Greitz heard a sound she could not identify. It was one of Daniel's teeth, which he had ground to pieces.

CHAPTER 20

June 22

Leo Mannheimer at last emerged from his office in a light-blue linen suit, grey T-shirt and sneakers, and Blomkvist got up to shake his hand. It was a peculiar meeting. Blomkvist had spent a great deal of time researching this man, and here they were, standing eye to eye. It was immediately apparent that there was something unspoken and painful hanging over him like a shadow, a phantom.

Leo was nervously rubbing his hands together. His nails were long and neat, his hair curly and a little dishevelled, and he seemed to be listening out for something. He looked tense and did not ask Blomkvist to come through, so instead they stood in the large lobby in front of the reception desk.

"I enjoyed your conversation with Karin Laestander at the Fotografiska Museum," Blomkvist said.

"Thanks," Leo said. "It was—"

"—clever," Blomkvist cut in. "And true. We're living in

a time when lies and false news reports have more of an impact than ever. Or should I say 'alternative facts'?"

"The post-truth society," Leo replied, and hesitantly returned Blomkvist's smile.

"Indeed, and we play around with our identities too, don't we? Pretend to be people we're not—on Facebook and so on."

"I'm not actually on Facebook."

"Me neither. I've never really understood the point. But I sometimes mess around with different identities too," Blomkvist said. "It's part of my job. How about you?"

Leo glanced at his wristwatch and looked out the window at the square.

"I'm so sorry," he said. "I have wall-to-wall meetings today. What is it you wanted to see me about?"

"What do you think?"

"I really have no idea."

"Anything you've had second thoughts about? Anything that would interest my magazine, *Millennium*?"

Leo swallowed hard. He gave the question serious consideration, and then, looking at the floor, he said:

"I suppose over the years I've done a few deals which could have been handled better. They're a bit of a mess."

"I'd be happy to take a look at them," Blomkvist said. "Messes are my speciality. But just now I'm interested in more personal matters, small divergences let's say."

"Divergences?"

"Exactly."

"Such as?"

"Such as you becoming right-handed."

Leo—if indeed it was Leo—seemed to be listening out for something again. He ran his fingers through his hair.

"I haven't, actually. I just changed around. I've always used both hands."

"So you write equally well with your right and your left hand?"

"Roughly speaking."

"Could you show me?"

Blomkvist pulled out a pen and his reporter's notebook.

"I'd rather not."

Sweat beaded on Leo's upper lip. He looked away.

"Are you feeling OK?"

"No, I can't say that I am."

"It must be the heat."

"Perhaps."

"I'm not in the best shape, myself," Blomkvist said. "I was up half the night drinking with Hilda von Kanterborg. You know her, don't you?"

Blomkvist saw fear in the man's eyes and realized that he had him. He could tell by his look, by the way he squirmed. But maybe—Blomkvist was watching him very carefully—there was something else too, something hard to define, a hint of impatience perhaps, and also doubt. As if Leo, or whoever it might be, was confronting a major decision.

"Hilda told me an unbelievable story," Blomkvist said.

"Is that so?"

"It was about twins who had been separated at birth. One of the boys was named Daniel Brolin. He had to work like a dog on a farm outside Hudiksvall, while his twin brother—"

"Not so loud," the man interrupted.

"Excuse me?" Blomkvist pretended to be surprised and looked at him.

"Perhaps we should go for a walk," he said.

"I'm not so sure—"

"—if we should take a walk?"

The man plainly did not know what to say. He mumbled something about the men's toilet and hurried off. The excuse was not in the least convincing as he took out his mobile before he was even out of sight. That was when Blomkvist became convinced that he had guessed right. He texted Salander that Leo was almost certainly Daniel.

As he continued to wait, he became increasingly worried that he had been outwitted—that the man had escaped through a back door. The minutes went by and nothing happened, employees and visitors came and went. The young woman at reception smiled and wished everyone a good day.

It was a stylish place with high ceilings and red-patterned wallpaper. Oil paintings of elderly gentlemen in suits, presumably one-time partners or board members, hung on the walls. In this day and age, the lack of women was an obscenity.

Blomkvist's mobile buzzed. It was Giannini, and he was about to take the call when the man—Leo or Daniel—came back down the corridor. He seemed to have pulled himself together, perhaps he had made some sort of decision. It was hard to tell. His throat was flushed and he looked tense and serious. His eyes were fixed on the floor and he said nothing to Blomkvist, just told the receptionist that he would be gone for a few hours.

They took the lift down and stepped out onto Norrmalmstorg. Stockholm was ferociously hot. People were fanning themselves with newspapers, with anything. Men had slung their jackets over their shoulders. They turned into Hamngatan, and Blomkvist noticed the man look nervously behind him. He briefly wondered whether to suggest that they hop on a bus or take a taxi. Instead they crossed the street into Kungsträdgården. They walked on in silence, as if they were waiting for something to happen.

The man was sweating more than he ought to have been, even in this heat, and again glanced around anxiously. They found themselves diagonally across from Operan, and although he could not put his finger on why, Blomkvist sensed a threat. Maybe he had made a mistake, and the people from the Registry could already be a step ahead of him. He turned around. Nothing. In fact the streets were peaceful; there was a holiday feeling in the air. People sat on park benches and on café terraces, their faces towards the sun. Perhaps his companion's nervousness was rubbing off on him. He went straight to the point:

"So, shall I call you Leo or Daniel?"

The man bit his lip and a shadow came over his face. A second later he threw himself on top of Blomkvist, and together they crashed to the ground.

Greitz, who had been waiting on a bench on Norrmalmstorg, had seen Daniel Brolin walk away with Blomkvist. She understood that elements had been set in motion which would lead to the story leaking out sooner rather than later.

She was neither surprised nor shocked. She had known

for some time that the stakes were high, but instead of elicit-
ing mere despair, this allowed her also a kind of freedom. She
appeared to have acquired the resolve of someone who has
nothing to lose. Plus, she had Benjamin. He was not dying
as she was, but he was bound to her by his lifelong loyalty
and by the unspeakable things they had done together. If it
all came out, his fall would be as great as hers. Without questioning it, he had agreed to put Blomkvist out of action and
take Daniel to a place where they could talk sense into him.

This was why Benjamin, in spite of the heat, was wearing
a black hoodie and dark glasses. He was carrying a concealed
syringe filled with ketamine, an anaesthetic which would
knock the journalist clean out.

Although she had been suffering from stomach pains all
morning, Greitz had dragged herself over to the avenue running alongside Kungsträdgården. In the glaring sunlight she
made out Benjamin moving along with quick steps.

Her senses sharpened. The city became one single concentrated moment, one sparkling scene, and she watched
intently as Daniel and Blomkvist slowed and the journalist
appeared to be asking a question. Good, she thought, that
will distract them, and in that moment she believed it would
go precisely as planned.

Further down the street a horse-drawn carriage appeared.
A blue hot-air balloon hung in the sky and people were walking by in every direction, oblivious to what was going on. Her
heart pounded in anticipation and she was breathing deeply.
But then Daniel looked up, saw Benjamin and threw Blomkvist to the ground. The journalist lay flat on the pavement
and Benjamin hesitated and missed his chance. Blomkvist

jumped to his feet. Benjamin lunged at him. But the journalist dodged him, and then Benjamin took to his heels. The coward! Furious, she watched as Daniel and Blomkvist ran towards Operakällaren. They jumped into a taxi and were gone. The heat settled like a wet blanket over Greitz and she felt only how unwell and nauseous she was. Yet she managed to pull herself up to her full height, and as rapidly as she was able she left the scene.

Salander was lying pressed against the floor of the grey van, being kicked at intervals in the stomach and face. The noxious rag was again placed over her nose, and she felt woozy and weak as she went in and out of consciousness. She had no trouble recognizing Benito and Bashir, no happy combination. Benito was looking pale and was bandaged around her head and jaw. She was having difficulty moving, so she kept still, which was good. Most of the blows aimed at Salander came from the men: Bashir, bearded and sweaty, dressed in the same clothes as the day before, and a thickset man of about thirty-five with a shaved head, grey T-shirt and black leather vest. A third man was driving.

The van rolled down past Slussen, at least she thought so. She tried to register every detail in the vehicle—a coil of rope, a roll of tape, two screwdrivers. Another kick, this time to her neck. Someone grabbed her hands. They tied her up, frisked her and took her mobile. That was a worry, but the bald guy stuffed it into his pocket and that was fine. She made a note of his physique and jerky movements, and his tendency to keep looking at Benito. He was obviously Benito's lapdog, not Bashir's.

There was a bench on the left side of the van. They sat there while she lay on the floor amid the smell of perfume, the stench of rubbing alcohol and sweat from their sneakers. Salander thought they were heading north but she could not be sure, she was far too light-headed. For a long time no-one spoke, the only sounds were of people breathing and engine noise and the metallic rattling of the old van, it must have been at least thirty years old. They drove out onto a main road and after twenty minutes or so began to talk. That was good, that was what she needed. Bashir had a bruise on his throat, from her blow with the hockey stick, she hoped. He looked like he had slept badly. In fact he looked like shit.

"You have no idea how we're going to make you suffer, you little whore," he said.

Salander was silent.

"Then I'm going to kill you. Slowly. With my Keris," Benito said.

Still Salander said nothing. Why would she, when she knew that every word spoken was being transmitted to a number of different computers.

Nothing too sophisticated, at least not by her standards. When they overpowered her in the street she had whispered "Harpy" into her modified iPhone. That had activated her alarm button via S.R.I.'s A.I. system and a boosted microphone was switched on automatically, triggering a sound recording that was sent to all members of the so-called Hacker Republic, together with the mobile's GPS coordinates.

. . .

Hacker Republic consisted of a group of elite hackers, all of whom had sworn a solemn oath to use the alarm only in cases of dire emergency. As a consequence a number of talented people all around the world were now breathlessly following the dramatic events in the back of the van. Most did not understand Swedish, but enough did, including Salander's friend on Högklintavägen in Sundbyberg.

Plague was as wide as a house at 330 pounds, but stooped from spending all day at his keyboard. His beard was a thicket and he hadn't had a haircut since the previous year. He looked like a case for social welfare, but he was an I.T. genius. He was sitting by his computer in his frayed blue dressing gown, nerves on high alert, following the GPS cooordinates northwards towards Uppsala. The car—it sounded large, and old—turned east onto National Highway 77 towards Knivsta, and that was not good. They were heading further out into the countryside, where GPS coverage was patchy at best. He heard the woman in the vehicle again, her voice hoarse and weak, as if she were unwell.

"Do you have any idea how slowly you're going to die, you bitch? Do you?"

Plague looked at his desk in desperation. It was strewn with scraps of paper, used coffee cups and greasy Styrofoam containers. His back hurt. He had gained weight, which did not help his diabetes, and it was almost a week since he had last been out of the house. What was he to do? If he had an address for their destination he could hack the electricity and water utilities, locate neighbours and organize a group of local vigilantes. But he had no idea where they were heading. He was powerless. His whole body shook and his heart pounded.

Messages came pouring in. Salander was their friend, their shining star. But as far as Plague could tell, nobody in the fellowship had any good suggestions, at least nothing which could be organized fast enough. Should he call the police? Plague had never contacted the authorities, for good reason: There were few cybercrimes he had not committed. In one way or another, they were always after him, *and yet*, he thought, *and yet*, even the outlaw has to turn to the law for help sometimes. He remembered Salander—or Wasp as he knew her—had once talked about an Inspector Bublanski. He was OK, she had said, and coming from her, "OK" was a major compliment. For a minute Plague sat paralyzed, staring at a map of Uppland on his computer screen. Then he plugged in his headphones and turned up the volume on the audio file. He wanted to hear every subtle variation in the voices, even in the engine noise. There was a buzzing and scraping in his ears. For a short while nobody spoke. Then somebody said what Plague least wanted to hear:

"Have you got her phone?"

It was the woman again. She may have sounded terrible, but she seemed to be in charge, she and the man who sometimes spoke to the driver in a language the hackers had uploaded and now identified as Bengali.

"It's in my pocket," one of the men answered.

"Give it to me."

There was a rustling and a crackling as the mobile was passed around. Somebody pressed some keys, turned it over, breathed into it.

"Is there anything fishy about it?"

"I don't know," the woman answered. "Doesn't look like it. But maybe the police can use this piece of crap to listen in."

"We'd better get rid of it."

Plague heard some more words in Bengali and the car seemed to slow. A door creaked open, even though the vehicle was still moving. Wind sounded in the microphone and then there was a swishing sound, followed by a clattering and an excruciatingly loud bang. Plague ripped off his headphones and slammed his fist on the table. Shit, damn, fuck! Expletives flooded in over the network. They had lost contact with Wasp.

Plague tried to visualize the situation. Traffic cameras—of course! Why hadn't he thought of that? But they'd have to hack the Transport Administration to get access to their cameras, and that took time. And time they did not have. He wrote:

```
<Does anyone know how to get into the
Transport Administration system quickly?
Like, now?>
```

He hooked them all up to an encrypted audio link.

"Some C.C.T.V. footage is publicly available online," somebody said.

"That's too jerky and blurred," he said. "We've got to get close enough to see the model of the car and the reg plates."

"I know a shortcut." It was a young, female voice. It took Plague a moment to identify her: Nelly, one of their new members.

"Really?" he exclaimed. "Great, get in there! Hook yourselves up to her, go for it. Give it everything you've got. I'll give you the times and coordinates."

Plague went onto the site www.trafiken.nu, which showed the location of cameras along the E4 motorway to Uppsala, and at the same time rewound the file from Wasp's mobile. The alarm had been activated at 12:52 p.m. The first camera on that route was likely to be the one at Haga South and, wait a moment . . . the vehicle seemed to have passed by there about thirteen minutes later, at 1:05 p.m. Then the cameras came in quick succession; that was good, he thought, good. Linvävartorpet and Linvävartorpet South, then Linvävartorpet North and Haga North Gates, Haga North, Stora Frösunda, Järva Krog, Mellanjärva, Ulriksdals golf course. There were plenty of cameras along the first stretch, and even though there was heavy traffic they should be able to identify the vehicle, since it was obviously an older, bigger model, a van or a light truck.

"How's it going?" he shouted.

"Just chill, man, we're working on it. Someone's really been messing with this, they've put in something new. Hell, 'access denied.' Wait. Shit, fuck . . . *yesss!* Now . . . yes . . . we're running, we're in, now we just need to get . . . What kind of idiots built this amateur shit!"

It was the usual. Swearing and shouting. Adrenaline and sweat and more yelling, only this time it was worse. It was a matter of life and death, and once they had figured out the system and how to get in and had gone back and forth on the surveillance cameras, they identified the car: an old grey Mercedes minivan with apparently fake number plates. But now what? They felt even more powerless as the vehicle passed one camera position after the next like a pale, evil spirit, and in the end disappeared beyond the reach of surveillance into the forests to the east of Knivsta, somewhere near the lake at Vadabo.

"Digital darkness. Shit, *shit!*"

Never before had there been so much shouting and swearing among Hacker Republic. Plague saw no alternative but to call Chief Inspector Bublanski.

CHAPTER 21

June 22

Bublanski was sitting in his office on Bergsgatan, talking to Imam Hassan Ferdousi. By now he understood how Jamal Chowdhury's murder had come about. The whole Kazi family—apart from the father—had been involved, along with some Islamists in exile from Bangladesh. It was a somewhat sophisticated operation, but no more so than the initial crime investigation should have been able to unravel without third-party help.

For the police, it was nothing short of a disgrace. Bublanski had just had a conversation with the chief of Säpo, Helena Kraft, and was now discussing with the imam how the police could do better at anticipating and preventing violent crimes like these in the future. But his mind was really elsewhere. He wanted to get back to the investigation into Holger Palmgren's death, and especially look into this Professor Steinberg.

"What was that again?"

The imam had said something which Bublanski did not fully understand, but before he could enquire further, his telephone rang with a Skype call from a user who called himself TOTAL FUCKING SHITSTORM FOR SALANDER, and that in itself was pretty weird. Who would call themselves that? Bublanski answered his mobile and at the end of the line was a young man shouting at him in rather graphic Swedish.

"I'm not going to listen to a single word you say until you've introduced yourself," Bublanski said.

"My name is Plague. Switch on your computer and open the link I've sent you, and then I'll explain."

Bublanski hesitated at first, but he kept listening to the man, who was using swearwords liberally interspersed with incomprehensible computer terminology, but who nonetheless was precise and clear in what he had to report. Bublanski was finally persuaded to open the link, and, overcoming his confusion and his scepticism, he sprang into action. He mobilized a helicopter and patrol cars from both Stockholm and Uppsala to head for Vadabosjö. Then he and Amanda Flod ran down to his Volvo in the garage. He decided it would be safer to have her drive as they sped northwards to Uppsala, blue lights flashing.

The man next to him had saved him from a serious assault. Blomkvist was still not certain he understood why. But it had to be a good sign. They were no longer in the same opposing roles of investigative reporter and quarry as they had been back in the Alfred Ögren lobby. There was a shared bond between them, and Blomkvist was now in his debt.

The sun was beating down outside. They were in a small, top-floor apartment on Tavastgatan with attic windows looking out over Riddarfjärden. A half-finished oil painting of an ocean and a white whale was propped on an easel. There was harmony in the painting, despite an unconventional combination of colours. But Blomkvist turned it to face the windows. He did not want any distractions.

The apartment belonged to Irene Westervik, an elderly artist who Blomkvist knew only a little. But he felt a certain fondness for her. She was wise and inspired confidence, and lived at a remove from the endless churn of current affairs. Sometimes she enabled him to look at the world from a broader perspective. He had called her from the taxi to ask if he might borrow her studio for a few hours, perhaps for the rest of the day. She had met them in a pale-green dress at the street entrance, and had handed over the keys with a gentle smile.

Now Blomkvist and the man, who was presumably Daniel, were sitting in the apartment facing each other. To be on the safe side, their mobiles were switched off and they had put them on a shelf in the galley kitchen. It was sweltering beneath the roof, and Blomkvist had tried and failed to open the studio windows.

"Was that a syringe in that man's hand?"

"Looked like it."

"I wonder what was in it."

"In the worst case, synthetic curare."

"Poison?"

"Yes. A heavy dose knocks out everything, including the respiratory muscles. You suffocate."

"You seem to know all about it," Blomkvist said.

The man looked sorrowful, and Blomkvist's gaze turned to the window and the blue sky.

"Can I call you Daniel?" he said.

The man was silent. He hesitated.

"It's Dan," he said. "I got a green card, became an American citizen and changed my name. Now I go by Dan Brody."

"Or Leo Mannheimer."

"Yes, that's true."

"A bit peculiar, wouldn't you say?"

"Indeed."

"Do you want to tell me the story, Dan? We've got plenty of time. No-one will come looking for us here."

"Is there anything stronger to drink?"

"Let me look in the fridge."

Blomkvist found several bottles of white wine, a Sancerre. This is my new normal, he thought bleakly—drinking through interviews. He helped himself to a bottle and found two glasses.

"Here," he said, filling them up.

"I don't really know where to begin. You said you'd met Hilda. Did she talk about . . ." Again Dan hesitated, as if reluctant to mention a name or an event that filled him with fear.

"About what?"

"Rakel Greitz?"

"Hilda told me a lot about her."

Dan just raised his glass and drank, grim and resolute. Then slowly he began to tell his story. It began at a jazz club in Berlin, with a guitar solo and a woman who could not take her eyes off him.

They had driven into a forest and stopped. The inside of the van was unbearably stuffy, and all that could be heard from outside was the sound of birds and insects. The engine idled. Salander was thirsty and she felt sick from the chloroform or maybe from the beating. She was still lying on the floor, tied up, but when she got to her knees nobody objected, although they glared at her the whole time. The engine was switched off and those on the bench nodded at each other. Benito drank some water to wash down a few tablets. She was ashen-faced and did not move as Bashir and the other man stood up. Salander could now see the man's tattooed fore-arms and the emblem on his leather vest: SVAVELSJÖ M.C. The same motorcycle gang which had been allied with her father and her sister. Had Camilla and her hackers cracked Salander's address?

Salander studied the back door of the van and tried to recall the action with which it had been opened when her mobile was thrown into the road. With mathematical preci-sion she recalled the force in the movement, or rather the lack of it.

She could not remove the rope around her hands, but she should be able to kick open the door. That was good, as was Benito's head injury and how jittery the men seemed. Bashir grimaced, just as he had in Vallholmen, and drew back his right foot to kick her. She absorbed it, over-reacting a little. Not that she needed to. It was a violent kick which caught her in the ribs; then she took another one in the face and feigned being dazed, but all the while she was watching Benito.

From the outset, Salander had had a feeling that this was first and foremost Benito's show. She would have the last word. Now she was bending over her grey canvas bag on the floor and taking out a red-velvet cloth. The men seized Salander roughly by the shoulders. This did not bode well, especially when Benito pulled a dagger from the bag—her Keris. It was straight and shiny, and it looked very sharp, with a long gold-tipped blade. The handle had been carved to represent a demon with slanting eyes. It was the kind of weapon that should have been in a museum, not in the hands of an ashen-faced psychopath with a bandaged head who was now examining the knife with a demented tenderness.

In a reedy voice Benito explained how the Keris was to be used. Salander did not listen attentively, it didn't seem necessary, but she heard enough. The Keris would be stabbed through the red cloth just beneath the collarbone, straight into the heart. The blood would be wiped off onto the cloth on its way out. It was said to require extraordinary skill. Salander went on making a careful inventory of everything in the van—every object, every accumulation of dust, every moment of faltering concentration. She glanced up at Bashir. He gripped her left shoulder and looked determined and tense. She was going to die, and he was fine with that. But he didn't look especially pleased, and it was plain to see why. Essentially he was the helper of a woman, and that can't have been easy for someone who thought of women as no more than whores or second-class citizens.

"Do you know your Koran?" Salander said.

She could tell right away by his grip on her shoulder that her question had unsettled him. She went on to say that the Prophet had condemned all types of Kerises—they belonged to Satan and the demons—and then she quoted a sura, one she had invented. She gave it a number and urged him to look it up. "Check it out and you'll see!"

But Benito stood up with her dagger and said: "She's full of shit. The Keris didn't even exist at the time of Moham-med. Now it's a weapon for holy warriors the world over."

Bashir seemed to believe her, or at least he wanted to believe her. "OK, OK, get a move on," he said, adding some-thing in Bengali for the benefit of the driver up front.

Suddenly Benito seemed to be in a hurry, even as she was overcome by dizziness and lurched to one side. There was a sound high above them, the reverberations of a heli-copter. Though it might not have had anything to do with them, Salander knew that her friends at Hacker Republic were unlikely to have been sitting around doing nothing. The noise was both promising because help might soon be at hand, and worrying because of the increased activity in the van.

Bashir and the other man were gripping her tightly as Benito advanced towards her, looking determined with her long dagger and red cloth. Salander thought of Palmgren. She thought of her mother and the dragon in Storkyrkan, and she braced herself against the floor.

Come what may, she had to get to her feet.

·   ·   ·

Dan sat in silence. He had reached a painful point in the story. His eyes flickered about and his hands shifted nervously.

"When Rakel said she would have me convicted for murdering my brother unless I cooperated, I felt helpless, I hardly knew what was happening. They made me wear sunglasses and a hat. It would be dangerous for there to be two Leos in the stairwell, she said—we had to get him out of the apartment while he could still stand. I saw an opportunity. If we could only get out, I thought, I'd be able to shout for help."

"But you didn't."

"We didn't meet anybody in the elevator or on the stairs. It was the day before Christmas Eve. Rakel's sidekick—I don't think John is his real name, in fact. She called him Benjamin several times. It was the man who attacked you this morning. Anyway, he . . ." Dan paused and took a deep breath. "He dragged Leo, who could only just stay upright, to a black Renault van parked outside. It was getting dark, or at least that's how it felt," he said. And he fell silent again.

DECEMBER, ONE AND A HALF YEARS EARLIER

Dan looked at the empty street before him—as weird as if he were in a stone-bordered, desolate nightmare. He might have run away to call for help. But how could he abandon his brother? It would have been impossible. They pushed Leo into the car and Dan asked:

"We're taking him to the hospital now, right?"

"Yes," Greitz said.

Did he believe her? She had just said there was no point, and had threatened him. He clambered into the car and focused on one thing: before she took his mobile he had managed to read online that a patient can recover from curare poisoning as long as respiration is maintained. He sat down next to Leo in the back seat. On the other side of him was the man Greitz called Benjamin.

Dan was concentrating on trying to help Leo breathe. Again he asked if they really were on their way to a hospital. Greitz, who was driving, was more specific this time. They were headed to the Karolinska hospital, and she even named the department.

"Trust me," she said.

She claimed to have called ahead to warn specialists, who were preparing to receive Leo. Maybe Dan knew it was all nonsense. Maybe he was too shocked to absorb what was happening. It was hard to remember anything at all. He focused solely on keeping Leo's breathing going, and nobody stopped him. That was something to be grateful for. Greitz drove fast. There was not much traffic and they came up onto Solnabron. The red hospital buildings seemed to rise like an apparition in the darkness, and for an instant he thought it might all be OK, in the end.

But it was no more than a smokescreen, an attempt to keep him quiet for a while. Instead of stopping, the car accelerated past the hospital, driving northwards towards Solna. He must have been shouting and lashing out because there was a sudden burning sensation in his thigh and he felt his protests grow weaker, less forceful. The rage and desperation did not leave him, but he felt his strength ebbing away. He shook his head and blinked. He strove to think clearly, to keep Leo alive. But he was struggling for words and finding it hard to move, and far away, as if through a fog, he could hear Greitz and the man whispering to each other. He lost track of time. At some point Greitz raised her voice. She was speaking to him now, and there was something hypnotic about her tone. What was she saying? She talked about everything he would get—about dreams fulfilled, about wealth, happiness.

With Leo gasping for breath beside him, the massive figure of Benjamin on the other side, Greitz sitting in the front talking about happiness and riches, it was . . . it was impossible to describe. It was beyond words.

Blomkvist might not ever be able to grasp it. But Dan had to try. There was no other way.

"Were you tempted?" Blomkvist asked.

The wine bottle was standing on the white coffee table and Dan felt an impulse to smash it over the journalist's head.

"You've got to understand," he said, trying hard to sound calm. "At that moment I couldn't imagine my life without Leo."

He was quiet again.

"What was going through your mind?"

"Only one thing: how we would make it through this."

"And what was your plan?"

"My *plan*? I don't know. I guess I thought I'd play along and hope a way out would present itself. As we drove further and further into the countryside, I managed to regain some of my strength. I was looking at Leo the whole time. He got worse. He began to cramp again, he couldn't move. Sorry, it's hard for me to talk about it."

"Take your time."

Dan reached for his wineglass and went on:

"I had no idea where we were. The road was getting narrower. We were in a pine forest. Darkness had fallen and the snow had turned to rain. I saw a signpost. Vidåkra, it said. We headed to the right, onto a forest track, and after ten minutes Rakel stopped the car and Benjamin got out. He took something out of the trunk, and there was an unpleasant rattling noise. I didn't want to know what it was. I was busy looking after Leo. I opened the door, laid him across the seat and started CPR. I had only a vague idea of what I was doing, but I tried. I've never tried so hard at anything in my whole life. I was dizzy and Leo had vomited without my even noticing it. There was a foul smell in the car. I felt like I was leaning over myself, can you understand that? As if I was giving breath to my own dying self. And the strange thing is that they let me keep at it. They were gentle with me now, Rakel and this guy Benjamin. It was odd, and I didn't really understand what was going on. Rakel said in a soft voice that Leo was going to die. Soon the effect of the physostigmine would leave him, and nothing could be done. It was horrible, she said. But the good thing was that nobody would be looking for him. No-one would even wonder where he went—as long as I took his place. His mother was dying, she said, and I could resign from Alfred Ögren and sell my interest in the company to Ivar. No-one would be surprised. They had all known for ages that Leo's dream was to leave the company. It was as if the scene was set for divine justice; I would get what I had always deserved. I humoured them. I saw no alternative. I mumbled, I hemmed and hawed. They'd taken my phone, I think I told you, and I was miles away in a forest and I couldn't see lights from a single house.

"Benjamin came back looking like a complete mess, soaked through with sweat and rain, muddy snow on his trousers. His woollen hat was askew. He didn't say a word. A nasty, unspoken complicity hung in the air as Benjamin dragged Leo out of the back seat. Leo's head hit the ground and I bent down to help. I pulled off Benjamin's hat, I remember, and put it on Leo. Then I buttoned up his coat. We hadn't even dressed him warmly: he had no scarf and he was wearing his indoor shoes, and they were untied, laces dangling. It was a scene from hell, and I wondered if I should run off to get help. Just take off into the forest or along the track and hope to find somebody. But was there time for that? I didn't think so. I wasn't even sure Leo was still alive. So I followed into the trees. Benjamin was dragging Leo along clumsily and I offered to help. Benjamin didn't like that; he wanted to get me away from there. 'Go,' he said. 'Get lost, this isn't anything for you,' and he yelled for Rakel. But I don't think she heard. The wind was blowing hard, rustling the trees. We were being scratched by bushes and branches and then we arrived at a large diseased-looking pine, next to which was a pile of stones and earth. There was a shovel lying nearby and for a moment I thought, or wanted to believe, that we had stumbled on some sort of excavation which had nothing to do with us."

"But it was a grave."

"It was an attempt at a grave. Not a very deep one. Benjamin must have had a hell of a time digging into that frozen earth. He looked exhausted as he put Leo on the ground and shouted at me to go away. I told him that I had to say goodbye, that he was a heartless bastard. He threatened me again, saying that Greitz had enough evidence to have me put away for murder. 'He's my twin brother, for Christ's sake. Show a little consideration, leave me in peace. I'll bury him myself. I won't run away, and Leo's dead anyway. Look at him,' I yelled. 'Look at him!' And then he really did leave me. I suspected that he hadn't gone far, but he did walk out of sight, and I was alone with Leo. I crouched on my heels under the pine tree and leaned over him," Dan said.

Giannini had eaten her lunch in the staff canteen at Flodberga and was back in the visitors' section in H Block, to take part in the continuation of Faria's questioning, which Modig was leading.

In the afternoon session, Modig was proving to be capable and efficient. She agreed with Giannini that it was important not only to establish the facts of the long-standing oppression Faria had suffered, but also to do what they could after all this time to investigate whether her attack on her brother might be a case of assault and manslaughter rather than murder. Had she really intended to kill him?

Giannini was optimistic. She had gotten Faria to summon up every possible aspect of her frame of mind at the time of the attack. But then Modig got a call, which she had taken in the corridor. When she returned she was no longer her cool and collected self. This shift of mood vexed Giannini.

"For God's sake, don't try that poker face on me. I can tell that something serious has happened. Spit it out. Now!"

"I know, and I'm sorry. I couldn't bring myself to tell you," Modig said. "Bashir Kazi and Benito have abducted Lisbeth. We have the whole team working on it, but it's not looking good."

"Tell me everything," Giannini said.

Modig told her, and Giannini shuddered. Faria shrank back into her chair, her arms folded around her legs. But then something shifted in her. Giannini was the first to notice it. Faria's eyes were not only filled with fear and rage. There was something else there, deep and intense:

"Did you say Vadabosjö?"

"Yes, the last sighting of them is from a surveillance camera. The van swung onto a forest track heading towards the area around the lake," Modig said.

"We . . ."

"Yes, what is it?" Giannini said.

"Before we could afford to go to Mallorca, my family used to camp at Vadabosjö," Faria said. "We went often. It's not far, so we could decide at the last moment to go there for the weekend. That was when our mother was still alive. Vadabosjö is surrounded by thick forest, you know, and it's full

of narrow paths and hiding places. There was one time . . ."
Faria hesitated, holding on to her knees. "Have you got a signal on your phone? If you can pull up a detailed map of the
area, I'll try to explain."

Modig searched and muttered and searched again, and
eventually she brightened. The Uppsala police had downloaded a map for them.

"Show me," Faria said, a new tone to her voice.

"They drove in here," Modig said, showing her the map
on her screen.

"Wait just a moment," Faria said. "Let me try to get my
bearings. There's something called Söderviken somewhere
around the lake, isn't there? Or Södra viken, Södra stran-
den?"

"Let me take a look."

Modig keyed "Södra" into the search engine.

"Could it be Södra Strandviken?" she said.

"That's it, yes, that must be it," Faria said eagerly. "Let me
see now. There's a small bumpy track, but still wide enough
for a car. Could that be it?" she said, zooming in. "I'm not
sure. But at the time there was a yellow sign where you drove
in. 'End of public road,' it said. A little way down the track,
a little more than a mile along, there's a sort of cave, not a
real cave, more like a sheltered space in the midst of a large
clump of trees with thick foliage. It's at the top of a hill on
the left, and you have to pass through a whole curtain of
leaves but then you come out in a completely secluded spot,
surrounded by bushes and trees. You can see a ravine and a
brook through a gap in the vegetation. Bashir took me there
once, and I thought he wanted to show me something excit-

ing, but it was to frighten me. It was when my body was start-
ing to fill out a bit and some guys on the beach had whistled
at me. When we arrived, he told me a whole load of rubbish
about how in the old days they used to take women there
who had behaved like whores, to punish them. He scared
me out of my wits, and that's why I remember it. Now I'm
wondering if Bashir took Lisbeth to that place."

Modig nodded gravely and thanked her. She took back
her mobile and made a call.

Bublanski was getting reports from Sami Hamid, one of the
police helicopter pilots. Hamid was circling Vadabosjö and
the surrounding woodland at low altitude, but had seen no
sign of a grey van. Nor had the walkers, the campers, or any
of the policemen patrolling the area. It wasn't easy, admittedly. The lake was bordered by wide-open beaches, but
the surrounding forest was dense and a jumble of labyrin-
thine paths crisscrossed the terrain. It seemed an ideal place
to hide, and that worried Bublanski. He had not cursed so
much in a long time, and he kept egging Flod on to drive
faster.

They were thundering along National Highway 77 and
still had some way to go before they reached the lake. Thanks
to voice identification they knew it was Benito and Bashir
Kazi whom they were pursuing, which meant the threat to
Salander was critical. Bublanski did not waste a second. He
was on to the coordinators at Uppsala police every few minutes and rang every conceivable person he could think of

who might provide information. He rang Blomkvist several times, but the journalist had switched off his mobile.

Bublanski swore and prayed by turns. Although he and Salander were hardly on friendly terms, he felt a fatherly affection for her, not least because she had given them the means to solve a serious crime. He asked Flod to pick up the pace. They were getting closer to the woods around the lake. His mobile rang. It was Modig, telling him to key "Södra Strandviken" into the car's GPS, and then she passed her mobile to Faria Kazi. He couldn't understand why he should be talking to her, but in fact the woman sounded quite different; she spoke with a fierce determination and with perfect clarity. Bublanski listened carefully and intently and hoped it would not be too late.

Just up ahead, they saw a yellow sign that marked a turn-off into the forest.

CHAPTER 22

June 22

Salander had no idea where she was. It was hot and she could hear flies and mosquitoes, wind rustling in the trees and bushes, and water babbling softly. She focused on her legs. They were skinny and did not look like much, but they were strong, and right now they were the only thing she had to defend herself with. She was kneeling in the van, her hands tied. Benito was grimacing in her bandages, the dagger and the cloth shaking in her hands. She really did look like death. Salander glanced at the door of the van. The men held her down by the shoulders and shouted at her. She looked up to see Bashir's face shining with sweat—he glared as if he wanted to punch her.

Salander asked herself if she might be able to play them off against each other. Time was running out. Benito was standing in front of her now, an evil queen with her long dagger, and the mood inside the van was changing. It became solemn and still, as if something momentous was about to happen. One of the men ripped Salander's T-shirt to expose her collarbone. She looked at Benito. Her red lipstick cut a slash across her ash-grey skin. But she seemed to be steadier on her feet now, as if the horror of the moment had sharpened her senses. In a voice which fell one octave, she said:

"Hold her still! Good, good. This is immense. This is the moment of her death. Can you feel my Keris pointed at you? You're going to suffer now. You're going to die."

Benito peered into Salander's face and smiled with eyes which were beyond all mercy and humanity. For a second or so all Salander could see was the blade of the dagger held out towards her exposed chest. A split second later a flood of impressions washed over her. She saw Benito had three safety pins in her bandage, she saw that her right pupil was larger than the left, and she saw there was a sign from Bagarmossen animal hospital just inside the van door. She saw three yellow paperclips and a dog leash on the floor and a line drawn with blue felt-tip on the inside of the van above her. But most of all she saw the red-velvet cloth. Benito was not comfortable holding it. However self-confident she might be with the dagger, the cloth was a foreign object, nothing more than ritual mumbo jumbo. She did not seem to know what to do with it, and suddenly she threw it onto the floor.

Salander braced herself with her toes. Bashir yelled at her to stay still, and she heard nervousness in his voice. She saw Benito blink and the dagger being raised to home in on the point just below her collarbone. She prepared herself by stiffening the muscles in her body and wondered if survival was even possible. She was on her knees, her hands bound, and the men were holding her tight. She closed her eyes and pretended to have resigned herself to her fate while she listened to the silence and the breathing in the back of the van. She felt excitement in the air, the thirst for blood, and also fear—a kind of pleasure mixed with terror. Even in this company an execution was a serious undertaking, and . . . What was that?

It was far away and hard to make out, but it sounded like engine noise, not from a single car but from several.

At that very moment Benito made her move and then it was time. Salander flew up in an explosive burst of energy. She scrambled to her feet, but she did not escape the dagger.

Flod braked so sharply that the car skidded and she looked angrily at Bublanski as if it was his fault. The Chief Inspector was oblivious, he was on the line to Faria and called out:

"We've found the sign, I see it." He cursed under his breath as the car swerved and shook. The yellow sign did indeed say "end of public road."

Flod controlled the skid and turned into the track, a swamp of mud with deep ruts. The rain, which had fallen relentlessly before the heat wave took the country in its grip, had made it almost impassable, and the car slipped and bumped.

"Slow down, for God's sake, we can't afford to miss it!" Bublanski yelled.

According to Faria, the place was at the top of a rise hidden behind a kind of screen of branches and foliage. Bublanski could see no sign of any rising ground. Looking at the density of the trees all around he did not think they had much of a chance of finding the van. It could be hidden any-where in this forest. It might even be on its way to some dif-ferent place. He tried to calculate the length of time that had passed since the van was last sighted. And above all: How could the girl be so sure where the clearing was? How could she remember so many details, or have the least clear idea of distances after so many years?

The forest looked the same to him on all sides; nowhere were there any distinguishing features. He was about to give up. The trees were closing in overhead so that it was practi-cally dark. Uppsala sent word that other police vehicles were behind them. That would be helpful, if indeed they were on the right track. He felt sure the forest would be able to camouflage an entire fleet of vans or trucks. But he did not see how they would be able to find anything in this impen-etrable jungle. He racked his brains as Flod negotiated the mud bath. Then, over there . . . it was not a hill, exactly, but still a definite slope. Flod accelerated gently, the wheels spun, and the car approached the top of the rise. Bublanski continued to describe what he was seeing. There was a large globe-shaped stone by the side of the track, which Faria might remember. But she did not. Damn it! They were get-ting nowhere.

And then he heard a bang, something striking tin or sheet metal, and he heard shouting, agitated voices. He put his hand on Flod's arm and she hit the brakes. He drew his service revolver and jumped out, flinging himself into the forest, under branches and through bushes, and in a dizzy-ing instant he realized that they really had found the place.

DECEMBER, ONE AND A HALF YEARS EARLIER

Dan Brody was kneeling in the wet snow in another forest at another time of year, under that pine tree not far from Vidåkra village, staring down at Leo as his face turned blue, the life draining out of his blue eyes. It was a moment of pure horror. But it cannot have lasted long.

Dan restarted the artificial respiration right away, though Leo's lips were as cold as the snow beneath him and his lungs were not responding. And Dan thought he could hear footsteps returning. Soon he would have to head back to the car as only half a person. *Wake up, Leo, wake up!* he muttered over and over, like a mantra, a prayer. He no longer had any faith in his plan, or in his ability to revive his brother.

Benjamin had to be close, maybe even spying on him in the darkness through a gap in the trees. He must have been nervous and impatient, desperate to bury Leo and get the hell out of there. The situation was hopeless, but Dan kept going, ever more desperate. He pinched Leo's nose shut and breathed into his airways with such force and violence that he grew dizzy; he hardly knew what he was doing. He remembered hearing a car far off, a distant engine. There was a rustling in the forest, the sound of a startled animal. Some birds flew up with a loud flapping, and then the silence returned, a frightening silence. He felt as if his very life had drained away, he needed to take a break, he had run out of breath and was coughing. It was a second or two before he realized that something strange was happening.

His coughing seemed to reverberate and echo from the ground. Then it dawned on him that it was Leo. He too was panting and struggling, Dan could hardly believe it. He just stared at Leo and felt—what did he feel? Not happiness. Just urgency.

"Leo," he whispered. "They're going to kill you. You've got to run further into the forest. Get up! Go! Now!"

Leo struggled to understand. He was fighting for air and trying to get his bearings. Dan pulled him up, and shoved him into the bushes. Leo fell badly, but staggered to his feet and stumbled away.

Dan did not watch him go. He began to fill in the hole with a ferocious energy, and then he heard what he had anticipated for some time: Benjamin's footsteps. He looked down into the shallow grave, sure he would be found out, and his digging became even more frenzied. He shovelled and cursed, throwing himself into the work, and now he could hear Benjamin breathing; he heard his trouser legs rustling and his feet crunching against the wet snow. He expected Benjamin to lunge at him, or to start chasing after Leo. But the man said nothing. Another car could be heard far off in the distance. More birds took to the air.

"I couldn't bear to look at him," Dan said.

He thought the words rang hollow, and when Benjamin did not respond he prepared for the worst and closed his eyes. Benjamin came closer, he smelled of tobacco.

"I'll help you," he said.

They shovelled and pushed the rest of the earth into the empty grave and carefully replaced the turf and stones.

Then they walked slowly to the car, their heads bowed. On the way back to Stockholm Dan sat quietly, grimly listening to Greitz's plans.

Salander shot up like a cannonball and was stabbed in the side. She had no idea how serious her injury was, nor did she have time to worry about it. Benito had lost her balance and was now stabbing wildly at thin air with her dagger. Salander stepped smartly to one side, head-butted her and sprang to the van door. She opened it with her body and jumped down onto the grass with her hands bound, adrenaline pumping through her veins. She landed on her feet, but with such a force that she fell forward and rolled down a short, steep slope to a small brook. She just had time to see the water begin to turn bloodred before she scrambled to her feet and ran into the forest. She heard the sound of cars pulling up, voices raised, doors slamming. She did not think to stop. She needed only to get away.

Bublanski did not see Salander through the leaves, but he spotted two men making their way down a steep slope. Up above them stood a grey van facing into the foliage. He yelled:

"Stop. Police. Nobody move!" and pointed his service revolver at them.

It was unbearably hot and humid in the clearing and his body felt heavy. He was panting. The men he was confronting were both younger and stronger, and no doubt more ruthless too. But as he looked around and listened out in the direction of the track they had come along, he still felt the situation was under control. Flod was standing nearby in the same stance. The police teams sent by Uppsala must be very close by now. The men were unarmed and had been caught unawares.

"Don't do anything stupid now," he said. "You're surrounded. Where's Salander?"

The men said nothing. They looked irresolutely in the direction of the van. One of its rear doors was open. Bublanski knew at once that something unpleasant was going to emerge. He could make out a figure moving slowly and with difficulty. At last, there she stood barely upright, a spectre with a bloodied dagger in her hand: Benito Andersson. She seemed to sway and put a hand to her head, and then she hissed at him, as if she were the one calling the shots:

"Who are you?"

"I'm Chief Inspector Jan Bublanski. Where's Lisbeth Salander?"

"That little Jew?" she spat.

"Tell me where Salander is."

"I'd say she's probably dead." The woman came towards him, her dagger raised.

"Stop right there. Don't move," he warned her.

She kept coming, as if his revolver was nothing, hissing more anti-Semitic remarks. Bublanski did not think she deserved to be shot—she must not be allowed to claim martyrdom in the hellish fraternities she inhabited—and it was Flod who fired. Benito was hit in the left thigh, and soon their colleagues came storming in and it was over. But they never found Salander, only drops of her blood in the van. It was as if the forest had swallowed her up.

Dan seemed exhausted. He clutched his head in his hands.

"So what happened to Leo?" Blomkvist said, gently.

Dan looked out through the studio windows.

"He stumbled about in the trees, going in circles. He fell over and felt sick, he ate snow or drank meltwater. As time went on he found the strength to start shouting. But no-one heard him. After hours of wandering in the bitter cold he was surprised to find himself at the top of a long slope, which he slithered down, ending up in a field. The open space seemed vaguely familiar, as if he'd been there before a long time ago, or maybe dreamed it. By the edge of the forest on the other side he could see light shining from a house with a large terrace. Leo reached it eventually and rang the bell. A young couple lived there—their names are Stina and Henrik Norebring, in case you want to check. They were getting ready for Christmas, wrapping presents for their children. They were terrified at first—Leo must have looked like an absolute wreck. But he reassured them, saying that his car had skidded off the road, he'd lost his phone and probably had a concussion. I suppose it must have sounded convincing.

"The couple took him inside and ran him a hot bath. They gave him dry clothes and fed him Jansson's temptation and Christmas ham, a little mulled wine and *snaps,* and slowly he began to revive. But he had no idea what he should do next. He was desperate to contact me, but he knew that Rakel

Greitz had taken my mobile and was afraid that my e-mails were also being monitored. Leo's smart, though—he's usually one step ahead of the rest of us. He thought it would be safe to send a coded message that looked innocuous, something I might easily be getting the day before Christmas. He borrowed a mobile from the Norebrings and sent me a text:

```
<Congrats Daniel, Evita Kohn wants to tour
with you in US in Feb. Pls confirm. Django.
Will be a Minor Swing. Merry Christmas.>
```

"OK," Blomkvist said. "I think I'm beginning to understand. But what did the message mean?"

"Well, he didn't want to give away my American name. He chose an artist he knew I never played with, so nobody would be able to trace me that way. But above all he signed off as—"

"Django."

"Right. That in itself would have been enough for the penny to drop, but on top of that: 'Will be a Minor Swing.'"

Dan paused for a moment.

"'Minor Swing' is a piece with incredible joie de vivre. Maybe that's not quite right. There's a dark streak too. Django and Stéphane Grappelli wrote it together. Leo and I must have played it four, five times already. We loved it. But . . ."

Blomkvist waited for him to go on.

"After Leo sent the message, his condition deteriorated. Apparently he collapsed and the couple had him lie down on their sofa. He had difficulty breathing and his lips turned

blue. I was unaware of all this. I was in Leo's apartment, and
it had gotten late. The three of us were there—Benjamin,
Rakel and me. I was downing glass after glass of wine while
Rakel went through the whole repulsive plan she had cooked
up. Shocked as I was, I played along. I agreed to become
Leo, to do exactly as she said. She told me how to order new
credit cards and get new passwords, and to go and see Viveka
at her hospice, Stockholms Sjukhem, as Leo. She said I had
to take a sabbatical and travel, and read up on the financial
markets and lose my American and my northern Swedish
accents. Rakel flew around the apartment and dug up Leo's
passport and some paper so that I could practise his signa-
ture. It was unbearable. And those threats were always there,
the threat that as Daniel I could be convicted for the murder
of my brother, or that as Leo I could go to prison for insider
trading and tax fraud. I sat there mesmerized, just looking at
her. Or rather, I tried to look at her, but mostly I averted my
eyes or closed them and saw in my mind's eye Leo staggering
off into the forest, disappearing in the darkness and cold. I
didn't see how he could possibly have survived. I pictured
him lying in the snow, freezing to death.

"I couldn't imagine that Rakel really believed in her plan
either. She must have seen that I'd never be able to pull it
off—that I would go to pieces at the slightest suspicion. I
remember how she exchanged looks with Benjamin and
issued him instructions from time to time. All the while she
was fussing with something, arranging pens, wiping table-
tops and chairs, looking in drawers, straightening things.

"At one point she took my phone out of her pocket and
saw Leo's text. She started grilling me about my friends, my

business contacts and fellow musicians, and I answered as best I could, some of it true maybe, but mostly half-truths and lies. I don't really know. I could hardly speak, and yet . . . You know, to save money I'd gotten myself a Swedish SIM card and hadn't given the number to many people, so the text made me curious. 'What was that message?' I asked, as casually as I could. Rakel showed it to me and, seeing those words, I felt like I'd gotten my life back. But I must have controlled myself well. I don't think she noticed anything. 'That's a gig, right?' she said. I nodded. She told me I had to turn down those things from now on. She took back my phone and issued even more dire warnings. But I was no longer listening. I went along with everything. I think I even managed to sound a little greedy: 'How much money am I actually going to get?' I wanted to know. She gave me a very precise answer, which I later realized was an exaggeration, as if my decision might depend on a couple of million one way or the other. By then it was already 11:30 at night. We'd been at it for hours—I was dead tired and also pretty drunk. 'Can we stop now?' I said. 'I have to get some sleep,' and I remember Rakel hesitated. Was it safe to leave me on my own? Eventually she must have decided she had to trust me. I was so terrified she would change her mind that I didn't dare ask for my phone back. I just stood there rooted to the spot, nodding at her threats and promises."

"But they left."

"They left, and I concentrated on one thing only— remembering the number Leo's text had been sent from. I remembered only the last five digits. I rummaged around in drawers and coat pockets until I found Leo's private mobile which, typical for him, needed no security code. I tried every conceivable prefix to those five numbers—I woke up quite a few people and dialled some non-existent lines. But none of them was right. I swore and cried, and I was sure that Rakel would soon get another text from him, which would be a disaster. Then I remembered the sign we passed just before the car stopped in the forest. Vidåkra, it said. I guessed Leo must have found help somewhere nearby and so—"

"You checked Vidåkra and the five digits you'd remembered?"

"Exactly, and I found Henrik Norebring immediately. His phone number came up with all sorts of information, including how old he was. There was even a picture of his house, and an estimate of its value compared to other properties in the area. Isn't the Internet incredible? I remember that I hesitated—that my hands were shaking."

"But you called, didn't you?"

"I did. Do you mind if we take a break?"

Blomkvist nodded, his face grim, and he put a hand on Dan's shoulder. Then he went into the galley kitchen, switched on his mobile and washed up the glasses while he waited. In almost no time the phone began to beep and buzz, and he looked at his messages to see what was going on. There was one from Bublanski:

```
<Call me. Salander in danger.>
```

He swore and rushed back into the studio.

"Whatever may have happened, Dan, I hope you appreciate that we have to make this public as quickly as possible—

not least for your sake," he said. "I'm sorry we don't have time to go through the rest now, but I have to rush off. Given the circumstances, it's important that you stay here in the studio. I'll arrange for my colleague—my boss, in fact—Erika Berger, to come and keep you company. Would that be OK? She's a good and reliable person; you'll like her. I have to go now."

Dan nodded and for a moment looked so confused and helpless that Blomkvist gave him a quick, rough hug. He handed over the keys to the studio and thanked him.

"It was brave of you to tell me. I look forward to hearing the rest."

As he raced down the stairs he called Erika on an encrypted line. She agreed to drive over right away, just as he had expected. Next he made several attempts to get hold of Salander. No response, so he tried Bublanski.

CHAPTER 23

June 22

Bublanski had every reason to be satisfied. He had arrested Bashir and his brother Razan Kazi. Plus the notorious Benito Andersson, and a member of the Svavelsjö M.C. gang. Instead he was upset and disappointed. Officers from both the Uppsala and Stockholm police forces had been searching the woods around Vadabosjö, but they had found no trace of Salander apart from bloodstains in the van and signs of a break-in at a holiday home further up the hill where they had come across bloody footprints from child-sized sneakers. What on earth was she thinking? Salander obviously needed medical attention. There were ambulances heading their way, but she had chosen to plunge into the forest, a couple of miles off any main road. Maybe she just ran for her life, with no time to realize that help was at hand. But if a vital organ had been perforated by Benito's dagger, Salander would be in trouble, maybe even dying. Why was she not like other people?

Bublanski had reached police headquarters on Bergsgatan and was just walking into his office when his mobile rang. It was Blomkvist, at last, and the Chief Inspector gave him a broad-brush account of what had been happening. It was clear that his words hit home. Blomkvist asked a whole string of questions and only then did he say that he was beginning to understand why Holger Palmgren had been murdered. He promised to come back to Bublanski with more as soon as he could, but right now he had no time to talk. Bublanski sighed and had no option but to acquiesce.

DECEMBER, ONE AND A HALF YEARS EARLIER

It was ten past midnight. Christmas Eve, finally. Heavy wet snow lay on the window ledge, and the sky was a canvas of black and grey. The city lay silent, save for the occasional car on Karlavägen.

Dan stood at the window, shaking all over, and dialled the number for Henrik Norebring in Vidåkra. The ring tone echoed in his ear. No answer. Then he heard a recorded message that ended with a repetitive: "Hope you're good, hope you're well." Dan looked around the apartment in desperation. There was no sign of the drama that had only recently taken place there, but instead an unfamiliar clinical tidiness prevailed, plus a smell of disinfectant.

He escaped into the guest room where he had been sleeping for the past week and tried the number again and again. He cursed—he was beside himself. He could see that Greitz had been at it in here as well. What on earth had she been up to? She seemed to have cleaned and wiped down every surface. He had the urge to create chaos and disorder, rip the sheets off the bed, throw books at the wall, anything to rid himself of every trace of her. Instead he looked out the window and heard music playing from a radio on the floor below.

Perhaps a minute or two passed before he picked up Leo's mobile again. Just then it rang in his hand. He answered eagerly. On the other end was the very same voice from the voicemail greeting. But now it no longer sounded so chirpy; it was serious and composed, as if something terrible had happened.

"Is Leo there?" Dan gasped.

For a while there was no answer. Just a silence which seemed to confirm the worst, and which also brought back the terrifying reality of the forest. He remembered the chill of Leo's lips, the absence of any light in his eyes, the lack of response from his lungs.

"Is he there? Is he alive?"

"Wait," the voice said.

There was a crackling in the receiver. He could hear footsteps. It took time, so much time. Then suddenly life returned and, with it, the world and its colours.

"Dan?" said a voice which could have been his own.

"Leo," he whispered. "You're alive."

"I'm OK. The cramps came back, but Stina here, she's a nurse, she sorted me out."

He told Dan he was lying on a sofa with two blankets over him. His voice sounded weak yet steady, and he was clearly unsure as to what he could say in front of whoever was there with him. But he did mention Django and "Minor Swing."

"You saved my life," Leo said.

"I think I did."

"That's pretty major."

"You mean it was swing."

"It doesn't get more swing than that, brother."

Dan did not answer.

"*Contra mundum*," Leo said.

"What's that?" Dan said.

"The two of us against the world, my friend. You and me."

They decided to meet mid-morning at Hotel Amaranten on Kungsholmsgatan, not far from Rådhuset, where Leo was certain they would not bump into anyone he knew. Dan sent a taxi to bring him into the city, and the brothers spent those hours on Christmas Eve in a room on the fourth floor, talking and making plans with the curtains drawn. They renewed their alliance and their pact and, just before the shops closed for the holidays at 2:00 p.m., Dan bought two mobiles with prepaid SIM cards, so that they would be able to communicate.

He headed to Floragatan, and when Greitz rang on the landline he repeated in grave tones that he had decided to do as she suggested. He spoke to a nurse at Stockholms Sjukhem who said that his mother was under sedation and would not live long. He wished all of them on the ward a Happy Christmas, and asked them to kiss Viveka on the forehead for him. He said he would visit soon.

That afternoon he returned to the Amaranten and told Leo as much as he could about the file Greitz said she had compiled on insider trading deals and tax fraud carried out in his name. There was depthless rage in his brother's eyes, a terrifying hatred, and Dan listened in silence as Leo went on about how they would take revenge on Ivar and Rakel and all the rest of them. He put a hand on Leo's shoulder to share his pain, but his own thoughts were less about revenge and more about Greitz's insistence on the mighty powers that stood behind her. He also remembered the car journey in the dark and the grave in the forest by the old pine tree. His whole body told him that he did not have the courage to retaliate, not right away. Perhaps—it occurred to him later—this had something to do with his background. Unlike Leo, he did not have the confidence to believe he could win against the establishment. Or perhaps it was simply that he had his eyes opened to the ruthlessness with which this group operated.

"Absolutely, we'll crush them," Dan said. "But this has to be planned meticulously, don't you think? We need evidence. We have to prepare the ground. Why don't we look at it as an opportunity to start afresh, try something new?"

He didn't know what he was trying to say. He was just floating an idea. But gradually it took hold and an hour later, after much discussion, they were forging plans, tentatively at first, then more and more seriously. They knew they would have to act quickly, before Greitz and her organization, whatever it was, would see that they had been duped.

On Christmas Day Leo made the first of what would be many transfers to Dan Brody's bank account. Then he bought a ticket to Boston for the following day, in Dan's name. But it was Leo who made the journey with Dan's American passport and papers. Dan stayed in Leo's apartment, where Greitz came to see him on the evening of December 26, to draw up guidelines for his new life. He played the part well, and if at times he did not look as disconsolate as he should have, Greitz seemed to interpret that as a sign that he was enjoying his new existence already. "You see your own evil in others," as Leo said later on the telephone.

On December 28, Dan was sitting at Leo's mother's bedside at Stockholms Sjukhem. He did not say much, and none of the staff appeared to suspect anything, which boosted his confidence. He tried to look upset yet composed, and sometimes he was genuinely moved, even though he was with a person he had never met before. Viveka was emaciated and pale, bird-like. She was sleeping with her mouth open, and her breathing was weak. Someone had combed her hair and applied a little make-up, and she had been propped up on two pillows. At one point—he felt it would be expected—he stroked her shoulder and arm. She opened her eyes and looked at him critically, which made him feel uncomfortable but not worried. She was heavily sedated with morphine, so it was probably safe to assume that nothing she could say would be taken seriously.

"Who are you?" she said.

Something harsh and judgmental surfaced in her delicate, pointed features.

"It's me, Mamma. Leo."

She appeared to be reflecting on this. She swallowed and gathered some strength.

"You never turned out as we had hoped, Leo," she said. "You were a disappointment to Pappa and me."

Dan closed his eyes and remembered everything Leo had told him about his mother. It was astonishingly easy to reply—maybe precisely because the woman was a stranger.

"You were never what I'd hoped for either. You never understood me. It was *you* who let *me* down."

She looked at him, surprised and confused.

"You let Leo down," he said. "You let us *both* down—all of you did."

He walked out and went back home through the city. The following day, December 29, Viveka Mannheimer died. The director of Stockholms Sjukhem telephoned to let him know, and Dan put the announcements and the funeral arrangements into the hands of an undertaker recommended by the hospice. They could organize it however they thought best, he told them, a week or so into the New Year. He himself would not be attending. When he told Ivar Ögren that he needed a long sabbatical, he got in return only coarse language and foul comments about how irresponsible he was. He did not bother to answer. On January 4, he too left the country, with Greitz's approval.

He flew to New York and met his brother in Washington, D.C. They stayed together for a week before going their separate ways.

Leo—as Dan—cautiously got to know the musicians on the Boston jazz scene. He explained he had started playing piano, but was nervous about performing in public. His Swedish accent worried him and he was homesick, until he decided to move to Toronto, where he met Marie Denver. She was a young interior designer with dreams of becoming an artist, and she was considering setting up a business together with her sister. She was not sure if she dared to take the plunge. Leo invested some capital and took a seat on the board. Not long after, the couple bought a house in Hoggs Hollow. He played the piano regularly with a small group of talented amateur musicians, all of whom were doctors.

Dan was rootless for a long time. He travelled around Europe and Asia, playing guitar and reading up on the financial markets. He found he had a burning thirst for knowledge. He felt—or rather believed—that as an outsider he would be able to apply a new kind of meta-perspective to the financial markets, and in the end he decided to resume Leo's place at Alfred Ögren, not least to find out about the dossier of evidence Rakel Greitz and Ivar Ögren had against his brother. He realized that it would not be easy to deny the allegations. When he instructed one of Stockholm's best business lawyers, Bengt Wallin, to look into them and was briefed on the extent and type of deals carried out in Leo's name through Mossack Fonseca in Panama, he was strongly advised to leave it alone.

As the weeks went by, life resumed its normal course, as it tends to do. Dan and Leo bided their time, and remained in close contact. When Dan left Blomkvist in the lobby of Alfred Ögren that day, the person he called was Leo. Leo was silent for a long while, and then told Dan it was up to him to decide if the time was right to tell their story, adding that it would be hard to find a more suitable outlet than Mikael Blomkvist at *Millennium*.

Now Dan had indeed started to talk, though he hadn't yet said anything about Leo's new life in Canada. Standing at the window of the studio, he called Toronto once again and was deep in conversation when he was interrupted by a discreet knock at the door. Erika Berger had arrived.

Earlier that day, feeling horribly nauseous, Greitz had dragged herself back along to Hamngatan, meaning to take a taxi to go home to Karlbergsvägen and collapse in her bed. But halfway there she became angry with herself and went to her office in the west of the city instead. It was unlike her to let illness or adversity get the upper hand. She decided to keep fighting and activated every contact and ally she could think of to find Blomkvist and Daniel Brolin—all except Steinberg, who had broken down after repeated calls from the police. She sent Benjamin off to the *Millennium* offices on Götgatan and to Blomkvist's apartment building on Bellmansgatan. But Benjamin only encountered locked doors. In the end she gave up for the day and let him drive her home. She needed to get some rest, and also to destroy the most sensitive of Project 9's documents, which she kept at home in a safe behind the wardrobe in her bedroom.

It was 4:30 p.m. and still unbearably hot. She let Benjamin help her out of the car. She really did need him, and not only as a bodyguard. She was groggy after all the stress of the day. Her black turtleneck was damp with sweat. The city swayed before her eyes. She stood straight and looked up at the sky, and for a moment her look was triumphant. She might ultimately be unmasked and humiliated, but she had fought—she was convinced of this—for something greater than herself: for science and for the future. She was determined to go down with dignity. She vowed to remain strong and proud to the end, however ill she might be.

At the building's street entrance she asked Benjamin to hand her the orange juice he had bought for her on the way and, even though it was a little undignified, she drank straight from the bottle and felt briefly restored. They took the lift to the sixth floor, where she unlocked the front door and asked Benjamin to go in ahead and switch off the burglar alarm. She was just about to step over the threshold when she froze and looked down towards the floor below. A pale figure was climbing the stairs, a young woman who seemed to have risen from the underworld.

•   •   •

Salander was more presentable than she had been, even if her face was white and eyes bloodshot, her cheeks scratched from brambles and bushes. She was walking with visible difficulty. But she had gone to the trouble of buying a T-shirt and a pair of jeans from a secondhand shop on Upplandsgatan and had stuffed her bloodstained clothes into a bin. She had also bought a mobile in a Telenor store, and dressings and disinfectant at a pharmacy. Standing on the pavement, she ripped off the duct tape she had found in a holiday home in the woods and used to staunch the flow of blood from her hip, and she replaced it with a new and better bandage.

For a while she had been lying semi-conscious on the forest floor. As soon as she came to, she sawed through the rope around her wrists on a jagged rock. She made her way to National Highway 77 and got a lift from a woman in an old Rover all the way to Vasastan, where she attracted a good deal of attention.

According to a witness named Kjell Ove Strömgren, she looked unwell and dangerous when she walked in "through said doorway" at Karlbergsvägen. She didn't bother to look at herself in the mirror in the entrance hall, as she did not expect it would be edifying. She felt like shit. The dagger had probably not damaged any vital organs, but she had lost a significant amount of blood and was ready to pass out.

Greitz—or Nordin, as the misleading sign on the door said—was not at home. Salander sat on the landing one level down, and from there she texted Blomkvist. He sent back a lot of sensible advice and other crap. All she wanted to know, she texted back, was what he had found out. Finally, he gave her a summary and she nodded as she read it and closed her eyes. The pain and the dizziness were getting worse, and she only just managed to resist the impulse to stretch out on the floor. For a moment it felt as if she would never be able to pull herself together again, or to do anything at all. But then she thought of Palmgren.

She remembered how he had come all the way to Flodberga in his wheelchair and she couldn't help thinking how much he had meant to her all these years. But above all she thought about what Blomkvist had told her of his death, and it was clear that he was right: only Greitz could have killed the old man. She drew strength from that—it was up to her to avenge Palmgren. She knew she had to strike with all her might, however weak she felt, so she pulled back her shoulders and shook her head, and finally, after another ten or fifteen minutes, the rickety lift stopped on the floor above her. The door was pushed open and through the banisters she could make out a large man and a much older woman in a black turtleneck. Oddly enough, Salander recognized her by the way she carried herself. It was as if the mere sight of Greitz's ramrod spine had taken her back to her childhood.

But she did not allow herself to dwell on it. She sent a rapid message to Bublanski and Modig and headed up the stairs, not very steadily and apparently not very quietly either. Greitz spun around and looked Salander in the eye, first in surprise and then—once she had recognized her— with fear and loathing. Salander stopped on the stairs, holding the wound in her side.

"We meet again," Salander said.

"You took your time."

"And yet it seems like yesterday, don't you think?"

Greitz ignored the question and growled:

"Benjamin! Bring her here!"

Benjamin nodded. He was a foot and a half taller than Salander and twice as broad, so he didn't seem to think he would have any trouble. But when he lunged at her, he was carried forward not only by the sheer mass of his body, but also by the downward slope of the steps. Salander stepped neatly to one side, took hold of the man's left arm and tugged. At that moment Benjamin's determination proved counter-productive. He went down headfirst on the stone landing, cracking his elbow on the way. Salander saw none of it. She was already hobbling up the stairs, shoving Greitz inside and locking the door behind them. Benjamin was soon hammering on the outside of the door.

Greitz backed away, clutching her brown leather bag. In a few seconds she had regained the upper hand, but that had nothing to do with the bag or its contents: Salander had expended so much energy on the stairs that her dizziness almost overwhelmed her. She looked around the apartment through half-closed eyes, and although her vision was hardly clear, she knew she had never seen anything like it. Not only was the place devoid of all colour—everything was either black or white—it was also dazzlingly clean and clinical, as if an android lived there rather than a human being. There could not have been a speck of dust in the entire apartment. Salander steadied herself against a black chest of drawers. Just as she was about to pass out, she saw from the corner of her eye Greitz advancing towards her, holding something in her hand. A syringe.

"I've just been hearing how you like to stick needles into people," Salander said. Greitz attacked, but to no avail. Salander kicked the syringe out of her hand, and it fell onto the shiny white floor and rolled away. Even though her head was spinning, she managed to stay on her feet and for a few seconds she focused only on Greitz. She was surprised at how calm the woman looked.

"Go ahead and kill me. I'll die with pride," Greitz said.

"With pride, did you say?"

"Absolutely."

"Not going to happen."

Salander looked sick and spoke in a flat, exhausted voice, but still, Greitz knew that this was the end of the road. She looked towards the window on her left, out towards Karlbergsvägen, and hesitated for a second or two. Then it became clear that she had no alternative. Anything would be better than ending up in Salander's clutches. So she made a dash for the balcony door and felt the terrifying pull of the urge to jump—but Salander caught her before she could climb over the railing. It wasn't exactly what either of them had expected. Rakel Greitz was being saved by the person she had dreaded more than anyone else. Salander held her firmly and led her back into her clinically clean apartment.

"You *will* die, Rakel. Don't you worry about that," she whispered in her ear.

"I know," she said. "I've got cancer."

"The cancer's nothing." Salander's tone was chilling.

"What do you mean?"

Salander stared at the ground.

"Holger meant a lot to me," she said, and she gripped Greitz's hand so hard it felt to Greitz as if her blood had frozen. "What I'm saying is that the cancer will seem like nothing, Rakel. You're going to die of shame too, and believe me, that'll be the worst part. I'll make sure so much dirt is unearthed about you that no-one will remember you for anything other than all the evil you have unleashed. You'll be buried in your own excrement."

She said this with such conviction that Greitz believed it. Then Salander calmly opened the door to let in a group of policemen, who had handcuffed Benjamin to a banister.

"Good afternoon, Fru Greitz. You and I have a lot to talk about. We've just arrested your colleague, Professor Steinberg," said a dark-haired man with a half-smile, who introduced himself as Chief Inspector Bublanski.

It did not take his men long to find the safe behind her wardrobe. The last she saw of Salander was her back as paramedics led her away. Salander didn't turn around once. It was as if Greitz no longer existed for her.

CHAPTER 24

June 30

It was another hot summer's day. There had not been a drop of rain for two weeks. Blomkvist was in the kitchen area at *Millennium*'s editorial offices on Götgatan. He had just finished writing his long piece on the Registry and Project 9. He stretched his back and drank some water and looked over towards the bright-blue sofa on the other side of the room.

Erika Berger lay stretched out in her high-heeled shoes, reading his article. He was not exactly nervous. He knew for sure it made for harrowing reading. They had a scoop which would be tremendous for the magazine. Yet he still did not know how Berger would react—not because of the one or two sections which gave rise to ethical questions, but because of their argument.

He had told her that he would not be spending the Midsummer weekend out in the archipelago or celebrating in any way. Instead he would be concentrating on his story. He needed to go through the documents he had received from Bublanski, and he needed to interview Hilda von Kanterborg again, as well as Dan Brody and Leo Mannheimer, who had come to Stockholm from Toronto in secret with his fiancée.

And Blomkvist had been working pretty much around the clock, not just on the report about the Registry but also on the Faria Kazi story. It was not he who had actually written it—Sofie Melker had. But he was involved from start to finish and had discussed the legal process with his sister while she worked to get Faria released and protected with a new identity.

He was regularly in touch with Inspector Modig, who was leading the newly reopened inquiry into what was now accepted as the murder of Jamal Chowdhury, for which Bashir, Razan and Khalil Kazi and two others were in custody and awaiting trial. Benito Andersson had been taken to Hammerfors Prison in Härnösand, and she too was awaiting fresh charges. Plus Blomkvist often got caught up in long conversations with Bublanski, and he was spending more time on the purely stylistic side of the story too.

But even he had gotten to the point where he could do no more. He needed a break. He was almost seeing double, and it was unbearably hot at his desk on Bellmansgatan. One afternoon he felt a pang of longing and called Malin Frode.

"Would you come over?" he said. "Pretty please."

Malin agreed to get a babysitter if Blomkvist promised to buy strawberries and Champagne and turn back his sheets, and not have his mind on other things like Kalle Fucking Blomkvist usually did. He told her the conditions sounded reasonable enough. And so they were tumbling about in bed, happy and drunk and oblivious to the rest of the world, when Berger dropped by unannounced with an expensive bottle of red wine.

Berger had never considered Blomkvist a model of good behaviour, and she herself was married and not overly scrupulous about dalliances. Yet it had all gotten out of hand. If he had had the time and inclination, he could have worked out why. One reason was Malin's fiery temperament, and another was the fact that Berger was upset and embarrassed. They had *all* been embarrassed. The women began to argue with each other, and then they argued with him too, until Berger marched off in a fury, slamming the door behind her. Since then, conversations at the magazine between her and Blomkvist had been strained and confined to work issues.

But now Berger was lying there reading, and Blomkvist was thinking about Salander. She had been discharged from the hospital and had flown in haste to Gibraltar—she said she had business to attend to there. But they had kept in touch every day about Faria Kazi and about the investigation into the Registry.

So far, the public knew nothing about the background to the story, and the names of the presumed suspects had not yet been published in any major media. Berger had therefore been insistent that they swiftly put out a special issue of the magazine so that no-one could scoop them. Perhaps that was why she was so upset when she found Blomkvist lying in bed drinking Champagne, though he could not have been more serious about getting the report ready.

Now he kept sneaking looks at Berger, who eventually took off her reading glasses and got up and joined him in the kitchen. She was wearing jeans and a blue blouse, open at the neck. She sat next to him at the table. He couldn't guess whether she would begin with praise or with criticism.

"I don't understand it."

"That's unfortunate," he said. "I was hoping I had shed at least some light on the story."

"Why on earth did they keep it a secret for so long?"

"Leo and Dan? As I say in the article, there was evidence that Leo had been involved in illegal transactions through various dummy companies. Although it's clear now that Ivar Ögren and Rakel Greitz had set him up, Leo and Dan couldn't find any way of getting at them. Besides, and I hope this is clear from what I've written, they were beginning to enjoy their new roles. Neither of them was short of money—large sums were being transferred all the time—and I think both of them were experiencing a new kind of freedom, a bit like the freedom that any actor enjoys. They could start afresh and do something different. I can understand the appeal."

"And then they fell in love."

"With Julia and Marie."

"The pictures are wonderful."

"That's something at least."

"It's good that we've got decent photographers," she said. "But you do realize that Ivar Ögren's going to sue the crap out of us?"

"I think we're well armed for that, Erika."

"Plus, I'm worried about defaming the dead—because of that fatal incident at the elk hunt."

"I'm sure I'm on firm ground there too. All I'm actually

saying is that the circumstances surrounding the shooting are unclear."

"I'm not sure it's good enough. Just *that* is already pretty damaging."

"OK, I'll take another look. Is there anything that *doesn't* worry you, or that you even . . . dare I say it, *do* understand?"

"You're a bastard."

"Maybe a bit. Especially after dark."

"Are you planning to devote yourself to one woman only from now on, or are you considering spending time with others too?"

"In a pinch I could imagine drinking Champagne with you, if worst came to worst."

"You won't have any choice."

"Will you force me?"

"If I have to, yes, because this article—the part we're not going to be sued for, that is—it's . . ."

She held back.

"Broadly acceptable?" he said.

"You could say that," she replied, and smiled. "Congratulations." She opened her arms to embrace him.

But then something else grabbed their attention, and later it would prove difficult to recall the exact sequence of events. Sofie Melker was probably the first to react. She was at her computer in the editorial offices and yelled out something incomprehensible, but it was clear that she was either shocked or surprised. Soon afterwards—or at the same time—Berger

and Blomkvist received news flashes on their mobiles. Neither of them was especially worried. It was not a terrorist
attack or a threat of war. It was only a stock market crash.
But gradually they were consumed by the events as they
unfolded. Step-by-step they entered into the state of height-
ened awareness which one finds in every press room when
major, world-shattering news events occur. They became
wholly concentrated and shouted out what they saw on their
computers. There were new developments every minute.

The crash accelerated. The floor was pulled out from
under the market. The Stockholm index was down by 6 percent, then 8, and fell further to minus 9 and 14 percent. At
that stage it showed signs of a small recovery, then continued
to fall again, as if plummeting into a black hole. It was a full-
blown crash, a galloping panic, and so far nobody seemed to
understand what was happening.

There was nothing specific, no apparent trigger. People
muttered: "Incomprehensible, it's madness! What's going
on?" Soon after, when the experts were called in, all the usual
explanations were trotted out: an overheated economy, low
interest rates, the over-valued market, political threats from
both West and East, instability in the Middle East and fascist
and anti-democratic movements in Europe and the U.S.—a
political witches' cauldron reminiscent of the 1930s. But
nothing new had happened that day, no development significant enough to have precipitated a disaster on this scale.
The panic appeared out of nowhere and was self-sustaining.

Blomkvist was not the only one reminded of the hacker
attack on Finance Security in April. He went onto social
media and was not surprised to find rumours and allegations

raging, all too often gaining a foothold in the mainstream media. Blomkvist said aloud, though it sounded more as if he were talking to himself:

"It's not just the stock exchange that's crashing."

"What do you mean?" Berger said.

"Truth is going the same way."

It was as if the Internet trolls had taken over to create a fake dynamic in which lies and truth were set against each other as if they were equivalent notions. An impenetrable fog of fabrications and conspiracy theories settled over the world. Sometimes the trolls did a good job, sometimes not. For example, it was reported that financier Christer Tallgren had shot himself in his apartment in Paris, devastated by the fact that his millions—or was it billions?—had gone up in smoke. Tallgren's own denial of the story on Twitter was not the only noteworthy thing about it; there was also the fact that it echoed Ivar Kreuger's death by his own hand in 1932.

A mixture of urban myths and apocryphal stories, both new and old, swirled in the air. There was talk of automated trading having run amok, about financial centres and media houses and websites having been hacked. But there were also reports that people were about to jump to their deaths from balconies and roofs in Östermalm, which not only sounded wildly melodramatic but also harked back to the 1929 stock exchange crash, when roofers working on Wall Street buildings were said to have been mistaken for ill-fated investors, and had contributed to the tumbling market merely by being up there.

It was claimed that Handelsbanken had stopped its payments and that Deutsche Bank and Goldman Sachs were on the verge of bankruptcy. News came pouring in from every direction, and not even a well-trained eye like Blomkvist's could tell the difference between what was true and what was fabricated by the organized groups of trolls in the East.

He had no doubt, however, that Stockholm was the hardest hit. The stock market crash was not as bad in Frankfurt, London or Paris, although there was rising panic in those cities too. The American exchanges would not be opening for several hours. Even so, futures prices suggested that there would be sharp downturns on the Dow Jones and Nasdaq. Nothing seemed to help, least of all when central bank governors and ministers, economists and gurus stepped up to talk about "over-reaction," saying that nobody should "rock the boat." Everything was cast in a negative light and distorted. The herd was already in motion and running for its life, although nobody knew who or what had frightened it. A decision was made to suspend trading on the Stockholm Stock Exchange, perhaps too hastily because prices had begun to recover only moments before. But investigations and analyses were needed before there could be a resumption of trading.

"Too bad about your twins story. It'll drown in this mess."

Blomkvist looked up from his computer and gazed wistfully at Berger.

"I'm touched that you're concerned about my professional pride when the whole world has gone mad," he said.

"I'm thinking of *Millennium*."

"I understand. But we have to delay publication now, don't you think? We can't put out a new issue without addressing this too."

"No new print issue, I agree with that. But we have to at least publish something of this finished piece online. Otherwise someone could get out ahead of us."

"OK," he said, "you're probably right. Whatever you think best."

"But then you'll have to get going again on this latest story. Can you bear to?"

"Of course, no problem."

"Good," she said, and they nodded at each other.

It would be a hot and oppressive summer, and Blomkvist decided to take a walk before tackling the next story. He came down Götgatan towards Slussen, thinking of Holger Palmgren and his clenched fist in the bed in Liljeholmen.

EPILOGUE

The cathedral was packed. It was not just that it was Storkyr-kan, and it was not as if the funeral was for some famous statesman. It was for an elderly lawyer who had never taken on any high-profile cases, but had rather spent his whole working life fighting on behalf of young people who had gone astray. *Millennium*'s recently published report into the so-called Twins Scandal may have had something to do with it though, along with the publicity around the old man's murder.

It was 2:00 p.m. The funeral service had been digni-fied and moving, with a somewhat unconventional sermon which had scarcely referred to the Almighty or to Jesus but portrayed the dead man with fine brushstrokes. It had been overshadowed, however, by the emotional eulogy delivered by Holger Palmgren's half sister Britt-Marie Norén. Many of those sitting in the pews were deeply moved, especially a tall, stately African woman by the name of Lulu Magoro, who was weeping uncontrollably. Many others had tears in their eyes or their heads lowered respectfully—relatives, friends, former colleagues, neighbours, a number of clients who looked to have done well for themselves. Mikael Blomkvist was there, as was his sister, Annika Giannini; Chief Inspector Bublanski and his fiancée, Farah Sharif; and Inspectors Sonja Modig and Jerker Holmberg; as well as Erika Berger and many others who had been close to Holger. But there were also those who had come out of curiosity and were looking around excitedly, which did not appear to please the priest, a tall, slim woman in her sixties with snow-white hair and sharp features. She stepped forward again with her air of natural authority and nodded at a man in a black linen jacket who was sitting in the second row on the left.

The man—Dragan Armansky, the owner of the company Milton Security—shook his head. It was his turn to speak, but he no longer wanted to. It was not obvious why. The priest accepted his apology and prepared for the mourners to file past the coffin, giving a signal to the musicians above.

At that moment a young woman stood up at the back of the church and called out: "Stop. Wait." It took a while before people realized it was Lisbeth Salander. That may have been because she was wearing a black tailored suit which made her look like a young boy, although she had still managed to forget to do something about her hair. It was as messy and spiky as ever. She made no effort to approach the coffin in a way appropriate to the occasion either. There was something aggressive about the way she moved, and yet—in a curious paradox—she appeared oddly indecisive. When she reached the altar she stared at the floor, refusing to meet the eye of anyone in the congregation. For a moment it looked as though she might go and sit down again.

"Would you like to say a few words?" the priest said.

She nodded.

"Please, go ahead. I understand you were close to Holger."

"I was," she said.

Then she fell silent. There was nervous muttering in the church. It was impossible to decipher her body language, although most thought she seemed angry, or stunned. When finally she began to speak, she was barely audible even to those in the first row.

"Louder!" somebody shouted.

She raised her eyes and looked lost.

"Holger was . . . a pain," she said. "Tiresome. He wouldn't accept it if people didn't want to talk and preferred to be left alone. He didn't know when to give up. He just barged right in and got all sorts of disturbed freaks to open up. He was dumb enough to believe in people, even in me—and there weren't too many people who shared that opinion. He was a proud old fool who refused to accept help, however bad the pain, and he always did everything he could to unearth the truth, never for himself. So naturally . . ."

She closed her eyes.

". . . there was every reason for them to murder him. They killed a defenceless old man in his bed and that makes me mad, really mad, especially since Holger and I . . ."

She never finished the sentence. She stared blankly to one side. Then she straightened up and looked directly out at the congregation.

"The last time we saw each other, we talked about that statue over there," she said. "He wanted to know why I was so fascinated by it. I told him that I had never seen it as a monument to a heroic deed, but rather as a representation of a terrible assault. He understood immediately, and asked, 'What about the fire the dragon is breathing?' I said it was the same fire that burns inside everyone who is being trampled on. The same fire that can turn us into ashes and waste, but which sometimes—if some old fool like Holger spots us, plays chess with us and talks to us, and just takes an interest—can become something totally different: a force which allows us to strike back. Holger knew that you can still get back on your feet, even with a spear sticking through your body, and that's why he kept on nagging and was such a pain," she said, and then fell silent again.

She turned and bowed to the coffin, her movements stiff and angular, and said, "Thanks," and "Sorry." She caught a look from Mikael Blomkvist, who smiled at her. She may have smiled back, it was hard to tell.

The church erupted with murmuring and whispers, and the priest had difficulty restoring order for the procession past the coffin. Hardly anybody noticed Salander as she stole along the rows of benches and disappeared through the church door, into the square outside and the narrow lanes of Gamla Stan.

ACKNOWLEDGMENTS

My heartfelt thanks to my agent, Magdalena Hedlund, and to my publishers Eva Gedin and Susanna Romanus.

A big thanks, too, to my editor, Ingemar Karlsson; to Stieg Larsson's father and brother, Erland and Joakim Larsson; to my friends Johan and Jessica Norberg; and to David Jacoby, senior security researcher at Kaspersky Lab.

Thanks also to my British publisher, Christopher MacLehose; Jessica Bab Bonde at Hedlund Agency; Nancy Pedersen, professor of genetic epidemiology at the Swedish Twin Registry; Ulrica Blomgren, assistant prison governor at Hall Prison; Svetlana Bajalica Lagercrantz, consultant and associate professor at Karolinska University Hospital; Hedvig Kjellström, professor of computer science at K.T.H. Royal Institute of Technology; Agneta Geschwind, deputy head of department at the Stockholm City Archives; Mats Galvenius, deputy managing director at Insurance Sweden; my neighbour Joachim Hollman; Danica Kragić Jensfelt, professor of information technology at K.T.H. Royal Institute of Technology; and Linda Altrov Berg and Catherine Mörk at Norstedts Agency.

And always, always to my Anne.